CITY OF DECEIT

CITY OF DECEIT: An Isandor Novel
Copyright © 2022 Claudie Arseneault.

Published by The Kraken Collective
krakencollectivebooks.com

Edited by S.L. Dove Cooper.
Cover by Gabrielle Arseneault.
Interior Design by Key of Heart Designs.

claudiearseneault.com

ISBN: 978-1-7778464-0-4

Published in the City of Spires Series

Book One
CITY OF STRIFE

Book Two
CITY OF BETRAYAL

Book Three
CITY OF DECEIT

Book Four
CITY OF EXILE

City of Deceit

An Isandor Novel

Claudie Arseneault

À MA BELLE MAMAN,

Pour son infatigable soutien et tout son amour.

Previously

THE SCENE:

Isandor, the City of Spires. A nexus of eccentric towers in which bickering merchant families vie for power through overbearing shows of wealth and endless trade wars. At its edge is an enclave from the Myrian Empire, a conquering mageocracy of dubious ethics and an economic powerhouse meddling in local politics.

A FEW KEY PLAYERS:

Diel Dathirii, Head of Isandor's only elven noble house, an eternal idealist.

Master Avenazar, Leader of the Myrian Enclave, ruthless and powerful mage.

Nevian Ollu, young Myrian apprentice, stubbornly trying to learn magic despite Avenazar's abuse.

Varden Daramond, High Priest of Keroth. Talented artist, loving soul, powerful fire-wielder.

Branwen Dathirii, Dathirii spymaster, master of disguise and owner of the greatest wardrobe.

Our story begins on a cold late autumn day, on a plaza surrounded by a great many shops. **Avenazar** has caught his apprentice, **Nevian**, there, and he intends to show his discontent in the traditional means: by shooting pain through his forearm until it overwhelms his mind. For **Diel Dathirii**, a witness to the event, this is one-too-many horrible acts from the Myrian. He interrupts, and tells Master Avenazar know that the Myrian Enclave will no longer be tolerated, and he will do all in his power to eradicate them from Isandor's politics.

Thus begins the hostilities that underpin our tale. Diel Dathirii returns home and musters his forces: cousins, nieces and nephews, lover and steward. The plan is two-pronged: to protect his network of local merchants, and to convince other Houses of Isandor to rally against the Myrian Enclave. Master Avenazar is, however, much more direct: he instructs the enclave's High Priest to walk into a Dathirii-affiliated shop and burn it to the ground.

Varden Daramond knows better than to refuse. His position is ever-precarious; in Myria, his people are more frequently slaves than titled priests. When he finds **Branwen Dathirii** inside, he knows he is expected to kill her. Instead, he whisks her away to his quarters, hiding her until she can escape. Winter solstice is coming, and most of the Enclave will be attending an all-night ritual to mark it, providing a perfect opportunity. In the meantime, their rocky start turns into mutual respect, then quiet friendship.

Little do they know, Varden will not make it through winter solstice unscathed. You see, all this time Nevian has been sneaking out of the enclave to meet with a mentor, and Varden, feeling kinship with another rebellious soul, has known and helped this. But when Nevian is spotted leaving—in the distance, unidentified—it is Varden, the outsider and easy scapegoat, who is accused.

Master Avenazar is all too happy to confirm the accusations by invading Varden's mind—and in the process, he learns of Branwen's ongoing escape and Nevian's outing in Isandor. He ditches the High Priest and teleports to his apprentice. While Master Avenazar carefully and painfully erases all of Nevian's knowledge of magic, Branwen interrupts him with a well-placed dagger throw then makes a narrow escape afterwards. Helpful, but not quite enough to save Nevian, who falls of the bridge.

And here we must interrupt, for there is another story unfolding in Isandor, one far from the high towers of nobles and the troubles of the Myrian Enclave. This second tale started in a Shelter, little more than a hovel squeezed between two towers, where those of meagre fortunes can find a roof and a meal for free. We should, perhaps, introduce **<u>some new key players.</u>**

Arathiel Brasten, drifter from the past, returned after 130 years in a magical trap, all senses drained.

Calleran Masset (Cal), servant of Ren, luckiest and most generous soul.

Hasryan Fel'ethier, secret assassin for the Crescent Moon Mercenary, open sass master.

Larryn, owner and cook of the Shelter, a bubbling stew of anger and spite.

Drake Allastam, firstborn son of House Allastam, uses the power and privilege to harass those less lucky.

Sora Sharpe, investigator for Isandor's Sapphire Guards. Quick of wits and pigheaded.

Lady Camilla Dathirii, centuries-old elven lady, dispenser of tea, cookies, and wisdom.

Now that we have that settled, let's rewind a moment, to **Arathiel**'s arrival in the docks of Isandor, wet and out of luck, a stranger in his own city, a ghost uncertain of his future. He finds his way to the Shelter, where through luck and **Cal**'s insistence, he integrates three friends'—Larryn, Hasryan, and Cal—regular card games. In particular, he bonds with **Hasryan,** with whom he shares an easy understanding; two outsiders struggling to let others in.

It is during one of these card games, up in a fancier tavern of the Middle City, that the group is interrupted by **Drake Allastam,** who has an antagonistic history with **Larryn.** It takes less than a minute for it to devolve into a fight, and while Hasryan gets a solid headbutt in, the fight lasts long enough for guards to walk in, and Hasryan is arrested.

Nothing would've come out of it if not for **Sora Sharpe**'s eagle eye. She ties Hasryan's dagger—an unique weapon with a jagged blade and the ability to produce electricity—to several unsolved murders, and pins him down for them, prolonging his stay in prison. One of these, the death of Lady Allastam, remains the highest profile assassination of Isandor's history. No big deal, Hasryan tells himself. He didn't do it. A bribe and a lie, and his boss will get him out of there.

Except she doesn't. The head of the Crescent Moon organization leaves him out to hang, confirming the dagger is his—a dagger she gave him, shortly *after* Lady Allastam's death. After a decade of working together, the person Hasryan trusted most, the woman who'd picked him off the streets and taught him to survive has scapegoated him through a ploy she had set up over a decade ago.

That knowledge shatters Hasryan as surely as his trust and, dejected, he is ready to give up and wait for his execution—but his friends certainly aren't. Unaware of their friend's real job and angered that he is being scapegoated, Larryn and Cal plan to use the winter solstice as cover to sneak into the prisons, pretending to be two priests.

And this brings us back to winter solstice, and to poor Nevian falling off a bridge—only to crash right in front of Cal. Cal, with his very limited healing skills and big heart, with his absolute faith in the randomness of life and his own, ridiculous luck. Cal, who is awaited for a prison infiltration but stops, knowing this teenager's life is in his hands. He can only interpret this happenstance as the will of his deity.

He patches what he can, and is running back to the Shelter to gather help bringing Nevian back when he finds Arathiel. Flustered, desperate to save Nevian, filled with guilt over his absence from the prison heist, Cal unburdens all of his worries on calm, patient Arathiel.

It is worth noting that Arathiel, who was alive in the city a hundred and thirty years ago, held a noble title at the time. He has been recognized by **Lady Camilla Dathirii**, with whom he has shared tea multiple times since, and to whose door he runs that night. She had offered help—any help he wished—and it is direly needed now. To send healers to Nevian, certainly, but that is not all he intends to ask. Arathiel has no intention of letting Hasryan's execution go through, but he'll need help to stop it and to hide afterwards.

Larryn is not one to be deterred by Cal's absence (although he is certainly one to be angered by it). He makes his way to Hasryan's cell and prepares to free him—until Hasryan, desperate for someone, *anyone*, to accept him without any lies left, tells him about his true job. Shocked, already primed for anger, Larryn tells him off, and is forced to flee before he can get over himself and fix his initial reaction.

When he reaches his Shelter once again, all of his anger is bottled tied and ready to blow at the one friend who should have been there. Cal's attempts to defend himself only infuriates him further, and in the heat of the yelling match, his fist flies faster than his brain, knocking Cal to the ground with a solid punch.

And thus the winter solstice night comes to an end. Branwen has returned to the Dathirii Tower and into her family's loving arms, but few others have had such luck. Varden is imprisoned in the Enclave, at Avenazar's mercy, and Nevian clings to life only through sheer stubbornness, his memory of magic erased. The long-standing friendship between Cal, Larryn, and Hasryan has shattered, existing fissures finally cracking.

But not all is lost, as they say, and in the following days, as Branwen and Lord Dathirii struggle to convince Isandor nobles to ally against the Myrian Enclave, Arathiel's plans solidify and come to fruition. On the morning of Hasryan's execution, he is ready.

So we come to our last scene, a park commemorating one of the city's founders with the delightful habit of hanging criminals above it. On bridges above, the high-born have gathered to celebrate the capture and execution of Isandor's most infamous criminal. Below, Lower City residents fume at one of their own once more sacrificed on the altar of politics.

Moving through the crowd towards the investigator responsible for it all is Camilla Dathirii, an old elven lady—perfectly innocent and respectable, here only for congratulations, of course. And when, in the process of doing so, she drops her purse and provokes a small commotion of guards trying to help pick it up before everything rolls off the bridges, it is also without malice, and not at all the distraction Arathiel has been waiting for. *Of course.* (It is.)

Nevertheless, Arathiel uses the opportunity to drop into their midst, blades drawn, and sprints for Hasryan. He is outnumbered, but he possesses one advantage no other has: he does not feel pain any more than he does cold or touch. Wounds that would stagger other fighters leave him unfazed, and so despite his profuse bleeding, he pushes through the Sapphire Guard surrounding Hasryan and they escape by leaping into the park below.

The landing is hard—impossible for one who does not feel the pressure of ground under his feet. Arathiel's ankle snaps when they hit the park, destroying any chance he has of walking away from his spectacular rescue and the chaos that will ensue. Only Hasryan slips away, clinging to the written address offered by Arathiel and the certainty he still has at least one friend in Isandor willing to risk it all for him.

He does not expect the safehouse to be Lady Camilla's quarters, nor does he anticipate the delicious butterscotch cookies awaiting him and the crash of emotions they will bring. He sits in the living room, cookies in hand, unexpected acceptance washing over him while on a balcony nearby—a few stories above, really—Diel Dathirii considers his few remaining options.

The nobles of Isandor refuse to help him, the Myrian threat is growing, and they hold a man to whom his niece owes her life. But today he saw a man who does not know pain—a man he knew, over a century ago, as caring and courageous. Arathiel's aid would destroy the political goodwill he has left, but what good is that, when all of his allies rebuked him? The choice is simple and dangerous, and he is ready to make it.

Here ends *City of Strife*, but certainly not their adventure.

CITY OF BETRAYAL

All of Isandor is searching for Hasryan, some for revenge, others to save their friend. Only Arathiel knows where he hid, however, and he is recovering from the dangerous escape, cuffed to a bed in the Sapphire Guards Headquarters. What time he has awake, he spends with Investigator Sora Sharpe, who is desperate to understand why this stranger—this unknown noble from a time long passed—has risked everything for the city's most infamous criminal. Arathiel has no answers to give: the bond he shares with Hasryan is not easily explained with words and his sense of rightfulness goes beyond the city's laws.

What could (and should) have been a prolonged stay in prison is interrupted by Lord Dathirii, who brings his political influence to bear in order to cut a deal with Arathiel: temporary freedom if the man is willing to lend him his aid against the Myrian Enclave.

The time eventually comes for his mission, and Arathiel has been allowed to call for help—a favour Cal is more than happy to grant him. They are to assemble in Lord Dathirii's office. However, on the same day, through circumstances and quick deduction, **Kellian Dathirii**, the family's guard captain, figures out that Lady Camilla is involved in hiding Hasryan and confronts her about it. She refuses to give in, and instead challenges him to arrest her for her crime and brings her to the Sapphire Guard headquarters—a challenge Kellian readily accepts.

Hasryan, a witness to the confrontation, refuses to let Camilla face prison on his behalf. As soon as possible, he sneaks his way up the Dathirii tower, to Lord Dathirii's office, and warns Diel Dathirii of his aunt's arrest, risking his own fate in the process. Instead of bringing him to the guards, Diel ropes Hasryan into his Myrian Enclave mission, adding invaluable assassin skills to the infiltration team.

And thus Hasryan finds himself part of a small team with Arathiel, who has saved him when he thought everything lost, and Cal, who had never given up on him and is thrilled to prove it through spontaneous hugs and squeals of joy. Their last member is none other than Branwen, the driving heart of the mission, who will gladly take any help if it lets them extract Varden from his terrible situation.

They set off as night falls, and their infiltration starts without a hitch—in no small part thanks to Cal's subtle luck-bending magic. Only, Varden is no longer in his cell. Master Avenazar has dragged him out of it, to the great brazier in Keroth's Temple, to try a brand new spell of his own devising. With it, he slams into Varden's mind, forcing him to channel Keroth's power through the flames, and uses the magic to further nourish his spell and wipe Varden's spirit out of his own body and mind.

Branwen's team arrives just in time to interrupt the ritual, but the confrontation is not without pain. They must also face not only Avenazar's deadly green whips of magic, but also Varden's streams of fire, as the High Priest has not regained control of himself. Hasryan's successful stealth-and-stab breaks the spell, but by that time Arathiel has been flung directly into the brazier's great flames. And here, several things happen at once.

First, the ritual's accumulated power goes haywire, causing an explosion which collapses the temple, and which the ragtag team only escapes with a magical bubble shielding them. Second, Arathiel's contact with the fire causes him brutal and entirely unexpected pain. His scream is what causes the third event: Varden, in possession of himself once again, pulls fire away from Arathiel and uses every inch of his power to keep them both safe. Although no one is left unscathed, the entire team is alive when the dust falls, and they are ready to head home.

Here we must pause again, for there are many agents whose story has unfolded in the sidelines, more quietly perhaps, but in a way no less essential to our tapestry, in House Dathirii and in the Enclave both. These **<u>key players</u>** are:

Vellien Dathirii, youngest Dathirii cousin, anxious singer and expert healer.

Hellion Dathirii, arrogance and drama incarnate. Convinced of his own cunning and the supremacy of elves.

Lord Allastam, Head of House Allastam, father to Drake.

Arrogant and choleric. His wife was assassinated a decade ago.

Master Jilssan Wich, second in command at the Myrian Enclave, transmutation specialist, irremediable pragmatic.

While his infiltration team made its way into the Enclave, Diel Dathirii attends a meeting of Isandor's ruling instance, the Golden Table. Here, nobles from the most prominent houses gather to decide of the city's future—or, in this case, that of House Dathirii's. **Lord Allastam** leads the charge against Diel, angered that he dared free Arathiel, the man who'd stopped the execution of his wife's killer. The price to pay for rescuing Varden is steeper than Diel Dathirii had expected, however: by the end of the Table's meeting, House Dathirii has lost all of its seats around it, and thus its claim at nobility.

The political downfall is only the first of Diel's problems tonight. Without titles, he and his family are unprotected, and he returns to his home to find it invaded by Allastam soldiers. Worse, he is brought to the elf who betrayed him and, with Allastam's help, claimed his place. **Hellion Dathirii** awaits him in Diel's own office, smug and convinced he can force Diel to yield his place publicly, but Lord Allastam has other plans. He has struck another deal, this one with Master Avenazar, and promised to send him Diel as a prize. In the dark of night, Diel Dathirii is shipped towards the Myrian Enclave, shackled and shattered.

He is received by **Master Jilssan Wich,** but their brief chat is interrupted by the temple's explosion. Jilssan immediately heads out, and on her way there she intercepts Branwen's team. Jilssan has been known for her ambition and ruthlessness, but over the course of this conflict, she has witnessed the depths of Avenazar's cruelty and, more importantly, his fickleness. By now, she knows neither she nor her apprentice are safe around him, and the only people foolish enough to openly fight him are Diel Dathirii and his people. So she tells them Diel is here, at the Enclave, allowing Branwen and the others to save him. When it becomes clear none of them can return to the Dathirii Tower, now under Allastam control, Cal offers his home as temporary shelter.

This should, by all means, have marked the end of their troubles for the night. Unfortunately not, but to understand what comes next, we must return to the lower levels of Isandor.

While political players make their moves, Nevian continues his slow recovery at the Shelter. He is aided by young **Vellien Dathirii**, who through frequent visits helps him restore his missing memories and slowly heal both body and mind. The rest of his time is spent relearning his spells, a fact not unnoticed by Larryn, who has been feeding and housing him. In exchange for these, Nevian accepts to work on a spell to try and track down Hasryan.

The scrying spell is cast on the night of the infiltration, with Larryn looking in, and they find Hasryan as he infiltrates the enclave, at a time where he is alone with Branwen. Larryn concludes House Dathirii is secretly holding him, and he takes it upon himself to arrange a hostage exchange: when young Vellien steps into the Shelter that night, he kidnaps them.

The ransom letter for Vellien is, shall we say, not well-received. It is, however, received in the presence of Hasryan, who offers to sneak to the Shelter and talk some sense into his old friend. It is their first meeting since the attempted prison break and it turns into a rocky one, but Hasryan is firm and clear: the Dathirii are helping him, and Larryn needs to get his shit together and his anger under control, both for his friendship with Cal and for his own sake. Vellien is freed and returns with Hasryan to Cal's house, where their healing talent will be welcome at Varden's bedside.

Here ends *City of Betrayal*. Master Avenazar is grievously wounded but House Dathirii is in disarray, its members split throughout the city—including three very important figures caught inside the Dathirii Tower who vowed to fight Hellion together. And so we leave with a final presentation and a final wish.

Jaeger Larethian, stalwart steward, the nerves of the House, Diel's lover.

Yultes Dathirii, liaison with a now-angry House Allastam. Arrogant elf in a bad position.

Garith Dathirii, Dathirii coinmaster and incorrigible flirt. Branwen's cousin.

Happy reading, everyone!

Still lost while you read? A Character Guide is available at the end to help you remember who's who, and what they mean to one another!

Chapter One

BRUNE HAD never meant to leave Kellian Dathirii alone in his cell for a full day, but an inconsequential elf hardly measured in urgency, when compared to the rush of meetings and scrying she accomplished with her time. The wait had fouled his mood, if the irascible pounding of fists on flimsy stone walls served as any indication. Perhaps she should have abandoned him still encased in rock, as he was when she'd brought him into the underground network of her headquarters. He'd be stiffer and equally disagreeable, no doubt, but at least his two guards would've been spared the noise.

She had warned him of the pointlessness of it when she'd first left him in the cell, explaining in very clear terms that she had crafted the walls of his prison with Gresh's grace, and very little could erode Their everlasting power. Only another priest of Gresh would stand a chance at escaping—provided they could best her own inner strength. Brune did not mention the keys; she'd rather let the Captain believe he wouldn't hatch from his egg-shaped cell until she desired it.

Kellian had paid her words no mind, of course. Stubborn righteousness ran in the blood—a peculiarity of House Dathirii that made them a wonderfully interesting player in any schemes one wove around Isandor. She hadn't expected any trading merchant family to lean into incorruptible ethics with such vigour when she'd arrived a decade ago, but Brune enjoyed a good challenge. Isandor, the renowned City of Spires, had held quite its share of surprises. Even now, she sometimes forgot how deeply melodramatic its inhabitant liked to be, especially when compared to Nal-Gresh's population. No wonder Lord William loved it so much. The eccentric towers and lush gardens were but a surface manifestation of the city's natural inclination towards sweeping gesture and overreaction. In that sense, Isandor was as firmly Allorian as the region stretching south of it.

Even with her low expectations for Kellian's willingness to heed her advice, his decision to punch a wall until his hands bled left her pondering. Brune enjoyed untangling what lay behind others' actions; it always paid to learn more about an adversary or ally. First of all, Kellian Dathirii was not hammering away out of panic. He had a reputation for calm under pressure, especially when faced with an enemy. While none of her troops had reported exceptional feats of cunning from him, he was not so slow of wit as to believe he could escape in such a fashion. She'd trapped countless merchants in there while competitors moved on a business opportunity, many of which had tried cleverer tactics—to no avail, truly. No, he was making a point. About loyalty, refusal to cave or give up, about forcing others to acknowledge your existence, about not playing by their rules, or such similar things. The exact reason mattered less than the act of futile defiance. Brune doubted he even knew precisely why he kept hammering at his prison cell's wall. He considered her an enemy—which was fair, since she had snatched him off a High City bridge and imprisoned him while House Allastam took over the Dathirii Tower and ousted Kellian's liege— but in truth, that assessment was a mistake. She wished for House Dathirii to survive a while longer, and it was increasingly clear it would not do so without her help.

Brune stopped outside the cell area, her fingers tracing the geometric markings etched into the walls. They reminded her of the hundred-foot high frescoes along the inside shell of Nal-Gresh, a masterpiece of art in honour of the Earth Shaper, each of its delicate lines illuminated by soft yellow lights. Hers glowed too, and everyone could navigate the headquarters by their radiance. The patterns themselves contained clues about paths and locations for those who knew the code—a simple way of allowing her blind lieutenant, Xan, to guide themself through touch.

It had been a decade since she'd carved this space for herself and her people under Isandor, but even now, she could hear Hasryan's laugh when he'd first witnessed the walls.

"Is it Emmior you miss, or Nal Gresh?" he'd asked, all smug adolescent mockery.

"Both," she'd answered, and her honesty had taken him aback.

It had been the truth then, and it still was today. Over a decade had passed since she'd sent Hasryan, her best assassin, to kill her partner—in crime, and so much more. They had been a perfect duo, their symbiosis blurring commonly understood lines, deadly and powerful … until he'd plotted to murder her. She had struck first, stolen their best mercenaries, and left the Stone-Egg City to build her own mercenary empire. Brune remembered staring at the crescent moon that night, as it reached the hole atop the city's walls, knowing that at this precise moment, Hasryan was plunging his daggers into the man's heart. She hadn't scried on it; there were some events even she had no desire to witness.

Brune chided herself for the melancholy—their partnership had been over, one way or another, and she always prevailed—and refocused on the present. Kellian Dathirii would not be a compliant ally, but she wanted to start smoothing out some edges before she had need of him. He'd festered long enough; it was time to clarify some facts. The faint pounding she'd felt through the stone echoed more strongly as she walked to the cell area, and when Brune nodded towards the two guards rolling dice at a nearby table, one of them didn't bother to hide his relief.

She stopped in front of the deeply carved ovoid lines characterizing the cell and slid her fingers into them, calling upon Gresh's power. A coppery taste filled her mouth, a sign of her deity's answer. Brune allowed herself to bask in Their presence, a reassuring aura, immovable and eternal. Xan had once told her she felt Them as a multitude, grains flying in a whirlwind, an expanse so large none could tame it. How many nights had they spent theorizing on whether these reflected their highly personal connection to Gresh, or if the manifestations represented Their duality of creation and destruction? No doubt some scholar had studied this and written something insightful about it. Not that it mattered. They were mercenaries playing at philosophy when alcohol ran too thick in their veins.

First, Brune sent her consciousness into the ground, quickly locating Kellian's feet. Stone rose around them, gripping his ankles and climbing until it trapped his legs entirely. A muffled curse reached her through the walls, and Brune smiled as she disintegrated the barrier before her, opening an entryway and stepping inside.

She had shaped the cell like a perfectly symmetrical egg—another bout of nostalgia—but the floor stayed flat, about ten feet in radius. Kellian stared at the wall across from her, his back stiff, and she stifled her laughter. He must have been knocking on the wrong side.

"Good evening," she said.

She waved her hand, and the stone holding him shifted, spinning him around to face her. Kellian crossed his arms, his shoulders squared with pride, as if no rock trapped his feet. Every muscle of his short, wiry body was tense, and he'd tied his blonde hair into a ponytail, giving prominence to his pointed ears. Her greeting was met with a scowl.

"It cannot only be evening." The harshness of his tone didn't entirely cover the hint of despair.

"There is no 'only'. You have been here for more than a day."

"Oh." The sound escaped him, and for a moment his stiff posture collapsed, fatigue weighing his shoulders. He pulled himself back together quickly, raising his chin and pinning her down with a defiant look. "How long is this supposed to last?"

"An excellent question to which I do not have a definite answer." Her gaze travelled around the barren cell and she added, "The full day of isolation was an unintentional lapse on my part, however. I'll give instructions to bring you regular meals. Should you stop pounding so relentlessly, I can also request a mattress for you, and I could embellish your dwelling."

Kellian snorted. "I don't want comfort. I want to leave."

"I'm afraid you're grounded here until it's safe."

"Safe for whom? Myself, or you?"

Brune smiled. She liked those who asked the right questions. "Both."

"I'm not scared of the Myrians. It's my job to risk my life for others. Let me go out there and protect my family."

That almost sounded like a plea, under all the gruffness. The poor elf was running on too little sleep and too little information.

"Sit down."

Brune gestured towards the ground and called upon Gresh, morphing the stone encasing Kellian's legs into a seat for him, wrapping the earth around his hip so that he had no choice but to obey. His grunt of disapproval warmed her heart, and she created a second pillar for herself.

"It's time for me to lay cards on the table."

As if, she thought, and Kellian's grimace reflected the same idea.

He leaned backward as much as the chair would allow, sneering. But just because she wouldn't tell him everything didn't mean she would lie about what she did reveal. "In the time you took to bring your aunt to the headquarters, Hasryan Fel'ethier left her quarters and climbed the tower to Lord Dathirii's office. There, he petitioned for Lord Dathirii to help Lady Camilla, and in the process gained his protection and joined the expedition to save High Priest Varden Daramond. You would have arrived to this meeting after Lord Dathirii's departure for the Golden Table, and as I could not predict your reaction to Hasryan's presence, I swept you off the street. When I can't control a player, I remove it."

Lord Kellian Dathirii had gone stiff, his jaw set, his eyes boring holes into her. He'd flattened his two hands against the stone at his hips and now pressed the butt of his palms into it, releasing what anger he could without moving. She admired his self-control—more proof his earlier knocking had nothing to do with panic. Slowly, Kellian brought his hands back on his lap. "How do you know all of this?"

She laughed, and he scowled at the deep staccato of her voice. "My dear Kellian, it's my job to know things, especially those affecting my people." And Hasryan would always be one of them, no matter what plans demanded or how much he hated her now. "When one of them goes underground, I keep them hidden, to the Sapphire Guard's great frustration. They must not enjoy the inconsistency of their poor divination spells."

"So your assassin is with our team. With Lord Dathirii's approval."

"Indeed," she confirmed. "I could have released you once they had left the Dathirii Tower, but it came to my attention a kill order had been attached to your name should you resist during the following takeover by House Allastam—which you would have, I'm sure—so I judged it best to keep you here. As I said, for your safety."

Kellian blanched and sucked his breath in, once again putting a commendable effort into remaining calm. "I would rather have died than let them run into our home unchecked."

"Yes, I'm well aware a pointless but heroic death would have been your first choice." She dismissed his answer with a hand-wave and leaned forward, meeting Kellian's eyes, unflinching at the hatred burning in them. May Gresh grant her patience, he was as overdramatic as the other nobles of Isandor. "None of your family perished, though at this moment most of the city has no idea where to find Lord Dathirii. Well, Diel, now. You've lost your titles. Did I mention a lot has happened? A veritable landslide of events."

"All of it while I'm stuck here," he countered, gritting his teeth. "What do you want? If you won't release me, you must want something."

Brune leaned back and waited before answering. She couldn't underestimate Kellian, even if the gruff captain was no master schemer. "I want many things, most of which are none of your concern. I have concluded, however, that the Myrians' continued presence in Isandor would be detrimental to several of these objectives. Which means that we want the same thing: we want Master Avenazar gone from our neighbourhood, and we want his new alliance with House Allastam to crumble before it has fully taken flight. It makes us allies, however temporary that might be."

"No better ally than the one who will stab you in the back as soon as they no longer need you." Kellian leaned forward, meeting her gaze. "I know a trap when I see one. You'll either demand something in return for your help, or place yourself in a position where you can grab it no matter what we think of it."

Brune lifted her hands, palms up, and countered him with a nonchalant shrug. "I'm a mercenary leader, not a charity. You'll find, I believe, that my prices are fair, and the benefits invaluable."

He rolled his eyes. Brune had not expected Kellian to dance with joy at her proposal—metaphorically, of course—but his attitude annoyed her anyway. She rose to her feet, lowering her stone seat in the process.

"We can discuss details later. Understand, however, that if I deem it necessary, you will have my help whether you like it or not, at the time and manner of my choosing."

"Not unlike now, is that it?" Kellian retorted.

"Precisely."

"If you seek an alliance…" He started his sentence slowly, doubt weighing his every word. "One would think releasing me would be a good show of faith."

And waste a precious resource? No. Brune might not know how Kellian fit in with all the moving pieces yet, but she had no intention of throwing away her chance to have him on hand when an opportunity arose. Alone out there, he'd simply join one group of Dathirii or another and become a predictable player in this ever evolving mess.

"I keep my shows of faith for the Earth Shaper, thank you."

She turned her back on him, releasing the stone holding him tight in a sharp movement, causing him to fall hard on the floor. Kellian hit the ground with a grunt but swiftly leaped to his feet, recovering with impressive fluidity. He surprised her by staying put instead of attempting to jump her. Perhaps the ease with which she wielded magic had convinced him not to waste his time in a pointless assault.

"Now, I will certainly return as the situation develops. Until then, however, should I have a mattress brought, or will you continue banging on the walls during every waking hour?"

Not that the sound reached her. This was a test of Kellian's willingness to negotiate, at least on a small scale. The ceaseless pounding had been a statement, but also a demand to be acknowledged. She had come and offered a deal, and if he took it, it meant he could accept having his needs met by an enemy. If that was true, then even Kellian Dathirii could, when presented with the right incentive, become a potent ally. Brune waited, too used to silence and games of power to let any impatience show. When Kellian sighed, she knew she had won.

"Bring me the mattress," he said, before sitting on the floor, cross-legged and thoughtful.

THE last days had tested Branwen's skills in brand new ways. She was used to sliding in and out of disguises as the situation required, flitting from one informant to the next or sitting in tea houses, taverns, and other locations ripe for debates and meetings. It was harder to accomplish those goals when her glorious wardrobe was inaccessible, drastically limiting her options to conceal herself at a time when discretion held even more weight.

The fall of House Dathirii and Diel's disappearance were the talk of the city no matter the height at which you lived, and residents of all stripes enjoyed speculating about which members of her family were missing, which remained inside of their own will, and which had been trapped there. Information was particularly scarce the first day, and she'd had to listen to numerous strangers declare with vehement conviction that as House Dathirii's spymaster, only she could have orchestrated this coup. Many argued her supposed capture by Myrians had been a ploy, and that the troops invading the great elven tower had only looked like Allastam soldiers, but had in fact been sent from the enclave.

The mysterious enclave explosion added to the mystique of this theory, as did the rumours that it had left Master Avenazar bedridden. Many residents of the higher layers of Isandor reported great smoke and flashes of light spotted from balconies and windows, and they were eager to speculate about their origins. When Branwen investigated the Upper City, she had to sit there, fuming, as nobles and upper crust merchants concocted the wildest stories, all of which subtly deflected blame away from House Allastam. That must be their handiwork; they hadn't wasted a second directing the flow of rumours.

So she got to work countering them. She invented witnesses that had watched the Allastam troops walk out of their tower, pointed out the strange timing of the attack and how it coincided with the Dathirii losing their titles—something Myrians could not have predicted. She spread rumours which facts would bolster eventually: that Branwen Dathirii was missing, that Dathirii nobles had escaped their home and wouldn't stand by the coup, that Hellion Dathirii now claimed the office of the Head of the House, that Lord Allastam himself had been sighted within the great tree spire that night. With a few well-placed coins, she convinced others to raise those same questions. She doubted they'd sway anyone. All she needed was to stop Allastam's version from being set in stone before Diel decided on their next step. Besides, you couldn't keep a whole household bottled up, and it was only a matter of time before facts emerged from the Dathirii Tower.

The indigo sky announced their third dawn at Cal's as Branwen snuck back into the cozy home they had invaded. Warmth sunk into her bones and she sighed in relief, slowly pulling off her gloves and allowing her frozen toes time to thaw. Three bundles of blankets and cushions marked people's sleeping spots in the living room, and her heart twinged as she noticed how Diel— unmistakable with his splash of golden hair—clung to a bigger pillow as if it was another body. He'd tried putting up a front, but he'd been frazzled and distracted ever since Hellion Dathirii had taken the tower—or, perhaps more to the point, ever since he'd been separated from Jaeger.

A soft melody drifted from the bedroom's door, draping itself over the quiet household. Vellien's voice soothed Branwen as much as the inside warmth, if not more. With a smile, she carefully picked her way across the room, striding around Hasryan, then over Cal, and slipped through the cracked-open door.

Hushed light bathed Cal's blue bedroom, its diffuse glow emanating from her cousin's palm. They sat by the bed, one hand on Varden's shoulder while the other formed a circle over their heart. The song must be a prayer to Alluma, then. Branwen found a nearby seat and settled in it, unwilling to interrupt. Even though they directed their magic at Varden, Vellien's crystalline notes acted as a balm on her nerves. She closed her eyes, and exhaustion sloughed off of her as she drifted to sleep.

A gentle hand on her shoulder woke her up, and she blinked her bleary eyes until they focused on her uncle. Someone had wrapped her into a warm blanket, and sunlight streamed through the windows. Varden still slept, his brow smooth and his breath steady—his usual state, these days—and Vellien had crawled into the second half of the bed, their back to the fire priest.

"You've been out all night, haven't you?"

Branwen couldn't help her smirk. Although concern weighed Diel's voice, she'd heard that same question from Kellian or him so often in the past, right before they scolded her and Garith, it was hard to think of anything else.

"Oh yes, out joining the wildest revelries I could find."

"I'm sure." He squeezed her shoulder. "A pile of pillows isn't a mattress, but it's still better than a chair. Please take mine and get a real night—or day—of rest."

How long had she slept? Two hours, maybe three? Branwen

stifled a yawn, pushing back against her fatigue. "Can't," she mumbled.

Diel's gentle smile faltered. "No news from our home?"

Watching the hope dim in his green eyes was almost unbearable. Every time she returned to Cal's house, Diel's gaze tracked her, searching with quiet desperation for a sign she had anything concrete about Jaeger. She hated disappointing him, and hated even more that she'd made countering Allastam's narrative a priority over digging out specifics about House Dathirii. As much as Branwen wished to find out how her family fared, she didn't see how the information would help them.

"Nothing new," she said. "Uncle… What would you do if you knew? What *could* you do?"

Silence met her question, and with every passing second, guilt gnawed Branwen more heavily. Perhaps she should have kept the thought to herself. Diel didn't deserve to be reminded of his powerlessness. Jaeger was out of his reach, at the mercy of Hellion's cruelty. Deserved or not, however … he needed the reminder.

"Nothing," he finally whispered, and his shoulders slumped. He set his gaze on the floor, a curtain of golden hair falling before his face. "I just… I need to know, Branwen. I can't think of anything else."

Branwen scooped his hands up, bringing them on her lap. "Then let's think about it. Let's think about what we can do to get ready! I don't want to wait for the hammer to fall, Uncle. Forget the news: let's gather our allies. We had trade deals all over the city. Surely some of these merchants would rather work with us than

Hellion."

"We don't have anything to offer them." Diel pulled his hands away and straightened, flipping his hair back. Branwen wanted to shut her eyes and lock away the sight of his exhausted hopelessness. It was so wrong, on her miracle-working uncle. "I'm a political pariah, with no titles and no gold behind my name. Who would risk the trouble?"

"We can't know if we don't ask." Her forced cheer wouldn't fool anyone, let alone Diel. "I'll check on our network of merchants. Stop worrying about how much I sleep, and try to think of nobles who could funnel gold or legitimacy our way. Waiting for the bad news to tumble to us won't help Jaeger."

"All right," he said, but his frown didn't ease.

Branwen doubted she'd get more from him today, so she slid out of the chair and stood up. "People love you more than you give them credit for. Titled or not, what Lord Allastam did was heinous. We'll find a way to use it against him, and then we'll have our home back, and you'll be with Jaeger again."

Diel's shoulders lifted as he breathed in deeply, then lowered. They didn't sag, not this time, and Branwen took heart in that minuscule change. She craved Diel's unrelenting optimism—it was too strange and too draining to be the one putting on the brave face and meeting despair with calm reassurances. Branwen wasn't meant for this role reversal, and she didn't know if she could keep it up. She'd try, though, for as long as her uncle needed her to. With a deep, steadying breath of her own, Branwen left the bedroom and readied herself for another long day.

She did not go rumour-hunting, not this time. It was time to stop trying to piece together what had happened in the Dathirii Tower from overheard conversations. Without a spy in her household, she had to consider that avenue a dead end. Her best bet in that regard would be Alton, whose work within House Allastam allowed him to catch quite a lot of gossip, but when she inspected the public flower pot in which they concealed messages, she found no discarded blue flower to indicate he'd left her something. She checked the cache anyway, in case someone had picked up the flower and erased the signal, to no avail. At least her own note, left on her first day out after the explosion, was gone, so he knew she wanted a meeting. It'd come. Altonhad never let her down before.

In the meantime, she'd prove what she had told her uncle—that among the merchants who'd remained loyal through the upheavals of the Myrians' financial and physical assaults, many would stand with them, if given a chance to rally. They only needed to know which ones, and what it would take to get them on board.

BRANWEN never got to the merchants at all—or rather, she got to *Jolyan's Joyous Jewelry*'s door and stopped short, her eyes latching onto the woman idly guarding it. Long russet hair, beautiful freckles, lean muscles, and an endearingly loud laugh. Cordelia. Cordelia, who had stood night duty when Branwen had escaped the Myrian Enclave. Cordelia, who had caught her as she fell and wiped dirt from her cheek to make her "presentable" before she crawled her way to Diel's office. Cordelia, who had a wry smile that sent flutters down her spine and biceps to dream of. Cordelia, who was definitely one of Kellian's guards, many of which had vanished after Allastam troops overtook their tower, and who had certainly ditched the Dathirii ceremonial armour Branwen had last seen her with.

She had replaced it with a indigo slim wool coat that skimmed her waist and split in two, allowing for warmth and freedom of movement, on top of which she'd draped a fur-lined pale grey cloak. Her winter hat matched the coat, and a long braid emerged from under it. The whole was far more stylish than Kellian's fancy breastplate, and the pleasant aesthetic effect dimmed Branwen's slight irritation that their guards had removed all Dathirii symbolism.

Branwen readjusted the knitted beret on her head, which did much to hide her tell-tale ears, and strutted to the guard, plastering her brightest smile on. She wasn't halfway there when Cordelia spotted her, her brow furrowing into confusion—points for efficient perception, Branwen thought, before waving at her.

"Miss Cordelia!" she called. "How strange, to find you watching another door than ours. That is what you're doing, right? Or are you available for a drink?"

Recognition hit Cordelia halfway through the invitation and her eyes widened. Her gaze flicked briefly at the jewelry door next to her. "Been guarding this place since the Captain asked me to, Miss Branwen—and that is the proper address now, isn't it?"

Light humour tinged her tone, but Branwen's heart twinged

nonetheless. She'd chided Cordelia for skipping over her title when she'd escaped from the enclave, in jest more than any real concern about propriety, but now the title was truly gone and its absence reminded her of Hellion's treachery, Allastam's arrogance, and all the ways this city had its head up its ass. Still, Cordelia remembered the exchange, and that knowledge slid into Branwen, warm and exciting.

"It is," she confirmed. "You didn't answer my second question."

New dimples appeared in Cordelia's cheeks as she smiled, making Branwen's heart stutter. "In half an hour I leave to have lunch," she said. "If you intend to exploit these liminal days where I'm not under your family's employ to flirt, you can take the spare time to browse jewelry for a gift, yes? I am fond of eccentric earrings when off duty."

Wow. Forward, wasn't she? And unafraid to call Branwen's act for what it was. Pink climbed to her cheeks and heat flushed through her. She'd never been one to refuse a challenge. Besides, this absolutely counted as a meaningful use of their limited funds, didn't it? Most of the gold they had left came from Cal's improbable luck and constant generosity, and if she'd learned anything about their gracious host, it's that he'd beg for her not to turn down this lady. She flashed Cordelia a grin.

"Let's see what *Jolyan's Joyous Jewelry* has in store, why don't we?"

Not that Cordelia wouldn't know. If she enjoyed the jewelry she seemed to guard, she must have browsed a few times. Which meant Branwen needed to unearth the piece she'd had in mind with that description. She roamed the modest boutique in search of it—and truly, while *Jolyan's* had plenty of options, Branwen had developed an expertise in sizing up others' sense of aesthetics and in finding the rare treasure in a mountain of choice.

When she laid eyes on a pair of asymmetrical earrings, one a sideways cat with its paw raised playfully, the other a ball of blue yarn with a single string of tiny aquamarines trickling down, she knew she had her winner. It was silly, to buy such a thing now, while her family struggled to survive and her home had been ripped from her, but her heart hammered with quiet joy at the idea, and the excitement jolted her awake, as if she'd rested for two days instead of two hours.

Cordelia's smile as she unveiled her choice was worth every doubt and future recriminations. It sparkled, warming her entire expression, and Branwen caught herself enraptured by the crinkle at the guard's eyebrows, the long and thick nose, the frizzy hair escaping her braid. Cordelia had always been a pretty, light-hearted sort of crush—a beautiful woman she loved to look at without any real intentions—but now that they sat at a table together, freshly baked bread and a selection of terrines, creamy cheese, and other deliciousness to combine between them, Branwen could tell why she'd been attracted. Cordelia had a mature, confident charm that challenged you to earn her attention.

"So you are flirting," Cordelia said after silently holding up the earrings, watching sunlight glint off the aquamarine.

Branwen busied herself with their meal, flattening the cheese on her warm bread until it melted. She wished she could remove her lighter cloak and hood, but this establishment was a small dinery at the frontier between the Middle and Upper City, and she'd rather not be spotted.

"Garith has taught me never to hesitate, and always be clear with my intent," she said, "so, yes, I am. But I also have questions for you."

"That makes two of us." Cordelia, despite the loud grumbling her stomach had emitted when they'd entered this place and caught a whiff of fresh bread, had yet to touch her food. She set the earrings down, and her smile vanished with them. "We've no news of our captain, Allastam soldiers are in our home, and many of the merchants we're supposed to protect from Myrian assault have received a missive from the Dathirii Tower voiding what arrangements they had. There are rumours, of course, but…"

"You say 'we'… Are you and other Dathirii guards still in contact?"

"Some of us. We'd all hoped colleagues had more information than us, so we reached out. Those of us on missions away from the tower knew better than to try and set foot within it. All we put together is these Allastam bastards killed some of our fellows, and no one's got a clue where Kellian was during this mess." She snatched up one piece of bread and tore through it. "What is he waiting for? We thought he was dead, same as his troops in the tower, but those who survived the night said they never caught a glimpse of him. Left his people adrift, grieving and angry."

Every word out of Cordelia's mouth doused Branwen's quiet joy at their casual flirt. So much for a pleasant chat; as always, they had bigger matters to attend to. She'd hoped, upon spotting her, that they might've heard of Kellian, that after failing to find any Dathirii not trapped in the Tower, her uncle had sought his soldiers throughout the city. No such luck. She grimaced.

"I wish I knew. He should've been with me that day, but he never showed up."

She shoved another piece of bread in her belly—terrine covered, this time, pork and apples—and Cordelia followed suit. Quiet dread draped them as they ate. Something must have happened to Kellian, who'd always been amongst the most loyal and reliable of them.

"I'll piece it together," she told Cordelia, "I don't believe he abandoned you, or any of us. Lord Allastam had planned this attack, timing it to move as soon as we'd lost our titles at the Golden Table. He might have something to do with it. But this isn't over, and we're about to start fighting back properly. Just hold tight."

Cordelia snorted. "Hold tight?" She played with a piece of bread, shaking her head. "You got a beautiful smile, Miss Branwen, and a great sense of people, but that won't feed me—nor will loyalty feed the others, or their family. Lots of us already found work elsewhere. We had to."

Of course. House Dathirii had been a job to them, no matter how much camaraderie had bloomed between Kellian's troops. They might want revenge, but that didn't mean they could afford to idle for their chance at it. She sighed.

"I understand. I'd love to speak with the others, though. Anyone inside and outside the Tower when this went down. You never know who might have key information, and we'll need all we can find."

"I'll get you in touch." Cordelia's smile returned, melting away the worry weighing on Branwen's heart. "They'll be happy to help however they can."

And that was all she could ask for now. Branwen wished they'd all been waiting for the Dathirii signal, but that had been foolish of her. House Dathirii had relied on them for security—or, truly, the prestige that came from hiring dedicated guards—and, in turn, they'd relied on them for income. With that relationship falling apart, they had no reason to trail behind except sentimentality, so they'd started moving on with their lives. Branwen would take what help they could give, when they could give it—which, from the sound of it, might still be a lot. She rewarded Cordelia with a bright smile.

"Then I'm glad fate brought us together today," she said smoothly, leaning over the table, "and I'll be even more so if you can take my mind off this awful business for half an hour."

Cordelia laughed, a booming sound that already did wonders to cleanse Branwen's thoughts.

"Then let me tell you about my family," she said and as they emptied the plates and ordered more bread, she brushed a vivid portrait of life with two cats and seven birds, in her two-room flat towards the lower end of the Middle City, peppering anecdotes with a wry humour that had Branwen's sides hurting from laughing. It didn't matter, if nothing came out of this flirt but a nice, relaxing lunch. She needed this break and drank in the solace Cordelia offered without hesitation, allowing her companion's frankness to seep through her.

CHAPTER TWO

"JILSSAN?"

At Isra's question, Jilssan startled awake and straightened in a hurry. Sunlight streamed through her window, splashing across her desk and forcing her to squint. How late was it? She must have fallen asleep at her desk, using a magic tome as a pillow—which, quite frankly, was not the best. Jilssan rubbed the back of her neck and turned towards Isra, who'd walked in and closed the door behind her.

"Is that a book?" Isra asked, leaning past Jilssan to peek at it. Her lips pinched in disgust. "That's unlike you. 'Practice overrules theory', no?"

"If you know what to practise," Jilssan replied.

Her gaze slid back to her night's reading. *From Emotional Empathy to Mind Control: A Survey of Mind Spells and Their Endless Possibilities.* Heavy with theory, dry as a desert ... a perfect candidate to fall asleep on, if one was honest. Not that she could afford such behaviour, not if she wanted to find a way to defend herself against Avenazar's most devastating magic.

It was only a matter of time before she or Isra became targets now, so Jilssan had roamed the enclave's small library and collected pertinent work. Most of her research, however, had been pilfered directly from Avenazar's office, where they'd stayed as he'd used them to build his latest spell for Varden. She'd have to return them if he showed signs of leaving his bed, so until then, she intended to decipher and understand as much of them as she could. As pointless as it was likely to turn out, she had to try.

"Knowledge is never superfluous. I should have been digging up this kind of information the moment I grasped how volatile our great leader is."

Isra threw a fearful look at the door behind her and scuttled deeper inside Jilssan's room, as if it could protect her. She settled on the bed, leaving her legs hanging. She had gathered her thick brown hair in a massive ponytail, leaving only strands to fall out of it and clearing her face. Jilssan still caught herself marvelling at her apprentice's transformation—the physical one, certainly, but even more so at the shift in her behaviour. She had grown more serious, often sinking into silent thoughts. Her previous chirpiness had vanished, replaced by constant worry.

"You don't think you can keep poisoning him," Isra stated. "Not without him noticing."

Jilssan searched for reassuring words, but none came. She had dosed Master Avenazar every day since the temple's explosion, convincing him to drink a concoction that threw him into a feverish sleep akin to infections. In his few hours of wakefulness, he railed against Priestess Yavia, the unfortunate soul who'd inherited Varden's responsibilities as the enclave's healer, for her incompetence. She hated small talk and avoided him to the best of her ability. The gist of his wrist injury might have been fixed, but Jilssan's little trick had kept him from recovering fully and she'd thought that would be enough. After all, Avenazar had plenty of enemies in Isandor who wouldn't waste such an opportunity to finish him off … right?

The first two nights, she had gone to bed expecting to be shaken awake by terrified guards or the enclave's magical alarms, or even to be greeted in the morning by the delightful news of Master Avenazar's assassination. She'd used the time to brush up on powerful communication spells and reach out to Master Enezi, Isra's father. Jilssan had confirmed with him that the girl by her side was indeed his daughter, not an impostor, and asked what help he could offer. Travel to the enclave would take too long, but he'd promised to do everything he could to get Master Avenazar demoted and asked her to keep Isra safe in the meantime. *Through whatever means necessary*, he'd said, but when she'd inquired about what protection he'd provide should foul play come to light, he'd mellowed and mumbled about limited influence on the Circle of Mages. Best not to get caught red-handed, in short, so she'd hoped someone else could put an end to Avenazar on her behalf.

No one had deigned to, not yet anyway. But how long *could* she keep poisoning Avenazar? If Lord Dathirii and his allies couldn't be counted upon, she would have to try the next best thing.

"Don't worry, Isra." She met the girl's deep brown eyes and forced a smile. "I have a plan, as always." More accurately, she had the first step of a plan: ruin the alliance with Lord Allastam, and make it personal. "It involves pitting two dangerously violent men against each other, which promises to be thrilling, but I'm sure it'll work out."

Isra paled, but she raised her chin defiantly. "How can I help?"

Another marked change in Isra: she no longer tried to dodge responsibilities, demanding them instead. It pleased Jilssan, although she had no idea what to entrust her with in this particular case. "For now, not much. You can keep the research up while I put things into motion. The more we know about how to defend ourselves, the better."

Isra's determined expression faltered—she enjoyed digging into books about as much as Jilssan, which was to say not at all. Sometimes one had to undertake tasteless tasks to survive, however, and she withheld any protests. "Do you think we can really learn that? To protect ourselves from him?"

Jilssan almost lied to her again, but it seemed too cruel to hide that particular truth. "No, I don't, but I've been wrong before." With that, she slid out of her chair and walked up to Isra, gripping her shoulders. "I know only one type of protection that works against Avenazar: deflection. Redirect his anger to a shinier target, and you might control his course to some extent.

So if he ever comes for you … if I'm not here to shield you, make sure someone else catches the brunt of the blow. Don't hesitate, Isra. It'll be you or them."

Isra's breath itched at the suggestion, her eyes widening in horror.

"Isra." Jilssan squeezed her shoulders and caught her gaze. When she spoke again, her voice allowed no disagreements. "Promise me."

Still, her apprentice hesitated. She swallowed hard, her head shaking even as she replied. "I… I promise."

It would have to be enough, Jilssan decided. She straightened up and sighed. It was time to face Avenazar's foul mood.

"Good luck with the books," she said, wishing she could stay, study, and steer clear from Avenazar. Jilssan reminded herself once more about what needed to be done, holding the mantra close to her heart as she left to prepare poison, in words and drinks both.

JILSSAN forced a smile to her lips before she stepped into Master Avenazar's quarters, building her walls and patience for the encounter to come. She brought her latest brew, a hot and spicy mix that would ignite his fever again, once it had time to settle into his system. She found Avenazar wide awake, angry eyes staring at the ceiling, skin pale and crummy. Bandages still wrapped around his right wrist, which he held close to his body, and he'd grown so thin his skin stretched against his skull. He glared at her as she approached the bed and set the drink down on a side table.

"Jilssan." His voice was a rattle of bones. "Useless wastes of skin have been fussing over my health for an hour. You best bring news that'll cheer me up, or I'm tearing this building down."

Ah, a warm greeting and dire warning all at once—just what she'd wanted! "I'm afraid I cannot create favourable events, Avez," she said, slowly at first before continuing in a singsong voice. "I got you something to drink the healers would hate, though."

Her phrasing melted away Avenazar's wariness. He snatched it up and downed the cup, eager for his petty vengeance, and Jilssan resisted the urge to grin. If everything went this smoothly today, she wouldn't complain. Her mirth lasted only until Avenazar slammed the cup back on the table.

"Whatever this is a diversion for, just be done with it. I have no patience for people beating around the bush. Out with the bad news."

Jilssan hesitated—long enough for him to scowl at her, and for her to decide she risked more by waiting. She grabbed one of the chairs the healers had pushed away and sat next to him, considering the best approach for this. "Have you spoken with the guard captain about the team that infiltrated the enclave?"

"And endure another fool? Why would I waste my time with his excuses? If he couldn't keep intruders out, he deserves to be fired."

Excellent. Unlike Avenazar, *she* had talked to the man. In their brief discussions following Diel Dathirii's escape, he had frequently implied Isra should be blamed for everything that had unfolded. "I'll be glad to take care of that for you. Especially since it seems he didn't have the courage to bring you disagreeable news, instead bestowing them on me."

Avenazar rolled his eyes and gestured for her to get on with it. Jilssan steadied herself, readying her lies. She'd killed the guards Branwen and her team had left unconscious to keep a lid on what had happened that night, and it was about to pay off. No one but her had the full truth.

"Here is what I learned: Lord Allastam is not as greedy as we'd anticipated. The carriage which should have contained Diel Dathirii instead arrived with his niece, Branwen, and several allies. This is why he freed Lord Arathiel Brasten—to send him in our walls and save Varden. Lord Allastam must have known all along. He played us."

Here lay the most dangerous part of her lie. Avenazar hated being wrong, and Jilssan's story implied he had misjudged Lord Allastam. He wouldn't like it, so she had been careful to use "we" and "us", sharing in the blame for this alliance even though he hadn't included her in any plans about it. She needed him to believe this and act upon it.

"You're sure about this?" he asked, scowling.

"Quite certain."

Years of half-truths and manipulation turned her answer into a smooth lie. Jilssan crossed her legs and waited, as if there was nothing else to add. Embellishing a lie was the best way to add contradictions in it. Master Avenazar's expression hardened, and he downed the rest of his drink then slammed the wooden mug on the table.

"So he betrayed us." Avenazar grew even paler—all except his cheeks, which had turned almost purple. Angry beads of sweat rolled down his face. On one hand, this was exactly the reaction Jilssan wanted from him. On the other, the slow build of magical power within him, swirling with his rising anger, was a terrifying insight into what would happen to her if he discovered her game. "He thinks he can get away with it—that I won't retaliate!"

Waves of relief hit Jilssan. It was working! All she needed to do was to fan Avenazar's vengeful flames in the right direction, and he would give her violent orders to enact. Crackling energy already emanated from him, and she suspected that if he wasn't recovering from the stab in his wrist and the poison in his body, he would have teleported to Allastam's chambers then and there. Jilssan allowed herself a smile.

"I heard he held a feast for himself and declared House Allastam had entered a new, glorious age," she said. "Babbled on about how great a legacy it was for his son. Drake's name is always on his lips, as if nothing in the world was more precious than his snivelling boy."

Perhaps it was mean to focus Avenazar's anger on the kid, but Jilssan had met him once and it'd been enough to instil in her a solid dislike for his person. Someone needed to take the brunt of Avenazar's vengeance, and the father and son pair deserved it.

"He needs to be taught about consequences. They dared to touch me!" He raised his bandaged wrist and shook it midair. "These good-for-nothing healers say I can't cast spell for days—not until it moves well and my fever is down. Utterly preposterous! That can't stand, Jilssan, it can't. Make him pay."

"How much?"

With Avenazar, asking that question was a formality. She would always remember how he'd boasted about killing Nevian's previous master over an almost-imagined slight. It had been her first warning sign of his volatile behaviour, and she should have heeded it more carefully and planned her escape ahead of time. After all, if Master Avenazar had razed an entire neighbourhood in Myria, where multiple more powerful wizards might resent him for it, how far would he go here, thousands of miles away from their country? She doubted this time would be any different, and Avenazar's enthused cackle quickly confirmed it.

"I want Drake Allastam dead, and I want the whole city to know we did it. Let it be a warning to everyone. Then we'll make our message infinitely clear with Lord Dathirii, and no one will dare whisper against us again."

Jilssan suspected they would be saying a lot of words *about* them, just not to their faces. Either way, she hoped Master Avenazar would never get to the 'Lord Dathirii' part. If he did, then she'd failed, and she had no doubt he would unearth the lies she'd planted today and would continue to do so in the coming weeks. When she had decided to help Diel Dathirii escape, she had irrevocably tied her fate to his. She'd have to speak with him so that they told the same story.

"I'm on it, sir." She stood up with a smile. "I never liked Drake Allastam anyway."

That, at least, wasn't a lie.

"Make sure you enjoy yourself for the two of us."

In other circumstances, Jilssan might have agreed with enthusiasm, but the pleasure Avenazar drove from his overblown revenge terrified her. She wasn't here to enjoy herself: she was here to ensure she and Isra escaped with their lives and mind intact. She hoped he wouldn't notice her smile stiffening.

"As you wish, Master Avenazar. Rest well, drink a lot, and you might join me before the fun is over."

He grunted, and Jilssan didn't hang around for a longer answer. He'd downed the poisoned beverage with such oblivious speed, he'd get sicker within an hour or two, and she'd rather be long gone by then. The quick degradation of his health would only worsen his mood. Let the healers deal with that. Jilssan had enough on her plate already.

She closed the door behind her and heaved a sigh of relief. This could have gone much worse. Sometimes Avenazar was hard to predict, but over the last two years—especially the last two weeks—Jilssan had learned which strings to pull, and how to avoid the biggest pitfalls. She'd set things in motion, now, and with Avenazar's destructive energy directed where she wanted it, there would be no stopping him.

CHAPTER THREE

FTER a week confined to his bed, nothing could have deterred Varden from undertaking the short walk to the living room. Each shaky step was a battle of will against his body. The world closed in on him, shapes and colours blurring together, his sight fraying at the edges as blood pounded in his ears. He refused to stop, however, straining muscles into another step, then another. By the time he'd reached the bedroom door, Varden had gripped Arathiel's forearm and leaned heavily on him, but still he went on, through the living room until he crumpled into a bright red sofa.

"You didn't have to stand up so soon," Arathiel said, his voiced filled with concern.

Varden squeezed his eyes shut, dizzy. "I did."

The warm mental glow of his success made his growing nausea worthwhile. He had needed this accomplishment to measure his recovery, minor as it was. Something, anything, to confirm he'd improved.

Since they had taken refuge in Cal's home, Vellien had been applying their considerable skills and previous experiences with Nevian to heal Varden. Continuous consent shaped the young elf's approach: Vellien always asked before slipping into Varden's consciousness, then made their own presence small, touching Varden's mind enough to communicate intent before every step of their work. Sometimes healing session consisted of what Vellien called "cleaning up"—smoothing out bruises in his mind and untangling the mess created by Avenazar's destruction—and while those certainly exacted their toll, the truly dangerous ones were times Vellien "relinked" his memories. They had no prior knowledge of what Varden would remember and how it'd impact him, so if he didn't have the fortitude to take the worst memories on, they waited for a better moment.

It was a gruelling process, leaving him exhausted physically and mentally, and Vellien's magic could never replace real, prolonged rest, so Varden had slept as much as he could. When Vellien had almost collapsed at the end of their last session, however, he had yielded the bed to them. A perfect occasion to test his limits, he'd declared.

Arathiel had only grudgingly conceded. Over the last days, he had made himself the self-appointed guardian of Varden's health, insuring the priest always had water at the ready, someone to talk to, and plenty of rest. More than once, he'd ushered Branwen and others outside, interrupting cordial games of cards between Cal and his friends. The noise could get overwhelming at times, but Varden otherwise enjoyed listening in. Everyone here was so warm with each other, so casual, and their gentle teasing relaxed him. It was, all in all, better than staying alone with his thoughts.

Arathiel might have guessed at the latter, considering he rarely let it happen. Even when Varden woke up in the middle of the night, he found the other man dozing nearby. And despite Arathiel's assurance that his senses were too numbed to hear Varden startling out of sleep from nightmares, he always seemed to stir within minutes of him. Arathiel called his timing a blessing and brushed it aside with a laugh, easily sliding the conversation to a different topic. They had discussed Varden's art and Arathiel's new friends at length, sidestepping heavy subjects to focus on calming ones.

The ghost of the enclave always clung to Varden, however, and his narrow escape stayed fresh in his memory. More than once, he'd insisted on seeing the burns Arathiel had acquired across his back when saving him, but his companion refused, reiterating that it no longer hurt—never mind that he slouched while walking or avoided leaning on walls if he could help it. When Varden pointed out the obvious lie, Arathiel instead replied that he was too fragile to do anything about it, and that Vellien's energy was better spent on him. Any mentions of Cal were pointedly ignored. Varden promised himself he would nag him again later, once he felt better. For now, Arathiel was right: if even a short walk left him weakened, calling upon Keroth for something as demanding as healing him would ruin him.

"I needed this for morale," he told Arathiel. I promise I'll be fine."

Arathiel answered with a pensive sound. "I'll fetch you water while you enjoy the new sights. Try to rest before everyone returns. We won't get this kind of quiet often."

As Arathiel left for the kitchens, Varden got his first good look at Cal's living room. It had quite a different mood from the bedroom, which was all dark blue and soothing. Here, vivid colours competed with each other for the chance to hurt his eyes. In addition to Varden's red sofa, Cal owned bright yellow and green seats, and a bunch of pillows covered in all colours of the rainbow at full intensity. He wished the room had a fireplace to light, and that he had something to draw with. Those would help even more than a short walk. He ought to mention it to Arathiel, or Branwen if he could get his hands on her. She'd barely been in the house at all.

No one but Cal and her had left the place on the first day. Everyone else sat in tense silence, worried that Lord Allastam and Master Avenazar would be hunting for them. The rumours in Isandor alleviated some of those fears, however, and their group had started circulating more. Today, Hasryan had gone snooping around his favourite spots from his time as a Crescent Moon assassin to gather information—although not after promising Cal he'd be extra careful, and accepting a blessing of luck from his friend. Lord Dathirii had stepped out for the first time, hoping to call upon Lord William, who'd once made him a clear offer for help. The thought didn't seem to enchant him, but Lord William had plenty of coin to his name, something they desperately needed. They also planned to visit Lady Brasten—a prospect than enthused him as much as it obviously frightened Arathiel.

Varden had tried to ask about it, only to receive either vague or snappy answer. Until now, Arathiel had always been open and warm with him—even when placating Varden about his burns, he'd stayed calm. It didn't seem fair to press him when Arathiel's steady presence helped Varden get through hard mood shifts, so they'd started avoiding the subject after a few sparks. It pained Varden that he wouldn't be solid enough on his feet to accompany them to the Brasten Tower, though. He wished he could return the kindness and be a silent anchor for Arathiel, but the day was fast approaching. Even now, Branwen and Cal were visiting a tailor who owed the halfling a favour or ten—something about unclaimed lost wagers—to put the finishing touches on their intended outfits for the visit, and Varden still couldn't walk more than a few feet.

Arathiel returned with the cup of water, and Varden wrapped trembling hands around it, tightening his grip to avoid spilling everything. He sipped slowly, under Arathiel's watchful gaze, letting the liquid flow down his parched throat.

"You like nursing others, don't you?" he asked.

Arathiel jerked back at his question, but his smile resurfaced in an instant, quiet and magnetic all at once. "I do. I spent a lot of time with my sister, and as her illness worsened, offering what care I could became part of the routine for us. Did you need space? I understand we barely know each other, and I don't want to be overwhelming."

"No, no ... I like it, actually."

The words slipped out of him, leaving his throat dry. Varden downed the offered cup of water, trying to douse the rising warmth within him. He could pretend the erratic beat of his heart and light-headedness were due to the walk's aftermath, but he knew himself better than that. How often had he caught himself staring at Arathiel, entranced by a simple laugh? It was unfair, how much he wanted to touch him—run a finger along the wide bridge of his nose, or around his lips and to his jaw, feel for the muscles of his back … or at least draw them! It had been dangerously easy to let Arathiel into his routine, to allow his calming presence to nestle close to his heart. A tiny voice whispered to be careful with his desires, that he could not forget the price of them, but Varden felt safe among Branwen's friends, and he was too exhausted to raise feeble barriers again.

He set the glass down and returned Arathiel's smile as best as he could. "It's easier with you around."

The front door opened before Arathiel could reply, and Lord Dathirii walked in, a cold wind slipping inside with him. Varden shivered and tugged the threadbare wool blanket tighter around him. The elven lord threw his cowl down, freeing a curtain of golden hair, then pulled off his gloves and rubbed his hands together, blowing on them for warmth. His every movement stayed fluid and at ease despite the worry and fatigue that had dimmed his smile. Varden remembered that about him: he'd danced through political gatherings like water, always fitting perfectly in the space granted to him.

"It's winter all right," Diel said as a greeting to them, "and Lord

William must hate proper heating. His manor is almost colder than the outside. I don't know how he can live in those conditions, but I'm freezing!"

A whole body shudder coursed through him, then he reluctantly removed his fur-lined coat and hung it on one of Cal's low hooks. The bottom trailed on the ground, pooling with Vellien's. How strange, that their host would have plenty of seats for human-sized guests and enough cutlery for all of them, but not a single higher hook for cloaks to dry upon. He itched to walk over, conjure fire, and fix the soaking wet pile of scarves and coats, but he knew better than to leave his chair. There were more than clothes needing some warmth, however.

"Perhaps I can help with the cold?" he suggested, before closing his eyes. A flickering flame burned within him—Keroth's power, close and comforting. Varden hadn't reached to Them since protecting himself and Arathiel from the temple's brazier, but Their very presence soothed him. He'd missed it, during his imprisonment. Gently, he coaxed the interior fire into his hand and created a small flame. Its dance over his palm brought a smile to his tired lips.

"Only if it isn't too much a drain on your strength."

Diel Dathirii crossed the room and offered his hands out, palms facing down. Varden placed his under and flattened the flames, letting the heat radiate upward. Simple though it was, the feat tugged at his energy, and he had to stop after a few seconds.

"Here you go, milord." Varden's head buzzed from the effort, but Diel's shook his fingers with a delighted chuckle, and that was reward enough.

"Lovely, thank you."

Arathiel placed a hand on Varden's shoulder—a plea not to exhaust himself any further, if Varden had learned anything of his personal nurse over the last week.

"How did it go?" Arathiel asked Lord Dathirii. "Will Lord William help us?"

"He will lend us funds, yes." It should have been good news, yet concern barred Lord Dathirii's forehead. He dragged another sofa closer and settled into it, linking his fingers. "I will admit, however, that I am a little wary of Lord William's willingness to help as this goes against his normal non-involvement policy. He clearly harboured a strong dislike for Lord Allastam, so perhaps this is our explanation. Talking to him gave me the impression that he found his politics to be excruciatingly … tiresome."

From the sound of it, Lord Dathirii wished 'tiresome' wasn't the proper word to describe Lord William's opinion. 'Violent' and 'relentless' struck closer to the problem, if Varden's brief experience with Isandor's politics was anything to go by.

"So if we petition Lady Brasten for support … we'll have something to offer." Arathiel's fingers dug into Varden's shoulder. Did he notice how hard he squeezed, or did his numbness to touch erase that? Varden turned around and took in the tightness in Arathiel's jaw and the worry in his rich brown eyes. Whatever ghosts haunted him had resurfaced. He set his hand on Arathiel's, returning the squeeze until the other man felt it and glanced down and caught his reassuring smile.

"Lady Brasten was the only person to stand up for me during the Golden Table," Diel said, "and she defended you, Arathiel. She is a shrewd politician with weight to her name, and I trust her priorities. We need her to dispute Hellion's claim."

"Besides," Varden continued with a layer of forced cheeriness, "it will give you something new to tell me. There's only so many times you can narrate your card games at the Shelter before I've memorized everyone's tells. I'd enjoy a different story."

Arathiel closed his eyes and his grip on Varden's shoulder lessened, relaxing with the rest of his body. "You're right … and I don't know how you endure the sound of my voice all day long, Varden!"

Endure? Varden laughed. He loved Arathiel's voice. It reminded him of glowing embers, warm and powerful, reminiscent of a majestic fire. And when Arathiel spoke of Lady Camilla's kindness, of Cal's eager friendship and of Hasryan's deep affection—of every friend, new and old, who had reached out to him since his return to Isandor—the flames rekindled, lively and beautiful. It made Varden yearn to kneel and blow on them, turning a flickering flame into a glorious brazier.

"It's good to hear you laugh." Lord Dathirii stared at them with a wide smile, and something in his expression made Varden flush—like "laugh" wasn't all he meant. "Branwen was right. You're not the same as the High Priest I met during those political events."

Varden stiffened. The comment betrayed how little Lord Dathirii understood. "You met a front and couldn't perceive the person under because I refused to let you, or anyone else, do so. I haven't changed: the risks to myself have. Why fear the ruination of a misplaced word when I've already survived it? There is no point in breaking myself into pieces until their shape fits someone else's desires."

Silence stretched between them as Varden squeezed his eyes shut. Even thinking of his time at Avenazar's mercy was almost too much. He fought the waves of fatigue and dizziness, focusing on the rough texture of the leather under him. This was his first opportunity to speak with Lord Dathirii since awakening, and he would not waste it.

"If I may ask, what are your plans for the Enclave? You saved me, and I'm thankful for it, but … if you do nothing now, while Avenazar is out of commission, it will not last."

A dark cloud passed over Diel Dathirii's expression, and he looked away, past Varden and Arathiel, refusing to meet their gaze. "I'm well aware, but as long as my family isn't safe—"

"They won't be," Varden snapped. "Not as long as Master Avenazar is alive. None of us will be safe."

"What would you have me do?" Diel spread his arms out, and his hands shook with the same frustrated despair that laced his voice. "We're but a handful, and my most trusted advisors are either hiding, or imprisoned in their home. Jaeger is in there, without protection, at the mercy of Hellion's whims! They will beat him up again at the slightest occasion—one wrong word, one imagined insult. I can't—I have to make this my priority. We'll never be in a position to strike against Master Avenazar without the whole of House Dathirii behind me." With a deep breath, Diel Dathirii steadied himself and brought his hands back to his knees. "Jaeger and Garith aren't optional. Without them, without my family… I'm sorry, I—"

"I understand, milord," Varden interrupted with calm he didn't feel. He was all too familiar with the terror of watching loved ones be ripped away because of a single, mistaken word. Perhaps that was why he could see past the immediate threat. "I understand, but you must set the fear aside. Master Avenazar is wounded *now*. Your advantage will not last. Have you not already successfully gone into the enclave? Isn't … isn't Hasryan an assassin?"

"I will not ask Hasryan to kill anyone."

Lord Dathirii's response was immediate and decisive, giving Varden no doubts he'd considered the possibility. Perhaps Hasryan himself had offered—he had always seemed open and relaxed about the nature of his profession. Varden's throat tightened at the blunt refusal. He'd known Diel Dathirii was an idealist at heart, and the suggestion felt tasteless to him too, but how else would they ever have peace? He raised his head and met Lord Dathirii's green eyes.

"You cannot wait. Do I need to remind you what Avenazar can do?" A quake wormed its way into his voice. Memories swirled in his mind, and for a moment his back hurt, as if still lined by burns. Calm escaped him, slipping through trembling fingers as a cold sweat covered his body. "Rules and reason are strangers to Avenazar. Nothing will stop him, and nothing will satisfy him. Do you think he'll stop at you and me? You-you don't know him like I do!" Unhelpful tears blurred his vision and he wiped them away in an frustrated gesture. "If-if you don't believe me, ask Nevian.

Avenazar's ire extends to relatives, friends, family—everyone. You can save your tower, can bring Jaeger by your side, but it'll do you no good once he's back. Hellion's petty anger is meaningless next to him."

Varden wished he didn't tremble like this, that the nausea didn't threaten to overtake him, lumping in his throat until it turned his breathing into a soft wheeze. He must look like a quivering mess of irrational fears to Lord Dathirii, an unreliable and scarred witness. He could almost feel Avenazar's mind creeping into him, cold, overwhelming, and relentless. Calm down, he told himself, and he tried to focus on the ground under his feet, or the sofa beneath his fingers.

A hand slid through his curls, startling him. Varden half-expected it to grab and pull, the harsh movement a familiar tactic with Avenazar. Instead, it stroke him, gently coming to rest down to his neck. Arathiel's warm voice reached him, distant yet clear.

"We're here, Varden. It's all right. Look at me."

Varden couldn't remember closing his eyes. No, he hadn't. His vision had blurred, and was gradually clearing up. He focused on the cool hand at his neck and blinked hard, then turned towards Arathiel and attempted a reassuring smile. Judging by the concerned stare he received, it wasn't too successful. They waited, giving Varden ample time to herd his scattered thoughts and slow the frantic beating of his heart. A sickening unease remained, piling on Varden's exhaustion.

"I'm… I'm all right." Not really, but it would have to do. He'd never truly be fine until Avenazar was no longer a threat.

"I'm sorry for everything that happened to you, Varden," Diel said. "I wish we'd been there sooner and I… I'll consider your words. We'll do our best to stop him when we can."

Varden straightened, drawing strength from the hand at his neck and gathering his dignity. "Branwen always said you could work miracles. My faith is deep, milord, but Keroth Themself could appear before me and vow delaying was the right path, and I don't know if I'd believe Them." He pushed himself up, holding tight to the sofa. When his legs threatened to give in, Arathiel caught him and supported his weight. "I'm sorry. You mean well and perhaps I am ungrateful, but promises are no longer enough. I cannot wait for you. I'm going to rest, and the moment I have the strength, I will walk back into the enclave and work my own miracles, through flames and blood if I must."

Keroth forgive him, he'd never desired to take a life. But Varden had lost faith in other solutions, and while he could not force Lord Dathirii to order a man's death, he'd wanted the lord to see eye-to-eye with him. Too many lives were at stake, and he wouldn't wish what he'd endured on anyone—not even Avenazar himself.

One tiny step at a time, Varden returned to the bedroom, Arathiel holding him up wordlessly. He slipped into the double bed near Vellien, too tired and angry to care about bothering the young elf, and tried to sleep. It was a long time before exhaustion overwhelmed the memories clinging to his mind.

Chapter Four

ARATHIEL huddled under his winter cloak, more for concealment than protection against the supposed stifling cold. Although it had only been a week since he'd holed up at Cal's, it'd felt like a small eternity—a peaceful one, watching over Varden, distracting him with long discussions, and exchanging quiet smiles. Arathiel would have taken a dozen more like this, especially if it kept this particular moment at bay. The Brasten Tower loomed above them, candles flickering in several of its windows, its main entrance down a single bridge. Luminescent vines wrapped around its railings, shedding a pale blue light and eventually stretching towards the tower proper, climbing partly along its stone walls.

"Well," Diel said, "I think it's time."

The elf stood on his left, his hood pulled even lower than Arathiel's. On Diel's other side, Branwen kept fidgeting with her hair, as if she could save her elaborate coiffure from the wind's relentless assault. The knots in Arathiel's stomach tightened. He'd hoped Branwen's carefully selected outfit would help ground him, but instead the silver-trimmed doublet had increased his unease. It was a fine piece of work, and Branwen had adjusted it so that it would fit him perfectly—scolding him as he squirmed with nerves, and threatening to stab him with a needle he would not even notice—but it felt like a lie. Arathiel hadn't donned anything so elaborate since leaving Isandor in search of the Well, a hundred thirty years ago. He missed the mismatched and threadbare outfit he'd worn, arriving in the city. Insulting though they might have been, those clothes would have suited his emotional state: he wasn't ready for this meeting.

What if she rejected him? He'd avoided House Brasten upon returning in Isandor despite Camilla's reassurances that he would be welcomed, first terrified at the prospect of being spurned, then unwilling to reconcile his old life in Isandor and the new one he'd built. Those two had smashed together when he had jumped above Carrington's Square, interrupting Hasryan's execution, and they mingled more and more with every passing day. It *was* time, Arathiel knew. The Dathirii needed this ally, and Lady Brasten had recognized his claim to the title during the last Golden Table.

"Let's go," Arathiel said, and he took another step closer, then another, certain with each of them that something inside of him would snap, that his courage would falter. The main great doors hadn't changed from when Lady Camilla had caught him staring at them, more than a month ago, nor from when he had left, in times long forgotten by anyone but the elves. The colour of maize, he recalled, although he could not tell in the moonlight.

Arathiel's chest ached and he closed his eyes, focusing on that distinct pain and the throbbing in his back. He might not endure the wind and the cold, but he felt those, and they grounded him. He belonged here, in Isandor. He belonged in the Brasten Tower too. It had been his home, his birthright. With a shuddering breath, Arathiel pulled his hood down, stepped forward, and pushed the grand doors open, leading his two elven companions in without knocking.

The entrance hall hadn't changed at all.

Columns the colour of sand rose up, branch-like designs etched with minutiae inside. They curved at the end, forming a graceful archway and gliding into a complex mosaic of blue, gold, and silver. The detailed pattern built from hundreds of carefully placed shards of glass sent a wave of reassuring calm through Arathiel. The mosaic's blues were no longer as rich—perhaps time had washed it away, or his greyed eyesight had stolen that pleasure from him—but they retained the familiarity of home. How often had he raced Lindi to the exit, and lost because he could not help slow down and contemplate the art? He could almost hear her teasing him, memories entwining with the present.

A steward's discreet cough broke the charm.

Arathiel's gaze snapped to him and he stared, briefly confused by the thin old man. He'd been expecting Kayin's chanting voice, as if the portly steward serving during Arathiel's youth would still be alive. In his mind, he was as integral to the entrance hall as the mosaic across its ceiling. The shock left him reeling, words drying in his mouth before they could escape it.

Diel Dathirii stepped forward with impeccable gravitas, his hood lowered and his tone firm. "Lady Brasten will expect us."

"She does," the steward confirmed. "If I may have your coats…?"

Two other staff members had materialized within the hall, along with a guard in simple chain mail, taking care of coats and scarves before vanishing into an adjacent room. Diel shook his long golden hair back into proper place. Branwen had braided part of it earlier, and the routine had turned them both wistful and silent, though neither had spoken a word about why. It had contrasted with Branwen's excited demeanour as she'd shown Arathiel his outfit, explaining her choice of colour and how "it was always gold and green with the Dathirii, and it was nice to change." Arathiel had decided not to tell her it all looked grey to him.

As soon as they were all ready, the steward led them to the main staircase.

The wide and steep steps that wrapped around the middle of the tower had been cut in half, and in their centre was a platform on vertical rails. No visible pulley system had been installed to lift it, but it featured a small wooden panel with several levers. Their guide asked if any of them required assistance up the stairs before beginning the climb. He explained they only used it when necessary, since numerous members of House Brasten could need its help at any given time. The office, Arathiel knew, would be at the top of the tower, in a room as large as the building itself, with windows covering the entire walls. The base of the Brasten Tower rested upon the cliff's upper end, and the family had constructed it to be thin but tall, adding small levels in rapid succession. The tower's flat roof was the highest point of Isandor, and the office under it offered a breathtaking vista of the City of Spires—the best view in Isandor and the coldest room in winter, as they used to jest.

Arathiel matched the steward's pace despite frequent impulses to peek into the doors they passed and see how much, if anything, had changed. He ought to think about the impeding meeting, but every familiar detail disrupted his concentration. Fresh paint covered the walls and decorations along the stairwell had been switched, but the exact same distance separated the floors, and more than once, he would have sworn he recognized the dents in the wall or the creak of a step under his weight. Arathiel was hyperaware of his surroundings in a way his numbed senses hadn't allowed since leaving the Well, and he had a hard time determining what came from perception, and what was a figment of memory.

When they passed the level on which his quarters had been, Arathiel couldn't help but stop. Branwen bumped into him and muffled an exclamation, before staring up. He pressed his palm against the door.

"Yours?" she asked.

"Not anymore, I'm sure," he answered. Diel and the steward had already disappeared around the bend. "Let's catch up."

He didn't want to linger. Nostalgia could wait until their alliance with Lady Brasten was forged—if it ever happened. They drew nearer to the top, with Diel and Branwen increasingly out of breath, and Arathiel found that with every new floor they passed, the anxious twists in his stomach lessened. He could no longer turn back now, and somehow that made it easier to breathe. Arathiel soaked the discreet familiarity of the tower and reminded himself Lady Brasten had acknowledged Arathiel as a member of her family in front of Isandor's leading nobility. They wanted him to return.

By the time they reached the last floor, Arathiel stood as straight as his hurting back allowed. He inhaled deeply as the steward knocked, pushed the door open, and announced them.

"Lady Brasten," he started, and the change in his voice startled Arathiel—he had gone from reedy and polite to deep and confident. "May I present to you Lord Arathiel Brasten, the Once Beloved, as well as his companions, Branwen and Diel Dathirii?"

Though subtle, Arathiel didn't miss Diel's flinch at the introductions. Was it their order, with his name last, or the absence of his title? It must have been a century since he was first formally introduced as "Lord Dathirii", his first name foregone while he stood as Head of his House. And besides … what was up with "Once Beloved"? Arathiel forced his unease down, stepping fully into the office first, as if leading the two elves.

They entered from the south side, and the bioluminescent lights of Isandor's Upper City unfolded before them in the great windows, their soft glow illuminating the spires' varied shapes. It was almost impossible to see beyond the brightness, where the towers plunged into the darkness of the Lower City.

Amake Brasten stood before a massive desk, arms half spread in a welcoming gesture. Delicate golden beads ran through her hair, holding the long twists away from her face, then tumbled to her bare shoulders. The deep embroidery of her dress reminded Arathiel of the patterns in the entrance's mosaic, their style reminiscent of those in communities near the Aberah Lake, to the south. The Brasten family had been in Isandor since its foundation, but their roots remained displayed proudly in the tower's designs and into the fabric wrapped around Lady Brasten's thick body. Again, Arathiel thought with fondness of Kayin—they both had large arms and legs, with round bellies and an easy, beautiful presence.

"Welcome to my not-so-humble office," she greeted them.

Once, glasswork birds had crowded the room, hanging from the ceiling or clinging to iron-wrought stands. The Lord Brasten Arathiel had known—his uncle twice removed—loved the way light played into them, and when time allowed, he often chased birds in the forest east of the city, trying to catch sight of the rarest species. None of the avian artwork remained, but Lady Brasten had filled the office with tasteful rugs and several potted plants. The room felt larger than in his memory now that it was devoid of its glass occupants.

"It is an honour," Diel said. "We're thankful for the audience."

Her bright smile stiffened. She gestured for them to follow her around the office without a word. Railings lined the inside wall, and a small lounge area waited for them on the northern end, with a set of teacups and a fresh brew. When Branwen inhaled and released a happy sigh so loud he could hear, Arathiel wondered what the tea smelled like. He hoped he wouldn't burn himself on it as he had with Lady Camilla during their first talk. They sat at Lady Brasten's signal, and Branwen reached for the pot immediately. Their host remained standing as they settled down, her arms crossed, her expression pensive.

"Isandor is awash with rumours of your fate, Diel, each more terrible than the last. I must admit I was surprised to receive a letter penned by you; it seems your situation is not as dire as I'd thought."

The tea pot smacked on the table as Branwen set it down, straightening up to glare at Lady Brasten. "I'm sorry, we lost our home to a treacherous asshole, many loved ones are stuck in there with him, and Uncle Diel could have been tortured for days, but our situation isn't dire enough for you? What more do you need?"

"Don't mistake my statement for ill wishes. Your uncle is alive and appears sound of body. Surely *you* have heard what is whispered in taverns and spy networks alike." Lady Brasten's tone cut through the air, but it was wrapped in softness, and she met Branwen's gaze not with defiance but with empathy. "I half expected him to be dead, and the city would have been worse for it."

"Only Ren's blessing kept those conjectures from turning into reality." Branwen returned her attention to the tea, serving it with controlled movements that seemed forced to Arathiel. When she set the pot down once more, however, her usual smile had reappeared and she wagged her fingers. "But no one takes my uncle without my say-so. We ruined that part of their plans, and we're looking to throw the rest of it down the shitslides."

She faked flinging something away, causing Diel to choke on a laugh. Fatigue remained etched into his face, but fondness for his niece softened the lines of exhaustion.

"If you would… I'd like to share the truth of that night." He waited for Lady Brasten's acquiescent nod before continuing, his tone even and numb. "Hellion Dathirii struck a deal with Lord Allastam to unseat me from my position as Lord Dathirii, and when I returned from the Golden Table, Allastam soldiers held my home. They captured Jaeger, too, hoping to make me cede the house leadership by threatening him." His voice cracked, and he picked up a tea cup from the table, wrapping his hands around it as he steadied himself. "Lord Allastam had concluded a second deal, however, this one with Master Avenazar—one for commercial advantages, I imagine—and I was a part of it. My life was used as a bargaining chip in a trade agreement, and I was shipped out to the enclave in secret."

Lady Brasten sat down in a slow, almost solemn motion, right across from Diel. She let the elf's words hang in the air, heavy with the weight of Diel's accusations. At length, her tone low and deliberate, she asked, "You would swear this?"

"I would—on Jaeger's life and my family's honour."

"He sold you."

Disbelief crept into her voice. Would she deny it and refuse them? Arathiel's heart pounded in his chest, and he could only imagine how Diel's head must ring. They'd chosen to come to Lady Brasten not only because of her direct support during the Golden Table, but because she'd seemed to think House Allastam's tactics and ethics abhorrent. If she saw the depths of his cruelty, perhaps she'd commit to more than a distant assistance.

"We intercepted Diel in the Myrian Enclave, shackles at his wrists," Arathiel said. "Is this acceptable in Isandor now? Have people become the new currency, just as lush magical gardens replaced the building of higher, ever more twisted towers?"

"It would seem so," Lady Brasten replied, "but that does not mean we have to stand for it. Lord Allastam must have known the full extent of Master Avenazar's ill intent and abilities—we all do, even if many prefer to look away. This is … vile, yet easy to believe. Lord Allastam has often demonstrated he cares little for others' lives, especially once he considers his family or its reputation harmed."

Silence fell over their small group. Arathiel sat stiffly, refusing to lean into the sofa and rest his burned back against it, too busy trying to puzzle out Lady Brasten to drink from her tea. This was the first he'd spoken to her, but she'd paid him no more mind than if he'd been a random ally to the Dathirii, otherwise unattached to her. Arathiel hadn't known what to expect, but he had expected *something*—joy, anger, sadness, anything. Her body language revealed nothing, however. At the moment, her entire focus was Diel Dathirii and his problem, with no thoughts spared to the 'Once Beloved'. Which was good, Arathiel reminded himself. They hadn't come for him, and this unusual bitterness ill suited him.

"Let me be clear," Lady Brasten said, "if I can erase Lord Allastam from the current political landscape, I will. He brings nothing but vicious pain and arrogance, pulling power to himself and refusing to build with it. In the ten years that have passed since his wife's assassination, we have stagnated and even regressed." She swept out of her seat and began pacing, considering her next words. "He is cunning, however, and his grief has garnered the sympathy of many. As long as an assassin had been running freely in Isandor, nobles did not feel safe. Someone had dared to kill one of theirs; they were no longer untouchable. The relief at Hasryan Fel'ethier's arrest was palpable—an entire city releasing a breath it had been holding." She turned to Arathiel, tilting her head to the side, her tone neutral and matter-of-fact. He froze under her gaze, as if the judgment she passed now would follow him forever. "You broke their chance at peace of mind."

Did she resent him for freeing Hasryan, then? Arathiel squared his shoulders, bracing himself. He regretted many decisions in his life, but not that one—never that one.

"That peace was an illusion," he countered. "Only the Upper City was releasing its breath. Down in the Lower City, they already know they are never safe. Anything can ruin their lives, from a noble's whim to a cold, unlucky winter. They felt no relief at Hasryan's arrest, only dismay and anger at losing another of theirs to the politics happening in bridges far above their dwellings and only trickling down to hurt them. What do I care for the nobles' peace of mind?" Arathiel laughed, surprised at his own bitterness and the disdain creeping into his voice. He could almost hear Larryn in his tone. He hadn't returned home to play these games of make-believe, however. "Assassins are hired. If they wanted peace rather than a pat on the back, they would hunt down the employer. That they don't is a testament to their hypocrisy, not an indictment of my actions or Lord Dathirii's support of them."

What surprise passed through Lady Brasten's expression was quickly replaced by a large grin. She laughed, and unlike his bitter chuckle from earlier, the sound was bright, honest, and warm. "I see why Diel likes you."

Arathiel flushed. It was a compliment in and of itself, but the affection in her tone implied she'd enjoyed the response too. His heart sped at the thought. It shouldn't matter whether she liked him or not, yet this spark of approval left him craving for more.

"I'm afraid, however, that we cannot guide your actions with truth, as it will not dictate the reactions around Isandor's Golden Table. Perception will." She clasped her hands behind her back and returned her attention to Diel, all business once again. "This is where you erred and why you failed. If we want to remove Lord Allastam from his position, we need to erode the sympathy our colleagues have for him. He is a symbol of Isandor's ways, of its stability—one attacked by his wife's assassination. You, on the other hand, provoke change. You're an aggressor."

Diel's knuckles had gone whiter from holding his tea cup. None of her words seemed to surprise him, however, and he continued her idea effortlessly. "We need to reverse the role. If he becomes the threat ..."

"He *is* a threat," Branwen interjected. "Your perception shift is nothing but the truth. He attacked us! There are Allastam soldiers in our home, right now, and Hellion would be powerless to oust them. How long before he hammers deals with other discontent nobles in House Lorn? House Balthazar? How long before he fractures more families that ought to stay together?"

"I agree, but Isandor's most powerful houses will comfort themselves with their titles, knowing that Lord Allastam orchestrated his attack to reap House Dathirii when it had lost its position—a mistake they'd never make." She rubbed her forehead and sighed. "It's not an easy angle to work. We could rally smaller houses, but to what end? At best, we could pass laws to prevent noble houses from occupying rising families with no titles and siphoning their resources through military might. It solves none of our bigger problems, but you'd at least be able to dispute Hellion Dathirii's claims without Lord Allastam's meddling."

"Then we'll start there," Diel declared, and he could not contain the fervent desperation of his tone. "If you can get this passed, and I can solidify my position as a House leader with a following and funds…"

He told Lady Brasten of the funds at his disposition through Lord William, and together they discussed plans to put them to good use. While they talked, Arathiel met Branwen's gaze. She'd heard of her uncle's confrontation with Varden and had seen first-hand Avenazar's power and volatility. Her mouth twisted into a frown, and she offered him a slight headshake—*let him he*, he understood. Arathiel kept his peace until Diel fell silent.

"Beyond politics, milady, I would ask that you receive my companions as guests of House Brasten." The words almost caught in his throat. As a member of this family, he was well within his right to make this demand, but she had yet to reaffirm that he belonged. Nonetheless, he went on. "There would be the three of us present tonight, Vellien Dathirii, and Varden Daramond, once High Priest at the Myrian Enclave, whom I rescued with Branwen that night."

Lady Brasten's eyebrows arched as she considered the last of his guest. Accepting Varden within these walls would make her a target for the Myrians, but they couldn't live at Cal's house forever. It irritated Arathiel that Hasryan would have to remain with Cal, but they didn't trust Lady Brasten with that particular truth. His friend had tried to shrug it off as "just the usual"—which it was. Arathiel knew how the usual could hurt, however.

"A request I will gladly grant," Lady Brasten said. "Return to us in time for dinner, and you'll have a warm meal and separate quarters for everyone. I'll pen an official message to inform other lords I consider each of you under my protection, to be sent tomorrow. Keep a low profile until then."

Diel rose from his seat, catching the inflections of dismissal in her tone. "We're most grateful, milady."

"It's always a pleasure to house friends of the family." Her gaze turned to Arathiel, sparing no doubt as to whom she meant by 'family' here, and he startled. There it was: the clear confirmation he'd been waiting for and dreading all at once. His eyes snapped to hers as if she'd magnetized him. "Lord Arathiel, I was hoping you would stay with me while the others carry back the news."

"I—"

"Just the two of us is plenty!" Branwen declared, cutting him off before he could protest or dodge the invitation in any way. She sprang to her feet, slipped her arm in Diel's, and began dragging her uncle away. Diel cast him an apologetic smile before they vanished around the curved wall, leaving him alone with Lady Brasten.

They stood in silence, Arathiel studying the discarded tea pot intensely while she stared at him. The door closed, its sound distant and unfamiliar. They must have changed it in the last hundred years. Of course they had. A lot had evolved in that time, and he was a stranger here, from another time and another family.

"You must have many questions," Arathiel said.

"I do, but they can wait." She set a hand on his shoulder, which he only noticed because he caught the movement from the corner of his eyes. Her smile was soft and inviting, strikingly different than any she'd offered while in the Dathirii's presence. "Quite frankly, what matters to me now is that I have a great-great-great-great-uncle whom I've never met!" She marked the 'greats' on her fingers with uncharacteristic childishness. "Mentions in archives don't count. You're here, bless Ezven for this miracle, and I wish you would feel at home with us. House Brasten spends enough time grieving. I'm glad that, for once, we get to celebrate."

She held her hands out, offering to help him stand, and Arathiel withheld his questions about the family's grief, accepting the lift instead.

"I'm not ready for *everyone*," he said quickly, still struggling to process her joyfulness. "Understand … the House Brasten I knew is dead. Returning here, for me …"

How could he explain this? His heart fluttered, light and curious, at the idea of meeting new generations of Brastens, of discovering their lives and passions and flaws. Yet every hall here was filled with memories of a cousin's laughter, or an aunt's anxieties. Every dining room held countless dinners with people he'd never see again, relatives he'd at best learn of from incomplete, dry archives.

"Ah." Hers was a quiet sound, filled with deep sadness. "Grief, of course. Is there anything I could do to help?"

Arathiel closed his eyes, his stomach churning with a jumbled mess of feelings. Where to start? She was right, it was grief tearing at his insides, leaving him breathless and shattered. Inevitably, his mind returned to his sister, whom he'd missed more than any others, and for whom he'd left in the first place.

"Who lives on the sixteenth floor now?"

"No one, not anymore." At her subdued voice, he forced himself to look at her. An invisible weight bent her shoulders and her grim mask didn't hide her exhaustion. "As I've said, we've had our share of grief through the years. Was that your floor?"

Arathiel nodded. "I'd like to visit it."

He had no idea how he'd react to it, but he needed to see, to at least step in and pay his respects.

Lady Brasten extended her arm, which Arathiel accepted. It was time to honour what he had lost. Part of him wished Hasryan was with him—or even Varden, whose calm had a strange way to spread—but at the same time he was glad for the space to collect his thoughts alone. For now, however, he was accompanied by the new Head of the House, who practically vibrated with excitement by his side. She was doing her best to maintain a somewhat stoic façade, so he naturally set out to break it.

"Does House Brasten still hold an annual glider competition?" he asked, as innocently as he could. "And are there still bonus points for going through the loops of House Lorn's tower?"

Lady Brasten burst out laughing, and her eyes lit with enthusiasm. "We do, and I won last summer's."

It had been a silly summer tradition to gather on the Tower's flat roof with apparatus meant to soar and fling them off the roof, to see who could land the farthest. Each of the gliders were stripped of magic, then marked with a colour spell to track their flights. Arathiel had been five during the first competition, and while at the time there had been size limits, the last two contest years he'd experienced had gotten rid of almost all the rules, leaving people to exploit the full depths of their imagination.

"Tell me about it," he said.

She launched into the story eagerly, sparing no details about her plans. Arathiel followed her down the stairs as she explained her original idea, gesticulating with her free hand. Her overblown excitement over a few gliders soaring across the sky was as familiar as the mosaic in the Brasten Tower's entrance hall; although changed by time, it held the same roots as the enthusiasm Arathiel's peers had shown, a hundred and thirty years ago. It instantly became easier to think of her as family and lose himself in her story. Perhaps the House Brasten he'd known wasn't dead after all, but lived on, transformed by its descendants.

Chapter Five

ADY Brasten invited Arathiel to join her on the roof when he was ready before leaving him alone on the sixteenth floor. He'd barely offered a nod in reply, slowly walking the round corridor at the heart of his old lodgings, a hand on its inner railing even though he couldn't perceive the texture under his fingers. His close relatives had occupied the entire thin floor, split in four sections: three bedrooms and a common area, with a small table and comfy seats. Arathiel stopped in front of his parents' door, its wood still marked by deep dents. Arathiel traced them with his fingers, but he couldn't feel the indentation under his skin. He'd done those with a tiny knife, all those decades ago, on the day they'd told him nothing would save his sister.

He had been twenty, and her, fourteen. Nothing could have contained the roiling anger, the stalwart denial, so he'd let the door have at it. Today, he tapped the marks, sighed, and moved on, leaving behind the bitter memories.

This floor hadn't changed as much as others, perhaps because it'd been the first to be transformed for increased accessibility, for Lindi's sake. Now the Brasten Tower had a central lift, railings, doors that slid within the walls with the touch of a rune, and several small rooms dedicated to rest. Lady Brasten had explained these adjustments on the way without clarifying the motivation behind them, except to mention they helped more and more members of the family. He didn't need to ask: as Arathiel looped around the corridor and stood once more before Lindi's quarters, the cause hovered at the forefront his mind.

He headed inside, steeling himself for the dissonance between the present room and the one from his memories. The only furniture left was the old birch bed, devoid of the mattress, and the railings along the wall. No dust had gathered anywhere, giving the empty room the eerie feeling of being inhabited nonetheless. Arathiel forced his feet to move and stepped towards the westward window, ignoring the crawling sensation of being an unwelcome intruder. Half the city spread before his eyes, the Reonne snaking at its feet, beyond the cliff, before vanishing into darkness. He soaked in the view, cloaking himself in its familiarity.

Whenever Lindi's illness had spiked, he had spent his afternoon here with her. Unless she had a migraine, sunshine bathed the entire room, flowing through the window. On bad days, Arathiel would read to her or talk until she preferred sleep, while on the good ones he would help her to the railing. She'd loved dancing, and used the support to practise without falling. The summer of her sixteenth year had been particularly blessed for her health, and she'd attended every social event in Isandor she could dance at. They'd joked about it for years after, calling it the Summer of Twirling—a brief season during which they had believed she might heal, no matter what others had said for years.

It hadn't lasted, of course. Arathiel remembered too well the afternoons of swollen joints and frustrated tears, the healers pointlessly trying to stave off her sickness. In the first years, Lindi had acted strong and defiant, as if nothing could truly touch her. By the end, she had been exhausted, seeking only company and reassurance when the spikes returned.

Arathiel had been twenty-six and Lindi twenty-two when he'd heard of the Well: a magical place that could cure all illnesses. The unexpected panacea, the one possibility to save her. Within a week of hearing the tale, his decision was made. He'd packed everything he could, strapped his sword at his belt, and shared his solution with Lindi.

I don't want you to leave, she'd said. *Don't do this.*

He'd told her he had to—that he couldn't let her die.

I might die anyway.

Arathiel had taken her hands, so frail and thin. *Promise me you won't.*

He shouldn't have asked that. Arathiel still heard himself, standing in his sister's room, a full one hundred and thirty-three years later. How could she make such a promise? But she hadn't. She'd stared hard at him.

I am dying, Ara. I want my brother with me at the end, not false hopes. Stay.

He should have listened to her, instead of seeking a vague miraculous cure. That would have required him to accept she would die, however. He hadn't been ready. When he had left for the Well, he had done so for his sake more than hers, disregarding her wishes. Arathiel stared at the empty room, angry at himself. She had wanted him with her in the last stretch, and he had deserted her.

It was too late now. Too late for regrets, and too late to cry over it. His tears remained stuck in the past, absorbed into the Well with the rest of his senses. Or perhaps he wasn't ready to grieve yet, despite the decades that had elapsed. Arathiel sighed and tapped the railing. He wouldn't push it—emptiness, he'd found, had a way to fill itself whether you liked it or not. For now, he preferred to ground himself in the present. The railings could still serve—Varden might need them until his strength returned. This way, he could take ill-advised walks around the room even without Arathiel to help. It would be good to breathe new life into these quarters. It almost felt like they had been waiting for him and for those he'd come to consider family.

With a slight smile, Arathiel left Lindi's bedroom and headed towards the roof.

HEAVY gusts slammed into Arathiel as he stepped onto the tower's rooftop, their strength enough to send him stumbling for a moment. He'd always loved the powerful winds at this height and was relieved to have them snap and push and pull at him once more. Protective fabric wrapped most of the garden, shielding the plants underneath from the worst of winter, and lamps—a soft blue, if they hadn't been changed—still shed a pale light across the area. Lady Brasten waited at the edge of the roof, draped in thick fur, and her palms rested on the low sandstone, similarly protected from freezing. She turned upon hearing his steps and shot a concerned glance at his bare hands.

Arathiel shrugged. He had no desire to mask his numbed senses. "I can't feel the cold."

"Is that not further cause for worry?" She smiled at him then returned her attention to the city, waiting for Arathiel to come to her side before continuing. "I won't pry. I hate questions about how I feel or how much I hurt, and I hate the useless advice that tends to follow. Understand, however, that we will accommodate your needs to the best of our considerable abilities. If there's anything House Brasten can do to alleviate your troubles, let me know."

Arathiel hadn't expected the straightforward offer, and for a moment he lost himself in the possibilities. House Brasten might not boast the largest wealth in Isandor, but they'd always dealt in magical items and accessed wizards at significant discounts. What if he had a spell to make his skin glow whenever he wounded himself? Or even better, alert him directly in his mind? He could forego his nightly examinations with a hand mirror without risking infections. And that was likely only the beginning…

"You are most kind, milady," he said. "I can't think of anything urgent, but I'm sure I will find ideas later, when I've had more time to consider it."

Lady Brasten's eyebrows shot up, and she laughed. "Please don't 'milady' me. Unless we're in an official space, it's Amake. The title … it makes me feel old and tired."

Arathiel's gaze slid from the crisscross of bridges below them to Lady Brasten. When Camilla had told him the new Head of his family was young, he had expected an exaggeration. Who wouldn't look young to the centuries-old elf, after all? Amake Brasten couldn't be over forty yet, despite speaking as though she had led this House for several years. He could think of numerous reasons she would have received the position early in her life, but between her talk of chronic pain and diminished family numbers, the modifications made to House Brasten, and his own sister's death, Arathiel understood the underlying story.

"How many…" He trailed off, searching for the right question. "We've been ill for quite a while, haven't we? The family?"

"Yes." Her voice hardened, as if in protection from the very words it spoke, but determination shone through her eyes. "Painful joints, dislocating bodies, sudden unexplainable migraines … we've become experts at predicting the numerous ways our bodies can twist and break and function, and when to call upon healers to manage the pain. It is what it is. So, yes, we've been ill. It progresses at different speeds depending on the person, comes with varying side effects…" She waved a dismissive hand and finally turned to him. "That's our reality. Some days it makes me want to take a week-long nap and give up. Most of the time, I forget not everybody is on constant watch for the next flare. In our walls, it is the norm, not the oddity."

They would be complete opposite, then, the other Brastens and him. He struggled to register the ground under his feet, and apart from mysterious throb that had been nagging his back since the enclave, he no longer experienced physical pain. Yet Arathiel felt a kinship with these strangers, not so much because of shared blood, but because he, too, had become an expert on the unusual ways his body acted.

Arathiel wished he had comfort to offer but he was still raw from his quiet time in Lindi's quarters and all he could say was "I'm sorry."

Amake laughed, her voice carrying far into the night. "Don't be. If you stay, however, you will have to learn to deal with it." Her mirth dwindled, and she hesitated, her lips split open as she searched for words. Arathiel had never noticed how decisively she always spoke until she suddenly wasn't at all. "You *are* staying, aren't you?"

"Yes." He answered with a conviction that surprised him. He had dreaded coming to the Brasten Tower only this morning, so how could he be so certain? Amake made him feel welcome— desired, even—and that assuaged a lot of his fears. Even the distortion between home remembered and present-home seemed easier to handle now. A short, exhilarated laugh crossed Arathiel's lips. "I am staying. Perhaps not forever—who knows what the future holds?—but regardless … I want to belong to House Brasten again."

"I'm glad."

Amake sounded surprisingly relieved, and it gave Arathiel pause. Until her brief hesitancy earlier, he'd expected her to take his agreement for granted—a natural conclusion to her decision to support Diel Dathirii, at the very least. He couldn't help but ponder at her reaction. There was something personal to it, as though she craved his presence not as a house leader, but as Amake Brasten. How much of the family's business did she shoulder on her own? Or did she have a team he hadn't met, the way Diel relied on Jaeger and the others? Nothing he'd heard indicated she had that sort of circle.

"You should know not everyone wanted you here," Amake said, leaning forward, her palms on the wide stone railing, "just as not everyone will want Diel Dathirii in our tower. They're afraid, and I think they have every right to be."

"Then why help us?"

"*I* am not afraid." She grinned and spread her arms, letting the wind buffet her. "Perhaps I should be, but cowering gets you nowhere in this city, and it's never been in my nature. That's why they voted me as Head of the House. I know this game and I play it without hesitation. We'll see if Lord Allastam is as good at politics as he thinks he is."

Amake's easy confidence appeased his worries. He had no idea what she was capable of and he was eager to find out. Arathiel turned his gaze once more to the city below. He'd missed this top-down view and the odd exhilaration of standing at the top of the world. Perhaps that was why fear didn't slow Amake Brasten—she could always come here and soak in the strange, invincible feeling. Arathiel grinned and let her boldness lift his mood and fill his chest with hope.

Chapter Six

Hours spent poring over numbers had numbed Jaeger's brain to the pain of stiff muscles and the void in his heart. Days slipped by him like surreal dreams, time trickling in an irregular stream while he, Garith, and Yultes devised ways to hide House Dathirii's wealth from its new leader. One of Hellion's first tasks for Yultes had been to scrutinize every inch of their finances and household needs and curtail, as Hellion put it, "the inevitable pointless charity Diel has allowed to bloat our expenses, particularly in salaries."

By which he meant, of course, that he wanted Yultes to fire a significant number of their staff, or cut their pay. It still escaped Jaeger *why* Yultes had brought this problem to them, to workshop solutions that would satisfy Hellion while keeping a maximum number of people hired, but they set to it, opening the Dathirii books.

Jaeger had sat with Garith before, to examine House Dathirii's finances and build concrete plans to support Diel's projects, and the two of them had easily fallen back into old dynamics. Jaeger had grabbed a list of the household employees, reviewing each individual pay in detail, explaining the reasons behind the amounts—Julian needed a bonus to cover for nir son's chronic food allergies, Fern lived within a well-off family and lacked very little, Lellyn had lower wages but worked less often, on a flexible schedule that allowed more free time, and so on. Garith scribbled numbers as Jaeger droned on, building the tangible information essential for their plan. Jaeger could almost lose himself in the minutiae and forget why they had to revisit the servants' wages. Then Yultes spoke up.

"What if we quantified every advantage besides the main salary, such as Julian's extra, cut it out of their official pay, and then slipped it under a generic label? Call it 'household expenses' and pretend this money is used for soap, dusters, new rugs, and so on …"

Yultes had made himself very discreet since the start, fidgeting with the many plants in his quarters while the two others worked, perhaps keenly aware of their reluctance to have him around at all. Jaeger tried not to dwell on this behaviour, no matter how unsettling Yultes' willingness to go against Hellion, or his mindfulness of their opinions. The barbed-tongued, arrogant lord Jaeger had contended with for decades would inevitably return, but until then, Jaeger would take what allyship was offered.

Garith turned to him, his brow furrowed. "We have 'household utilities' for that. How would we then justify those?"

A pause, heavy with the churning of potential solutions. "A fair point. Instead, split the recovered gold between kitchens, cleaning, guards, and so on, then call them 'unexpected expenses'. All consequences of our war with the Myrian Enclave. He might pay less attention if he anticipates the numbers to vanish with time."

"That might work. Jaeger, can you return to the start of the list? Let's see how much the benefits amount to."

They began again from the top, Jaeger going through the motion on the strength of habit alone, his heart shrivelling. This, too, was a familiar dynamic, except Diel had always been the one listening to their work, staying silent until he had a suggestion and provided a new direction. It hurt to watch Yultes slip into that role, but Jaeger grit his teeth, pushed down tears and emptiness, and focused on his duty. He had promised Diel he wouldn't let the family down, and he would keep his word even if Diel was gone forever. Grief could wait for the long nights alone, when no one could see him cry.

He held on as they continued to trim down spendings over the next days. The task was grim and gruelling: Garith had already pruned a lot of unnecessary expenses when the Myrians had begun applying pressure, leaving them with few real options. When they ran out of ideas, slept on it, and *still* couldn't find new ways to conceal gold from Hellion, they still needed to cut four people from their staff. Jaeger inherited the agonizing responsibility of choosing whom, and as such, resolved to be the one to share the decision with them.

Jaeger never truly slept well anymore, but Yultes' flock of plants had a strangely soothing effect on him, as if simply being surrounded by living, breathing things helped alleviate the restlessness of insomnia. Even they couldn't salvage the night before his meeting with the staff, however. They all knew Hellion, and they must have been expecting the axe to drop since House Dathirii had fallen into his hands. Even so, Jaeger couldn't predict how they would react to his news, and he hated to bring this pain to them. He had run this household for decades now, and never before had he needed to do such a thing. It weighed on him through the night and all the way to the meeting, when he slipped into the room, clutching the four sealed letters, his heart and steps heavy.

They rose from their seats as he entered, the perfect synchronism of their movement lending it a strange solemnity. Jaeger met each of their gaze in turn: Sikando, an old cook who had talked about retiring for almost four years now; Ylvetta, who had friends within House Serringer who might help her find another position quickly; Nero, their new and dynamic recruit in the cleaning crew; and Fern, who could take the financial hit more easily than anyone else. People of different ages and circumstances, less vulnerable than many. Good people who did not deserve this. They must have understood why he had called them, because they remained silent.

"I'm sorry," Jaeger said, the words bitter and inadequate.

"We know." Ylvetta stepped forward and guided him firmly to a chair Fern had grabbed and set out for him. Jaeger sat down, unable and unwilling to resist their pull. "You'd never choose this."

"Is it just the four of us?"

Sikando placed a hand on Jaeger's shoulder as he asked, his voice soft, his touch light and filled with care. They crowded around him and their concern wrapped him like a warm hug, solid and real and comforting. Jaeger's self-control, so meticulously cultivated over the week, melted away. A few thick tears rolled down his cheeks before he could catch them, betraying the frailty of his emotional buffer. He'd managed to hold it in with Garith and Yultes, focusing on the work at hand, but he couldn't anymore—not surrounded by those who paid the price.

He wanted to keep them all, to pay them what they were worth, to forget the choking weight on his chest that never left him now. He wanted for Branwen and Camilla to return and brighten the tower with their laughter, for Vellien's songs to echo down the halls when they thought no one listened, for Kellian's grumpy rants to travel up the stairs as he tried to preserve order in a house of carefree elves. But most of all he wanted Diel's enthusiastic greetings, his compassionate speeches, his low flirts when they were alone. It had vanished so brutally, ripped from his grasp before he could fathom what had happened, and now he spread that pain to others.

Hands squeezed his shoulders as he wiped away the treacherous tears and attempted to compose himself.

"It's awful that they make you do this," Fern said. "If Yultes has got your job, he should be kicking us out himself. But Nicole says he's always been a coward."

"I asked to do it," Jaeger said. He hadn't given anyone the chance to take this responsibility away from him. "I chose your names, in the end. When it came down to *who* and not *how many*, I made the decision." He fumbled for the four messages he had written that the morning, extending one to each of them with shaking hands. "These are letters of strong recommendation, which explain our current situation and encourage others to hire you. I hope it will make your future easier."

Nero huffed as xie picked the parchment. "I liked this place. It's a mess since the soldiers came, but I liked it. You think we can return, once it's all resolved?"

A murmur of agreement spread through the four at xyr question. Jaeger frowned, uncertain what to do with their confident and determined attitudes. Even Ylvetta, more prone to fits of pessimism, seemed convinced this situation would pass. How strange of them.

"If you've not settled elsewhere, yes, I imagine we'd be glad to have you back, but ..."

Without Diel, he didn't see how House Dathirii could ever be the same. Even without Hellion, or the Myrians, or any Allastam soldiers... How could anything fill his absence?

"He'll take the tower back." Fern crossed his arms with a smirk. "That's what my zucchini keeps saying, anyway. The mood's shifting, and people like him more than the Myrians. Ne said Mister Dathirii's just one miracle short of setting everything right again, and it'll be coming his way, just you watch."

It took a moment for Jaeger to remember Fern's zucchini, Lai, a teenager who visited him often in the tower, and whom Kellian had described as suspiciously lurking more than once. Ne did have the confidence and daring to be snooping for information, but Jaeger couldn't be bothered to worry about it—especially as his mind pieced together the implied meaning in Fern's answer. *Mister Dathirii's just one miracle short of setting everything right.*

An act for which aforementioned Mister Dathirii needed to be alive.

The sudden, stunning hope crushed the breath out of him and he fumbled with words. "W-what do you mean? Diel is ... Is there … news?"

Jaeger whispered the last word, and silence followed. They drew back from him, looking at each other, horror and excitement spreading across their faces in equal measure.

"You don't know?" Sikando asked.

"He's back!" Fern exclaimed with a burst of joy. "Was hiding all this time, but now he got Lady Brasten sendin' letters to other fancy nobles, telling them he has her protection and all! Walked right in there with this Arathiel he'd released from prison and Miss Branwen, or so the Brasten staff say."

"He's alive." Very little else made it past his shock. "He's alive and he's free."

The tears returned, relief overflowing, and Jaeger grinned through them, light-headed. A tiny bead of hope, hidden deep within him, began to grow. Diel was alive and fighting. He had Branwen and others by his side, and it could only mean one thing: he would be coming for his home, and for Jaeger.

Urgent knocks at the door startled them. Everyone stepped away from Jaeger. They knew this would be about him and wanted nothing to do with it—not that he could blame them. Jaeger pushed himself up, keeping one hand on the chair to steady himself.

"Yes?" he asked, inordinately calm.

Garith opened the door. Agitation had washed away the bleary eyes of the last few days. "Jaeger, you gotta hide." He paused, running fingers through his already dishevelled hair as he caught his breath. "Start from the beginning, Garith," he admonished himself. "I have good news and bad news. Really good and really bad. The good is that—"

"Diel is alive," Jaeger cut off, and even though he sensed the bad news would crush the joy out of him, he grinned. "They've told me. What is the bad, Garith?"

"Word reached Hellion. Lady Brasten had a letter just for him, and I don't think he'll like it."

EVERY time Hellion flipped a page of the clean and concise report submitted to him, Yultes lost a decade of his life. He had written the document with Garith, rereading it over and over until dawn peeked through the curtains, casting pale grey light on the unturned bedsheets. Every sentence, every number, every word … it had to *look* perfect, to cover their trickery while seeming to build a realistic plan. More than once, Garith had muttered about how he'd never have dared to present figures like these to Diel.

"It's not even subtle!" he'd exclaimed, gesturing at the pages. "Only a complete beginner would be fooled. If I had done anything like this to our finances for the Golden Table, they would have ripped me apart."

"Hellion *is* a beginner." It had always surprised Yultes how averse to numbers he had been. "He is the honey pot, bringing interesting merchants to him and charming them until they sit at a negotiation table. But tracking amounts once a signature has been obtained? Filling in the balance sheet? Those tasks are for subordinates, Garith. Those are what he trusts *me* with."

He'd been so confident when he'd said it, but now that Hellion was examining the report? The spectre of impending failure loomed over Yultes, crushing his lungs and tightening around his heart. Only decades of practice helped him keep his outward calm when his insides shrivelled so. How long before Hellion began questioning the vagueness of certain changes? How long before he picked up incongruous details and pulled at them, unravelling the tapestry of lies hidden within these pages? It would happen. This wouldn't succeed. Defying him had been a terrible idea. He'd lose Hellion's trust and friendship, and he'd lose the title he'd worked all his life to deserve, and for what? What had Jaeger and Garith done for him all these years? Always, Yultes' thoughts returned to this, to the loyalty he owed Hellion, the debt of gratitude for teaching him so much—and always, Yultes clung to Diel's last words to him.

Think about how much power is in your hands now, and what you want to do with it.

What *he* wanted, not what Hellion wanted, or Hellion told him he should want. He wanted to be a part of the House Dathirii that had taken him in, along with his brother. The one that hadn't minded their commoner bloodline. The one that cared for one another. And Hellion's house, in which cousins could be cut loose or sold as assets, was not his.

Yultes clasped his hands behind his back and steadied himself with that quiet certitude and wait for Hellion's comment on the report. It did not take long: his friend skimmed through to the end, clacked his tongue, and slapped the deerskin with their notes onto the table with obvious discontent.

"Only four? In the entire household?"

"And we'll have brought the salaries expenses to a minimum, yes." Yultes met Hellion's gaze, hoping it would make the deception more convincing.

"You are telling me that Diel had only four extra individuals running this house? This is the most we can cut? Four?"

Yultes resisted the urge to point out Hellion's request had not been to fire people, to avoid Hellion making it the new one. "The numbers don't lie." He almost choked at his own audacity, then, bolstered by it, added, "I grilled Garith about them to make sure he wasn't trying to cheat on us."

"Was he?"

Hellion drummed his fingers on the desk, all casual, and fear jolted through Yultes as he realized only one answer would ring true. He shouldn't have run his mouth and insinuated he'd had doubts. Too late now. He forced a smile to his lips.

"Of course," he said, his tone dismissive. "I'm sure he will again."

"Let him know that Jaeger will pay the price for this behaviour. A threat may be unlikely to stop him, but perhaps the subsequent consequences, once you catch him, will cool down further attempts." They could have been discussing a bad choice of wine rather than Jaeger's next beating, and it wouldn't have changed Hellion's attitude. With a dramatic sigh, he tapped the top of Yultes' report. "I imagine I might have underestimated the efficiency with which Diel oversaw this house."

"Four full-time positions are a lot of extra cut," Yultes replied, hoping to reassure him enough that he wouldn't look into other options, such as demanding more work hours for an equal pay. "We'll save mountains in the long run."

"You're quite—"

In a perfect example of poor life decisions, someone burst into

Lord Dathirii's office—Diel's office, Yultes reminded himself—and interrupted Hellion's sentence. Outrage flashed through his expression, and he sprung to his feet, slamming his palms on the table.

"What is this?" he demanded.

Yultes hurriedly stepped aside, more than happy allow Hellion to focus entirely on the twenty-something woman in the doorway, panting, her cheeks beet red from running up the Tower's many stairs.

"Milord ..." she breathed out, and Yultes silently commended her for the use of the title, even though none of the Dathirii held one anymore. She brandished a single scroll, held tightly wrapped by a blue ribbon. "I have a missive for you that could not wait."

"I decide what waits or doesn't," Hellion retorted, but he nonetheless motioned for her to come closer. "I do not appreciate commoners barging in on important meetings without so much as a knock!"

Yultes very much appreciated it, in fact, and prayed the distraction would keep Hellion from mentioning the report again. He was surprised the Allastam soldiers at the door had let this woman in, however, and the relief he felt for his own position was immediately replaced by worry about this 'news'. The woman stayed put for a few seconds, each making Hellion mouth twist into a deeper frown, then half-jogged to them. As soon as she extended the scroll, Hellion snatched it out of her hands.

The wax sealing it had been stamped with House Brasten's sigil.

Hellion glowered at it as if his gaze could melt it away, and the messenger used the opportunity to slip out of the room, escaping before he opened the missive. Yultes wished he could follow. He also wanted to snap at Hellion to get on with it. His already-frayed nerves wouldn't hold much longer.

Before any ill-advised words crossed his lips, however, Hellion finally broke the seal and unfurled the scroll. Unable to read it, Yultes instead studied every micro change in his body language—the twitch of his eyebrows, the flare of his nostrils, the ever-tighter grip on the scroll, crinkling it, and for a brief instant, blank horror. Then it all smoothed away into a calm, smug smile as Hellion crumpled the letter.

"How nice of Diel to drain another House's resources until they've been run into the ground." He laughed—a sound which melodic charm had turned into jagged edges.

Cotton had filled Yultes' mind. It was about Diel, then, and Diel could not possibly drain another house's resources if he was dead. Somehow, he'd escaped Avenazar's grasp and found his way to Lady Brasten. A burst of warmth expanded through Yultes' chest, one he struggled to conceal. Only once he trusted his voice not to betray him did he dare speak up.

"What does it say?"

Hellion sniffed. "I supposed you ought to know. Lady Brasten hereby declares, on behalf of her House, that Diel and his assorted cohort are welcome guests in her halls and under her protection. Any attempts on their person will be considered one against her family. Furthermore—and this is where it gets delicious, Yultes— furthermore, she supports Diel's claim to leadership of House Dathirii, as Lord Allastam supports mine, and will help him rebuild what was stolen until he can reclaim his ancestral home."

A sharp, strangled noise escaped Yultes. He'd known Diel would fight as soon as he'd learned the elf was still alive, but he hadn't expected the weight of a public declaration. How many Houses had received such a letter? All of them? Diel meant to take this confrontation into the public eye, to leave no room for secret deals that'd end with him in chains.

Hellion's eyebrows shot up at his reaction. "Wait, my friend, you've yet to hear the best part. I am, according to them, welcome to abandon the Dathirii name, find a new tower to inhabit, and start my own family—in which case I, and any who would follow, would not suffer any consequences for our treachery." Hellion scoffed and flicked the message away, letting it fall to the ground. "He's learned nothing, it seems."

On that, Yultes agreed, and this time there was no stopping the smile breaking through his face. "All the better for us," he said, hoping to cover his childish joy at the idea Diel hadn't lost his brazen idealism despite his brief visit to the enclave. "If he still believes he can win with pretty words and no sacrifices, proving him the fool will be child's play."

"Of course."

Hellion's replied came too quick, its confidence brittle. Yultes wondered how it'd felt, to read these words, if his ears had rung as fear blocked all thoughts away. He'd never forget the split second of pure horror he'd caught. Hellion might quip and laugh and handwave it all as pointless, but if his early reaction was any indication, he *knew* he would lose, that he didn't have what it took to cling to his position, that only Lord Allastam kept him there. His doubts weighed heavily in the silence that followed, the pressure stifling Yultes' breathing. He needed to move this conversation.

"You'd mentioned interesting mercantile targets for us. Tell me more, and I'll get us in touch before Diel has even settled in the Brasten Tower."

"No."

Hellion's hollowed tone, entirely devoid of its honeyed smoothness, rattled Yultes. He stared as his old friend sat back down, his back rigid.

"Leave me."

Despite the clear order, Yultes stayed rooted to his spot. What dark thoughts swirled in Hellion's mind now? Was it wise to leave him to them? Should he provide more reassurance that they could beat Diel? Mock the letter openly? Comfort Hellion? Perhaps he—

Hellion annihilated the thread of his ideas with one wide sweep of his arm, sending Yultes' financial report along with several quills and unlit candles flying to the side. Yultes froze, throat so tight no air made it in, as Hellion glared at the desk for a few, infinite seconds and then, without a sound, snatched a small ink bottle and flung it at the wall of golden flowers. Panic coiled inside Yultes as black liquid clung to leaves and covered buttons of luminescent gold. With every drip of ink sliding to the ground, he managed an inch backward, until the spell of terror holding him lifted, and he turned tail and left.

CHAPTER SEVEN

GAINST her deepest wishes, Sora Sharpe had returned to the Shelter.

This occurrence, all-too-frequent over the last month, never heralded good news for those inside. Her first visit had come in the wake of Hasryan's arrest and the investigation about his assassinations, both framed and real. Sora hadn't even spoken with Larryn at the time, instead snooping around long enough to confirm most of the locals refused to talk with her—no surprise there.

The welcome hadn't improved when she'd returned after the prison break attempt. Patrons had glared at her, and Arathiel had covered for Larryn's actions without the slightest hesitation. She'd strode in certain to find her culprit, only to leave with thick lies. These people didn't care about the law.

On her third visit, Sora had understood they might, if the law ever cared about them. Arathiel had planted those seeds when he'd come to ask Cal for help. Her fondness for Hasryan coupled with Larryn's fury had nurtured them. She'd spent a lot of time mulling over his accusations when he'd demanded to see Hasryan. They'd sounded so unreasonable, at first, yet she'd watched colleagues falsify paperwork or attack people of the Lower City on a whim without repercussions, and she'd endured plenty of nobles dictating her priorities, either directly to her or to her commanding officer.

The worst? It worked. Isandor's guards were rotten to the core, and she cared little what they expected of her anymore. As Camilla had so deftly put it, Sora trusted her personal compass over laws voted by the Golden Table. And right now, her compass pointed towards the missing members of House Dathirii. No doubt this had a lot to do with the old elven lady fretting in her house every day.

As of now, she still had two unaccounted for: Vellien and Kellian Dathirii.

She'd spoken with Lai, her informant with access to the Dathirii Tower. Ne hadn't managed to snoop in, but nir zucchini worked in the kitchens, and he'd confirmed Garith's and Jaeger's presence inside. No one else, though. After that, she'd wasted a lot of time trying to follow rumours about Diel Dathirii over the last week, only for him to show up with Branwen at Lady Brasten's door. Safe and sound. According to Camilla, Kellian should have been with them. He'd gone with Branwen into the Myrian Enclave the day of the coup, as demonstrated by the massive explosion of their temple to Keroth. Perhaps the elven captain had chosen to remain hidden while they reorganized. Either way, Sora figured that if Branwen had made it back safely, he must have too. And if not … She doubted she could help that.

This left her with Vellien, and their trail started at the Shelter, the night everyone first vanished, supposedly healing a teenager. According to witnesses, it seemed young Vellien Dathirii had entered the Shelter late that afternoon—shortly after leaving Sora's office, she reckoned—and never left. So now she returned, uniform stiff on her shoulders, dread gnawing at the pit of her stomach.

She didn't look forward to another chat with Larryn, but Sora reminded herself of Lady Camilla's quiet nervousness that fateful day, and of how Vellien had soothed it with a sweet melody. She latched onto the love there as motivation. She'd face Larryn's shit attitude if needed. Hopefully their verbal spars wouldn't end in an interrogation room.

Everyone hushed and glared at her the moment she stepped in.

The tangible hostility didn't cow Sora. She squared her shoulders and placed a hand on her hip, sweeping her gaze over the patrons, hunched at their tables with empty bowls. When faced with adversity—whether rooms full of assholes doubting her competence or dark alleys surrounded by criminals—she didn't back down. Never had, and she certainly wouldn't now. She ignored the nauseating scent of anise permeating the Shelter, forging through the crowd towards Larryn, sitting at a stool on their counter. Flour whitened his dark hair, red sauce lined his cheeks, and he'd seemed lost in thoughts before the mood shifted. His scowl returned as he caught sight of Sora, its familiarity almost reassuring.

"What in Keroth's Blazing Ass is your problem this time?" he asked. "Will we ever be rid of you, or is the harassment our new normal?"

Sora's eyebrows shot up at the creative swearing but she continued forward, walking at him like a charge. "Depends on how much you cooperate," she stated, stopping just short of Larryn, who had not bothered to slide down his stool. "Where is Vellien Dathirii?"

Colour drained from Larryn's cheeks until they matched the flour in his hair. His jaw worked as he searched for an answer, and Sora cursed inwardly. Could he look any more guilty? What had he done this time? Larryn angered her to no end, but she didn't want him behind bars, his Shelter abandoned. Sora clenched her fists, pushing down her urges to scold him for getting mixed up into trouble again.

"Not here," he finally managed. "They're not here, and haven't been for a week."

Sora crossed her arms, looming over him. "Thing is, I asked around and no one saw them leaving."

"Not my problem if your spies suck," he retorted before sliding down his stool, forcing her to take a step back. "They're not here. That's all I got to say to you."

He made to push past her, but she grabbed his forearm, shoving him back against the counter. He winced as he hit it, then glared at her. As if she hadn't dealt with folks ten times more intimidating. "Anyone ever told you how bad a liar you are? Don't make me arrest you, Larryn. What are you hiding?"

His gaze went to the handcuffs, and instead of scoffing, or berating her with some choice words about corruption and bullying, he turned even paler, the brown of his skin almost all white. Under her grip, he leaned harder on the counter, as if for support, then he pulled both hands closer to himself. Sora noticed his crooked fingers, and memories of colleagues joking about breaking thieves' fingers swarmed her mind. Larryn had his name in their books quite a few times, and she suspected the Sapphire Guards were to blame for the state of his hands.

"All I want is to find them, Larryn," she said more softly.

"Then look elsewhere. We like Vellien. They fix people's wounds nicely, don't think they're better than everybody here, and they don't linger pointlessly."

"Then *help me.* Soldiers are all over the Dathirii Tower, and I don't know what Allastam plans to do with those who weren't home when the place was taken. Vellien never returned to their quarters, and they didn't show up at Lady Brasten's door either."

Larryn tensed, sliding along the counter in an attempt to shrink away. Behind them, she could feel several patrons moving closer, as if to form a protective circle around their host. She stiffened at the unspoken threat there but didn't turn. She needed to focus on Larryn. He was staring at her, hesitant, fear beating back his anger.

"You think they could have been intercepted? Caught by Allastam soldiers out on the street? 'cause I'm telling you, they left this place. I haven't harmed them."

Sora released Larryn's forearm and leaned back, both to give him space and to be better prepared should the crowd behind her decide to become violent. Larryn straightened but kept a hand on the counter to steady himself.

"Considering how much time has passed since they've left here … perhaps. Allastam soldiers, or anyone else with ill intent." Vellien didn't have an imposing frame and the very fabric of their clothes marked them as wealthy—an easy target, for many. "You say they left. No one saw them, but if I can discover where they were headed …"

Larryn drew a sharp breath, and her stomach flipped. He *knew*. He knew where Vellien had gone but didn't want to tell her. Which meant some stinky crime was wrapped in all of this again. Curious as she was, she'd rather find Vellien than dig out whatever secret Larryn tiptoed around now, so she held her questions and waited.

"Maybe I can help," he muttered, "but you follow my rules. I got a contact, someone who might know, but they don't like guards sniffing around and won't want to meet you."

If Larryn could get the info out of them, Sora didn't care to meet them either. Well, a little—her curiosity couldn't be stopped. She'd let the mystery be if it led her to Vellien, however. Besides, she could always circle back to it later. For now, she withdrew, offering even more space to Larryn, and the patrons behind slowly drifted back to their previous conversations. Larryn closed his eyes, as if mentally preparing himself for a difficult trip. "All right. Let's move. I don't have all day for your little hunt."

He wiped the sauce off his cheek and ran a hand through his hair, shaking out part of the flour—apparently all he needed to get ready, considering he then went straight for the door, snatching a tattered fur cloak on the way out. Sora fell into step behind him, eager for a break in her long, otherwise frustrating search.

⁂

THIS was a mistake.

Larryn was halfway up to the Middle City by the time he admitted this to himself. Vellien and Hasryan had left the Shelter. If the young healer hadn't been seen since, they might still be together. He shouldn't help Sora find the kid, not if it led her back to Hasryan. But if both House Allastam and the Myrians were hunting for Vellien, then perhaps … Fear tightened Larryn's stomach, same as it had down in the Shelter. What if neither was safe and no one discovered it because he had kept his mouth shut?

It wouldn't matter that Sora never located Hasryan if his friend was dead, body thrown in tiny pieces down the shitslides. Larryn needed reassurance they'd at least reached Cal's place. Which meant they needed to visit Cal.

He could have gone later, on his own, rather than dragged her along. She knew he was covering something up, though, and he'd seen the way her hands twitched for the handcuffs. Small knots had lined his spine when she'd threatened to arrest him, each a prickle of unwelcome memories. He'd been arrested over and over as a youth, but the last time … The Shelter had been a hunk of planks back then, put together by Jim's relentless work and love. That day flipped Larryn's life around. He'd humiliated Drake Allastam too hard, without thoughts of the consequence, and the asshole had come to the Lower City for revenge. Jim paid first.

They were following the same path of arching bridges and steep stairs as he had back then, chained by two guards and led by Drake. Larryn's thumbs ached as he remembered how he'd escaped his arrest. He could almost feel the weight of the shackles around his wrists, the way they'd pressed into his thumbs and shattered his weak bones as he'd leaped off the bridge. The grind of it had reverberated through his whole frame, washed away only by the blinding pain hot on its heels. His hands had slipped out of the holes, each taking less width with the base of his thumbs crushed. He'd landed hard on another path below, his entire body shaking, and ran.

Apparently, the Sapphire Guards called him Bonebreaker now. His thumbs had never recovered from the stunt, much like his other fingers. Sometimes Larryn wondered if a single bone of his hands had made it through his first sixteen years of life unbroken. Doubtful. He had managed to avoid arrest since that day, but even the thought of it sent terror coursing through him again. He wouldn't risk it, not if he could placate Sharpe another way.

Larryn stopped a dozen feet before the spot where he'd jumped, in the small rest area with benches and a few potted plants right before it, and he rubbed the base of his left thumb, breathless. On most days, he managed to push the memories far enough away not to care when he passed this place, but Sharpe's threat had shaken him. She slowed a step behind him.

"Are you all right?" she asked. "I'd expected an hour-long rant on the way."

Was that … humour? Larryn whirled around, unsettled. "You asking for one? They're never far away, even when I'm… " He trailed off as he caught Sora's stare, pointedly following his slow, reflexive rubbing of the base of his thumb. Larryn dropped his hands by his side. "You don't care anyway."

"It's not that simple and I think you know it." Heavy winter winds buffeted Sharpe's hair, and she pushed strands out of her eyes.

"I'm glad you're helping. You don't trust me and that's fair, but Vellien doesn't deserve to pay because of what's between us."

"You mean, they don't deserve to pay because you've been hard at work trying to get my best friend to hang, is that it?" He wouldn't let her weasel out of facts. She was right; he didn't trust her. Not with Hasryan, anyway. Nobles, though? You could trust most guards with a noble's safety. "You wait here. Don't follow. I know how to spot and shake a tail. You try that and you're on your own."

Sharpe tightened her winter cloak around her shoulders, to shield herself from the cold. "I won't. Whatever else you're hiding, I trust you on this."

Larryn stared back, as uneasy with this as with her attempt at a joke earlier. He knew how to deal with Sora Sharpe barging into his Shelter demanding answers and accusing him—rightly—of one illegal act or another. She'd always been hostile, quick to retort and put him on the spot, and difficult to placate and turn away. Without Arathiel's help, she'd have had his ass behind bars after the prison break. This trusting and concerned Sora left him wary, uncertain of his footing. He was still trying to figure out how to react when a third hated voice cut the winter air.

"Now that's not a mistake I would make, Sharpe," Drake Allastam said, and Larryn spun around. That he knew how to deal with. His pamperedship stood on the other side of the tiny park, right where Larryn had jumped off to escape him over two years ago, the eternal sneer curling his lips. "This runt deserves a deep prison hole, not our esteemed guards' trust."

Larryn snorted and bunched his hands into fists, ready for a fight. He had so much pent-up anger to release, and who better than Drake? Between the constant harassment, Jim's murder, and Hasryan's imprisonment, this asshole managed to displace even Yultes on Larryn's mental list of nobles he despised. At least his father had mustered enough guilt to try and assuage it with gold. Drake had breezed through life without ever experiencing the consequences of his actions, unless you counted Larryn's infrequent retaliation.

"Is your nose healed yet?" Larryn asked. "I can break it again, if you want. In Hasryan's honour."

Healers must've put their skills to good use on Drake, because no trace of Hasryan's glorious headbutt remained. What a shame. Larryn stepped forward, hoping to rectify this mistake and ignoring the casual threat of the rapier at Drake's hip. Sharpe's hand clamped down on his shoulder and pulled him back.

"You don't shove residents striving to better their communities into deep prison holes—not when you want your home to flourish." Anger strained her calm voice, and her fingers dug deep in Larryn's bony shoulder. "How is your father? Has Lord Allastam destroyed enough of the House disagreeing with him, or does he plan to extend his dictatorial leadership to others?"

Drake grew red as a beet and sputtered. Only surprise kept Larryn from laughing. What was happening with Sora Sharpe?

"Watch your mouth, guard, or your commanding officer will hear of our dictatorial leadership and its demands."

A bitter chuckle escaped Sora. "As if that's not already the case."

Drake's lips parted and closed twice, but he failed to answer, as if he couldn't fathom Sora knew he could take her job away and still dared to contradict him. Larryn twisted around and found her grinning and wide-eyed, fierce determination shining through her expression.

"I can answer to my superior when the time comes. Until then, I will not bow to a snivelling crybaby who deliberately provokes fights with others and complains when he gets hurt. I have better things to do than to validate the constant harassment you've subjected Larryn and his friends to in the last years."

Larryn froze, certain now they'd entered an alternate dimension. Or this was a twisted dream. How did Sora Sharpe even know about that? Had Hasryan told her of their history? With a squeeze to his shoulders, she motioned for Larryn to follow her, turning back the way they'd come. Larryn scrambled after her, giddy from Sora's support. If that was her opinion of the Allastams … He couldn't resist swivelling back and gracing Drake with a victorious grin and a rude gesture.

"You little—"

Drake's rapier slid out of its scabbard with a musical shlink. In three long strides, he reached Larryn and grabbed his coat, yanking it to spin Larryn around as he struck. Sora reacted faster, her sword slicing through Larryn's cloak to parry Drake's, knocking it away before it could pierce his breast. Drake released the torn cloth with a frustrated scream and locked eyes with Sora. Larryn stepped back, his heart slamming against his ribcage, the world unsteady under his feet. A second later and he'd have been dead.

The terrifying thought was still worming its way through him, turning his muscles into lead, when a wall of shimmering, dark blue energy formed in the public square. The eight-foot-tall entity towered over Sora and Drake, translucent and menacing, unlike anything Larryn had ever seen. It swept forward before he could cry out and slammed into Sora. Larryn's stomach climbed up his throat as she flew off the bridge with a surprised yell, pushed over the edge in a single painful second.

"Sora!"

He hurried to the bridge's edge, hoping another road—his road, from two years ago, the one he'd landed on in his escape—had caught her, but the wall surged towards him before he could get a good look. Larryn scrambled back, barely avoiding the advancing wall. This thing was almost as large as their tiny park! He reached into his boot and retrieved the dagger he kept hidden there, before spinning around to search the source of this threat.

Two cloaked figures had dropped into the park: a muscular woman with a broad sword, and a man in robes, the circlet on his brow shining the same blue as the wall. At the bottom of their cloaks was a pattern Larryn recognized from Nevian's apprentice robes, and he stiffened. What did Myrians want with them? The warrior approached them, her gaze set on Drake.

"Drake Allastam?" she asked in a thin voice.

"Who else?" Drake countered. Larryn had to admit, all the Allastam sigils etched into his rich-ass outfit and upon his fancy scabbard warranted the disdain in his response.

"Excellent."

The bloodthirsty look she threw him left no doubts about her intentions. Drake fell into a technical stance, meant for fights with rules—nothing like what you'd see on the streets. Nothing like this one. Larryn suspected she'd only need a few swipes to gut him. The city would be better for it.

Then Larryn didn't have time to worry about Drake, because the mage's eyes unfocused, and the wall spun above Larryn, coming down to squash him like a fly. Larryn dashed out from under, and the flat bridge rumbled under his soles as he scrambled forward, sprinting towards the wizard. Why couldn't they leave him alone? If they wanted to kill Drake, let them! But that wall was moving again, sliding after him at a terrifying speed, gathering a thin layer of snow as it swept all on its way. These Myrians would see him dead as surely as Drake, and he wouldn't reach the mage before the wall shoved him off to splatter a hundred feet below. His heart hammering, Larryn flipped his grip on his dagger, prayed that Hasryan's many throwing lessons would bear fruits, and flung it at the wizard.

It sank into the Myrian's flesh with a thunk, and the circlet flared a deep blue before going out. Behind Larryn, the wall fizzled out. With a rush of relief, he barreled into the thin mage, bringing him down on the ground. Larryn had been in enough fists fights for the rest to come naturally. He ignored the clanging swords and the grunts and yelps from Drake as he struggled to stay alive, and smashed his fist into the mage's face.

Sharp pain spread through his fingers as his knuckles hit rock-solid skin. Larryn cried out, confused, and snatched his fist back. Hadn't the dagger sank in just fine? What horseshit—The Myrian's hand wrapped around his throat, interrupting his internal swearing. The strength in his grip shocked Larryn as much as the throb in his hand, and the mage flipped him over and pinned him to the ground with stunning ease. Through his panic, Larryn registered a blur, cold stone under his shoulder blades, and thick fingers crushing his windpipe. He wheezed and struggled under him, desperate for a sliver of fresh air. The mage didn't even bother to look at him as Larryn clawed at the stone-solid arm holding him. With the casualness reminiscent of someone used to murder, the Myrian turned to his partner.

"About done?" he asked.

"You're always in such a hurry."

Sickening panic surged through Larryn in waves, threatening to crush his mind. He couldn't let that happen. Needed to think, to plan. Black spots crowded the edge of his vision already and his lungs burned and burned, screaming for air, anything. Larryn pawed at the man's torso, each movement weaker than the one before. His fingers touched his dagger's hilt, and a jolt of hope coursed through him. He pulled with all his flimsy strength.

Stuck, as if embedded into rock. Curse that stonelike skin! Head light, nauseated and desperate, Larryn shook and twisted the blade, pleading for it to move and come free.

It sliced through flesh underneath.

The mage cried out, relaxed his grip—and fresh air rushed into Larryn's lungs. Emboldened, he stabbed his left hand's fingers into the man's eyes. The wet, squishy sensation sickened him, but this time the Myrian let go entirely, and the dagger loosened. No rock-hard skin anymore. Larryn pulled it out. Instincts overruled every other thought, and he closed his eyes as he slashed the man's throat open.

Warm blood drenched his forearm and face, sliding down his cheek. He rolled away, the taste of copper on his lips, his stomach twisting into a hundred knots. Larryn heaved, dizzy, unable to do anything but stare at his slim dagger and hands, crooked fingers covered in red, and the pool of the wizard's blood slowly crawling towards them, across the snow-flecked bridge. He'd killed someone. The body was bleeding, right there next to him, lifeless because of him, because he'd sliced its throat open, spilling it all out. He didn't—couldn't—look at it.

Drake cried out in pain, pulling Larryn from his daze, offering a perfect distraction from the corpse. The noble was stumbling away from his opponent, a bright red line traversing his torso. His rapier had slid halfway across the park—out of reach from Drake—and the Myrian warrior was stepping over it, advancing on Drake.

It left the weapon directly between Larryn and the Myrian.

He didn't even think twice about it. He'd never beat that warrior in a fair battle, but she had her back to him now. He scrambled up and dashed across the park, snatching up the rapier as he passed it. She lifted her broadsword, ready to strike, unaware of his quick steps right behind her. Larryn grabbed her shoulder, pulling her down as he plunged the blade between her shoulder plates. It slid in with sickening ease and she stumbled backward, a ragged breath crossing her lips. Larryn let go of the hilt, slipping out from under her as she fell. He stared at the body as it hit the ground, unable to avoid it this time, and blood rang in his ears, banging against his temples.

Twice. He had killed twice.

Larryn stared and stared and stared, the world narrowing to the corpse at his feet and his hand twitching as if it still held a hilt.

Fingers grabbed the front of his shirt, snapping him out of it.

Drake, eyes wide, expression twisted in a sneer. "If you think I'll forget about you just because—"

Larryn punched him, releasing the horror building inside of him in one powerful swing. He couldn't deal with Drake, not now, while his mind buzzed from the kills and the rush of battle drained away. Blood from the mage left a satisfying red smear on Drake's face and he fell on his ass, stunned. Shaken and out of breath, Larryn glared down at him.

"Shut up. I saved you because I would've been next. I hope they come back for you."

He pushed the mentioned ass with the tip of his now-bloodied shoes, for good measure, then walked away, ears still ringing, to the edge of the park. Sora had fallen here. He needed to know, even if that meant another body. His gaze swept the city below, and his insides squeezed when he spotted her. She'd hit the bridge he'd leaped to, all those years ago, and she lay sprawled on the dark grey stone, her leg at an awkward angle. Unconscious, but probably alive—after all, he hadn't broken anything when he'd made that jump. Around her, people either stared from a safe distance or hurried on their way.

Larryn had meant to reach Cal's house alone in case Hasryan still slept there. Not an option anymore, not unless he left her for dead. He gathered the remnants of his shaky energy and ran towards Sora, never looking back at Drake or the two Myrians he had killed.

CHAPTER EIGHT

CAL'S heart quickened when someone hammered at his door. That was it: his luck had run out. Myrians had traced Varden to his house, or the Sapphire Guards had discovered he was hiding Hasryan, or-or anything like that. He'd known the risks, packing so many fugitives all at once, and he didn't regret it. Even now, as a short prayer to Ren crossed his lips, he prepared to make a stand. After all, he still had Vellien and Varden sleeping in his bed, and he refused to let anyone get to them. He'd figure something out—a stroke of luck, sudden inspiration—or their friends at the Brasten Tower would come back for them. *Something*, he promised himself.

Then Larryn's voice pierced through the door, seeped in despair. "Cal? Cal, are you home?"

Cal's quick and terrified pulse turned into an angry stammer. Larryn? What had he done this time? Did he think he could show up and ask for help as if nothing had happened between them? Cal stomped to the door, flinging it open, a scolding at the tip of his tongue. His frustration morphed into horror as soon as he laid eyes on his friend.

Larryn was cradling Sora Sharpe in his arms, thick sweat rolling down his temples and neck from the exertion of carrying her. It traced paler lines into the dark red blood covering his cheeks and staining his clothes. Under it all, Larryn shook and shook and shook, pale as the grey sky above. He staggered a step forward, hesitated. When his lips parted, only a strangled sob slipped out, and it washed away the rest of Cal's indignation. He rushed to his friend, promising himself they'd talk about Larryn's non-existent apology later.

"I'm here, I'm here," he said, reaching for Larryn's forearm and squeezing it. He coaxed him towards the pillows on the ground, motioning for him to set Sora down. Tears streamed down Larryn's face as he followed Cal's direction and the moment he'd freed his hands, he wiped them away.

"Tell me she won't die," he whispered. "I can't—not another one."

His voice broke and he stayed there, kneeling, trembling from head to toe. Cal couldn't help but stare. Last time Larryn had been in such a sorry state, Drake had just stabbed Jim and he'd had to shatter his thumbs to escape arrest. But he didn't even *like* Sora, so what had him so shaken? Could he have done this? Was that guilt, wracking through him?

"What happened?" he asked.

"J–just … please just … save her."

"A–All right. I'm saving her." He set a firm hand on Larryn's leg and looked at him. "It'll be fine, Larryn. I promise."

Cal dug into his pocket for his silver coin, his physical connection to Ren, and ran his thumb over the burnt relief. Fire had blackened one side, melting it out of shape, yet the distorted piece remained perfectly balanced between heads and tails—a miracle of chance. He placed the coin on top of Sora's knee and tried to keep his mind off Larryn. As much as he craved to hug his friend and wrap him in love, he had to take care of Sora first.

Well, Ren, let's see if I'm getting any better at this healing thing.

He knew he was. Months ago, he'd never have been able to perform the kind of healing he'd done on Hasryan in the Myrian Enclave. Vellien had taught him techniques while they helped Nevian at the Shelter, explaining to Cal how to follow Ren's divine energy into a wounded body. In theory, that granted him a sense of what was happening in the body, how tissue was damaged and how to better fix it. It'd taken Cal several attempts to succeed—at first, it had only made his temples pulse and his head hurt, as if something hammered from inside it. Practise provided him with a firmer perception of blood flow, but nothing as detailed as Vellien described. They advised more training, but Cal suspected thorough healing was simply not in Ren's nature. Even Hasryan's leg had continued to ache until Vellien had looked at it.

All that healing required focus and energy, though, and Cal had been sleeping on pillows and caring for everyone sheltered in his home. That took its toll, and when Cal tried to dive into Sora's wounds, pain blossomed in his own knee and shattered his concentration. He yelped, found Larryn staring at him with wide eyes, breathed in deep and prepared for the sharp agony before plunging back in. Cal reached for the snapped bone, fusing it together before knitting the muscles and nerves around. Yet as he fixed Sora's leg, a new pain grew in his back as an echo of hers, intensifying until the hot spikes along his spine forced him out. Vellien managed to numb their own echoed pain when they healed, but Cal had never mastered that either. Sora needed more than he could give her. With a sigh, he lumbered up and set a hand on Larryn's shoulder.

"I have to wake Vellien," he said. "Her leg's fine now, but she hurt her back hard too. Don't you want to sit somewhere more comfortable?"

He gestured at the sofas, and Larryn gave him a blank stare. "Whatever. All right."

Larryn unfolded from the ground and dragged his feet to the seats. He crumpled into the green one, as if all the energy and emotions had been drained out of him. It wasn't right. Larryn never stopped moving, yelling, *doing*. Cal tried to find words to light that spark in him again, but he'd no idea where to start. The air between them had stayed thick with Larryn's punch and everything unsaid since. With a sigh, Cal left his living room and hurried to the bed. He stretched up near Vellien's sleeping form and shook them alive as gently as he could. Vellien woke with a moaned yawn, eyes bleary until they caught Cal's expression.

"What's going on?" they asked, slipping out of the covers

without pause. "Does someone need me?"

"Sora Sharpe." Vellien's proactive question sent relief coursing through Cal. "Larryn brought her … She had a broken leg, and her back's all wrong. I–I tried to heal her and let you rest, but …"

Cal interrupted his rambling as he caught the deep exhaustion in it. Vellien didn't need to hear about that. Everyone here had so much on their minds. His little bouts of tiredness could wait.

Vellien ruffled their copper-tinged hair and rubbed the base of their neck, shaking themself fully awake. Behind them, Varden groaned and rolled over, spreading out in the bed. The smile it brought Vellien vanished as they reached the door, a hand on the handle. "Is … Is Larryn in the room?"

"Yeah." Vellien might not want to see him after the kidnapping. Cal still couldn't believe Larryn would threaten someone as gentle as them, but when it came to Larryn and nobles, one could expect the worst. "Sorry."

"I'll manage," Vellien replied with a thin smile. "This is nothing. Sora needs my help."

The young elf took another moment to straighten their hair and clothes, gathering their courage before they stepped into the living room. Cal followed close behind in case Larryn reacted badly, but his friend didn't even glance their way. He was playing with his bloodied sleeve, pulling at threads as if to unravel the entire thing. While Vellien hurried to Sora's side, Cal slid towards Larryn.

"You look like shit," he said. "I can get you water to wash your hands."

"I don't want to talk. Isn't Hasryan here?"

Cal stiffened at the rebuttal, hot tears prickling his eyes. He fought them off, forcing himself to step back and wrench calm words from his tight throat. "Out spying. Sorry I'm not good enough for you."

"That's not—" Larryn lifted his head, horror transforming his expression, the first solid emotion he'd shown since wiping away his tears. "I just … I don't think I deserve that kindness from you."

"Oh." But he wanted to help so bad it tore him up inside. Cal frowned. "Larryn—"

"No, please, listen." Larryn squeezed his eyes shut. "We both know you're just waiting for a reason to forgive everything. I'd say sorry and that'd be it, wouldn't it? But I … I haven't changed, have I? I'm still angry and impulsive, and now I'm even more a-a mess. It's not fair." He shook his head, and the faintest smile touched his lips. "I want to earn it, Cal, and you're too kind to make me."

Cal gaped at him, every word of protest dying before he could utter them. They'd all be lies, anyway. He *had* been ready to embrace Larryn again, because that's what friends did—that's how he was.

"You have changed," he whispered, before forcing his natural cheer back into his voice. "That's more insightful than I've known you to be!"

A choked laugh escaped Larryn. "Yeah, well … I didn't use

to *think* so much."

The tears rolled down Cal's cheeks despite his best attempts to contain them. He missed Larryn and the evenings running around the Shelter while exchanging snippets of conversation, the quick teasing between two patrons or a game of cards. And he missed the softer parts too—sharing Larryn's dreams for a children-only floor for the Shelter or commemorating Jim's death under a starry night, outside the Shelter. Larryn had always been difficult, but it had been worth it.

"It's all right," he said. "I think I get it."

Larryn brought his legs back to him, wrapping arms around his knees. Cal resisted the urge to squeeze his friend's leg in reassurance, and they watched Vellien work in silence, almost at peace despite everything still unresolved.

The rattling doorknob and creaking door eventually broke that daze, and they both stiffened until Hasryan slipped in. He'd draped half his face with a scarf and hid his wine-coloured winter coat under a fur cloak. Hasryan pulled the hood down as he stepped in, but his warm greeting died as he took in the scene: Vellien healing Sora on a bed of pillows, Larryn covered in blood on Cal's green chair, and Cal hovering nearby.

"What's going on?"

Larryn's head thunked against his knees. "I killed two Myrians and Sora's trying to die on me."

"She's not dying," Vellien replied, their voice firm and calm.

"It will be fine."

"Nothing's fine!" Larryn gripped his knees with a snarl. The blood staining his cheek was streaked through with tears again, the diluted red running down his neck. "One moment they were alive, and then I slashed and stabbed and–and they weren't. I killed them. I've never … I don't want to be …"

The words died on their own. Hasryan pulled his gloves off and flung them far, crossing the room in a few swift strides. He knelt on the other side of Larryn and cupped his chin, moving with a soft protectiveness Cal had rarely seen, as if about to fuss over a child. Perhaps that made sense. Hasryan had executed two guards in the Myrian Enclave and brushed it off like routine.

"Look at me, Larryn." He waited until Larryn stared back, still holding his chin, calm and serious. "This doesn't make you anything you don't want to be, and you certainly don't have what it takes to be a cold-blooded killer. I would know." Hasryan smirked, which dragged a smile out of Larryn. "Do you feel sick? Lightheaded?"

Each time, Larryn nodded. Hasryan turned to Cal and whispered "water" before refocusing his attention on Larryn. Cal reluctantly peeled himself from them, and it felt like a cocoon closed around the pair, as if Hasryan had isolated them from the rest of the world, leaving only his gentle questions behind. Even as he moved to the kitchen, Cal continued to listen, captivated.

"Do you feel like you're drowning? Yeah? All right."

Cal pushed one of his steps next to the sink and climbed on in, reaching for the water pump. He placed a large wooden cup under it and started pulling.

"Listen, everyone reacts differently to this, but here's what I think. You'll be sick. Maybe not now, but you'll throw up eventually. Especially if you've seen the body. Did you?"

"Y-yeah. One of them."

Larryn's voice barely covered the sound of running water. The cup overflowed in Cal's hand and he hurriedly pulled it away, sloshing water. His heart hammered as if caught eavesdropping. Cal gripped the cup tight and paused, trying to control himself. It was hard, not to hug or touch Larryn, not to brush away everything that had come between them to be the friend he needed. But Hasryan was doing that, filling that role better than Cal could have, in the circumstances, and Larryn was right. They hadn't worked anything out—another emergency had dropped on them. They could talk more later, when their lives had regained a semblance of normalcy. For now, he would need to hold his love steady.

As Cal returned into the room, Hasryan was going through reactions he had experienced or seen in others with the casualness of someone listing meals they had enjoyed.

"Newcomers get a day or two without tasks after their first kill for the Crescent Moon, to give themselves time to deal. Some would have needed more. Don't try to hold it in. No matter how it happened—no matter how justified—it's always rough." Hasryan ran a thumb over the scar at his neck, a strange inflexion in his voice at the word 'justified'. "Doesn't make you a bad person, this killing business. You saved Sora, didn't you?"

A sad laugh escaped Larryn. "I even saved Lord Asshole on a Stick."

"Drake was there?" Cal offered the cup.

Larryn wrapped shaky hands around it and sipped. "Yeah. It sounded like he was their target."

"Are those finger marks on your neck from him?" Hasryan asked with a low growl. "Was that prick trying to strangle you?"

"No, that's one of the Myrians. Some mage. His skin was so hard. I had to …" His voice trailed off and he shook his head. "I feel sick."

"Drink more water." Hasryan tapped the cup. "And open your ears. I've killed more people than I can count, most for a pouch of coins. You don't hate me for that, so you don't get to hate yourself for killing Myrians in self-defence. You did the right thing out there. It won't feel like it for a while, but you did."

"Thanks."

Hasryan straightened up and mussed Larryn's hair the way he often did with Cal's. Larryn downed the cup of water in silence and one by one, they turned towards Vellien. The young healer had rearranged the pillows around Sora. When they realized the attention at shifted back to them, they flushed a deep red and cleared their throat.

"She needs rest now, and she'll feel sick upon awakening." Vellien rubbed their arm and stood up. "Larryn. I—that's a lot of blood. If you're wounded …"

Larryn's gaze clasped upon Vellien and his eyes narrowed. "Thanks. I'm fine. I mean, I'm not fine, but I'm not wounded. Only bruises."

Vellien stepped forward. "I could still—"

"Don't." He waved Vellien back with a tight smile. "You're sweet, but keep your strength for others."

"All right. Will … will those sick at the Shelter manage without me for a while?"

Surprised flitted through Larryn's expression and he cast his gaze down. "We've done so before. You don't have to come back. We can cancel the rules."

Vellien drew themself taller, squaring their shoulders to take as much room as possible. The effect would have been more impressive if they hadn't flushed red as they answered. "I'll return. I have ties in the Shelter now, and I won't abandon everyone. But if Myrians are attacking nobles openly and we've no news from our home … it's dangerous for me. Will you tell Nevian that I miss him and that he still needs to take breaks from work?"

A rush of joy coursed through Cal and he hopped up. "Oh,

can I? Please, I want to see his face when I do!"

Hasryan laughed and Vellien got even redder. Larryn looked at the young elf and this time his smile seemed more genuine. "Ties in the Shelter, huh? I see what's going on." He turned to Cal. "Not sure it's fair to inflict you on poor Nevian. If you end up squealing with romantic delight in front of him, he'll be mortified."

"Or maybe he needs someone to talk about it!"

"I don't think—" Vellien started.

"Don't worry." Cal set his hands on his hips, grinning. They all looked terrified of what he'd do or say to Nevian, which in itself was almost as amusing as the idea of poking the grumpy teenager about his budding love. "I need to talk to Nevian anyway. Someone ought to tell him we retrieved Varden without getting caught before he loses too much sleep over whether or not Avenazar will come knocking."

"All right. Permission to carry the message in my stead granted," Larryn said. "While you're there, reassure everyone that I'm safe. No one was at ease after I left with Sora. She threatened to arrest me in front of the whole room."

Cal tilted his head to the side, wondering what exactly had transpired. The miracle here was that Larryn hadn't immediately given her cause for an arrest, if only to spite her.

"Consider it done," he said, opting against more questions. He trudged to his entrance and picked up his mismatched winter attire, along with his one gift from the tailor: a tuque of a stark yellow reminiscent of his bright door that fit him perfectly. "Don't wreck my house while I'm gone, and let Miss Sharpe know she's welcome to stay as long as she needs."

Cal left his warm and colourful living room with a lightness in his steps he had to fake. Even though Hasryan seemed to have everything under control, Cal felt like he'd failed Larryn. But that was wrong. All this distance between them, it was Larryn's doing—and for once, his friend had been right to keep it there. Cal might crave their old relationship, but it'd been a broken thing, its jagged edges all pointed at him. If they didn't figure out how to remove those, any attempt to get closer would only end in fresh new cuts. Cal refused to let that happen. No matter what, they would find a way to repair the Halfies Trio.

Chapter Nine

BRANWEN'S first foray into assessing the goodwill left in the network of merchants House Dathirii once sported had yielded awful results. The general response had been clear: their House was no more—Golden Table seats lost, leader vanished overnight, rival soldiers with the Tower's walls—and after Hellion had cut off mercantile relationships with most of them, the financial instability of the last weeks had taken a turn for the worse. Until they had more than empty promises, partnerships wouldn't be worth the risk. Some had been gentler about it than others, their regrets genuine, but the end result had been the same.

That was before Lady Brasten's support.

If they intended to compete with Hellion for legitimacy, they needed to rebuild their family's business, so Branwen had been sent out for a second foray, this time with Lord Oloan Brasten, one of the House's twin coinmasters, to convince previous allies to revisit old deals. Branwen appreciated the seriousness this lent her; she suspected several merchants would have outright ignored her without such undeniable support. Lord Oloan was a calm man, with broad shoulders and dark brown skin. When he entered the room, he commanded attention, and his genial smile quickly put many at ease.

This allowed her to put a foot in the door, but little more. One of the first shopowners, a pale and straight-backed silversmith by the name of Albert Duvigny, could barely bother to look up to them, his focus fully directed to polishing a beautiful cup with leaf designs etched into it. Branwen kept a wide smile plastered across her face, unwilling to lose a potential partner along with her temper, and begun explaining the Brasten-Dathirii alliance. She'd not even finished relaying Lady Brasten's official declaration when he set his cup down and raised a finger, interrupting her in one simple and dismissive gesture.

"Let's not further waste our respective times," he said. "House Allastam has a heavy hand in silver supplies for the city. I cannot afford to anger them by allying with Diel Dathirii, no matter the supplementary income you propose, as no amount of gold will let me ply my craft if I cannot access silver. I have learned one truth since this trade war with the Myrians has started: I'd rather sink alone than do so because of strangers' incessant political manoeuvres."

And that had been the end of it. He could not be convinced joining them might save him from decline, cutting off most of

Branwen's argument with a wave of his hands or a grunt, and guiding them back towards the door. By the time they both stood on the connecting bridge once more, winter winds buffeting them, Branwen's words had given way to impotent rage, and Lord Oloan hadn't said a single thing. She spun on him.

"Aren't you here to help?"

"I am." He offered a shrug, but there was nothing apologetic about it. "Did you listen to him?"

"Of course! I—"

"Then you know as well as I what we'll need to do if Mister Duvigny is ever to join us."

Branwen's lips parted for a retort, but her mind caught up to his meaning before she could make a fool of herself. "The silver supply," she said instead.

"Precisely. We'll investigate the solidity of House Allastam's control over it. In the meantime, however, our time is better used speaking with House Dathirii's other lost merchants."

Branwen agreed with a stiff nod, trying to ignore the flush at her cheeks and bitter splash in the pit of her stomach. He shouldn't have needed to tell her that. Needling valuable knowledge out of others was her bread and butter, and she should've latched onto the silversmith's mention of supplies on her own, filing it away for later. Branwen hadn't come into the conversation thinking about information gathering, however. Diel had tasked her with convincing these old allies to join them by presenting a deal favourable to them, and she'd been so focused on succeeding at that and making her uncle proud, she'd lost sight of the bigger picture.

Perhaps Lord Oloan's pointed observation had made her feel like a beginner because she was one, at least where deal signing was concerned—the kind who got so caught up in the task they forgot the rest of their skills. It wouldn't happen again.

They continued on their route, meeting traders and artisans in their shops and homes, entertaining brief conversations or tight negotiations in turn. Many had enjoyed their long-standing deals with House Dathirii, which a halfling weaver described as 'his guaranteed gold to sail down the Reonne and see his family once a year,' and rejoined without needing much convincing. Most, however, still readily expressed their doubts. The first to do so had been Branwen's favourite inkmaker, Amma, whose wife created beautiful designs Branwen had always wanted inked into her skin. The portly woman had been lining up bottles on higher shelves, listening to them with disinterested deference at first, but by the time Branwen had laid out the details of their offer—monthly stipend in exchange for supplies, personnel to help with accounting, and access to magical inks from House Brasten's unique network of trivial enchanted goods—she'd stopped and climbed down her stepladder. Her sharp gaze moved between her two visitors.

"This is all riveting, but I'm not concerned about the details. Been dealing with House Dathirii long enough to know it'll be fair." She'd set her elbow atop the stepladder and leaned on it as she turned to Branwen. "No, I'm worried about its stability. Agreements are all nice and good, but what's our guarantee your House will exist in a week? A month? A year? You make enemies faster than I can track."

"If I may?" Lord Oloan's polite request didn't match his step forward, placing himself almost between Branwen and Amma. "Should House Dathirii fail to fulfill their end of the bargain, then House Brasten will in their stead. We've grown in importance steadily through the decades, have never encountered major obstacles in our dealings, and enjoy a unique stock of magical paraphernalia that can be turned into a revenue stream with a flick of the wrist. Our stability is not in question." He brushed the air before him with his last, dismissive sentence, then granted the inkseller with a beautiful smile. "Certainly, if House Dathirii falls, you'll lose a regular and beloved customer, but everything else will remain the same. House Brasten will gladly take its place."

Branwen's polite smile froze as a cold dread coiled in the pit of her stomach. *House Brasten will gladly take its place.* Was that supposed to be comforting? When Lady Brasten and Diel had discussed this plan, it had been as equal partners, two leaders joining forces to oust House Allastam and the Myrian Enclave. Certainly, Diel had come to her in a position of weakness, but Lady Brasten had offered protection, insight, and help. They'd chosen to rebuild the Dathirii network of merchants to prove their house, as a political entity, existed beyond the Dathirii Tower and would keep fighting. A symbolic gesture, almost, although the income would be welcome.

According to Lord Oloan, however, House Brasten would replace House Dathirii in these deals should they be annihilated. And wouldn't it be so convenient, then, if Diel Dathirii's last bid for his home—for survival, really—failed, and all these partnerships transferred to House Brasten? Had Diel not noticed? Did he have a plan? Why not warn her about this?

She ground her teeth as Lord Oloan retrieved the documents to sign, wondering if she should say anything. Amma had been clear: without House Brasten's stability, she wouldn't rejoin. Branwen opted not to squabble with her supposed ally in front of the ink merchant, and once they emerged into the cold winter air again, she let Lord Oloan's praise about a smooth transaction slid off her shoulders. No point arguing now. They'd never meet the entire network today. If this transfer rights tactic had malicious intent, there'd been plenty of time to counter it, and Branwen would rather not tip her game this fast. She kept her smile bright and inviting as she led Lord Oloan to the next merchant.

"UNCLE, their help is a trap."

Branwen strode into her uncle's newly acquired office—no knocks, no patience for them. She'd spent her entire day watching Lord Oloan Brasten conclude perfect little trade deals—a beautiful noose to tighten around their neck as soon as they were ready.

Diel sat behind the chestnut-coloured desk, his long fingers tracing the lines in the wooden surface. He hadn't looked up despite her noisy entrance, and she stopped dead. How deep must he have lost himself? She'd barged in without a hint of subtlety, her words as inflammatory as her attitude, yet still he stared at his desk. Branwen's anger dissipated, a profound unease sliding inside in its stead. She crouched in front of him.

"Uncle?"

Diel startled, his head snapping up as he gasped. "Oh, Branwen!" He pushed jovial notes in his voice and forced a smile to his lips, as if it could mask the lines of fatigue under his eyes and the heaviness hanging over him. "Can I help you?"

Everything in her screamed to act as if nothing was wrong here and he was still her miracle worker. He'd explain this afternoon away with simple logic that she, as a beginner negotiator, had not seen. Branwen could stop worrying about their only real ally setting them up for a dramatic fall, and she could instead celebrate a day of good work. It'd be fine, all fine.

Except it wouldn't.

Diel hadn't been himself, only summoning energy in brief bursts before returning to this listless anxiety. She'd thought the alliance with House Brasten had helped—he'd seemed more hopeful since they'd moved into the new quarters—but perhaps his fallow periods had simply lessened in length.

"Just wanted to check on you," she chirped. "Have you eaten? I've been out with Lord Oloan all day and could use some warm soup or something."

Weariness sloughed off Diel's shoulders as he tilted his head to the side. "Making sure your poor old uncle is eating all his meals?"

"Did you?" she asked.

He laughed, then, and although Branwen's ears picked up the strain in it, the sound heartened her more than soup ever could.

"No," he admitted, sliding out of his chair. "Let's see what we can acquire."

Branwen smiled back at him, taking his arm as if he was an old man. Her desire to burden him eroded away with every step. If Diel was not her miracle worker anymore, then what was he? Still her beloved Uncle, emotional and ragged from the recent events, in need of his family to rebuild himself before he leaped back into the fight with his full might. It unsettled her, to think of Diel as frail on any level, but Branwen resolved to let him be for now, and to tackle this problem head-on, by herself.

Not before soup, however. Never before soup.

WITH her belly full and the reassurance that her uncle, for all his staring into the void, did have that spark of joy within him still, Branwen climbed the long and narrow stairs to Lady Brasten's office for an impromptu talk. She was the one pulling the strings, after all, not Lord Oloan, and not Diel. Branwen wanted answers to her questions, and she wanted them from the source.

Amake Brasten stood in front of her desk, holding a delicate flower made of thin, dry leather in one hand and a parchment in another. She'd invited Branwen inside yet paid no mind to her until she'd finished the missive, leaving her to wait awkwardly there. Branwen didn't mind; she never begrudged an opportunity to study another's space.

Lady Brasten's office consisted of a series of bubbles, each organized around a central piece with everything within easy reach.

The desk, for example, was accompanied by a low table with a few key tomes, extra parchment and ink bottles, and a sculpted hand Branwen had seen elsewhere in the Brasten Tower. Mage hands, as they were called, allowed their user to lift small objects in an area around them. Thus, the rest of Lady Brasten's day-to-day implements had been placed in bookshelves flanking the desk in a half circle, within the spell's reach. The tea area of their first meeting had been similar, but the circular disposition hadn't been unusual, so Branwen hadn't paid it much mind.

Now it was impossible to miss: half-circles for every station, railings along the walls to move in between, the occasional extra long chair in darker corners—other elements that had been equally present throughout the Brasten Tower. Except that here—in the room where she received friends and foes alike, all eager to judge her worth—Lady Brasten used lush rugs and verdant potted plants to divert attention from them. It was well known in Isandor that the lords and ladies of House Brasten shared an illness, but the consensus had always been that the healthy members worked for all. It hadn't taken long for Branwen to realize there wouldn't be enough 'healthy' members for such a set-up and, more importantly, that they didn't need them at all.

"I've been expecting you."

Lady Brasten's calm declaration startled Branwen out of her examination. She'd set her letter down but was still playing with the crafted flower.

"I didn't announce myself," Branwen pointed out, already on edge. She didn't like being predictable.

"Perhaps, but Oloan summarized your joint work together. He was of the opinion you'd have … discontentment to share."

Well. Predictable it was. They'd both save time, at least. Branwen crossed her arms and leaned against the wall behind her, near the entrance. "Why, yes, I do have an issue with an arrangement that sets you up to eat House Dathirii alive and reap all the profit. Good allies typically don't have everything to gain from eliminating you."

"And yet here we are," she said with a smile, "and it's true that if you look at it from a purely monetary perspective, this stinks of a trap. I am using your pre-established network and the lingering trust between House Dathirii and its many partners to access new deals that could bolster House Brasten's status by a significant amount, once transferred fully to me. So you, rightfully, question whether I can be trusted at all, and want an explanation."

"I—yeah."

This also felt like a trap closing in on her. Perhaps that was why Branwen kept the wall at her back even though Lady Brasten was peacefully twirling her artificial flower. Should that have put her at ease? Because if so, the other woman needed to stop staring, as if it wasn't Branwen's fear keeping her to the wall, but Lady Brasten's gaze pinning her there.

"There are multiple reasons. The simplest is that I am Lady Brasten, Head of my House, and my people trust me to keep us safe and afloat. As I've told Lord Arathiel … They are afraid, and they have every right to be. The material comforts offered by our wealth have allowed us to adapt this environment to our needs, instead of trying to fit a world not meant for us. If I had no guarantee this alliance would not ruin us, I would not have their support."

"I came here to ask what's our insurance, not yours."

Lady Brasten laughed—an honest, somewhat startled sound that did more for Branwen's trust than any of her previous words. For all that she hated their set-up with the trade deals, Branwen liked this woman. Conversations with her felt like long nails scraping off dead skin: they stung and left you raw, yet cleaner and more clear-headed. She wanted to believe her, so she'd walked into the office to ask her questions instead of snooping about to find proof of one plan or another. Hopefully it wasn't a mistake.

"The truth, Miss Branwen, is that we need you. What we're doing, your Uncle and I, is declaring that a House—a family's political entity—isn't tied to its home at all. It's the people that matter, and legitimacy should stay with a leader who is respected by their peers. Never forget that in this city, prestige and appearances count as much as the gold. Certainly, I can backstab Diel and amass his trade deals, but now instead of having a network of mercantile allies that trusted Diel Dathirii enough to follow him through the most terrible upheavals, I'd have, what, a handful of small-time merchants I mooched off Lord Allastam's victims. Clever, perhaps, but nowhere near as powerful."

"We're the symbol," she said. "You don't care if it's empty."

Lady Brasten grinned at her. "Exactly."

"Well, I care." Branwen pushed herself off the wall, and for the first time since entering the office, she met Lady Brasten's gaze without feeling cowed by it. Perhaps she wasn't an experienced politician like her or Diel, but she knew something wrong when she heard it. "Your empty symbol is my family. I grew up with them—fought with them, laughed with them, cried with them. Diel would fling your symbol down the shitslide in an instant if it let him save the people."

"So would I," Lady Brasten interrupted—which might have been for the better, as Branwen had no idea where she'd been going. Lady Brasten set down her flower on the desk near her, then strolled closer, her tone much softer. "I understand your care, Branwen, and I have no ill wishes for your family. This is the strategy I chose because I believe it'll benefit everyone, and because my responsibility is to mine first."

"And all I have on that is your word," she said, but there was no bitterness in it, no anger or want, not anymore. That's how faith and trust worked, and they'd decided to ally with Lady Brasten because of her perceived personal ethics and public animosity for Lord Allastam. Those things hadn't changed, even though Branwen hadn't been given a chance to witness them first-hand. She had welcomed Arathiel with open arms, however, and was risking Avenazar's fury for Varden. No amount of trade deals would safeguard her family from that. "Thank you for the explanation."

Amake Brasten dismissed her thanks with a wave. "Honesty makes a good foundation for trust, however difficult it is to prove. But you may want to get used to the uncertainty, Miss Branwen. You'll find allies in unsuspected corners if you can accept that we all have our own agenda, and sometimes it's worth the eventual risk to make them line up now."

CHAPTER TEN

Y ULTES stared at the three piles of letters on his desk, all requiring a proper response: one for inquiries he needed to bring to Hellion, usually from other noble houses, a second for missives he could deal with on his own, and a third they could afford to leave unanswered, or that were purely informative. He had been sorting through the messages all morning and already regretted not splitting the middle pile into urgent and non-urgent— he'd never expected there'd be this many! Did Jaeger's days vanish in replies to petitions made for Diel's attention? How did he find time to organize anything else? Even with the steward's help concerning the household tasks, Yultes spent most of his waking hours at this desk. Ink stained both his fingertips and the pale bangs he kept pushing away from his face, and he'd discovered new muscles along his shoulders and lower back. He wrote and wrote and wrote, and still more letters arrived for Hellion, sealed with fancy sigils identifying a noble house, or plain wax and ribbons from commoners.

By now, Yultes had seen the Allastam seal so often he almost flung everything bearing it into Hellion's pile without even peeking at the content. Only the dried flowers pressed into one parchment slowed his movement, and he belatedly realized his name, not Hellion's, had been inscribed under the seal. His heart sped and fondness brushed away his exhaustion as he broke the wax, his fingers trembling with unexpected anxiety. Yultes could easily guess at its sender, and he both longed to read Lady Mia Allastam's words and feared the recent events would have irremediably changed their relationship. As House Dathirii's main ambassador in House Allastam, he had spent more time in their Tower than in the Dathirii home, and watched Lord Allastam's children grow. Young as she still was, Mia Allastam had already gifted him with a few years of striking conversations—witty and wise and calming all at once, but never indulgent. He had missed them terribly since Hellion had taken power.

Dear Yultes,

News of your position have finally reached me, and I would love a chance to congratulate you in person, perhaps over a mid-morning tea? Enclosed are two sheets of paper on which I marked folding instructions. It is a simple craft, and together they make a potted plant. Use it as proof of invitation when you find time for a visit; my staff will recognize it.

I have missed your conversation, and look forward to it.

Lady Mia Allastam

He flicked the letter to his desk, excited to lay eyes on the accompanying paper. Ink marks and numbers served as his instructions to fold them, and Yultes set to following them with childish eagerness. He'd helped Mia Allastam with the occasional folding project while they spoke, more out of courtesy than extreme interest at first, only to discover the process relaxed him in a way not unlike gardening—and the Shepherd knew he needed the release right now. With all but his purple miseria left with Jaeger in his old quarters, the little paper plant would be a welcome addition to his desk.

He was halfway through the paper leaves when a door slammed farther down the corridor, and Hellion called his name. What serenity Yultes had achieved vanished at his friend's brusque, high-pitched tone. His meeting with Mister Beriol, the owner of a sizeable mercantile fleet who'd only recently started sailing up the Reonne, must not have ended well. Again.

Since Diel had re-emerged with House Brasten's support and publicly reaffirmed his position at the head of House Dathirii, Hellion's dinners with potential merchants had taken a turn for the worse. They were worried, they said, about signing with a House embroiled in internal turmoil. One had even gone on to conclude his deal directly with Lord Allastam after Hellion had mentioned the bigger family's backing.

Hellion's frustration had found a wide variety of expressions, and Yultes struggled to curtail him. The guards at Jaeger's door had stopped kitchen staff from bringing him food for almost two days before Yultes had learned about it and intervened, the maids who'd attempted to clean up the mess left on the wall of golden flowers had been yelled at for an hour before he'd walked in and provided enough distraction for them to slip away, and Yultes himself had been snapped at and blamed for the deals' failures repeatedly. The latter was not entirely wrong; Hellion's trade offers would be infinitely more appealing if Yultes and Garith didn't conceal as much of their available coin as possible.

Yultes' door flung open before he'd even set down his folding project, let alone stood from his chair. He dropped it, scrambling to his feet as Hellion strode in, then stopped after a single step.

"I called." The flatness of his tone perfectly conveyed his unsaid reproach. Yultes should have come running. He knew better than to delay.

"Y-Yes." His heart hammering, Yultes scooped up the pile of letters he'd meant to bring to Hellion's attention. "I have your correspondence—the significant one, at any rate."

If Hellion heard, he gave no sign of it. "When are you bringing your desk back into the audience hall? You know how I value your presence by my side, and your absence pains me when I sit in the morning."

Yultes could only offer a blank stare in response. He'd expected a number of things from Hellion—a rant regarding this most recent meeting, ridicule about the correspondence Yultes had just proffered, demands for Yultes to miraculously convince more merchants to come to them—but not complaints about the desk. Not when Hellion himself had requested its removal two days ago, berating Yultes for bothering him with the incessant scratching of his quill then arguing his presence during negotiations impeded them. Shame had burned through Yultes, but when he'd tried to apologize, Hellion had simply waved him off, saying he wanted silence not excuses.

So Yultes had had Jaeger's desk removed, even though its absence in the main office jarred him—even though his position felt almost meaningless, once physically removed from proximity with the Head of the House. There had been times, working alongside Hellion, when he'd managed to forget his torn loyalties and pretend everything was as it should rightfully be. He didn't dare admit these times were when he imagined Diel in the room with him instead of his old friend.

"Are you all right, dear friend?" Hellion asked, all solicitude. "You're paler than usual. I hope I've not foisted too many responsibilities on you. I thought you could handle this, but if not …"

He pinched his lips, and the pensive expression, combined with the hint of disappointment in his tone, sent Yultes' heart thundering. He'd wanted this position all his life, and even though his entry into it was rough, he refused to give up or lighten his load. He could do this. He was good enough for the role, he always had been, whether or not Diel acknowledged it.

"I'm fine," he said firmly.

"Then don't hide from me." Hellion gestured at the desk again before swooping in, throwing an arm around Yultes' shoulders. His cologne wrapped around them as surely as his arm. "We're a team, you and I. I knew you'd be my staunchest supporter the moment I laid eyes on you, and I understand how hard you've worked to surpass your unfortunate origins. We don't need words anymore, do we?"

Yultes could only muster a slight nod as answer. The familiarity of Hellion's proximity settled into him, a comforting weight he'd long since learned to rely on. Yultes had been angry to be summarily thrown out of the office alongside the steward's desk. He'd taken it as a disavowal of his importance. Maybe he'd read too much into it. Maybe he was letting Jaeger and Garith get into his mind. He should be more careful. After all, they still treated him with suspicion, unlike Hellion. Hellion was the one who believed in him.

"My quill's scratching won't bother you?" he asked. "I've quite a few responses to write."

Hellion squeezed his shoulder with a laugh. "Don't be absurd, Yultes. Why would you think such a thing?"

Because that's what he'd said … wasn't it? It'd only been two days. Yultes hadn't invented that conversation, he was sure of it. But before he could reply, Hellion pulled him towards the door.

"You definitely need a breather," he said. "The balcony from my quarters has a splendid view of the city, and the day is unseasonably warm. Let's enjoy it while some servants move your things."

Yultes followed with a muttered "certainly," too confused to put up much resistance. Was Hellion simply not angry with him anymore? Was that why his desk was being reinstated? Or had his friend realized Yultes' perceived insult and now sought to make amends? Perhaps he should see this as a peace offer, or perhaps

Hellion did miss his presence for its own sake. Either way, he should be happy about this. His value was being recognized.

So why did his chest tighten with worry all the way to the balcony, where a cold gust cleared both Hellion's perfume and the buzz in his mind? Why did it take a deep inhale, fingers freezing on the railing and Isandor hidden behind closed eyes, before his doubts eased away? Yultes pushed the questions aside, focusing on the prickle under his palms and the force tugging at his clothes, clinging to the illusion of being alone.

Hellion broke the latter within a minute.

"So, tell me your solution."

"What?" Yultes' eyes flew wide open. He gripped the railing tighter, taking in the sights before him—the city's pale, snow-covered bridges, the mismatched towers rising across the landscapes, the occasional flat platform creating a public park ... the beauty of his home.

"Your solution," Hellion repeated. "We're a team, yes, and you have all this free time while I deal with endless meetings and negotiations."

Free time? Yultes spent nearly every hour working, and the few minutes he'd had to himself, folding Mia Allastam's paper plant, were the only break he'd enjoyed in the past few days. Hadn't Hellion been concerned about his fatigue moments ago?

"No idea?" Hellion asked when Yultes' stunned silence stretched on. "Don't worry about it, then. We do have an expert in Diel psychology close at hand, and I had him fetched."

Despite his friend's amicable tone, Yultes understood the threat for Jaeger there. The steward would never help Hellion coerce Diel into retracting, not willingly, and even then. Neither of them had any illusion about that, though, not unless Hellion had grown foolish overnight. So why bother? Yultes tore his gaze away from the city, forcing himself to look at Hellion, to really see him—see the cruel twist in his smile, the eagerness in his forest-green eyes at the prospect of releasing his frustrations on Jaeger—and see, under it all, the unease and the fear. This was his pretend solution, but if they both knew it wouldn't work, then Hellion had nothing else to fall back on, no way to cow Diel Dathirii into disappearing from the landscape. The cold creeping into Yultes' bones had nothing to do with the howling wind.

"Forget Jaeger," he said. "Forget Diel, even. They're meaningless."

Hellion's head whipped to him, his glare so intense that Yultes almost apologized and begged forgiveness on the spot. Fear paralyzed him, and he remembered every time Hellion had shut down one of his ideas, every smooth ridicule he'd endured when arguing with him. He didn't want to lose Hellion's respect—no, no, it wasn't about respect, or shouldn't be. He didn't want to lose his trust, undeserved as it was, because they needed it. Jaeger and Garith needed it. That was the side he'd chosen, wasn't it?

"I'm serious, Hellion. You're wasting your time," he continued, and to his surprise the words flowed out, forceful and convincing. His idea was coalescing, and with it the confidence he could push it through. "They're nothing, and if we pursue this—if we put our energy into responding to Diel's claims, we're giving them more importance than they're worth. That is not where your focus should be."

"Then where?"

Hellion asked the question through gritted teeth and Yultes' heart sang. He'd baited his curiosity, implying another path to follow, another option. Hellion might hide it as best as he could, but there was something lost about him—control of the situation had slipped through his fingers, and he couldn't imagine what his next step should be. It was always easier to destroy than to rebuild, and for all his speeches about leadership, Hellion had no idea how to be constructive with his time as Head of the House. Yultes turned his back to the city and gestured at the great tree tower House Dathirii called home.

"House Dathirii is more than the handful of elves Diel relied on. Correct me if I'm wrong, but our prospective partners seem unconvinced by the solidity of our House because a single elf and his few followers declared it illegitimate, no? There are almost thirty others who bear the name, Hellion—thirty potential allies. Have you spoken with them?"

Hellion scowled at his question, and Yultes raised a hand to stall any reply, as if signalling he hadn't meant it as an attack.

"They've heard of Diel's claim by now, and they will want to see your retort. Pursue Jaeger and you give him more importance than he's worth. It's them you should be concerned with. They are House Dathirii. Not Diel and his close guards, not even you … Them." Doubts still marred Hellion's expression, and he waited for the rest with his arms crossed. Yultes let the pause lengthen, walking to his friend and placed a firm hand on his shoulder. "Every time you focus on Diel, you give weight to the past. But Hellion, you are the future of this family. Make them see that."

A spark lit in Hellion's eyes and he looked over Yultes, at the city sprawling before them, then slowly strode to the edge of the balcony and set his palms on the railing, hands spread wide and shoulders straight. Regal as the wind snatched his long golden hair, blowing it about. Spikes of victorious excitement rushed through Yultes, almost burying his guilt at so easily manipulating his friend—almost. He'd chosen what he wanted to build, and with whom, and he'd have to bear the weight of his betrayal to get it. Hellion was listening to him, daydreaming of Yultes' grand words, Jaeger and Diel all but forgotten. All he needed now was to seal the deal with concrete steps for him to occupy him.

"Call a meeting for all the Dathirii elves in the Tower. No, not a meeting … a reception. Delicious bites and a glass of exquisite wine to reassure them and prove we once more have the financial ease for such extravagance, thanks to your hard work. Then woo them with a speech. Make them see your vision, Hellion. Sweep them off their feet and they'll forget all about Diel. Who needs him when they have Lord Dathirii before them?"

Yultes gestured at him as he asked the question and was rewarded by Hellion's frank and sudden laugh. His friend repeated 'Lord Dathirii' dreamily, then closed his eyes as if listening for imagined acclaim. He looked ecstatic, almost drunk. Yultes tried to convince himself the red on his cheeks was the unrelenting winds.

"Perfect," Hellion said. "I knew I needed you for something."

Warmth spread through Yultes at his approval, warding off the biting cold and setting him more at ease than he'd been in a long time. Despite all the work he did to undermine his friend, Yultes still craved his goodwill, the gratification of that smile, and the pride it always brought. He clasped his hands behind his back, hating the confused bundle of feelings spinning inside him. Part of him yearned to truly, completely support Hellion, to organize the most splendid reunion House Dathirii had seen in years and to complement his friend's moving speech in every way possible. Hadn't he and Hellion worked for years to achieve this? But always, always Diel's voice and the hope in it haunted him.

"Focus on your speech," Yultes said. "Conquer them with your eloquence, and I'll take care of everything else."

"Thank you."

Deep sincerity coated Hellion's words, layer upon layer of meaning the other noble would never utter out loud. Thank you for your help. Thank you for the precious advice. Thank you for dragging me out of a bad mood, for opening new possibilities and preventing mistakes. Thank you for being a close ally—a trustworthy friend. And it hurt to hear it all, knowing full well all of it had been not only a diversion from Jaeger, but a trap for the future, one designed to appeal to Hellion's arrogance and ignorance.

Diel Dathirii had always grasped the vital importance of his household staff in the running of his family. Although they bore no titles, they contributed to his success just as much as every Dathirii who plied their trades, acting as ambassadors in Isandor's other families. The staff loved Diel, in no small part because Jaeger had earned their trust and loyalty over the decades, and they were invested in his prosperity because they understood Diel's vision included them. Hellion's did not and never would. Yet for a reception like what they now planned, with more than thirty Dathirii elves, beverages and food, and an impressive decor … one needed the logistical help of the staff. Without them, there was no main event.

Yultes met his Hellion's gaze, angry and amazed at himself for keeping his cool and smiling as though nothing was amiss. He had always been a good liar, and it served him better now than ever.

"The cycles turn, my friend, and I will always be there when you need me."

He walked back inside then out of the office, his mask falling as soon as he crossed the threshold and left quarters that had once belonged to Diel Dathirii and that should never have changed hands.

JAEGER couldn't tell which he hated most: the low throb of pain in his body, still present despite the passing days, or the torturous restlessness that was slowly replacing it. He spent most of his days alone in Yultes' quarters, with nothing to do with his hands but care for the greenery around him, and nothing to turn his mind to but dreams of Diel's tender smiles. It had been decades since he'd been this idle, and he couldn't even use the opportunity to relax. How utterly foreign, not to have half a dozen distinct projects to oversee along with Diel's schedule, and how awful.

By now, he'd written seven different notes for Garith, which he'd passed by hanging them off the window from a branch of one of Yultes' vine-like plants—a rare non-edible one. It was something of a crime, to have removed it from the specimen, but he had no ropes or ribbons long enough and with the soldiers at his door every hour of the day, he couldn't walk downstairs. Besides, this was precisely why Yultes had moved him into his old quarters, wasn't it? And with nothing else to do, Jaeger was more than willing to freeze his fingers while he waited for Garith to notice the unexpected green at his window—an exercise he'd gotten better at with time. It didn't matter that the notes ranged from ideas to subtly hinder Hellion's movement and life in his own home to scrappy, ill-conceived poetry and absurd humour. They distracted him from the emptiness of his days, and that was enough.

When his door burst open and an Allastam soldier came to fetch him, rough hands grabbing his arms and denying him the dignity of walking out on his own, he immediately regretted the emptiness. His wrestled his panicked heart into submission as they dragged him through the floor's corridor, then found his footing as they climbed up the stairs, yanking his arm out of the grip with a sharp "I can walk, thank you."

The beak-nosed guard responded with a bleak, compassionless glare, and clasped his elbow again. Jaeger memorized the cold blue eyes, the unhappy wrinkles at the corners of his mouth, the three crescent-shaped birthmarks along his jaw: the face of the man who was a few flights of stairs away from beating him. They both knew it, and where Jaeger's stomach clenched with dread and indignation, the Allastam man appeared taken only by professional disinterest. Perhaps it should have brought Jaeger relief that he didn't seem to relish the idea, but the result would be the same. Still, he froze fear out of his expression, his chin high as he climbed towards the office Hellion had stolen from Diel.

It had only been a matter of time, he told himself. He'd known it'd happen again, known the risk when they'd decided not to attempt an escape. Yet with every step, his mind slipped deeper in denial, leaving his body to walk as it tried to withdraw, floating behind himself with a strange disconnect, as if it'd save him the pain.

He never noticed Yultes coming down the stairs, didn't even truly understand the other elf's sharp voice as he argued with the guard, using the full height of his extra step up the stairs to glare at Jaeger's escort.

"If you don't believe me, go right ahead and ask Hellion

yourself," Yultes snapped. "You'll find him on his balcony, contemplating the aforementioned change of plans. I, however, have my own business with Jaeger."

A terrifying surge of relief welcomed him back into his body—elation at Yultes' voice that he deeply mistrusted. Decades of animosity still hovered between them, and while Yultes had helped undermine Hellion so far, Jaeger could not forgive him so easily. His excitement was manufactured, a reflection of his utter boredom and desperation, and it might well have been maliciously planned.

Yultes paused long enough for one of these haughty glares Jaeger had so often received, then gripped Jaeger's elbow right next to the guard's hand, and started turning him around. For a moment, the Allastam soldier squeezed tighter—a single, awful second during which Jaeger imagined him calling Yultes' bluff and drawing the sword at his hip—then he let go, and Jaeger spun so fast he almost tumbled down the stairs. He caught himself, and Yultes released him to instead set a firm palm against the small of his back, pushing him back towards his quarters.

The heavy stare of the guard followed them all the way to the last step, then around the corner, but while Jaeger relaxed once out of sight, he didn't dare speak. Yultes kept silent, too, his jaw tight as he hurried Jaeger along. Were they truly going back to his quarters? Wouldn't it be a matter of time before Allastam soldiers returned, sent by an even angrier Hellion? All this would have accomplished is to delay and worsen the beating. But if not his quarters … Jaeger's pulse quickened as they reached another flight of stairs, this one leading below his quarters. Could Yultes mean to try and walk him right out of the tower? It would forever blow his cover, but …

"What—"

"Garith's."

Yultes' clipped interruption served as a demand not to talk again, in addition to crushing his fledging hope. Jaeger hadn't realized how much he longed to escape until the possibility of simply being outside—of running all the way up to the Brasten Tower and into Diel's arms—had entered his mind. He fought the surge of disappointment. Something must have happened if Yultes wanted them both in the same room. That hadn't been permitted since Diel had declared Hellion an impostor.

Yultes rasped his knuckle on Garith's door, and as they waited for the coinmaster, he glanced up and down the corridor and added, "We'll have to be quick. There has been a change of plans, but there's a limit to how long I can spend with you and Garith before it becomes suspicious."

Garith's bored expression when he opened turned into a genuine grin when he spotted Jaeger. Yultes cut short any exclamation of joy with a sharp shake of his head, and the unrelenting pressure of his hand guided Jaeger inside. Only once the door clicked behind them did Yultes relax: his shoulders sagged, and he leaned against it with a bone-deep sigh. Jaeger glanced at Garith, and saw his own worry reflected in the coinmaster's face.

"Looks like I missed quite the party," Garith said. "Do I need to get the Emergency out? I stocked up."

The recent events had led Jaeger to learn more about Garith's drinking quirks than he'd ever cared for. The Emergency designated whatever strong bottle he'd pilfered from their supply and kept hidden in his quarters, and was by the far the most frequently used.

"I believe Yultes has just spared me a second beating." Jaeger trailed off, watching Yultes. He'd yet to move from the door, and if anything his breath had turned more erratic.

Garith stepped up to him, frowning, and snapped fingers in front of Yultes' eyes, startling him. It earned him a glare, but Garith laughed it off. "You didn't knock on my door to have a breakdown on the other side, I'm sure."

Yultes' eyes widened at the mention of a breakdown. For an instant Jaeger swore he saw deep fissures of fear and pain in them, and the elf's mouth twisted into a wry smile that bordered on vulnerable. Then it was gone, smoothed away under an upturned nose and a smirk.

"Of course not," Yultes replied, the crack in his voice almost imperceptible. "I've just finished a tactical meeting with Hellion, however, and steered his next move. We have to lay down the foundations of our plan to counter it, and fast, so we can work with minimal contact."

Yultes summarized the last hour for them, glossing over the details of his cozying up to Hellion, a kindness for which Jaeger would always be thankful. He did not need reminders of Yultes' shifting loyalties and of the beliefs he'd so often parroted, and might still hold close to heart. It was hard enough to trust him already, even if his glib tongue had just convinced Hellion to classify any physical harm to Jaeger as bad strategy. They had no idea how long that'd last, but they could hope it'd remain until this grand reception Yultes had dangled in front of him. Jaeger would take every extra day he could get. Even so, the more he listened to Yultes explaining how he'd persuaded Hellion, the more he worried.

"Not to be ungrateful," Garith said, his fingers playing idly with a coin, "but wasn't Hellion floundering like a beached fish until you showed him the perfect way out?"

They'd naturally moved around his quarters and assumed the positions they'd occupied while working out the misleading financial report: Jaeger by the window, Yultes pacing through the room, and Garith sitting at the desk.

"It's not perfect, but it's better than letting him directionless and eager to vent some frustration." Despite his protest, Yultes' cheeks had taken a rosy colour at the compliment to his plan. "Jaeger, do we still have those big Dathirii banners that hung in the grand reception hall and Lord Dathirii's office, when I first joined the family?"

"In storage, yes, as far as I know."

They had been woven by some of the city's finest artisan, and the House's deep green had decorated every wall of import in the tower. Jaeger doubted the decades would have been kind to them, however.

"Good. Hellion's target audience is his own generation and older Dathirii. He will paint memories of the glorious days, before Diel took the mantle of Lord Dathirii, to appeal to the family's past prestige and convince the nobles not already in his pocket he can lead them back to that wealth. So I think we want to emulate those decades, but … wrong. Let him wax poetic about better times, of that night being a taste of the future with him, and let the setting around him speak against his words in a hundred innocuous ways."

Jaeger did not need to ask how to achieve such a result. So many small elements went into building a successful soirée: food, seating, decor, entertainment, and so on. Taken in isolation, any of these could be found lacking without ruining the gathering, but if dozens of otherwise inconsequential failures added up … Planning a smooth event demanded great organizational skills and the support of a full household. Hellion relied on Yultes for both, and Yultes had come to them.

"I'm in," Garith said, "but if you're to get those ugly banners out, you'd better drop one on his head. The message doesn't have to be subtle."

That would be a sight to behold, though even Hellion would smell the sabotage then. And, if he was honest, that was his biggest qualm with this plan. "When all is said and done, and Hellion demands accountability for his awful reception, who will take the fall, Yultes? Someone will pay for this, and the more humiliating it is, the higher the price."

Yultes stopped his pacing and closed his eyes. They all knew there was only one right answer here, if he wanted Jaeger's help—only one way to prove he'd changed at all. Yet he hesitated. "If he learns I'm behind this, it would destroy my cover."

Jaeger's enthusiasm for the plan vanished. Any employee aiding Yultes would get blamed and fired for their supposed incompetence. How ironic, that Yultes had worked so hard with them to keep as many as possible on staff, only to set them up as a scapegoat for his scheme mere days later.

"Tell me, Yultes, what is the point of your cover, if you must let everything slide to maintain it? Why pretend you care for the household, if you're so eager to sacrifice them?" The question hung between them, and when Yultes' opened his mouth to protest, Jaeger cut him off again. "It's not enough to save me from a few punches. You want our help? Then you need to be their shield, too."

Yultes pressed his lips shut, and with every passing second he paled. Yet the resolve hardened in his eyes, too. It was strange, to watch him absorb the lesson, indignation sliding into panic and then into careful determination. Stranger, still, to acknowledge that Yultes Dathirii wanted to learn at all, or was so dangerously good at faking it that Jaeger couldn't help his growing trust.

"You're right," Yultes said. "I'll deal with him, and I'll take the fall if need be."

He could be lying. By all means, Jaeger should assume he was, that nothing about this Yultes was heartfelt, yet he believed every word. With a sinking feeling, he realized it would be his job to convince the rest of the staff to do so, too. They had a lot of work ahead of them to make this plan a reality.

CHAPTER ELEVEN

M Y DEAREST *nephew,*

I've had a long, beautiful life, yet of all the joyful memories I carry with me, few have filled me with such a rush as the news of your wellbeing. Forgive an old lady for worrying so; I should know that nothing is beyond you, or our youngest generation. It pleases me to learn Lady Brasten is in agreement and has welcomed our family under her roof in our time of need.

As for me, I have been with Sora Sharpe, providing soothing blends of teas and the occasional mount of cookies to better her days. She has taken great care of me, as you had requested, and I've not lacked company, for she shares her lovely space with a feline youth by the name of Kirio. He plays with just about anything that moves, including my feet, and loves to perch on high counters and shelves before he pounces. It has taught me not to tie my hair with ribbons or strings

Nevertheless, I look forward to reuniting with you. A week without a

Dathirii smile has weighed heavily on my soul. You might wonder why send a letter, then, when I could simply climb a few staircases and come in person? But I am loath to abandon Kirio alone, and another worry has slipped into my heart. You see, since Allastam soldiers have taken our home, Miss Sharpe has been relentlessly searching for those of ours who had gone missing—you, Diel, but Kellian, Branwen, and Vellien as well. She left yesterday morning and has not returned.

Sora is a bright young woman, quick of wits and sword, and that should suffice to reassure me. I'm afraid it does not. Again, forgive an old lady for worrying so, and for the request that will follow. I know you have much on your mind, Jaeger first and foremost, but I cannot help think that we are responsible for whatever befell Sora, and that we should seek to lend what aid we can. As I am caring for the excited ball of fur she adores, I had hoped you could direct some energy towards locating her, whether your own or that of Lady Brasten. Regardless, you will understand, I'm sure, that I intend to remain stationary until my fears are put to rest.

Write back—or visit, even, if you find the time! It always warms my heart to hear of you.

With all my love,
Camilla Dathirii

Diel finished his recitation to Branwen and Vellien, who had both rushed to his quarters at a mere mention of news from their aunt. They must have felt her absence as he did, a quiet hole where reassuring words and warm tea should be. Reading Camilla's flowing handwriting had been like plunging into the Reonne's affluents on a hot summer day, or finding Jaeger's arms after a frustrating meeting with other nobles. It loosened the painful knots of tension along his shoulders, filled his lungs with fresh air, and cleared his mind from the dark clouds that had hung in it. Strange, how she had that effect even when she offered no advice—even when, in fact, she brought news of more trouble. Diel wished she would return to them. He craved her presence more than he cared to admit.

"It'd seem a cat has your aunt trapped," he said, "and she needs Inspector Sora Sharpe to free herself from its clutches."

Branwen flopped back in her seat, her arms thrown wide. "Why doesn't she just bring it along? Steal the cat until we find Sora and everyone's happy! I want her here, with us."

They all did—her, and Jaeger, and Garith and Kellian too. Diel had relied on the rest of his family all his life, and being cut off from them had wreaked havoc on his ability to function. Ironic, when he desperately needed to stay sharp and active if he stood a chance at reuniting with them.

"Uncle, you should write her back immediately." Vellien's calm, factual tone didn't prepare Diel for what came next. "Inform her Miss Sharpe is safe and recovering from an injury I treated, and that she's resting by my orders."

Branwen sprang right back up, staring at her younger cousin. "She is?"

"I—yes." Vellien's confidence cracked, and they clasped their hands together, eyes cast on them. "I'm sorry, I should've let you know faster, but I've been with Varden a lot and sleeping the remainder of the time, and—"

"It's all right, Vellien," Diel cut them off, firm but calm. "You're here now, so share your information with us."

Diel hadn't expected their shy healer to be the one with knowledge of Sora's whereabouts, let alone to bring the good news that she was not, in fact, in any danger. So when Vellien told the story in full and added tidings of the first Myrian actions since the temple of Keroth had been destroyed, he stared at the young Dathirii with open surprise. Vellien must have noticed, as they started stuttering more and more, their cheeks flushing a deep red, until they trailed off. Branwen jumped in with the most obvious question.

"Why would the Myrians attack Drake? Is this a feint?"

"It seems unlike both of them," Diel agreed.

Lord Allastam spoiled his son like no one else and wouldn't risk this sort of feint. A slippery patch of snow or stray blade could transform a choreographed display of aggression into an actual disaster in the blink of an eye. Besides, Lord Allastam had never pretended to care about the Myrians, so why even do this? No, something else was up.

"Branwen, how would you like to speak with Miss Sharpe and your aunt?" He hadn't truly needed to ask: Branwen turned to him with open eagerness. "I'll write to Camilla with the information we have on hand. Vellien, when you next visit Miss Sharpe, please let her know we'd be grateful for an opportunity to … share breakfast, let's say, and collaborate further. I want us to learn all we can about this Myrian attack and anything she's found during her search for us." He frowned, then added, "I'm sure Hasryan had the good sense to hide, but if either of you can gauge how much of our involvement with him she's surmised, that might help avoid a bad surprise."

They nodded in unison, and a quiet warmth filled Diel. They still listened to him, even though he'd spent days tracing mental circles, paralyzed by his fears for Jaeger. He'd let them down recently, but Camilla's casual confidence in him pushed at the frazzled inertia of his mind. He needed to kindle back his will to fight, and fast.

SORA'S memory contained one large hole between the moment she hit a bridge at full speed, shoved off from another by an unknown force, and the moment Hasryan's voice startled her awake.

"Relax," he was saying, "I've handled Sora before."

Her heart clenched in a painful jolt and she sat up, one hand reaching for the sword at her hip. Instead of a hilt, her fingers found a soft object. She stared at the bright yellow pillow for one intensely confused second, then her vision blurred and nausea rushed up her throat. Flinging the pillow away, Sora bent to the side and threw up.

"Shit, Sora!"

Hasryan's voice sounded miles away, but he crouched at her periphery, and the hand on her shoulder was as solid as the floor under her. "Settle down. You can't get up so fast."

Sora groaned and stared at her splashed fingers, waiting for the tiles underneath to stop shifting and for the throbbing in her head to subside. She'd been lying down on a spread of cushions in a wide array of stunning colours—stunning in the sense they hurt her eyes, not that they were beautiful. Shelves lined the walls, covered with statuettes of deities and demigods. Some were in wood, others in glass and ivory; many had been painted in full or in part. A thick fishing net hung from the ceiling, but only a weird-shaped pillow remained in it. The numerous ones scattered across the floor left little doubts about where the rest had been emptied.

Hasryan offered a handkerchief so she could wipe her mouth and hands. She snatched it up, cleaning herself as best as she could, while her gaze latched onto Larryn. Blood covered his forearm and had clotted in his hair, and he seemed exhausted. He leaned against a doorway, arms crossed in an attempt to appear steadier than his paleness indicated. Her eyes moved between him and Hasryan. *Of course* Larryn had known where to find him. Why, however, was *she* allowed to see him?

"What …" The rest of her sentence caught in her dry throat. "Water."

Larryn slunk away with a nod, while Hasryan offered a mischievous grin.

"We kidnapped you!" he exclaimed.

Sora's stomach dropped so fast she thought she'd be sick again. Before her body could react to the sudden spike of stress, Larryn yelled from the other room.

"Hasryan! I told you not to say that!" He rushed back in, spilling half his mug of water. "Don't listen to him. He's being an ass."

"A funny one," Hasryan countered.

"In what world?"

Larryn placed one hand against Hasryan's temple and gave his head a playful shove before offering Sora her cup of water. She downed it without a word, struggling to get her bearings—physical and mental both. The unusual, easy back-and-forth between Hasryan and Larryn set her on edge, as it provided nothing familiar to latch onto. Her back ached, a dull and constant reminder of her fall, but with the initial garbled awakening passed, she realized it should have been worse. Larryn had briefly left them again, returning with old rags to clean up her mess. Embarrassed, she stared at Hasryan—and noticed how he kept running a hand through his hair. She remembered that nervous habit.

"Explain yourselves, maybe?" Her voice remained an uncertain croak. She cleared it. "Where am I?"

"Cal's home," Larryn said. "It's where we'd been heading, and the closest place I knew to where you fell."

"It wasn't." Sora's brain might be jumbled, but she hadn't lost track of all spatial awareness. "The guards' headquarters were almost right next to us."

Larryn snorted. "If you believe I'd have been safe carrying your unconscious body into the Sapphire Guards' Headquarters while covered in blood, you hit your head harder than I thought."

Fair. She forced herself to take a deep breath and put her thoughts in order. She'd reacted like she'd awoken among enemies, but if Hasryan or Larryn had wanted her dead, she'd never have opened her eyes. Hard to reconcile 'mortal enemies' with the blood-soaked man cleaning her vomit, or with Hasryan's concerned crowding.

Sora brushed away the black strands falling over her hair, trying to piece back the events leading to this. She'd parried Drake's strike before he could hurt Larryn, then something had moved at the edge of her vision. Larryn had screamed. It had slammed into her, sending her flying. He'd still been up there, however, with Drake. With a frown, she turned to him.

"What pushed me? Did you fight Drake?"

"I saved him, if you'll believe that." Larryn reached for his neck, where finger-shaped bruises inferred a specific tale. He'd paled again and sat on the ground, next to her, the stinky rag in his other hand. Perhaps he didn't trust his legs to hold him. "A pair of Myrians attacked. They were after our snotty Allastam friend. I guess you and I were in the way. Now they're …"

"Dead," Hasryan finished. "Larryn defended himself."

Heavy silence followed. Larryn hunched his shoulders and brought his knees closer, staring at a random spot on the floor. Hasryan glared at her, as if daring Sora to utter a single word about murder. She had no desire to. "I'm sorry, Larryn. You shouldn't have had to do that."

A brief smile passed over Larryn's lips, the only acknowledgment she received. Sora granted him the space he needed, instead reviewing what she had learned. Why would the Myrians attack House Allastam? House Dathirii's fall had made it clear any alliance remaining between the two houses was long dead, and the enclave gained nothing from making new enemies for itself. Only one person would benefit from this.

"Is this what Diel and Branwen Dathirii have been up to the last week?"

She hadn't meant to speak the words aloud—neither Hasryan nor Larryn had any reason to know about this. To her surprise, Hasryan shook his head with a chuckle.

"Nah, none of that, but I bet they won't cry over it."

He'd refuted her hypothesis with a certainty he shouldn't have, and Sora stared at him. Slowly, her tired mind put puzzle pieces it'd long held together. According to Camilla, Hasryan had been hiding in her very quarters when Kellian had arrested her. She'd been worried he'd stay still and wind up caught in the Allastam takeover, but he must have moved out and spoken with Lord Dathirii. *That* was why Diel knew Camilla had awaited Sora in the headquarters when he'd met her and Arathiel in his entrance hall. Which meant … Sora's jaw dropped, and a dozen different curses crossed her mind before she could formulate her conclusion.

"Did Diel Dathirii have the nerve to ask me to protect his aunt, promising to collaborate in any investigation of her role in hiding *you*, pretending to know nothing about it, while you sat in his quarters? Did he—" She stopped at Hasryan's widening grin—all the confirmation she needed. The gall of this elf! "How many Dathirii have contributed to your continuous escape from the law, exactly?"

Hasryan spread his arms with a laugh. "An assassin never reveals his secret."

She huffed, and at the sound, his smirk returned—the mix of mockery and arrogance she had so often encountered during interrogations. Except now genuine mirth underlay it, and

Hasryan's eyes shone from contagious amusement. Sora found herself half-laughing, her head light, and the sudden rush made the world spin. She rubbed her eyes and set a hand down, trying to steady herself again.

"I will assume that means all of them except Kellian from now on."

"Make sure you include Vellien," Larryn said. "They sneaked out of the Shelter with Hasryan, but I wasn't about to tell you that."

"So they're safe."

"They healed you." Larryn jerked a thumb towards another door. "Still sleeping it off in there."

"Once rooms are ready in House Brasten, they'll leave for it too," Hasryan added.

Sora let her head rest on her folded knees, allowing a few knots of stress unwound in her stomach. Camilla would welcome the news, and perhaps she, too, could soon join her family. Inaction hadn't sat well with the old lady, and she'd taken to baking one batch of cookies after another, stopping only for tea and silent fretting. And now Sora could not only reassure her about Vellien, but about Hasryan too—which, truly, was a nonsensical turn of events. Part of her wanted to let it be, to simply rest without questioning the assassin's presence and kindness, but that had never been in her nature.

"So what's the deal here?" she asked. "I'm supposed to arrest you. Why am I allowed to see you at all?"

Hasryan tensed, and for a moment Sora thought he would bolt, as if he'd just realized the risks involved for him. Larryn glared at her. "It means we both trust you not to blow Hasryan's cover in the name of unidirectional, tampered justice. You stood up to Drake for me—why can't you see this is the same?"

Because it wasn't. Several of Hasryan's assassinated victims had nothing to do with nobility. Larryn was a small-time thief who spent his energy and money in providing for others around him. When it came to the delicate balance of ethics and law, they weren't the same at all.

"Don't get ahead of yourself. Drake's petty harassment can't compare to the lives cut short or broken by your friend. It's not just Lady Allastam—I found at least six families without titles, and they deserve justice, too."

"Damn it, Sora!" Hasryan sprang to his feet, and the intense hurt in his voice caught her off guard. What had he expected? "I can't give them justice. Not short of dangling myself off a noose, and I won't—I refuse. You know that's the wrong answer. You told me … you said you'd never wanted to hang someone less than you did me."

"I—The right answer is not up for me to decide." That's why they had laws. People had spent considerable energy thinking about morality, ethics, and justice before writing them. Her job was to see them applied properly.

"It is today." Hasryan crossed his arms. "I don't have anywhere else to hide."

It should have been a hard choice. Sora had dedicated her life to upholding Isandor's laws, and the last month to Hasryan's crimes. Through it, her reputation for efficiency and thoroughness had reached new, notable figures. If she arrested Hasryan now, she'd solidify her position and bring a measure of peace to his victims.

Would an execution truly help the latter, however, when those who'd contracted an assassin remained free? Beyond that, the very idea of selling him out to Lord Allastam repulsed her. He'd given the case such a high profile, demanding swift and public retribution—a demonstration of his importance and power more than any semblance of justice. She'd understood that when she'd told Hasryan she didn't want to hang him, and her guts rebelled against it once more. Only this time, she knew to trust her internal compass over the laws of Isandor.

It would have been a hard choice, if she hadn't freed herself of her illusions.

When she met Hasryan's gaze and smiled, when the words "Your assassin secrets are safe with me" passed her lips, it filled her with a sense of rightness. Then a grin bloomed across Hasryan's face, sending her heart spinning and leaving her light-headed, galvanized at bringing such a genuine show of joy from him, entirely different from his confident smirk. His hands flitted in the air for a moment, as if he didn't know what to do with the excitement, so he shoved them in his pockets.

"I'm so glad I can trust you," he declared, as if trust was the most precious thing in the world, as if he'd wanted this badly. Was she having concussion-induced hallucinations? He should hate her—without her hard work he'd never have even reached the noose. "Will you tell Camilla I'm safe? She's with you, isn't she? Diel said you'd promised not to accuse her of anything before he spoke with her, and he never had the chance, so I thought—"

"She is," Sora confirmed, interrupting his excited string of words. Camilla would be delighted to learn about this conversation.

"Wonderful." Hasryan grabbed a handful of pillows, building himself a comfortable seat nearby with almost childish enthusiasm. "Vellien warned us you'd need rest. Lots of it. I'm also stuck here for the foreseeable future, so if you want, I can catch you up to our mysterious week of adventures. I've been helping House Dathirii!"

At that, Larryn groaned and stretched. "You two enjoy your storytelling hours. I gotta clean myself, and the Shelter's not gonna feed itself." He tugged on his bloodied sleeve as he spoke, tension underlying his otherwise light tone. "And, Sharpe? Thanks for that parry against Drake. Don't think I could've dodged in time."

Sora replied first with a dismissive wave. Even though instincts had driven her parry, she was glad for it. Drake had been ready to impale Larryn, as if he had every right to his life, and it still made her blood boil.

"He's lucky those Myrians shoved me off a bridge," she grumbled. "Look, Larryn … I know I haven't been an ally, but I won't forget what I saw—what he tried, right in front of me. This won't be the last time he curses my name."

"Yeah, sure." Her support did not bring Larryn a fraction of the joy it had Hasryan. He grabbed the bloodied, threadbare cloak from the hanger by the exit. "Take care."

Larryn slipped out without another word, leaving Sora to stare at the door as it closed behind him, disturbed. If she never saw Larryn this subdued again, her life would be better for it. When she turned a questioning look to Hasryan, he only shrugged.

"Rough day," he said, and she'd interrogated him often enough to recognize the purposeful evasiveness. Sora let it go.

"It's not how I imagined mine would unravel, certainly. Pain excepted, I'd call it a nice surprise, though."

Hasryan's bright smile returned even as he ran a nervous hand through his hair again. "Been there. I once started a day debating cookie recipes with Camilla, hiding in a hostile city who wanted me dead, and ended it here, surrounded by friends and allies. Sometimes ya gotta learn to roll with the scary turnabouts to get to the best parts of your life."

"Why don't you tell me more about that," Sora said, and Hasryan laughed.

"I bet you never expected me to comply with *that*."

No, she hadn't, and the thought he'd willingly do it left her downright giddy. She must have hit her head hard, back there, to be so taken in by his undiluted excitement.

Once he'd settled into his nest of pillows, he started the long tale of his last day in Camilla's quarters and how he had wound up under Lord Dathirii's protection. She sat and listened, painfully aware of how open and talkative he was now. This was the Hasryan she'd glimpsed at times, in prison: the one whose voice caught as he spoke of Camilla's loyalty, or of Cal wrapping him into a hug. The one who valued his newfound team and allies, who weaved a great tale of infiltration and ratcheted her tension, building his story as he would a scary legend by a campfire, enjoying every reaction he drew out of her.

Sora couldn't remember when someone had captivated her this way. Hasryan had always held himself tight when with her, controlling smirks and body language alike, hiding behind walls. He was letting her in, now, revealing an entirely beautiful person and leaving her breathless with the charm of it.

Chapter Twelve

HE days without Vellien proved harder than Nevian had expected.

He lay in his bed, staring at the ceiling, uninterested in the book open on his desk. Since Larryn's attempted kidnapping had stripped him of his young healer, Nevian had struggled to focus on his study of protection spells. Too many questions bumped against each other in his mind, obscuring his efforts to unravel runes and words of power. Where was Vellien now? Had they found a safe home to stay in? Why hadn't they sent a message? Maybe now that they weren't around Nevian all the time, they remembered how agreeable good company was and had forgotten about him. But no, no. That was unlike them. They had promised Nevian would always be enough, and they had meant it. He had to believe that they had a lot on their hands and no simple means to communicate. It was fine. It hadn't even been that long.

Nevian pinched the bridge of his nose, annoyed at himself. Logic dictated that he put this matter aside until the letter arrived, so why was he wasting time in bed? Why couldn't he get his mind to ignore the worries gnawing at it as easily as he had under Avenazar's duress? This was new, and he didn't like it. Perhaps he'd manage his distress better if he had news, but that required leaving his room. Nevian turned his head to stare at the door. Outside lay the common room, where the Shelter's patrons were no doubt exchanging the day's rumours. A crowd of strangers, none of whom he'd ever talked with before. He swallowed hard and immediately discarded the idea. He wasn't that desperate, not yet. Larryn or Efua would come around first, and he could ask them. In the meantime, however, he really ought to work.

Nevian spared one last thought for the freckled, smiling face that was missing in his life, preparing to roll out of bed and return to more serious occupations. Knocks at the door froze him into place, and for a brief instant he believed Keroth or some benevolent deity had been listening in. Then he realized these weren't Vellien's knocks—he'd recognize the shy sequence anytime. Still a familiar sound, though.

"Enter?"

He turned his head to stare at the newcomer—maybe Vellien was with whoever had knocked—and tried not to let his disappointment show when Cal slipped into his room. Cal had been at the enclave. He would know what was happening out there. The halfling stopped after a few steps in, frowning. His gaze went from Nevian to the empty desk, then back at Nevian.

"Is everything all right?"

"I'm … No." He should have lied. Nevian had always been awful at lying. "I'm confused."

He returned to staring at the ceiling. Soon enough, the bed shifted under Cal's weight as he climbed next to Nevian, putting his head within his field of vision. "Do you want to talk about it?"

Did he? Nevian frowned and pondered his options. He'd never had anyone he'd consider talking about these things before—not that it'd actually happened to him. Most people refused to stop touching him, and that told him to stay away and focus on his studies. Cal hovered nearby expectantly, and Nevian had the distinct impression he was hoping for a positive answer.

With a sigh, he admitted, "I miss Vellien. I think. I can't stop thinking about them?" Was that a repressed squeal from Cal? Nevian pushed himself into a sitting position to glare at him. "Don't laugh!"

"I'm sorry, it was just too adorable!"

No it wasn't! It was frustrating, and wrong, and confusing, and Nevian wanted it gone—or, well, no, maybe not? He didn't know!

"I don't understand it. Is that—is that what it's supposed to be like? To fall in love? It's so absurd."

"I have no idea, actually. I've never been there. That's what people say, though. Slight obsession, flutters in the stomach, hyper self-consciousness, and feeling like you're floating in clouds of wonderful bliss."

"The only clouds are in my mind, and they prevent me from studying. Can't they wait for Vellien to be here, at least? We're not even … This is ridiculous."

He huffed, and this time there was no stopping Cal's laughter. "*Adorable*, I tell you! Both of you, in fact. Vellien wanted you to know that they miss you, too, and that it was important for you to continue to take breaks from your work. It seems *that* wasn't an issue after all."

Relief coursed through Nevian—Vellien missed him, too!—and he grinned, light-headed, only to realize this was exactly what Cal must have meant by 'floating in clouds of wonderful bliss'. Vellien's reciprocation felt like a victory, as satisfying as scribing a functioning spell or deciphering what made two runes work together while others failed to synergize. Nevian slapped his hands over his face and flopped back down onto the bed with a sigh.

"I-I don't like this!"

Love, it seemed, meant losing control of himself, his discipline crumbling away for a pretty smile. Which was unfair to Vellien. Nevian didn't care about their smile, or even any other parts of their appearance. They liked Vellien because they could trust them with the deepest layers of his mind, because Vellien had proved over and over that they would respect his boundaries and love him for who he was, not who they wanted Nevian to be. Why would any of that make his chest hurt and his head float?

Cal crawled closer to him, and his smile had vanished, replaced by a much more serious expression. "You sound like this is your first time. Haven't you ever … craved to know someone? Obsess over whether they would notice you, or like you, or if you'll get a chance to talk to them? Wondered what you'd be like together, an unbreakable pair?"

"Why would I? That sounds like absolutely irrational behaviour."

Cal pressed his lips together. Was he withholding a laugh again? "It's just how people describe early love all the time. Even the one that leads nowhere. I kinda get it, too, for friends."

If he hadn't spent the last days unable to concentrate on his studies, Nevian would have thought Cal was trying to string him along. Perhaps he hadn't talked enough to other teens in Myria. He recalled overhearing similar things, but they'd always felt like an exaggeration. He'd been too busy striving to soak knowledge to investigate any further.

"So what are you saying?"

"I'm saying … aromanticism isn't black and white. I don't experience romantic attraction at all, but it's not the same for everyone. There's an elf—Elloren—who even studied those variations, and gave them names, definitions, and descriptions. I bet ol was like you and enjoyed well-defined things!" He mimicked a box with his hands and smiled at Nevian. "I scoured bookshops and bazaars looking for ols work when I was younger and trying to figure myself out. Eventually found the one I needed, of course. Ren wouldn't leave me stranded!"

"You have a book on this." Waves of excitement rose within Nevian, and he stared at Cal in wonder. "There's a book with words to explain this—to explain me. Words and definitions and concepts."

"And examples and essays, too!" Cal grinned at him. "It's *amazing*, Nevian. I'll bring it around for you next time, and you can see if you think anything in there fits you. On one condition: you make sure to look at demiromanticism in it. Call it my best guest for what you're going through."

Nevian pushed himself up into a sitting position once more and crossed his legs, taking as solemn a pose as he could. He meant to place a hand over his heart, but buried it under the blankets when he saw its shaking. He hoped Cal hadn't noticed. What if he thought Nevian was overreacting and silly? But they were discussing books—and one containing obscure knowledge he'd only ever caught in hushed whispers, back home. Myria's libraries proudly displayed tomes on the intricacies of necromancy or mind control, but Nevian couldn't remember resources on sexuality. Master Sauria had given him the word for asexuality in a late-night conversation and promptly advised him to avoid using it too loudly. In Myria, you learned to fit in or you were set aside. He'd never been talented at fitting in.

"I promise I will," he said, "and that no harm will come to your book."

Cal laughed again, and Nevian had forgotten how fond he'd grown of that sound, too. Cal's bouncy chuckles never felt like a mockery of him.

"I never doubted it would stay safe with you."

Nevian wished he held this book already, that he could sit down and read right away. When Sauria had spoken about asexuality, it had been naming an experience he understood in detail. Cal was offering something completely different: words to explore one that confused him, knowledge to battle uncertainty. Nevian could be patient, however. He had learned to bide his time long ago.

"I had other messages for you," Cal said, "from Varden, who's recovering. We told him that you're alive."

Nevian froze, fear jolting through him. Avenazar would be coming for Varden, and he could learn of Nevian's survival in the priest's mind now. His throat tightened with his rising panic, and he forced himself to think it through. Everyone who'd gone in the enclave was a target, and they all knew about him. Varden just made one more door, but his secret was already out there, within easy reach. He made his jaw to work despite the cold dread seeping into him.

"What … what did he say?"

Nevian had let Varden down, returning his rekhemal back without warning him about this false accusation of treachery. He could have given the kind priest a chance to defend himself, but he'd been convinced it'd have allowed Avenazar to learn Nevian was the one sneaking out. Guilt had dogged him ever since.

"First, that he'd enjoy the opportunity to speak with you in person, but that you should stay wherever you feel safe." Cal raised a finger and bit his lip, trying to remember what else. "He said he didn't blame you for what had happened during the Long Night's Watch, and that you should continue protecting yourself from Avenazar." A second finger went up, then he smiled and added. "Then he said he was glad you had support and friends around you to help! You were right when you told me he was really nice. He's so calm and warm."

Cal discussed his first impressions in detail, but Nevian only half-listened. These messages … How had Varden known? He'd taken Nevian's guilt and doubts and turned them into ashes, blessing him with unexpected peace of mind. He wished leaving the Shelter was easier, that he'd dare go to Cal's place and speak with Varden. He resolved to write instead. Efua would know where to find him, and this way he didn't have to risk the outside again. Nevian waited for Cal to finish his little story about Varden helping Branwen cheat at one of their card games before chipping in.

"It sounds like he has friends to support him, too." None of them were him, but that was his fault. He'd always pushed him away, certain Avenazar would have punished them for any proximity. "Will you tell me what happened at the enclave? How you found him and saved him? I'm sorry I didn't come, but I …"

Cal started reaching out when Nevian's voice trailed off, but stopped just short of touching him, withdrawing his hand. "It was a good decision. We ran directly into Avenazar, and if you'd been there, he'd have learned to look for you. Settle in, though. It's a long story!"

Nevian shifted to set his back against the wall, eager to hear it yet fearful of its content. It horrified him that they'd met Avenazar face to face, but they'd survived, hadn't they? And despite the terror coiling in his stomach, he needed to hear that, needed to know it was possible. Perhaps then he could believe they'd do it again, when the time came.

Chapter Thirteen

HE whip-sharp crack of Lady Viranya Dathirii's voice bouncing through the corridors set Yultes' stomach to churning. She had the unique talent of sliding her words from warm honey to deadly shards on a whim, most often after a poor interlocutor had triggered her displeasure. He'd witnessed it wielded against servants, and she'd always made it clear to Yultes his acceptance within the small circle of Dathirii she shared with Hellion was conditional on his proper noble behaviour. Hellion's friendship had been a shield the first years of his arrival in the family, but he'd done all he could to prove himself, and over the course of decades, it'd felt like they'd not only tolerated his presence, but grown to enjoy it.

Still, he'd avoided Viranya and the others as best as he could since acceding to his role as Hellion's steward. The loss of their titles would turn their mood foul, and he didn't want that harshness directed at him. Truly, he did not envy the poor soul who'd triggered it now, regardless of the reason. Yultes inhaled deeply, calming the nervous fear coursing through him, and continued up towards the next staircase, intent on walking right past this level without even glancing towards the fight.

"—will have you on the streets, your name so sullied no house of respect will dare to hire you."

Yultes' step faltered as he reached the landing. Viranya must be threatening a servant—threatening them with a fate only he, as steward, could carry through. He could ignore this now, but it'd wind up on his desk sooner or later. The staff was his responsibility. His duty, a voice added—one that sounded suspiciously like Jaeger. Besides, he needed the household to help him hinder Hellion's rallying speech, and what little goodwill he'd earned would dwindle if he let this happen.

Or so he told himself, at least, as he turned towards the fight and set his gaze on the pair. Viranya Dathirii towered over Sallin, one of their maids, her broad shoulders amplified by a wide, multilayered dark green skirt. Her very presence dominated the corridor, and although the servant must easily be almost six feet herself, she seemed small and insignificant in comparison. Yultes' heart thundered and his voice twisted on itself as he called out, producing a squeak that hadn't wanted out at all.

"Lady Viranya!"

She turned her glare to him, and he wished he could melt into the floor. But it was too late now, and her hostility morphed into a cold smile he'd often seen over the decades. The familiarity eased his fear.

"Yultes, just the person I wanted to see." Without ever breaking eye contact with him, she grabbed Sallin's wrists and pulled her forward. "Why is this clumsy fool in our employ? She just spilled soapy water all over me!"

Yultes allowed his eyebrows to lift. He could trace the darker shapes along the skirts' pattern now, along with the puddle a few feet behind. "How unfortunate."

"Unfortunate?" she repeated, obviously scandalized by his own lack of indignation. "This is—"

"A grievous slight, yes," he cut off, "and she shall be reprimanded accordingly. I, however, have need of her immediately."

"Of her, specifically?" Her scepticism sizzled through every word, and the corridor walls seemed to close in on Yultes. "Not anyone else in our still sizeable household."

"Yes, her." He placated her hostility with the humblest smile he could muster and forced himself to walk closer, each step smooth and calm. "You see, Viranya, one of my duties as Lord Hellion's right hand has been to take over the steward's responsibility, and thus to learn about our staff. Miss Sallin here has been employed, among other things, for her expertise in woodwork, and it so happens that the new lectern we've commissioned is being delivered in the coming fifteen minutes. I'd like an apt eye to go over it, to ensure the final product is satisfying."

"And you're gonna trust her judgment? This girl who can't even keep her hands steady enough to hold a bucket?"

"I must." He allowed a hint of distaste into his voice and pinched his lips, as if the very thought of it was unpleasant. "Woodwork is a commoner's craft, and as such none of us have more than very basic understanding of it. We pay her for her expertise; I'll rely on it."

She could not argue against that, and from the disgusted twist of her mouth, she knew it as well as he did. Sallin had kept her gaze on the floor, but she threw him a confused glance.

"Very well. But I want her punished for this." Viranya gestured at her skirts with a wide, dramatic movement. "And send someone else to help me change."

"Of course, milady."

Yultes set a firm hand on Sallin's shoulder and pulled until she snapped out of her daze and hurried along. Lady Viranya's disgusted scoff followed them as they reached the stairs, and as soon as they were out of sight, the maid started.

"I-I didn't—I was holding it very tight, sir, and something—"

"I don't need your excuses."

The shortness of his voice strangled the rest of her protest. Yultes gritted his teeth, knowing she was stewing in her fear, that every second of glacial silence was a small torture, but he did not want to risk someone overhearing them. He led her down two separate flights of stairs, until they'd left the upper tower floors where most nobles lived and reached an area of parlours and quiet libraries. It wasn't entirely safe yet, but House Dathirii did not receive nearly as many guests now.

"I don't need your excuses," he started again, much more softly, "because I already know what happened. Lady Viranya has dabbled in magic and, most notably, mastered limited telekinetic skills to impress others. She's trying to get you fired, so she provoked an incident. It's a game they play."

He understood the game because he'd played it once, too, alongside Hellion's friends. Sometimes it was overt and egregious: they would sit together and laugh at the mistakes they'd pushed staff into, discussing how they could use them to get a maid thrown out or a cook demoted. Most often, though, nobles took a dislike to any of the staff and whispered to each other about their failings, as if to confirm they weren't the only one dissatisfied. Not in aggressive conversations, but always within earshot of other Dathirii elves, seeding doubts in more benevolent members of the family who would inevitably become more inclined to notice the servant's mistakes. It built over time, an insidious and unshakeable reputation that usually led to a resignation or a dismissal.

But these tactics had stopped almost completely some twelve years ago, shortly after Nicole had been named as the head of the kitchen staff. She'd dogged Jaeger for months until he convinced Diel to institute a new House rule and forced every firing to go through the steward. Many had been outraged to no longer have control over who served them food or cleaned their quarters, and for a while they'd grown more aggressive, but it'd calmed with time.

Now that he had the final say, other nobles must have concluded they could start this cycle again. Sallin too, from the wary tension in her steps.

"Are your lies part of the game?" she asked. "I haven't worked with wood once in my life."

"I beg to differ. You sweep our cabinets and desks every day, making each of them clean of any dust or stain. I cannot think of a more practised eye to comb for scratches and imperfections."

A hint of pride squared her shoulders, but she still narrowed her eyes at him. "That wasn't the question, sir."

"I have no intention of firing you," he said, "and while we're indeed heading towards the lectern, it so happens that our coinmaster will also be there. It should make it easier to devise a monetary punishment that'll show on paper but not in your pockets."

"Wh-what do you mean?"

Yultes stopped, glanced around to make sure the corridor was clear, and turned to Sallin, trying to gauge what he could say. Servants were terrible gossips, weren't they? Not to be trusted with secrets of any sorts, or so he'd always believed. But that had been a fact repeated by Hellion and his friends—the same who set up these folks in order to fire them. Jaeger instead loved his people deeply, and Yultes had no doubt he'd trust them over most of the Dathirii nobles.

"Viranya is not one to forget you simply because you're out of sight. She'll want proof you've been reprimanded, and I cannot have her tell Hellion I am taking the household's side over hers."

"You're not, if you dock my pay."

"Precisely. So it must look as if I did in our accounts, and I'll need you to lie where any noble can overhear." Hopefully, she'd opt not to speak of it at all while in the Dathirii tower's walls. "Let your colleagues know they can petition for similar arrangements if these incidents happen."

Yultes had no idea how long they could play this game. They'd stretched the limits of their lies while responding to Hellion's first request to trim the household to its bare bones, and he wouldn't put it past some of the nobles to get whatever punishment they could, even if Yultes opposed firing the staff. Perhaps they could squirrel some of the fake expenses into the budget for this feast, however.

"I … I can do that, sir." Her voice held more suspicion than gratitude. "Might even make a few believe those pretty words you had Jaeger write for you, if you follow through with it."

Jaeger had penned a few messages to key staff members, assuring them his demands for less-than-stellar work about some aspects of Hellion's great reception were in good faith, and that they wouldn't be blamed for deficiencies or misfortunes over the course of the evening. It was a lot of trust to ask of them, and without their old steward's reassurances, Yultes doubted they'd have accepted. Even now, many had protested and questioned him at length, but they'd eventually relented—all but the kitchens.

Nicole had grabbed his wrist when he'd offered the letter, almost crushing the bones beneath with the force of her grip, and dragged him past the stoves and into the pantry. Everyone had hurried out as soon as they caught sight of them together, the last person closing the door behind Yultes, trapping him inside.

He'd swallowed hard, reminding himself Nicole had every right to be outraged and that he needed her help. Yultes had stood still, holding tight to Jaeger's message while she'd glowered at him. Then she'd slapped a wooden spoon over his knuckles, as if he was a child trying to dip his fingers into her soup, and he'd brought up his hand with a yelp.

"What was that for?"

"Fun. Don't act like you don't deserve worse." She'd extended an open palm and he'd obediently dropped the letter into it. Nicole had scanned it, her frown deepening with every word. Yultes knew the gist of its message, but Jaeger might have written more in it, however. He'd insisted on giving Nicole a personalized one. She'd evidently disagreed with the content and scoffed as she rolled it back up. "He's deluding himself. I love that boy, but Lord Dathirii's absence has clearly altered his judgment if he thinks you will shield any of us from harm."

"Nicole—"

"No. I'm not risking any of my staff to your little political games. We'll do our job and we'll do it right until the day Lord Dathirii returns, so that none of you assholes get an excuse to fire more of my people. You want to ruin his event? Spit in the drinks yourself."

Yultes had once again opened his mouth to protest, but before he could get a single word out, Nicole had snapped the wooden spoon on his hand. "Not a word." Cold, irrepressible anger emanated from her. "You ruined her, you know that, I hope. Whatever you told her, it shattered her. She refused all of our help, refused to even see me by the end. You killed her, as sure as cold and hunger and sickness did."

"I know." The words had slipped out, ill-advised. Yultes didn't remember what he'd been thinking, exactly—panicked ideas about bloodlines and proper noble conduct and being discovered, really.

All of it was already vague in his memory, buried under the waves of regret.

"I know what I did. I … I'll go, now." He'd taken two steps towards the door and stopped. Nicole had wanted to help Trish. Perhaps it wasn't entirely too late, in a way. "I found him. Our son. He doesn't want anything to do with me, but he'd like you better. I could tell you where to reach him."

Nicole had blanched, her hands tightening over the wooden spoon. Yultes had been glad for the distance between them; he'd suspected she'd have hit him again otherwise. When she'd spoken, utter disgust filled her voice. "Are you bargaining for my help using your son's life and happiness?"

"No! No." Horror had spread through him, and yet a deeply cynical part of him had marvelled at how efficient it would have been, how impeccably shrewd. Perhaps he should have tried. After all, the biggest risk was to bring Nicole's opinion of him even lower—if that was even possible.

In the end, he'd told her Larryn ran a homeless shelter at the bottom of the city without asking for anything in return, and had left knowing he'd have to ruin Hellion's day without the kitchens' help. He still requested less food than he should have, hoping to strike the delicate balance between having enough for everyone to eat a few bites but run out early and allow part of the family notice. Whether or not Nicole would see the ploy and add to the original order was beyond him, at this point.

It had been such a relief, to tell Nicole about Larryn, to let someone—anyone—know that he existed, that Yultes had found him. He'd always kept that truth to himself, out of self-preservation for years, but eventually for Larryn's sake, too. His son had been abundantly clear he wanted no association whatsoever between them, steady income excepted. The clear-cut answer had been a relief, at first, a simple way to dampen what he'd caused. Yultes had buried any longing deep under his much more prolific shame. He'd gotten a lot wrong in his life, but imposing himself on Larryn would not be one more.

Still. The jumbled mix of yearning and guilt stayed, rekindled by helping Sallin now when he'd doomed Trish. The brief visit to the kitchens had dragged memories of Larryn's mother to the forefront of his thoughts, and her laughter trailed him as he worked, directing staff to unearth the great Dathirii banners of old or penning invitation to everyone. It echoed in his mind now, as he watched Garith sweep Sallin into a conversation the moment she'd stepped in, flirting unabashedly while he guided her to the lectern, bringing a smile back to her face. He was so lost in ancient grievances he didn't notice the coinmaster had sent her on her way until Garith waved a hand in front of his eyes.

"Don't daydream about the staff, Yultes, it's bad form."

A flush crept up his cheeks and he shook himself awake, meeting Garith's grin with a roll of his eyes. "You were the one flirting."

He laughed, then. "Ah, yes, the incredible sexiness of a man leaning in close to whisper 'don't worry about your pay' into your ear. It's the huskiness that sells it."

Yultes' eyebrows shot up, but before he could comment on Garith's assertion, the coinmaster interpreted his reaction as doubt, set a firm hand on his shoulder to get him to bend forward, and then brought his lips close to his ear, tone dropping into a suggestive lull.

"Now let's move to my quarters and play with some numbers, hm?"

Yultes leaned away with a chortled chuckle. He never knew how to react to Garith's silliness, or to the very fact the coinmaster allowed himself this type of humour around him, as if they were friends.

"Refrain from doing that again, if you please."

It earned him a snort of laughter and a gentle squeeze from Garith. "Sure, sure. For what it's worth, I'd never do something as unfair as direct the irresistible Garith Dathirii charm on our staff. I like women to follow me because of the pull of my smile and wits, not because they won't risk me making their life hell."

Yultes' chest constricted painfully. That hadn't been it, had it? He hadn't turned on any charms, had only found himself sending notes back to the kitchens regarding the quality of his meals, eventually insisting to meet the cook responsible for it. But Trish had noticed his quarters' edible plants and asked about it, and they'd fallen into the first of many easy conversations. Yultes hadn't flirted; he'd craved her presence in a way he'd almost never experienced in centuries of life, and hadn't since. It had panicked him. Everyone around him was clear about the rules: nobles were too good for commoners, and he could not afford to lose their support. He'd known not to tell Hellion about his affair, but when Trish had told him of her pregnancy, he'd sought advice in a roundabout way.

Yultes would never forget sitting in Hellion's quarters, the bottle of wine between them already almost empty, digging for the courage to open up. It had come with a lull in the conversation, and Yultes had let a question unasked for decades slip out.

"Hellion, how do you know you're in love?"

"What an odd question," his friend had said. "You simply know. Everyone does."

And that had been the end of it. Yultes certainly had not simply known, and his suspicion that this might have been it was laid to rest by Hellion's firm assurances. He did not love Trish, he concluded: he enjoyed her presence, and its cost had become too great.

He'd been foolish and arrogant, and she'd paid for it with her life. Garith, for all his propensity to bring women to his bed, already understood a hundred times better what was at stake for his partner. Or partners, really, and it occurred to Yultes that Garith had a few decades of experience himself, yet he'd never had a stable relationship that he was aware of. Would he even know? Amidst Hellion's friend, they had rarely spoken of Garith except to sneer at his 'base escapades' with countless women, and their impact on House Dathirii's reputation.

Surely, he must only have missed it. After all, Hellion was also still unattached, having pointedly kept his relationships secret until he was certain they were worthy of the Dathirii name—something no one had yet achieved. How often had Yultes consoled him after an inevitable separation?

A deep, long buried part of him wanted to prod Garith about his past loves, to know if he was alone, eschewing romantic attachments entirely, but to even ask left him vulnerable. It wasn't until they'd reached Garith's quarters that he devised a way to breach the topic without exposing himself. His throat parched, he closed the door behind them and adopted the most casual tone he could.

"With all the women you do pull in, it's a miracle you haven't found the right one to settle with."

Garith turned back to him, one eyebrow raised sceptically, amusement stretching his lips. "There is no right one."

Not unlike Hellion, then. He should stop there, consider his answer acquired, but he couldn't. Garith's easy smile seemed to welcome further questioning.

"No one good enough for the amazing Garith Dathirii, then?"

Garith bowed as if honoured by the title, then shook his head with a pleased laugh. "You mistake me. I've met many a woman far better than I, with great wits and energy, a smile or look to melt your insides, and passion that can only be admired and beloved. I could have married any and all, if I had been so predisposed. I've thought about it, even, but it is wrong for me. I don't love in this fashion, and I have no inclinations for the communal life building it involves. This life—the flirting and sex with possible recurrence, limited expectations, and openness as to the future—that is what suits me. If romance awaits me, well, let it. Until then, I've been happily making my way without it for decades and see no reason to strive for it, or worry over such things."

"Aah, I see."

Yultes could barely push the word out. Not like Hellion, but like him, to some extent. He'd buried a lot of these questions over the years, as thinking of them meant thinking of Trish, but having that confirmation now lifted a weight off his lungs.

"Well now," Garith said, throwing himself into his desk's chair with a grin, "I never guessed my love life would get that big a smile out of you."

A smi—Yultes' heart jumped as he realized his cheeks ached from it. Curses, he hadn't meant to be this transparent! But Garith only dismissed his just-as-transparent panic with a wave of his hands.

"Look. You've been a tremendous asshole and I'm not about to forget that, but I'll grant you the gift of honesty: every now and then when we work together, you let someone surface who's more real and enjoyable than the shitty airs you put on for decades. That's the someone who just smiled at me, and if that someone needs an open ear to talk about relationship, then I'm willing. He sounds like he's been isolated for too long."

Yultes stopped moving, stopped breathing, stopped thinking altogether. Garith's words pierced something undefinable in him, leaving a sense of pain and possibilities he couldn't contend with. He hated the confusion burning through him, how it robbed him of his usual smooth tongue and quick wits. Instead, Yultes only managed a stiff nod—the barest of acknowledgments. Garith took pity on him, and kindly moved on.

"Now let's deal with Sarrin's case," he said, turning to his desk and withdrawing the most recent logbook. "The simplest, in my opinion, is to pretend the lectern's cost was higher, and use that gold to discreetly pay her the supposed penalty. Unless you expect Hellion to verify the quoted prices we've received?"

The direct and straightforward question dragged Yultes out of his daze. They had work to do, things far more important and urgent than his inner crises, whether recent or decades old. He leaned closer to Garith, bending his mind towards the Dathirii finances, yet he could not help but wonder at this someone Garith had perceived, and what it would mean to allow him a bigger presence in the future.

Chapter Fourteen

NEVER had Hasryan imagined he'd spend so much time with Sora Sharpe. He'd babbled for hours when she'd first woken up, spilling everything he knew about their current predicament with spontaneous, baseless trust that had later left him reeling with anxiety. All it had taken was one promise she wouldn't try to hang him anymore, and he'd thrown away all pretence at secrecy, alongside all the walls he'd so carefully built around himself over the years. Worse, he'd loved every second of it—how she drank his words, clinging to a pillow as she listened, never interrupting unless she had a sharp, intelligent question. He could have gone on forever, if she wasn't keeling over from exhaustion by the time he'd finished the tale proper.

He'd let her rest, and in the silence that had followed, Hasryan had taken full stock of just how much he'd said. Everything, really. All she'd ever need to not only hang him, but bring everyone else down with him. He told himself not to panic, that Camilla had lived with Sora since the Dathirii Tower had fallen, that she'd been looking for Vellien—that she was trustworthy, in short, and would never betray them.

Hasryan had thought that about Brune, too. He had been so sure she would save him, in that cell, so sure she would always be by his side, and he had been so wrong. What if this was the same? What if in one single conversation, he'd unravelled all the Dathirii had done for him and set his closest friends up for prison in one fell swoop? Before long, every thump overhead sounded like heavy boots, and Hasryan kept staring at the vivid yellow entrance door, as if expecting the Sapphire Guard to come knocking. Sora was still resting peacefully, and already he imagined them all in chains.

She slept through the night, and he could not. By the time the sky lightened again, the inside of Cal's home left him stifled and panicked. Hasryan gave up trying to reason with his body and mind, cocooned himself in Camilla's gifted red-wine winter coat and a layer of black cloak to mask its bright colour, then slid outside.

Thick white snowflakes drifted from the deep, pre-dawn sky, not unlike those that had fallen on his first outing with the old Dathirii lady, to see Esmera. Thoughts of the old woman's barbed tongue brought a smile to his lips and calmed the frantic beating of his heart. She'd call him a fool, and she'd be right—though whether it was for worrying about talking with Sora, or for talking in the first place, he had no idea.

He let his feet carry him, drifting through the quiet city.

Isandor's unrelenting winds had died down, wrapping the looming towers in eerie silence. The snow crunched under his every step, and a fine mist followed the shape of his breath. He was alone with himself, no guards and no tasks to accomplish, nothing but his aimless wanderings, to cease or start at his own impulses. Hasryan couldn't remember when that had last happened.

He closed his eyes and let the cold prickle his cheeks and nose, allowing the city's serenity seep into him. When they'd first come here a decade ago, he had been thrilled at the sight of it. The eclectic towers felt like a promise of varied philosophies, of hundreds of possibilities among which, surely, he'd find his place. The diversity had turned out to be more façade than anything, outward differentiation while the nobles closed ranks, and Brune had remained his only safe support until he'd met Larryn. He wouldn't have been able to navigate Isandor without her help, not as a teenager, but now? Now he knew the city well, and he had his own network—one that included Sora Sharpe.

It was harder to worry, here in the dampening snowfall, and Hasryan opted to stay outside. He wandered across bridges and along stairs, migrating to less travelled areas once the sun had risen and people emerged from their towers. By the time he returned to Cal's bright yellow door, it was well past noon and his stomach had much to do with his chosen path. Hasryan hurried inside, hoping there'd be a warm, delicious meal waiting for him. He found Branwen crouched by Sora's side, sitting on the ground with a wicker basket. A tasty, spiced oil scent drifted out of it.

"Missed Cal's delightful decor?" he asked, clicking the door shut behind him.

Branwen's nose scrunched up in disgust and that, along with her disbelieving chuckle, washed away the rest of his melancholy. "This room is a crime, and we all know it—Cal included."

"He wouldn't have it any other way." Neither would Hasryan, really. He adored the unabashed honesty of Cal's taste in colours and statuettes. "So what you got? Gifts from the lands of the rich?"

"Only the best," she replied before withdrawing a cloth and unwrapping it. Inside sat several flat slabs of a fried dough containing the gods only knew what deliciousness. "The Brasten's chefs could teach ours a few tricks. This has crushed nuts, honey, and a bunch of stuff I couldn't name but taste with great joy. Come get yours."

She'd picked one up and waved it around before biting in it. Hasryan didn't need more invitation; within a minute, he'd rid himself of his winter attire and snatched one of the deep-fried delicacies. Sora stared at both of them, eyebrows way high, and it wasn't until Hasryan had eaten well over half of his that she sighed, shook her head, and partook in the meal.

"Something up?" Hasryan asked.

"Knowing you've been working with House Dathirii and watching you banter with their spymaster are two very different experiences." She reached into the basket for her own share. "Don't mind me."

Easier said than done when she'd just reminded him everyone was supposed to hate him. He plastered a smirk over his face and forced a shrug.

"You tried to hang me, what, ten days ago? And yet here we are."

He'd chosen to trust her, just like he'd chosen to trust in Camilla and, from her, in Diel and Branwen. What else could he do? Avoid everyone but a few, always? He'd tried that, to miserable results. Besides, now that his little network of trusted folks was expanding, Hasryan was slowly discovering how much he enjoyed other people's company. He didn't want to lose that.

"Everyone settled in?" he asked Branwen.

"We got rooms, but I don't know about settled. Not sure any of us wants to do that." She looked at the wall, and after a moment Hasryan realized she'd turned towards the general vicinity of the Dathirii Tower. "But we're settled in enough to receive letters, I guess. I was telling Sora before you arrived that Aunt Camilla penned a missive for us, worried that her gracious host hadn't returned overnight."

Sora let her face fall into her hands with a quiet "Oh no" that drained away all of Hasryan's joy at news from Camilla. Why was she so unhappy about it? But he didn't need to ask: Sora rubbed her eyes with a dramatic sigh. "She'll have baked so many cookies by now."

Hasryan's laugh burst out, frank and relieved. Of course she would. "Need help emptying out the plates?"

"Yes, actually." She said it so casually, but his heart flipped and he froze. What did she mean by that? Sora's lips curled into a shy smile. "You could come over for breakfast, perhaps?" The offer hung between the three of them, unacknowledged while Hasryan struggled to conjure forth words in response. The erratic ache in his chest was so visceral he couldn't fight past it. Whatever Sora read in his expression, however, her smile stiffened and she inclined her head towards Branwen. "Both of you, actually, unless I've strayed in my conclusion and Miss Branwen knows where to find Kellian."

Branwen choked on her bite, caught off guard. She shook her head as she coughed, her eyes watering from the errant chunk. When she managed to swallow and speak again, her voice had turned raspy. "We don't."

"So come," Sora reiterated. "I should be in shape to go home tonight, and Camilla would be thrilled to see both of you."

Hasryan's mind was quick to conjure a hundred different ways in which he could butt heads with Sora and ruin this invitation, yet a strange, pleasant buzz filled him. He'd expected her to keep his secret, no more, and now she was offering his home to him, knowing the dangers involved. She trusted him, truly … and he'd get to see Camilla! With childish excitement, he wondered if any of the cookies had been butterscotch and if they'd taste as sweet as they had, right after his escape. He desperately wanted to sit down with Camilla, to have the chance to thank her properly for standing for him even at the risk of her freedom and safety. How many could have been said to have done the same? Kellian might not deserve his help, but Hasryan couldn't refuse this opportunity to see the old elven lady.

"All right," he said, "but I'll be leaving with those cookies—as many as I can carry."

Sora laughed. "Please, go ahead! These are far from her first, and

I've eaten more than my share."

Fond warmth spread through Hasryan—a feeling reflected in Branwen's chuckle and easy smile. They'd both witnessed Camilla's anxious baking habits, and there was something special in that shared space, too, something Hasryan had rarely experienced before. He was one strand in a bigger web, existing in a community united by their love for one delightful old woman.

SORA left the following evening. Hasryan watched her collect her belongings, pain stiffening her movements, and he wondered if he shouldn't have stopped her. He suspected Vellien wouldn't approve, but they'd have to scold her at her domicile. They'd come once and made the mistake of telling Sora everything was healing properly. She'd taken it as permission to leave as soon as she felt able.

With Cal once more gone—to the Shelter or to gamble, Hasryan wasn't sure—the house's silence grew heavy. He'd slid from the strange elation of connection with others to a lonely quiet, and the melancholy sank into his bones, threatening to lodge itself permanently. The more Hasryan spent time with friends, the more he realized he needed them. So when the door creaked open, he sprang to his feet—partly in fear, as he shouldn't laze about the living room if he'd left the front unlocked—but mostly in excitement. Only the latter remained when he recognized Arathiel.

"Friend!" he greeted, and the word felt so comfortable on his tongue, so right. "You won't believe what you missed. I ..." He set a hand on his chest, pausing for dramatic effect. " … got invited to morning tea with Sora Sharpe."

Arathiel snorted, but before he could rebuke him, Hasryan wiggled his eyebrows and met his gaze. The beautiful wave of shock and confusion spreading across Arathiel's face brought him great joy.

"Please explain," he said, removing his coat before sitting on a close chair to unlace his boots.

"And ruin the suspense so quickly? No way." Hasryan very pointedly yawned and stretched, as if he had all the time in the world and wasn't, in fact, eager to tell Arathiel. "First we settle comfortably. Then you recount everything about your grand entrance into House Brasten. How were they?"

His question tailed into a softer tone. Arathiel had concealed his affiliation with House Brasten upon returning to Isandor and avoided any contact with them. He'd expected hostility or, at best, denial—and besides, no one he'd known in it was alive today. When Diel had explained how Lady Brasten had defended both Arathiel's and House Dathirii's actions during the Golden Table, hope and wistfulness had threaded their way back into Arathiel. He hadn't said anything, but something in the pinch of his lips and tilt of his shoulders had tipped Hasryan—one of those wordless messages he could always decipher from Arathiel. Amake Brasten was the obvious ally to petition for help, and he'd grown ready to do so.

"Welcoming," Arathiel answered. "There's no other way to put it."

They gathered a bunch of pillows, then Hasryan grabbed

leftovers from Cal's last trip to the Shelter—a bean-beet-carrot salad of some sort—and dumped several slabs of Cal's humongous cheese collection in a plate besides the bowl. Arathiel snatched away some of the cheese as they sat side by side and rearranged the pillows for their comfort.

Arathiel started slowly, and it was obvious to Hasryan that he struggled to put words on the mix of nervousness, nostalgia, pleasant surprise, and reignited grief his night had been. One had to read between the lines, in Arathiel's sighs as he described the washed out mosaic overhead, in his rising tone as he related the lift apparatus now at the centre of the Brasten Tower, or in his awe when he repeated Amake's direct offer for any support he'd want to help manage his new physical needs. More than anything, however, it was the regrets seeping into his words and hunching his shoulders as he mentioned the visit to his sister's quarters that caught Hasryan's attention. He set his hand on Arathiel's leg and squeezed hard enough to be felt. It drew a thin, grateful smile, and Arathiel's voice lightened as he finished his story.

"I made sure they arranged the rooms to everyone's liking, but I couldn't stay again tonight. I had to get fresh air and distance."

Hasryan nodded, keeping silent for a while. Arathiel didn't need platitudes. He needed a friend to listen and sympathize without judgment. Not that Hasryan had any idea what it could be like, to return to your home and find it irremediably changed, the family you loved gone, replaced by worthy but unknown descendants. That would require ever having a home and loving family in the first place.

"You have good timing," he said. "Cal's humble abode is miraculously quiet tonight, and I'm always great company."

It had been a jest, but Arathiel's face split into a grin. He reached for the plate of cheese again. "You are. Where is Cal, by the way? I'd have loved to thank him for the hospitality."

"He's spending the evening at the Shelter, I think. Or gambling elsewhere."

Arathiel froze right before he could bite into his chunk of cheese. "With Larryn?"

Hasryan hesitated, unsure how to respond to the unasked question. Had Larryn apologized? Was the broken parts of their group mended? How Hasryan wished he had a positive answer to offer. Whatever had happened between Cal and Larryn recently, however, only heavy awkwardness had remained after his arrival.

"They … talked, I think," he said at length. "It's an improvement, but we've not reached a place where the four of us could blissfully play cards. I don't know if there will ever be such a time again."

It hurt to admit it out loud, yet with the shattered trust between Larryn and Cal and his own forced hiding, he didn't see how they could return to never-ending nights pointlessly trying to beat Cal at cards in the Shelter, sharing meals and laughter alike. It had barely lasted two years, this oasis of joy, less so with Arathiel. Now it was gone, reminding Hasryan of how fleeting every scrap of happiness he carved always turned out. Even his decade-long partnership with Brune had been brutally ripped away from him. Hasryan scooped up the beans salad and shoved it all in his mouth, trying to bury the melancholy and anger. He was building new relationships, too, with several Dathirii and even Sora, and not everything had soured as he'd thought, the day before his execution. He didn't have to start over, not this time, even if some things were gone forever.

"Cal would never abandon the card games," Arathiel said. "He'll figure out something. We all will."

Hasryan tilted his head back, sifting through his complex feelings on this. He wished for Larryn and Cal to find common grounds, but not at the price of Cal's well-being. Whether they all played again depended less on their too-gracious halfling friend, and more on Larryn's questionable ability to grow. Hasryan wanted to believe in it, though: for all of his angry rough edges, Larryn cared deeply about others.

"So …" Arathiel nudged him. "How long will you keep the suspense? Tell me how Sora wound up inviting you for tea!"

Hasryan grinned, glad for the change of topic. He picked up a last piece of cheese with deliberate movement, staring at Arathiel as he took his sweet time chewing it, dragging out this wait as much as possible. Arathiel pinched his lips, obviously trying not to laugh.

"It starts with something even more incredible: Larryn and Sora cooperating without tearing each other's head off."

"Ah! Now I know you're pulling my leg."

Their mirth didn't last long into the tale. Larryn and Sora had both come inches from death and no amount of jests about Larryn's rashness could erase the day's impact on their friend. Hasryan had never seen him so shaken, so out of sorts. It'd been a shock to learn he'd never killed anyone before despite living on the streets when it'd been such a fixture of Hasryan's youth.

Arathiel listened to the story in his usual patient silence, and his eyebrows shot up when Hasryan related the conversations he'd had with Sora, and how he'd told of his entire time in the Dathirii Tower. He seemed surprised at the openness, and while he didn't comment on it, it made Hasryan question it again. It was terrifying how quickly he'd decided he no longer needed secrecy and walls, how excited it made him. He never wanted to guard his joy as he had before, consequences be damned.

The two of them finished the salad as they spoke, setting their bowls aside, and soon enough they were leaning against one another more than on the wall behind them. Arathiel's legs were half-folded, providing perfect support for Hasryan's back. Hasryan didn't mind not seeing his friend's expressions. For once, he had no desire to watch someone else's face for clues of hostility or disapproval—he knew he would never find any with Arathiel. This conversation felt safe, a bubble in which he could fully relax—one Arathiel shattered with a few terrifying words.

"Hasryan, there's something important I have to ask you."

Hasryan's voice withered halfway through a hypothetical list of the breakfast and tea combinations he expected Camilla to have ready for him, words dying on his lip as dread filled him. What could Arathiel possibly want to ask?

"Sure," he said, a casualness to his tone he didn't feel in the least.

"What … what am I to you? What are we?"

May the demigods have mercy on his soul, what was he supposed to answer that? Hasryan almost quipped 'important' because it was both true and a non-answer. Why was Arathiel inquiring about their relationship? Had Hasryan missed clues? Should he not lean on him this way? He scooted away, turning on himself to stare at his … friend? The word that had seemed so perfect earlier now dripped with dangerous questions. Would Arathiel be disappointed? Was it even true? He'd never had this kind of easy connection with anyone before, yet it didn't feel like the big rush of romance he'd so often heard described. Could it be neither? Hasryan wished he could talk with Cal. Cal would know.

"I'm … not sure," he said at length, and he watched Arathiel for every hint of disappointment, or anger, or any clue at all, really! Arathiel's brow furrowed into a frown and for an instant, Hasryan's heart sank.

"It's hard to define, isn't it?" Arathiel said. "When they held me at the headquarters, Sharpe asked me what you were to me, and I had no idea how to convey it." He gestured at the air with slight exasperation. "We just are. And I like that, that ease of understanding, like we're always in tune without needing to explain."

Hasryan clenched his hands, shivers crawling up his arm. He knew exactly what Arathiel meant. When they'd met they had both felt like outsiders, too often judged, questioned, and distrusted. It'd only taken that first conversation for a bond to form, and from there it'd grown with disquieting natural.

"Then why did you ask? What was the point?" Hasryan bristled. Why had Arathiel put him on the spot like this if he already understood how much he meant to Hasryan?

"Because I ..." Arathiel closed his eyes and a soft smile reached his lips. "I need to know if whatever this relationship is feels, er ... exclusive to you. I didn't want to assume. Some things shouldn't be left unsaid. The risk is too great."

"You mean like romantic exclusivity."

"On our non-romantic thing, yes. I think I do." Arathiel laughed and rubbed his eyes. "Is that weird?"

If it was, Hasryan could still see where Arathiel was coming from, how mistakenly assuming they could both pursue whoever else could quickly lead to shattered trust. In fact, Hasryan suspected it wouldn't feel strange at all, if not for the fact he'd never entertained the idea of a deep and exclusive pairing of any nature, with anyone. He still counted his blessings with every new person in his close circle, every friend. Yet Arathiel had wanted to be extra certain, had chosen this conversation over any risk of breaking his trust. Hasryan's fears ebbed away, replaced by gratefulness so powerful it stole his words for a moment. He reached out for Arathiel and squeezed his forearm hard, until at last his ability to speak returned.

"I don't need exclusivity. I don't believe I remotely want it, even. I'm ... everything around love and romance is still so confusing. I wouldn't know where to begin."

"Aah, great."

Arathiel's relief was palpable and contagious. Hasryan couldn't help but think he'd given the right answer, even though there shouldn't be a wrong answer to such a question. Non-exclusive was what Arathiel had hoped for, either way, and it suddenly occurred to Hasryan something must have prompted the initial inquiry. Something must have changed for Arathiel to need to define more clearly the limits of their relationship and Hasryan had an inkling what. He grinned, warmth blooming in his chest, and he leaned towards his friend.

"Who is it?" he asked. "Is it Varden? It has to be. You've been all over him since he woke up."

Arathiel laughed, his smile so wide it threatened to break out of his face, and he stared straight ahead, refusing to meet Hasryan's gaze.

"It is Varden, yes."

The soft awe in his tone surprised Hasryan. It felt as if Arathiel held a precious and delicate possibility in his hands, sunrise glittering on a thousand dew drops, a vista that could change in a second, the moment lost forever, pure and fragile and perfect. Hasryan heard reverence and fear and eagerness, and he found himself yearning to understand.

"Can I ask …" He trailed off, instinctively shying from awfully personal questions. But if he couldn't ask them of Arathiel, then who would be left? Arathiel nodded, granting him quick permission. "Can you describe it? You're in love, right? What's that like?"

"That's … let me try to explain but …" He rubbed the back of his neck and grimaced, slowly picking his words. "When he smiles, my mind ceases to function for a moment, like my heart and lungs expand spontaneously to make room and cradle the beauty I have just witnessed. When he held me through pain and flame in the enclave's brazier, I forgot to breathe. Every minute I spend with him feels as if I have been blessed. I want to know him. It makes me unreasonably giddy, and in Varden's case it's also very soothing." Arathiel leaned forward and sighed. "Still … I'm worried. Attraction used to make me very grounded in my body. Heart pounding, skin tingling, the intense need to hold and touch. Now I … float, you could say, detached from the ground, from me. I still want to touch—gosh, how I want to kiss him!—but I'm nervous of being disappointed, of not feeling it hard enough. Of … having to grieve for that, too."

Hasryan frowned. Wasn't there a lot of overlap between Arathiel's description of giddiness and impulsivity and his own unexplainable thrill at Sora's presence? He wanted to parse through that, but it could wait. What Arathiel had just expressed couldn't.

"Wouldn't it just be different? You can feel our touch if we press enough." He sought Arathiel's gaze and held it fast. "If he's worthy of you then you should be able to talk to him about this stuff." He smirked and added. "Tell him to ram you hard."

It had been half a joke, but from the way Arathiel bit his lower lip, some very explicit ideas were running through his mind.

"Experiment," Hasryan said. "With the right partner it might even be fun!"

Arathiel threw back his head and laughed. "With the right partner, Hasryan, it can only be fun. But you did not want to talk about my prospective sex life. Something's bothering you."

"Oh, nothing serious." He smirked, but it had none of its usual smoothness, and Arathiel would have seen through that anyway.

"Just trying to understand myself, is all."

It was frustrating, how everyone he spoke with seemed to have figured themselves out. Arathiel had his worries, but he knew without a doubt he wanted to be with Varden. Cal was the exact opposite: both his aromanticism and asexuality had long been a clear certainty to him, and he never doubted either. Yet all of it—friendship and romance and everything else around them—was so confusing to him. Was he falling in love with Sora? Was that why his heart refused to be prudent concerning her? Yet it didn't quite feel like what Arathiel described for Varden, not as pressing. Hasryan flopped back down to the ground, to stare at the ceiling.

"I spent so much of my life convinced I would be alone and hated, I thought it was pointless to contemplate what I wanted. Now all my options are opening up and I discover that I can't even interpret my own feelings."

Arathiel leaned forward enough to re-enter Hasryan's line of sight. He smiled at him. "At the risk of sounding cheeky, perhaps you ought to experiment. With the right partner—and good communication—you might even have fun!"

Hasryan couldn't help his laugh. Maybe Arathiel was right and he would need to try, but that path led to vulnerability. He didn't know if he could handle it, and for the time being, he'd had enough of the restless self-questioning.

"I will consider your advice," he said with exaggerated solemnity, "but not tonight. I want to hear more about Varden. I didn't get much chance to speak with him while he recovered. Tell me about his smile, his laugh, anything you like in him!"

"Really?"

"Yeah." He lifted his arms, spreading them wide above him, as if reaching for the ceiling's net. "I want to hear you talk. You were always so silent during our games."

"I'm much better at listening," Arathiel said with surprising shyness.

Hasryan grinned, stretching out and shifting until he was perfectly comfortable in Arathiel's lap. It was a marvel that he dared this position, that he'd found someone he trusted enough to be this physically close to. Hasryan silenced the voice inside of him promising another disappointment. Arathiel would never let him down and Hasryan loved the solid reminder of his reliability under him. With Arathiel once more living in the Brasten Tower, their chances to talk might grow rare, and Hasryan didn't want to waste this opportunity.

"Not tonight, my friend," he said. "Not tonight."

Hasryan closed his eyes as Arathiel emitted a joking whine then slowly picked his first words. A warm excitement imbued his voice, a sense of wonder and awe Hasryan adored. It was as if Arathiel could not believe his own luck. The enthusiasm was contagious, and before long Hasryan's face hurt from smiling so much. He could spend hours listening to his friend ramble like this, and he had every intention to do so.

CHAPTER FIFTEEN

W HEN Branwen next checked, Alton's flower pot drop point had contained a reply—one that startled her. She'd expected a rendezvous in one of their usual spots, where she arrived in disguise and paid his meal he filled her in about House Allastam's ongoing, but the markings on his parchment called her directly to the tower. She'd wondered what he could want that couldn't be shared over an ale in some smoky hole.

The answer, it turned out, was a once-in-a-lifetime chance to infiltrate House Allastam at the precise moment Yultes had been invited for tea by Mia Allastam.

Branwen was no newcomer to using disguises and deceit to slip through enemy corridors undetected, but she typically had far more time to plan—weeks or months of studying her target, gathering information about the routine back and forth, learning names of notable figures. She had a decent idea of the Allastam's inside organization from regular communication with Alton, but nowhere near enough for comfort. His proposition gave her cold feet. So much could go wrong. And yet she could hardly say no, could she?

So she met him at the specified hour, her hair braided tight against her head, under a simple bandanna. He handed her the uniform customary of service staff, and its close-fitting vest made her glad for the binder holding most of her breasts. The rest of it suited her almost perfectly—unsurprising, considering Alton's eye for such elements.

"Think you can handle the improvisation?" he'd asked, his voice muffled by the door of the closet in which she'd changed. "Lady Mia Allastam is already with him. She has asked for tea and I've prepared it. All you need to do is knock, serve them each one cup, place the tray on the small table by the door, and leave. Few servants circulate near Lady Mia Allastam's quarters, though, so you'll be able to hover before and after. Just don't wait too long."

Branwen had finished buttoning up the disguise and slipped out. "I know how these go."

"And I know you're not usually rushed into them," he replied. "May Ren watch over you."

"Oh, I think I've got Xyr ear for a while."

And for a time, Branwen had believed her quip accurate. No one had intercepted her as she made her way up the Allastam Tower, tray in hand, and the initial frantic beat of her heart had steadied to a rapid, controlled pace. Improvised though this was, she'd undergone similar missions dozens of times before. The hardest part was acquiring the right outfit and getting inside, two steps Altonhad facilitated for her. By the time she hovered near the door to Mia's quarters, unscathed and with no alarms raised, she thanked Cal for Ren's blessings and bent her thoughts towards the voices within. Yultes' was the first she recognized, and it sent a spike of bitterness through her.

"We have been hard at work following up on every suggestion offered by your father, and we'll certainly return the House's finances to a normal state." He sounded tense and stiff; unusual, for one who lied as smoothly as he breathed.

"That's not what I asked, Yultes," Mia chided him. "How are you adjusting—you, the person? I've heard only rumours, but it seems you have the delicate and complicated task of getting Jaeger and Garith to cooperate. Surely they cannot be so eager to listen to you."

"I—no, they certainly are not. I merely make it work."

Branwen held back her snort. There couldn't have been anything simple about it.

"How?" Mia asked, voicing Branwen's main concern.

Yultes, however, did not explain. She heard the shuffle of a body, then a tight, controlled, "You are full of questions today."

"Am I being indiscreet?" An upward lilt in her tone added a layer of challenge to it, under the pleasantness. "You don't have to answer. I am merely ..." A pause. Branwen leaned in. This had been intriguing before Yultes protested and she wanted Mia to push for more. "May I be bold, Yultes?"

Another silence. She hoped he was squirming in his seat, that he experienced the tightness in his own chest tenfold. Mia took his lack of refusal for assent.

"I am concerned about you. You are one of the only adults who has ever shown an honest interest in me. Others ask about my health as if my illness is all that I am. You inquire about my hobbies, my love life, my moods. So when I see the bags under your eyes, the slump in your shoulders, the weight of every word, I worry. You have desired this new role for as long as I have known you. Perhaps I am too young to understand, but in that case, then that is why I ask so many questions. To understand, and be reassured."

Branwen's fingers tightened around her tray as Mia spoke, a burning acrid rising in the pit of her stomach. So Yultes had been kind towards Mia, huh? He'd cared about her as she grew up, inquiring about her life like she'd been family or something? How nice of him. How surprising, too, considering he'd never spared a second for his niece. Only Diel had cared, and Branwen had thought she'd been over it—who wanted Yultes to dote on them anyway?—but hearing Mia now, it was all she could do not to let the overpowering jealousy overtake her and slam through the door, all ruses be damned.

"It is not the position that brings me such trouble, but the price it came with. I may never have been satisfied with my role within House Dathirii, but now I feel entirely apart from it. My mind wanders to the family I've forgotten, lost, or outright denied through the years, those sacrificed for this achievement, and I ..." His voice cracked and fell, and Branwen pressed her ear against the wood to catch the rest of his words. "I do not know if it was worth it all."

Her feet hit the door as he finished, surprise stealing her care. Branwen bit back a curse. Was their silence because they'd heard, or a natural pause after Yultes' admission? She'd never know unless they called to her in suspicion. Perhaps it'd be best to beat a hasty retreat, but she hadn't learned anything yet. She hadn't come here for Yultes' regrets.

Branwen breathed in deeply, schooled her features into a mask, and knocked, the sharp rap of her knuckles in perfect sync with the hammering of her heart.

"Ah, it must be the tea at last," Mia said, her tone too delighted for Branwen's taste. She'd been heard. "Come in."

She could still flee; she'd have enough of a start to escape the Tower. It'd be the sensible decision. But when had Branwen ever been sensible? If Ren truly was watching, now was the time to prove it. She squared her shoulders, pushed the door open, and strode into the quarters.

"Thank you," Mia said as way of greeting. She sat with perfect poise, a porcelain statue in a perfect doll-room—tea set, flower paintings and motifs, and tasteful cream rugs and seats. "Please close the door behind you."

The demand, quiet though it was, startled Branwen. Close the door? She'd swear it wasn't customary for staff to stay during meetings. Alarm spread through Branwen, but it was too late now. She'd made her choice and would see it to the end.

She forced herself to continue moving, steps fluid and practised, but subdued—like a youth with years of experience in service. Her gaze snapped to the side table mentioned by Alton—it had enough room for her to pour while keeping her back to them, so she veered in that direction. The clinking of tea cups cut through the heavy silence as she prepared them, and Branwen could barely breathe as she poured. Were they staring at her? Could they see the tension in her shoulders? Had her elven ears tipped them off to who had been listening? Perhaps she should give up, or—

Her panicked planning ground to a halt as Mia Allastam returned to her conversation with Yultes, commenting on the recent weather with obvious boredom. Branwen recognized the meaningless banter of one waiting for more privacy and hurried along, filling the cups, placing them back on her tray, and sliding towards the pair. She kept her head bent for the most part, only risking a quick glance at them. While Mia Allastam settled deeper in her wide chair, clearly at ease, Yultes stayed at the edge of his, stiff shoulders and fingers laced tightly together—a common trick to avoid fidgeting.

His earlier words clung to her, most of all the intense longing when he'd spoken of family lost. She was still mulling over them, setting down the tea cups, when Mia Allastam surged from her seat, her delicate fingers clamping around Branwen's wrist. She froze, her head jerking up to meet Mia's dark blue eyes. Mischief shone in them, but no anger or malice, so Branwen waited, her breath stuck at the bottom of her lungs.

Mia Allastam smiled and, without ever taking her eyes off

Branwen, she said "Have I told you I've started learning the harp? My skills are paltry, but I find its melodies invaluable to drown out the noise of the outside world. It would be lovely if you stayed for a song at least."

That last had not been directed at Yultes, but at her. Branwen's long experience in piecing out the implicit meanings let her understand the offer despite her frantic heart: music to cover a conversation. A chance to speak with Yultes unimpeded. Mia Allastam must have known she was coming; Altonhad set her up, albeit less as a trap, and more as a helpful nudge.

"Certainly, milady," Branwen said in a whisper.

Yultes' sharp inhale warned her he'd finally recognized her, and the fact he'd taken so long sparked two conflicting emotions within her: pride at her skills, and bitterness that this uncle had never cared enough for her to immediately spot her. She turned to him, eyebrows raised, daring him to say anything as Mia Allastam rose from her seat and walked towards the graceful harp casually waiting in the parlour. Yultes had quickly masked his surprise, his expression neutral besides the thin tense line of his lips.

The first notes played, filling the silence between them, and still they didn't speak. Branwen tilted her chin up, bracing for Yultes' inevitable sneer. He'd been Hellion's shadow for as long as she could remember, always parroting his ideas, working so hard to please the other asshole. It must be quite the victory, to be granted Jaeger's desk at last and become Hellion's right hand.

Branwen's anger churned and rose at the very thought of Yultes sitting in that chair.

"Branwen—"

"Shut up," she snapped, cutting off his quiet voice. Hearing him speak her name had been too much, the final drop in the ocean of fears—her own and Diel's—she'd try to contain over the last weeks. "You don't get to say my name anymore."

His eyebrows shot up in a bemused, unimpressed mimic. "Please, Branwen, you—"

"No." She kept her voice down, but it sliced through his smug little words all the same. She glowered at him, thankful he'd remained seated so she had the height advantage. "I'm not sure what the point of this is, because I have nothing to say to you—nothing except that I will never forgive what you did, and I will ruin you for it."

Yultes smiled, then, and something about it threw her off balance. Branwen knew well his cutting, arrogant half-smiles, the hints of pleasures that preceded a scathing retort, but this one was different, amused and exhausted all at once.

"What I did," he repeated, as if tasting the accusation. "Which part, pray tell? Attempting to flee the tower with Jaeger? Manipulating our accounts with Garith to stave off the worst of Hellion's demands? Deflecting our leader's attention from petty, violent revenge on Diel's lover? Or, oh, I'm sorry, you must mean accepting the position where I can do these things."

His tone had reversed to its usual haughtiness, and it fanned such anger within Branwen that she stumbled on his actual words, unable to fully comprehend them. "What?"

"I've been helping them," Yultes hissed, leaning forward.

"Helping. You?"

He snorted. "Yes, that was their reaction when I offered."

Because none of it made sense. At best, Yultes disdained everyone in Diel's close council. At worst, he despised them. The latter was absolutely Jaeger's case. Why would he help, instead of gloating about his victory? This had to be a joke—a cruel one. Anything else required her to accept both Lord Allastam's darling daughter and her slimy uncle were her allies. Branwen crossed her arms. She'd love to believe it—they desperately needed more support, especially from the inside—but she refused to let the harp's tranquil melody lull her into false security.

"Prove it."

She didn't even know what she expected, exactly. Part of the demand served to buy herself time while her mind scrambled to make sense of this entire situation. If this was a ploy, then what for? Information? Did they want to manipulate her into doing their bidding?

Yultes' brow furrowed—a frown, or deep thoughts, or both maybe. Branwen stared, desperate for a revealing glimpse in his expression, something to ground her into trust or distrust, but her uncle had always been good at masking his feelings. He gave her nothing until he bwas ready to speak, and then he grew animated, words spilling out in a strange frenzy.

"Garith keeps three bottles of alcohol under his desk: the Flirt, the Cheer, and the Emergency. The Flirt is for unexpected lady visitors he seeks to impress and tends to be wine, light and fruity. His current was imported from Northern Mehr, but he hasn't touched it since Hellion took over. The Cheer is to celebrate small successes in private. The current bottle, a full-bodied delicacy from Aberrah Lake, was drank in full after we swindled Hellion about household expenses and salaries, effectively keeping most of the staff employed. I know this because he'd emptied the last, the Emergency, well before I came to him, the night Diel was shipped to his death, and that had made him talkative."

Shit.

Shit, shit, *shit*.

Garith called these three bottles his secret friends. She'd known about them since forever, but he'd never shown them to anyone else. Not that most others would care—half the house suspected he had wine on hand for his flirtations—but he enjoyed the secrecy of the joke. Why would he share something both trivial and private with Yultes unless they spent a ridiculous amount of hours together?

"That's disturbing," she finally said, not bothering to hide her dismay.

He laughed—and again, as with his smile before, it stunned her speechless by its open warmth. Vulnerable, she thought, and that was not a word she'd ever associated with Yultes.

"To all of us, yes." He waved his hand midair, as if dismissing the awkwardness of it all, and that was all it took for the brief glimpse at this other Yultes to vanish. "I'm sure you'd rather work with someone you don't despise, but—"

"I don't care," Branwen cut him off. "Save your self-pity and tell me how they are."

If her abruptness startled him, Yultes hid it well. "Restless, angry, and exhausted, I'd say. Jaeger has avoided any further injuries, but he's developing a rebellious streak that won't go unnoticed forever."

"Don't tell him Uncle Diel's a mess, then, or it'll become worse." It amused her that Yultes expected Jaeger to be subservient in any way. He'd played his role and let nobles snub him, but that rebellious streak had always lain in wait. Still, she'd hate for him to get hurt because he couldn't be bothered to contain the well-deserved snark. "Just say he misses Jaeger and we're all working hard to reunite them. That's true, anyway."

"Very well, I will transmit your message if …"—Ah, there it was, Branwen thought. The if, the conditions, the real trap— "you tell Diel that I will not build while Allastam troops are within our home."

"That's it? That's all you want from me?"

"He'll understand what—"

"Well, I want more from you." If he meant to help them, she'd make him. He startled at her brusque tone, but she only crossed her arms. "No offence, but your previous answer is lacking. Are they all together? In separate quarters?" She leaned forward, pitching her voice too low for Mia Allastam to hear. Her trust only went so far. "What is Hellion's next move? He needs new deals, so can you provide his next target? You've read Lady Brasten's declaration, Yultes: we're still House Dathirii. This is another trade war, except hostile soldiers have split our forces. So give me something to work with."

"Jaeger and Garith are kept forcefully apart, but I've moved Jaeger to my personal quarters, right above Garith's. Open windows let them pass messages. There will be a feast to celebrate Hellion's leadership, and we're coordinating to make it lacklustre at best. I doubt you could help with that particular task, unlike the stalling of our current trade efforts." He spared a glance for Mia Allastam before continuing on in a brisk, business tone. "We're moving on three potential associates that Lord Allastam provided. The deal is all but sealed for two of them, but the third won't arrive in town for another week. His wares include magical seeds that can grow giant vegetables year-long, plants with flowers that'd change colours—some according to the weather, others with the mood of people around. Hellion's goal is to use Allastam's money to acquire all of it, create a false scarcity, and ratchet up the price for profit. That only works if he has a monopoly, however."

If this was true, they had a golden opportunity to stop Hellion from pulling ahead while they recovered from losing their home along with Jaeger and Garith. Branwen wished she'd had the info from a source she trusted. It didn't help that Mia Allastam had set up the meeting, either. Both of them would benefit from Diel wasting resources on hindering or stealing a pointless deal. She studied her uncle, poised at the edge of his seat, the cup of tea untouched. Unreadable once more.

"One last thing: find out what happened to Kellian."

Alarm flicked through Yultes' expression. "Wasn't he—"

"He's missing, and it was timed too well to be coincidence. Hellion will know."

The grim line of his lips held no encouragement. "I'll try."

Well. That was more of a lead than she'd had coming here. She'd still need to talk to Altonon her way out and make sure he kept his ears open for rumours around the household. Her gaze drifted to Mia Allastam, her blonde hair brought into a frontal braid woven with paper flowers, her deft fingers running across the harp's strings, pinching each in turn.

Could she be trusted? They'd had a cordial relationship before Lord Allastam soured the alliance between their family to hell and back. Branwen had often sat with Mia when the soft-spoken girl had attended social events. Their shared love for flowers and Mia's passion for her craft made conversation an easy, pleasant affair, and more than once, Branwen had found herself taken in by Mia's clear, delighted laugh. She could ask her, but … Lord Allastam had never involved his daughter in his games before, lavishing all his praise on his asshole son instead, so how much could she know, really? Besides, something about today set her on edge—the rushed infiltration, how Mia Allastam had made her close the door from the start, how calm she remained while covering for their discussion... Branwen had been expected, which could only mean Altonhad set her up. Could she trust him at all, now? She had no better ins for information about the Allastams, sadly, and up to this point, Yultes and Mia had both proved useful.

Wary though she was, it still felt like Kellian's best chance.

At least she didn't have to decide how to handle the information about Hellion's deal now, or alone. They were a family, and Diel led them. He and Lady Brasten could choose whether to follow up on this lead or not. Her job had been to find the info at all, and she'd heard quite a lot worth her while today. Best to make sure to turn that into a repeat performance.

"All right. Got all of that stored right up in my head," she said, tapping her temples with her knuckles. "You hear anything else, write me. Scribble something and send a messenger to deliver it to the bright yellow door in the Middle City. Tell them it's for a bee friend. The owner will know to transfer it to me."

He would once she warned him about it, anyway. Branwen didn't want to risk any of her other drop spots when she'd sent most of her people scurrying for activity. Everyone except Hasryan had moved out of Cal's now and she figured their assassin fellow knew better than to hang by the door, visible to anyone outside, so this felt safe. Even if Yultes was playing her … As long as they all thought Cal was just one knot in her big network, they had no reason to go barging there unannounced looking for great reveals.

"Right," Yultes said, "I will keep you informed as needed."

His voice had fallen into a whisper so low the harp's gentle chords almost buried it. Regrets, maybe? Either way, Branwen didn't want to linger and analyze her uncle's strange moods. She tugged at her disguise, smoothing it back into perfect position, and slipped out before any of them could change their minds.

Chapter Sixteen

RANWEN pushed the door to Varden's brand new quarters without knocking, a bottle of red wine under her armpits, two glasses in one hand and Varden's gift in the other. She had scoured the Brasten Tower for cute fabric to wrap the latter, hoping to at least offer him the pleasure of a surprise. The wine was for her; even if he didn't want to drink, she certainly did.

Varden's room contained a minimal amount of furniture: one small desk, a pale baldaquin bed, and a large rug of bright orange and dark red patterns that seemed destined for Varden. Had the servants who set up the place known who would occupy it? That'd also explain the dozens of candles littered across the desk, windowsill, and floor—none of which had been present in her own room. Only the window ones cast any light, and Varden himself stood near them, clenching the railing that lined the walls. Branwen was pleasantly surprised to find him on his feet despite the hour.

"How are you feeling?" she asked.

Varden startled at her question, and the candles flared up, calming down only as he turned and offered a strained smile.

"I'm …" He shrugged in lieu of finishing his sentence. "Vellien imbued me with a surge of energy today, so that I could walk and exercise my stiff muscles. I try to enjoy it while I can. It's easy to see why Nevian always insisted on it. I feel more alive than I have since the Long Night Watch. Only in body, though." He sighed and returned his attention to the window. "Being here—being free—it's still so surreal. I wish I could appreciate it more."

Her heart clenched at the wistfulness of his voice, coating his words in a subtle distance which might never vanish. She forced herself to keep smiling, burying her sadness and anger. She wanted to be good company, not to remind him they hadn't finished this fight yet. Branwen moved into the room, setting her gift package on the desk before retrieving her bottle of wine and clinking the glasses.

"Let's focus on enjoying tonight while you're up to it." With Garith, she'd have forced the cheerfulness. That was how they dealt with horrible days: they smiled and jested about it. Varden had never shied from his feelings with her, though. He'd prefer honesty. "Just a calm celebration of your temporary home—which, I might add, has been tailored to your tastes way more than mine."

She pointed at the candles and the rug, lifting her eyebrows. He laughed, and with a snap of his fingers, the remaining candles flared to life, spreading flickering light across the area.

"This room, you mean?" Varden asked, and the amusement in his tone warmed her more than the new flames. "I think I have Arathiel to thank for the décor. I distinctly recall mentioning I missed having a fireplace or some manner of flames nearby, and that the dark blue of Cal's bedroom weighed on me. I'm surprised he remembered and followed up on it."

"Gotta admit, I'm not." Branwen snatched a bottle opener from the fold in her dress normally reserved for lockpicks and set to work on the wine. "That's what Hasryan said about him. He listens more than he talks, but his kindness shows when you don't expect it. He was like that with Uncle Diel, too, the night we saved you. Asked after Jaeger before any of us could. It's easy to see how he cares about people, and he has been caring *a lot* about you."

The bottle popped as she pulled the cork out, gloriously punctuating her unsubtle insinuation. It drew a second laugh out of him—personal victories she intended to count. Branwen leaned the bottle towards him, and he snatched one of the glasses. "All right, I see where this is going. You're bribing me for crunchy details."

"Oh, because there are crunchy details?"

"Not yet."

Her own laughter—a quick and honest burst—took her by surprise. Varden's eyes were shining, and part of Branwen wished she could freeze this moment in time: nothing but her easy teasing, and Varden's candid admittance that he was interested. She filled his glass.

"Now that's what I like to hear." She served her own glass then placed the cork back on the bottle. "First, however, I got you a gift."

Branwen lifted the wrapped package and extended it proudly to Varden. She had gone hunting with Cal. He'd brought her to a tiny shop with shelf upon shelf of pure chaos, miscellaneous objects thrown about with the barest semblance of order. The redhead owner had emerged from behind a section of different types of bags and started talking. He had started, and stopped only for breathing. Cal somehow managed to guide the conversation nonetheless—a skill Branwen suspected he'd honed through the years—and before long they had found the general area for art supplies.

It wasn't the sleek highbrow selection she had envisioned. Sketchbooks had their corners folded, scratch marks on top of them, or the leftovers of ripped pages within, while the fusains' various lengths attested to their previous use. A professional might have been baffled, but Branwen had had no idea what the best should be, and she loved these second-hand supplies. Varden had learned with charcoal from fireplaces, anyway, so he'd probably think these simply already had more life to them. She'd assembled a basic kit and picked two sketchbooks while Cal chatted with his shopkeeper friend. They'd insisted to drop by the religious trinkets section, and as Cal pondered over which statuette to add to his considerable collection, she'd found the perfect box to store her gift.

Engravings of Keroth's different depictions had been carved into the small case's top. Branwen recognized the Myrian's thin white man from her time in Varden's quarters, but also the portly black woman, more widespread around the world. Three others completed the array: a masculine elf with low monolids and a Tuenese outfit, an androgynous halfling, and a third being that seemed more flame than person. Branwen had never seen any of the last three, though the way fire linked them proved They represented the Flame Master. The heavy lines in the artwork reminded Branwen of some of Varden's sketches, and she hoped he would enjoy them.

Doubts rushed in as she watched him unwrap the gift, hundreds of irrational questions trying to convince her he would hate the art on top, hate the case, hate the gift and the very idea behind it. She fidgeted with the end of her sleeve, preparing apologies and excuses—all of which flew out the window at Varden's delighted gasp. His eyes widened and he ran his fingers over the art, whispering "That's ..." without ever completing his thought. He glanced at Branwen, lifted the case to stare at the two sketchbooks under, then looked right back at her.

"I know what's in the little box, don't I?"

"Do you?" she replied with a grin, and he laughed before sliding the top off. "It's not retrieved directly from the fire, but you'll manage."

Varden didn't answer. He picked up each stick one by one, handling them with reverent awe, as if they'd been blessed by Keroth Themself. Branwen sipped her wine while he examined his material, his smile never faltering, and flipped a sketchbook open to test them out. He traced a few quick lines, rolled the fusains between his fingers for a thoughtful moment, then launched into a full-blown drawing. Varden's hands moved fast over the paper, thick black lines appearing in rapid succession before he spread them, and Branwen stared with utter fascination as her likeness emerged in a manner of minutes, sitting at the desk with her glass of wine. She was unmistakable from the thickness of her arms, the almost barrel shape of her body, and the way she slouched, rarely holding herself straight, in addition to the quick lines suggesting the thin flowing dress she wore. It had taken only a moment, after which Varden leaned back with a happy sigh, but she felt like she had watched magic.

"Wow."

"Thank you. That was … I had missed it more than I realized. It's perfect."

He ran his blackened fingers over the sketch, smearing it intentionally in places, then stored the fusains back in their box and set the gift aside. Peacefulness settled across his traits, and Branwen was glad she'd had this idea, that she could at least contribute to his recovery this way. She had let him down, abandoning him for ten days in Avenazar's clutches, but she wouldn't fail again. She'd make the best of their brief time together to help him now.

"I'm glad. There's a fire in the floor's common room if you feel like drawing those, too. And if you need to talk instead …"

He met her gaze, and she could sense him weighing the option before he shook his head. "I want to move forward. Talking about what he did … I think it will only bring back the pain. He failed to erase me, and that is what matters. I am here, living, and he'll never get me again. In the meantime, I try to distract my mind."

Uncle Diel had told her about his confrontation with Varden, and although his tone stayed pleasant, she could feel anger and impatience simmering under his words. She couldn't blame him. As much as she missed Garith and worried for him, she doubted Hellion represented an immediate danger. It was just … easier to tackle, more accessible. Branwen didn't know what they could do against the Enclave. In many ways, House Dathirii's takeover remained a distant reality, unlike the raw power she'd witnessed Avenazar wield. She had stood in a temple as his magic reduced it to ruins, debris smashing against the meagre shield, and she'd never forget it.

"We absolutely don't have to talk about Myrians or politics tonight," she declared. "Let's stretch on the bed while you explain to me why you haven't been flirting with Arathiel more intensely."

Varden almost choked in surprise, but he swiped his glass of wine off the windowsill and obeyed. Soon enough, Branwen had her back against the wall while he sat cross-legged on the mattress, leaning against one of the baldaquin's buttresses. He'd brought the sketchbooks with him and played with the fusains, and she had no doubt he'd draw again before the night was over. When his silence lengthened, she decided to spark the conversation back to life with a small "so?"

Varden rolled his eyes at her insistence but gave in. "I'm not flirting because it feels wrong. I should be cooling my heels and recovering, not jumping at the first interesting prospect. It's tempting, but …"

Branwen bit back her urge to tell him he should absolutely jump at the first interesting man, if only because she happened to trust said person. She'd spent a lot of time since the enclave's expedition either touching base with her spy network, countering Lord

Allastam's rumours, or working with Lord Oloan—hours she couldn't stay with Varden. Arathiel's steadfast care for Varden had assuaged her guilt. Whenever she returned to Cal's to find the priest fast asleep, she'd turned to him for the latest news.

"Ask yourself what makes it wrong, then. Kissing and cuddling and late-night pillow talks with someone you love won't wash away your problems—it sure never did mine, anyway—but sometimes it can help. Usually, it's not the action itself that is wrong, it's the reasons behind them. So *why* would it be wrong?"

Varden set his fusain down and lifted his head to stare at her in a deliberate movement. Although he tried to keep his expression neutral, the hint of a smile curved his lips.

"You, my friend, haven't drank enough to dispense such wisdom." Branwen snorted and downed part of her glass in answer. He smiled but didn't drink his wine, still pondering her words. "Do you realize how mind-boggling it is, that I now live in a world where I could walk up to Arathiel and simply flirt? Just tell him he has a gorgeous voice, or the most precious laugh, and that I will never forget that moment in the temple's brazier, his hands digging into my arms as he clung to me, terrified and awed? Tell him I would very much like a kiss, or more, and the worst I'd expect to happen is a no? It's exhilarating, and that scares me."

Branwen hoped it was a good kind of scary, that he would have the chance to fully enjoy this change. Before she could answer, however, urgent knocks resonated through the corridor outside, echoing either from Arathiel's room or hers. She frowned. Of *course* something would interrupt her night with Varden. Her irritation vanished as her uncle's voice reached them, coated in worry.

"Arathiel? I think I need you."

Branwen and Varden left the bed without a word. Arathiel had returned to Cal's, hoping to see Hasryan, and he was unlikely to be back. As they moved towards the exit, Branwen caught Varden's arm.

"Are you sure you're up to this? Vellien's energy won't last forever."

He hesitated, then shrugged. "I'll risk it. Something is happening and I don't want to miss it."

Branwen didn't argue; she would have done the same if the roles had been reversed. Her palms sweaty, Branwen pushed the door and peeked her head out.

⌘

DIEL Dathirii had avoided the bed for a long time, knowing how little comfort the soft blankets and fluffy pillows would bring him. Every time he gave in to exhaustion and attempted to sleep, he wound up on his back, his hand sliding over the second, empty half of the bed. Diel missed the warmth against his back, the arms around him, or Jaeger's gentle breath on his neck. He needed them back, needed Jaeger to anchor him and stop the endless spinning of his mind.

His conversation with Varden still haunted him. Avenazar was not a threat they could ignore, but he couldn't focus on it, in a very real and physical sense. His thoughts always drifted back to the

Dathirii that should be by his side. It was so hard to function without Jaeger and Kellian and Garith, even with members of House Brasten to fill the roles, and it felt far easier to fight Hellion and Lord Allastam than Master Avenazar, for whom the only solution seemed one he could not stomach. Hasryan had offered to sneak back into the enclave and kill him, but Diel couldn't bring himself to ask that of him. Even after having his home ripped out of his hands, even after being shipped like merchandise, he could not cross that line.

Diel squeezed his eyes shut, telling himself they were moving forward, exerting pressure on Hellion and rebuilding his family, that it was only a matter of time before they ruptured the Myrian-Allastam alliance, too. Telling himself it was fast enough, that no one would die because of his hesitation.

He wished he could believe it.

Sharp knocks at the window startled him.

No bridge passed under it, offering space for someone to stand and rap on the glass—not unless one counted the stairs about five floors lower. He sat up, squinting in the dim light, trying to make out a shape against the stars. Were those wings? His heart hammering, Diel fumbled to light the candle near his bed and get a better view. The bird looked like a small swift, its plumage a pale beige instead of the darker colours Diel would have expected. He frowned. Didn't swifts fly south when winter came?

Diel stared at the bird, and it stared back. Long seconds trickled by, and the absurdity of the situation increased with time. He didn't want to open his window. Why would this strange bird knock at it at all, then wait for him to let it in? And it was waiting, obviously so, unblinking eyes set on Diel, never rustling its feathers. At most, it occasionally hopped from one leg to the other as if trying to keep itself warm. Diel licked his lips and slid out of bed. He needed to know what this was about, but he wouldn't make the mistake of opening the window alone.

As soon as Diel headed towards the door, the bird started knocking, hitting the glass with its beak harder with every step Diel took. Disturbed, Diel motioned for it to wait. It stopped instantly, flapping its wings as if to say 'hurry'.

Diel's dread only increased and he sped into the corridor, past Varden's door and to Arathiel's, wishing he could reach Kellian instead. Arathiel would make a fine bodyguard, but he wasn't *his* bodyguard, and Diel hated that they hadn't found his cousin yet. He knocked hard, letting his fear shine through the strength of his hammering, even calling for him, but never received an answer. Instead, Varden's door opened, and both the priest and Branwen leaned out, concern etched into their faces.

"What's going on, Uncle? Arathiel isn't here."

"A suspicious bird is knocking at my window."

It sounded ridiculous, but before he could give any details, Varden asked "More like a hawk, or a swift?"

Icy fear spread through Diel at the precision of his question, and he stuttered before answering. "A swift. It's definitely a swift, and it behaves like a person."

"That's because it is one." Varden clasped his hands in front of him, and Diel had the distinct impression he wanted to stop them from shaking. "Master Jilssan is not a fan of shape-shifting transmutations, but she has mastered them regardless. The swift was her favoured bird while training with Isra."

"We could leave her to freeze," Branwen suggested. "It'd serve her right."

"Perhaps, but she must be here with a good reason." Diel cast one last look at Arathiel's door, wishing he had a proper fighter by his side, then started back towards his room. "Let's see what she wants."

The swift—Master Jilssan—hadn't moved from its spot. It flapped its wings and hopped as they re-entered and spread out. Tiny flames licked Varden's skin and he glared at the window, his hostility palpable. Branwen stayed close to him, tense and silent. For a moment, all three of them waited. The bird pecked at the thick glass, clearly irritated at the delays, and Diel finally gave in to its desire and flung the windows open.

Cold wind blasted in as the bird flew inside, and Diel hurriedly slammed the window shut as soon as he could. He was putting the latch back on when the swift's shape distorted midair: its claws extended towards the ground, its wings grew into arms, and the beige plumage became pale skin and blonde hair. In a matter of seconds, Master Jilssan stood in the middle of his bedroom. She shuddered and rubbed her arms with force, trying to warm herself.

"I will never get used to the utter ridiculousness of winters around here," she declared, before throwing her hair back and smoothing her skirt. "Many thanks for not letting me freeze to death."

"I can help with the cold," Varden said, and the flames near his hands lengthened briefly. No gentleness touched his voice as he offered.

Jilssan laughed, so relaxed you'd think she hadn't flown into a room with three supposed enemies. "Why do I hear a threat in there, Varden? I'll pass."

"Suit yourself." The flames vanished, but he did not smile back. "Why are you here?"

And wasn't that the essential question? Jilssan had mocked him for losing to Avenazar and Allastam, only to warn Branwen and her team he'd been captured a few seconds later. She might lead the Myrian Enclave while Avenazar recovered, but Diel doubted she'd come to ruin them. Judging from Varden's tone, however, he did not trust her. She stared back at him, straightening and holding his gaze without flinching.

"I need Master Avenazar dead, and so do you." In the heavy silence that followed her words, Jilssan set her hands on her hips and focused her attention on Branwen and Varden. "I don't think any explanation about Isra's presence in the temple during the ritual will satisfy him. No one except terrified healers and me talk to him at the moment, so he has yet to learn of it, but when he does, he will go after her. Sooner or later, he will discover we helped you. We all know how he deals with traitors."

Her eyes lingered on Varden—a perfect example of her words. He stiffened. "Traitor? How does one betray a side they never belonged to? But you did. You're his right hand and have been for two years. You've never defied an order from him."

Jilssan snorted. "I've never been caught doing so, you mean. It's not the same. Circumstances demand that this be more overt than usual, and I will need allies if I'm to succeed. Hence my presence here tonight."

"Allies," Varden repeated, letting every bit of doubt drip from his tone.

Branwen set a hand on his forearm. "She did warn us we should save Uncle Diel."

Varden's eyes never left Jilssan. "It's her price I worry about. Nothing is ever free with her."

"Now you wound me. I healed you free of charge, didn't I?" Her voice hovered between seriousness and a teasing tone, and Diel couldn't tell if she was playing them thoroughly, or if the layer of amusement covered real hurt. Perhaps that was her goal: she let just enough sincerity shine through to instil doubt while never fully revealing her truth. "All I want is for our stories to match. You won't even need to kill Avenazar yourself! After a week without an assassin showing up on our grounds, I concluded I couldn't count on that."

Everyone's gaze simultaneously slid to Diel. He lifted his chin in defiance. "There are other ways."

"Perhaps, but I'm not risking them. Since I figured you wouldn't go through the necessary steps to see Master Avenazar dead, I decided to rely on another noble who has more power and has already demonstrated he'd have rivals killed over minor slight."

Branwen whistled. "That's why Myrians attacked Drake Allastam. You sent them!"

"Even better: Master Avenazar ordered me to."

Jilssan squared her shoulders, obviously proud of her work. Diel pinched the bridge of his nose, trying to put together all the political pieces here. The Myrian Enclave fighting with Lord Allastam was good news, but something about it bothered him. Why would Avenazar give such an order?

"You said you wanted our stories to match," he started, Jilssan's purpose growing more defined, "and this is the kind of actions you've established we should expect Master Avenazar to take with regards to traitors. So … What lie did you tell Master Avenazar? It's a lie I will hate, isn't it? You need to make sure I won't outright deny it and blow your cover."

"Excellent, yes!" She snapped her fingers, and Diel almost strode forward to grab her hand and wipe that proud smile off her face. She was playing with their lives with a nonchalance he could barely endure. "It'd seem you're not as naive as they pretend. Master Avenazar is now convinced you conspired with Allastam to sneak an elite team into his enclave to rescue Varden. He believes the little caravan meant to bring you instead carried Lady Branwen Dathirii and her friends."

"That won't work," Branwen said. "The Myrian guards around Diel will know it's all wrong."

"Those guards can't talk."

Rocks dropped to the bottom of Diel's stomach and he

grabbed the nearby bed support as his legs turned to wool. They had knocked them out, not killed them, but Jilssan must have ensured they would never wake up.

"Lady Brasten already knows the truth," he says, "and your plan makes me an ally of Lord Allastam, preventing me from throwing him out of my home. People will think I never genuinely lost it, that Jaeger is safe. You want me to sacrifice half my family for this lie."

"They're not dead," Jilssan pointed out, "but they will be if you allow Master Avenazar to run unhindered."

Diel ignored her. She was right, but couldn't admit it aloud, not yet, and he had more to say. "If I let this slide—even if I say nothing to support it—Lord Allastam will conclude this is my idea, taking the brunt of his anger off you, and back to me."

"All true, and all part of the plan."

He hated the plan. He wanted to publicly lay out every horrible action Lord Allastam had inflicted upon him and expose the other lord for the scum he was, but with Jilssan's lies, he would need to imply a non-existent allyship and exonerate him from his crimes. He sat down on the mattress, shaking his head at the enormous injustice this would be. All for a plan that would crumble at the first contradictory information.

"This is a messy idea."

"If you have a better one, you're welcome to make suggestions. I don't see how else we'd keep our two gentlemen off our tail."

In the brief silence that followed, Diel realized he had none. His ability to come up with sleek plans had not improved over the last days. Lady Brasten had laid the groundwork for their public declaration as the true House Dathirii, just as Jilssan was doing to fight the Myrian-Allastam alliance, and he couldn't help feeling useless. He wished Jaeger was with him, to give pointed advice or even simply anchor him. A hand settled on his shoulder, and he looked up to find Branwen, serious and determined.

"This is a good opportunity. We can take down Allastam once Avenazar isn't threatening to exterminate every one of us. Lies don't have to be forever." She straightened to glare at Jilssan. "When his turn comes, you won't be able to protect Allastam from us."

She laughed, bitter and dismissive. "I sent killers after his son. Do you really think I care about his future? I care about mine and Isra's, and I'll do whatever I need to in order to keep us safe. Even—" She stopped, and the fissure in her walls she'd almost revealed vanished in a second. Jilssan turned to Varden. "I have a final request, for you more than anyone else. The enclave won't stay safe for Isra. She can't linger there, but … She told me the two of you had talked, while you were in a cell."

Varden's expression had remained closed and hostile through the entire conversation, yet a smile now softened his face. "I remember. I called her obnoxious and it surprisingly didn't drive her away." Varden's shoulders sagged and he shook his head. "I wouldn't let anyone endure Avenazar's wrath, not even you. If she needs protection, we will do our best."

Jilssan slowly nodded, before turning towards Diel. He grimaced.

"Deal, then. I will let your lies slide, and I'll look for ways to make Lord Allastam more inclined to think Avenazar played him, too. This is a dangerous game. I hope you know what you're doing."

"So do I," she said, and although her tone was smooth, her body language betrayed her fears. "I have an audience scheduled with Lord Allastam tomorrow. In the meantime, I should return before my absence is noted." She rubbed her arms, as if to warm them up, then glanced at the window. "You have my thanks for this impromptu imposition on your time, milord."

Jilssan gave them no time to answer. Her form shifted, shrinking back into a swift. Branwen flung the window open and she flew out, vanishing quickly into the night. Diel watched her disappear before collapsing back at the edge of his bed.

"It seems we have unexpected allies," he said.

"Don't count on it to last," Varden retorted, his voice pure ice. "She'll betray us at the first opportunity."

"Then we'll have to hope she causes them more damage than she does us."

Diel wasn't as certain as Varden about her betrayal. Jilssan had essentially saved his life by informing Branwen and her team of his location, and she hadn't directly benefited from it. Regardless, he believed in her desire to protect her apprentice, for which she clearly needed allies against Master Avenazar. As long as that remained true, Diel would trust her to do her part.

Chapter Seventeen

A MOUNTAIN of cookies awaited Hasryan at Sora's home. They were piled on top of one another in a precarious mound, more numerous than he'd expected, and certainly more than he could ever hope to eat. Hasryan had stopped short upon catching sight of them, so stunned that he didn't notice Camilla springing to her feet with the energy of a young lady until she was sweeping him into a tight hug. Blessedly familiar lilac perfume filled his nose as she squeezed him, and Hasryan fought his rising tears. He wrapped Camilla in his arms, releasing a content sigh as he relaxed into her embrace.

"Ah, it is good to hold at least one of you," she whispered.

Her voice was frailer than Hasryan had ever wanted to hear, but it was her words that stunned him. One of them? What them? Who could she be referring to, if not the missing Dathirii, either trapped in their homes or now holed up in the Brasten Tower?

Her family.

Hasryan forced a smirk upon his face and pulled back before the strength of the realization ripped tears out of him. How was he supposed to answer that? He'd known Camilla cared for him—of course she did, she had risked the Dathirii's reputation and personal imprisonment to hide him—but to be so casually included with her family ... The depth of the love dousing him threatened to drown him.

"Not even a hundred evil Myrian wizards could keep me from your delicious cookies," he promised.

She laughed and stepped back, gesturing for him to reach for the plate. Hasryan sauntered over, taking his first good look at Sora's home. A large central area was dominated by a table, with the kitchen's counter to the side, while partitions separated a second room—probably her bedroom. To his right was a wooden cabinet, its doors opened to reveal a small altar consisting of a warrior's statue, the Sapphire Guard's seal, a handful of candles and coins, and a tiny dish currently containing two of Camilla's cookies.

Sora cleared her throat as his gaze lingered. She had come in after him, closing the front door and shutting out the cold. "Here you are," she said. "Nothing outstanding, but I spend almost all my time at the office or in the city."

"Too busy investigating assassins to enjoy your cozy home?" He smirked when she huffed, then turned away from the altar and back towards the table. He snatched a cookie up. "I like it."

It was certainly nicer than his small room in the Crescent Moon Headquarters had been, a dull affair with plain wooden furniture and a hard mattress. Hasryan had always been careful to leave no personal markers in it on the very slim chance that the Sapphire Guard searched the place and that Brune let them. He wondered if it'd been reassigned already or if it'd stayed empty, waiting pointlessly for his return. The former, probably. Brune was not the type to waste resources—not even her most trusted assassin. Hasryan chomped down on the cookie, burying bitter thoughts under the delicious butterscotch reminder of all he'd gained.

"I'm thrilled my living space has earned your approval," Sora countered, her voice dripping with sarcasm but her smile honest. "Lady Camilla, if you would please prepare our tea? Branwen should be here soon."

Camilla smoothed her robes and tucked loose strands of hair into her braid. The small nervous habits drew Hasryan's attention to the subtle signs of disarray in Camilla. Her eyes were dark and sunken, tiny drops of blood marked her fingertips, where she'd pulled the skins near the nail, and the wrinkles around her thin lips seemed to have multiplied. Rest and relief would smooth them away, he was almost certain, but it was unsettling to see the ever-solid elven lady in this state. She smiled at Sora and instantly shed decades—or centuries, perhaps, for her—of ages.

"With great pleasure," she said. "It's the least I can do for all your efforts." She hummed as she headed to the small counter opposite the altar's wall. Camilla picked through delicate jars of tea, explaining each option. "While I would normally recommend this green jyoku to complement the cookies' sweetness, it doesn't seem appropriate this early in the morning. Not to mention Branwen will prefer something stronger, spicier." By now she was mostly muttering to herself. Hasryan and Sora exchanged a knowing look; even alone, Camilla voiced her tea opinions aloud, as if asking the gods for approval.

Three loud knocks interrupted the decision-making process, but before Sora could get the door, Branwen strode in. She'd chosen a wide floral skirt despite the weather, and it flared out from her coat, partly covering the tights under keeping her legs warm. When she pushed down the fur-lined hood concealing her ears, Hasryan realized the entire ensemble was a single piece—skirt became classy coat which then returned to a heavily textured hood to protect from the cold. He shook his head, both amused and impressed by Branwen's wardrobe decisions. He would stick to black wool and touches of red, thank you, but she managed to look striking in that strange outfit.

"Here I am! Your most special guest has arrived!"

"Yes, you're special all right," Hasryan replied with a hint of mockery while Sora's eyebrows shot up.

Neither of them had time for more. Camilla abandoned her all-important tea selection and strode towards Branwen. The young Dathirii's gaze lit up and she exclaimed, "Aunt Camilla!" as she quickly dropped her bags to the floor and met her aunt halfway, sweeping her up and spinning the much older and taller elf in a short circle. Their respective skirts briefly mingled and then Camilla was back on solid ground, flushed and grinning.

"It is good to see your enthusiasm untouched by recent events, dear," she said.

"And let pretentious buffoons get to me? You've taught me better." She set her hands on her hips, and there was something undeniably attractive to her confidence. "But really, Aunt Camilla, I thought you were past the age of concealing handsome young men in your quarters! Give the new generation a chance; we can't compete with you."

Camilla and Branwen burst out laughing, and even Sora snorted, unable to quite hide her amusement. All three women looked his way and Hasryan grew hot and somewhat mortified. He ran a hand through his thick white hair, scrambling for a comeback, unused to being the subject of that particular type of teasing. Camilla must have taken pity on him, as she let her laughter die down and clasped Branwen's shoulder gently. "I'm sure you don't need any help catching the eyes of others."

Hasryan cleared his throat as loudly as he could and searched for another topic, desperate to move the conversation away. His gaze landed on the heavy bag Branwen had carried with her. Why would she bring that much stuff with her? "What's in the bags?" he asked. "Did they send you out shopping instead of spying?"

"You make it sound like the shopping is less interesting and important than the spying." Branwen snapped her sack up and caught his eyes. "Appearances count for too much in this city for us to neglect them. And no, they didn't send me out shopping—you did. I have a gift!"

Camilla returned to the array of tea options as Branwen rummaged through her large bag, eventually coming out with a thick package wrapped in coarse and dark fabric, tied together by a blood-coloured string. At first he was extremely confused. He didn't need Branwen to buy anything for him, so what could she possibly have brought today? She extended the bundle to him, a fierce glint in her eyes. Hasryan picked it up, throwing Sora and Camilla a glance, hoping either of their expressions would reveal something. They seemed every bit as intrigued and confused as he was.

Slowly, almost afraid to know, Hasryan opened Branwen's gift. He couldn't quite keep his fingers from shaking as he tried to undo the knot. Not even Cal and Larryn wrapped their gifts, and the last time had been Brune's special dagger, the magical and electrified weapon Larryn had returned to him a few days ago and which she had used to trap him. Fear tugged at his belly. Branwen wouldn't do that, yet it was hard to forget the dire consequences of Brune's first present and the deep wound her betrayal had left. Whatever was hidden inside was soft, pliable. The knot still resisted him. Frustrated, Hasryan snatched the dagger at his belt and cut it off. The coarse fabric opened, revealing … red pants?

No.

These weren't pants. They were much shorter, underwear length in fact, and they looked to be a tight fit. When Branwen had gone to the tailor for Arathiel and Diel, she'd inquired if he wanted anything, as if he'd ever get a chance to prance in public with a custom-made doublet. He'd smirked, asking her if she could find bright red underwear to replace the lucky pair his time in prison had ruined, pushing the joke as far as saying Alluma might bless her and let her be the first to see them on him. She'd laughed, and they had left it at that. There were other priorities for their rare coins.

Branwen must have disagreed, or the security provided by House Brasten had washed financial concerns away. Hasryan slowly lifted up one of the pairs, his head hot. Why did she have to give this to him now, of all times? Right in front of Lady Camilla Dathirii, a centuries-old elven lady who had just implied him to be family, and Sora Sharpe, the investigator who'd nearly got him hanged yet had triggered a small, existential crisis over potential romantic attraction? This was torture, and from the smirk on Branwen's lips, she knew exactly what she was doing.

"I sewed them myself," she mentioned. "They should fit. I have a really good eye for measurements."

Way to say she'd been staring at his ass. Hasryan slapped the underwear down to hide it while Camilla's hand hovered above her mouth, as if she could conceal her laughter. Sora scowled pointedly at the table.

"I—hum … thanks." He squeaked out the words, then cleared his throat. "We have tea. And work! So many things to do that are not contemplating this particular gift! Let's get to them, right?"

"Sure, but I'll hold you to that blessing from Alluma." Branwen grinned and her eyes sparkled in a way that made Hasryan even hotter. He swallowed hard, fighting his fast-drying throat, but forced himself to keep staring. They'd been playing this game of unbalancing each other since the start, and he wouldn't give her the satisfaction of learning how deeply unprepared she'd caught him. Laughing, she swept past him and collapsed into one of the chairs around the table. Sora followed suit, albeit in much more controlled movements.

"Based on my conversations with everyone here, I have concluded Kellian was last seen leaving the Sapphire Guard headquarters." Sora picked up one of the cookies and slowly tore a chunk from it. "He disappeared between there and the Dathirii Tower. None of my informants had any idea how."

When had she had time to look into that? She'd returned just yesterday, and she was supposed to head home for rest. Hasryan examined Sora more carefully—between his reunion with Camilla and Branwen's teasing, he hadn't paid her much attention. She held herself buckled forward, her mouth a thin line, and when she ate the chunk of cookie, the movement was stiff, controlled. She was in pain. He'd have to make sure Branwen sent Vellien over.

"Nothing from mine either," Branwen admitted. "Whatever happened was so efficient it didn't even provoke a scuffle."

"If I may ..." Camilla threw her chosen tea—dried black leaves Hasryan couldn't hope to identify—at the bottom of the pot and sighed. Her gaze met Hasryan's and the hint of regret in it twisted his stomach. He wouldn't like whatever followed. "Very few in Isandor could abscond with Kellian without provoking a fight, and one such person had just been spying on us. She spoke with us, and I cannot help but believe she wanted us to know she was up to something."

"Brune."

The name came unbidden, unwelcome, and Hasryan spit it out, his voice cracking as he did. Couldn't she leave them alone? But of course not. That was a naïve thought. Brune was a powerful mercenary leader, with influence reaching deeper into the city than most nobles realized. Diel's conflict with the Myrian Enclave and House Allastam had upset the balance of power and it would be preposterous for her to stand aside. She would nudge events in whichever direction she preferred.

"I'm afraid so," Camilla confirmed.

"She was at Allastam's yesterday," Branwen said. "Walked right in, like—"

Loud clatter interrupted Branwen and they all turned to Camilla. She'd dropped a tea cup on the counter and now snatched it up quickly to examine its state. No one said a word until she set it back down, but every passing second strengthened Hasryan's dread. This time, Camilla didn't look his way.

"When Kellian brought me to the headquarters, Brune ... intercepted us. Only for a chat. She made it quite clear she had always known where to find Hasryan. I'm convinced she could prove it, if she so desired."

Hasryan's throat had gone completely dry. He grabbed the table with both hands, trying to focus on its hardness under his palms as a low throb rose into his mind, like a tidal wave washing out his thoughts. Of course she knew. Nothing escaped Brune, not unless she allowed it to, and why would she lose track of him when so much hinged on his guilt? She hadn't laid a trap for him ten years ahead of time just to let fate and an unexpected friendship save his ass. His throat tightened and he fought a rising nausea. He wasn't safe. He would never be.

A dark shape slung out from the bedroom's door, small and fast. Hasryan sprang to his feet in alarm, shoving his chair to the ground in the process, daggers in hand before the shape leaped upon the table and gave him a better view of the creature. Four soft paws, two large and curious eyes, and long soft grey fur. A cat. He had his daggers pointed at a plump grey cat, which tilted its head to the side as if confused. Hasryan lowered the weapons, careful to avoid everyone's surprised stare, his breath still short and every muscle in his body tense.

Sora pushed herself up and grabbed the feline in the centre, forcing a smile to her lips. "Kirio, you're not supposed to scare my guests! Couldn't you come in purring and looking adorable for once?" She rubbed the top of his head, flattening his ears before striding towards Hasryan, cat in her arms. He stored both weapons back, uncertain of what Sora had in mind, but when she extended Kirio to him, he accepted the gift.

"I promise Kirio has only ever assassinated birds," Sora said. "Though I do suspect him of spying for unknown cat overlords at times."

Hasryan snorted. As he secured his grip on Kirio, the cat rubbed his head under his chin, pushing hard. Message received, Hasryan thought, and he started scratching him behind the ears. The hiss of boiling water filled the uncomfortable silence that followed. Camilla rose to get it and casually continued their conversation. "If Brune decides to tell Allastam we've hidden Hasryan, we lose any goodwill we have left. But I don't think she will."

"Why not?"

Hasryan's voice was still rough. He wanted to believe he hadn't doomed the Dathirii with his very presence, that he wouldn't once again be used as a weapon. Camilla poured hot water into Sora's intricate tea pot, perhaps buying herself time as she considered her words.

"She thanked me." Camilla tapped the surface of the tea pot, her lips a grim line. "I thought at first she was trying to rile me up, and that may still be the case, but if she has known all this time and meant to wield it against us, why wait? What is the point now, when we've already lost our seats and home? No … the idea does not please me, but I believe her thanks were sincere, whatever logic lay behind them."

"It's great blackmail material no matter how you look at it," Sora pointed out.

Branwen huffed, crossed her arms, and threw her chair back, balancing herself on its two hind legs. "How did she pull that off, though? How in Alluma's good name did Brune learn Hasryan was hiding in Camilla's quarters? Because I would love to have that kind of spy network on hand.

"Scrying," Hasryan answered, and although he held no loyalty to Brune anymore, spikes of guilt stabbed him at spilling this information so casually.

"My quarters are shielded against such things," Camilla said, although judging from the way she played with her still-empty teacup, she doubted the efficiency—rightly so. Hasryan had never bothered to learn the details, but he knew Brune had dealings with most of the city's specialists in scrying and protections.

"Pointless against her."

Sora huffed. "They were good enough to keep our best scryers out."

"Oh? And which one of them ever successfully spied on Brune?"

He'd asked to poke fun at their mages' competence, yet as the question flew out, it hit him. Perhaps that was exactly the right one. Hasryan sat down, dazed, still holding Kirio tight. He focused on the thick fur under his fingers, trying to parse through one reeling possibility: what if the one reason no one had managed to scry on him was because Brune had stopped them? What was she playing at? First thanking Camilla, and now this? He had no proof, nothing but a gut feeling, and yet … Perhaps he was deluding himself with hope again, trying to convince his poor soul that he hadn't been thoroughly betrayed. It was better not to think of it. Camilla placed a cup of warm tea before him, drawing him out of his gloom.

"However Brune got her hands on this knowledge is ultimately irrelevant. We can't do anything about it except pray she doesn't tell Lord Allastam, and I believe that had she done such a thing, we would have already paid for it."

"She'd gladly accept Lord Allastam's gold to keep Kellian away from the Dathirii Tower while it was under attack." Hasryan dug his fingers under Kirio's ear and smiled as the cat pushed his head against his hands, purring. He'd rarely been with domestic cats and petted one, but he loved feeling the animal react to his ministrations. It stilled his whirling mind. "Brune isn't the type to let a conflict pass without profiting from it."

"So we can safely assume she took him." Branwen leaned back and downed her tea in one impatient gesture. "She knew where to find him, she has the power to overwhelm him quickly and efficiently, and she's conniving with Lord Allastam."

"I have a question." Hasryan slowed his petting and cringed as Kirio moved on his lap, as if preparing to leave. Perhaps he sensed Hasryan was about to ruin everyone's enthusiasm at their progress and he wanted to be ready to dash out as soon as needed. "What makes you all believe she hasn't executed him and ditched his body in the Reonne?"

Camilla paled at the suggestion and looked away, but Branwen instead jumped to her feet. "He's not dead! That's not how these things work. You don't kill nobles in a trade war and Uncle Kellian would never …"

She trailed off, her voice cracking at the end. Camilla replenished her niece's cup of tea before setting a hand on her shoulder and slowly forcing Branwen back down into her seat. Hasryan waited for them to calm down to push his point.

"You're not nobles, not anymore."

Branwen shot him a flat glare from across the table. "We were when he was kidnapped."

"It doesn't matter." Sora cut in. "We'll assume he's alive because I refuse to stop searching until I have proof of the contrary. If Brune seized him on behalf of Lord Allastam, then he is either secreted away in the Crescent Moon Headquarters, or he's been handed to Lord Allastam. There aren't many channels I can use to properly investigate this."

"I'll take it up," Branwen said. "Talkative cooks, disgruntled soldiers, perceptive maids … there are many in the Allastam's household who would love to gossip about suspicious changes, and I have my contacts."

At least they were getting somewhere. Hasryan wished it hadn't involved Brune and Lord Allastam cooperating. It hit like a whole new betrayal, and he berated himself for such silly thoughts. She'd set him up a decade ahead of time and he needed to stop feeling hurt and start feeling angry. Whatever she was up to, he'd mess with it. Make her regret she'd dumped him so unceremoniously.

"Find him in the Allastam Tower and I'll get him out," Hasryan said. "Find nothing and, well, I know the most protected corners of Brune's empire. It won't be easy, but we can crack that egg when we get there." He didn't think they understood how accurate the egg metaphor might prove, in that case. "Best to start with anything we can dig out from the Allastam Tower. I'll be a one-man rescue team if that's what we need. Me and Kirio."

He brandished the cat, who retorted with a small rumbling sound and decided he'd had enough. He wriggled in Hasryan's grasp, who let him go and laughed as the poor thing darted out of the room. Hasryan rewarded himself with a cookie. Camilla followed the cat's flight before turning back towards him.

"You'd be putting yourself at great risk. After what Kellian has said about you—"

"I'm not doing it for him," he interrupted, his mouth was half-full and the sweet and salty mix of Camilla's delicious cookies at the forefront of his mind.

He would do it for them—for the Dathirii and Sora—just as he'd joined Varden's rescue party for Camilla and Arathiel. For himself, too, as a way to shatter any link with Brune. Whatever game she was playing, thanking Camilla or even perhaps protecting him from prying eyes, he wanted no part of it. Hasryan pushed the cookies down with some tea. "Can't say I'm not looking forward to Kellian's face when he discovers the terrifying dark elf has come to save him. Life can offer you precious memories, if you but reach for them."

Chapter Eighteen

HE extravagant contests the nobles of Isandor participated in had always amused Jilssan. After two years living alongside Master Avenazar's ego, very little impressed her, least of all silly competitions to build the fanciest, tallest spire in the neighbourhood, or their more recent passion for creating the weirdest, most outlandish garden they could imagine.

Still, the blue forest in Lord Allastam's audience chamber had its charm—as far as anything part of a dick measuring contest could be called charming—and Jilssan pointedly took her sweet time exploring it as she strolled down the main alley. She stopped within Lord Allastam's sight, lowering a white branch to study it, revelling in the noble's huff of impatience. Hadn't he wanted to show off? He ought to appreciate the care she put into examining his mages' handiwork, then. A smirk dancing on her lips, Jilssan continued her painstakingly slow progress.

She used the occasion to mentally revise the many words of power she had prepared this morning—strength, speed, stamina—and the other spells she might need in case Lord Allastam saw through her game. He might be a bitter man eager to sate his ego's desire for revenge, like Avenazar, but that did not make him Avenazar. She had not dealt with Lord Allastam as often, and she needed to stay alert. Testing his patience in this innocuous way was a good gauge for his ability to withstand contests of wills—and without surprise, Lord Allastam lost patience before long and closed the distance between them.

"Impressive, isn't it?" he asked, his voice strained under the attempt to remain diplomatic.

"After a fashion." She twirled a blue leaf between her fingers, pensive. "Whoever worked this must have great skills with transmutation magic. I can't help but wonder what else their talent could have been put to, rather than wasted on fancy trees."

The veneer of politeness fell from his expression. Lord Allastam scowled, knuckles whitening as they tightened on his cane. His face had grown so red Jilssan half-expected the colour to taint his greying temples. "Less a waste than you people and the air you breathe." He spun on his heels and stalked back to his throne—an ostentatious and massive chair of pale wood threaded with blue veins, and a source of infinite amusement to Jilssan. The five guards spread behind it, however, doused her desire to roll her eyes. "Your agents tried to murder my son, and you dare traverse my hall as if on pleasant stroll? Are you that eager to discover the dark walls of my cells?"

Tight fear coiled at the bottom of Jilssan's stomach. This had always been dangerous, and she'd known it, yet she'd expected the threats to be less straightforward. Perhaps he was more like Avenazar than she'd thought. At least he'd given her a chance to explain instead of seizing her immediately. He must be trying to understand what had gone wrong.

She let her smile slide and stared back at him hard. "Don't insult me, Lord Allastam." She dropped the blue leaf with disdain and strode forward, mustering as much bluster as she could. "Your ploy to assassinate Master Avenazar almost succeeded, I'll give you that, but you won't win such a game. Isandor isn't half as cutthroat as Myria. I'm not here to explain myself. I'm here to warn you."

Delightful confusion spread across Lord Allastam's face. He must be dying to ask what ploy she was referring to, but pride and experience kept his lips sealed. After fifty years of political games, he'd know better than to ask questions that revealed the depths of his ignorance.

He leaned forward in his seat and hissed out, "I held my end of the bargain. But you? You allowed Diel to escape and gather support, and you dispatched killers after my son?"

"Escape? You never sent him to us." Jilssan's voice rang, ice-cold, and kept walking towards Lord Allastam with a determined glare. In Myria, most men found it unsettling to have women almost charge at them. Allastam turned out to be no exception and he sank deeper into his throne at her approach. "Every Myrian guard assigned to your carriage was killed after it entered our enclave. Witnesses glimpsed your team traversing our grounds to escape shortly after destroying our grand temple to Keroth, but no one ever noticed Diel himself. Did you think we wouldn't understand what had happened? We are not fools, Lord Allastam, and Master Avenazar does not like to be crossed. You're dead the moment he can walk again."

"What even—" Allastam interrupted his sputtering to jump to his feet, perhaps unable to take Jilssan looking down upon him. Once he had an inch on her, he gathered his thoughts and continued. "We shipped him to you, all packaged with manacles. Ask Hellion or Diel's own precious steward—ask anyone present! If you lost him, that is your problem, not ours."

"How convenient. All your witnesses are our enemies and I cannot trust a single one of them." She clacked her tongue and dismissed his words with a wave of her hand. The coolness she displayed was all faked, a front to hide her hyperawareness of the guards nearby, the lack of clear, easily accessible exits, and the tension rising. But Jilssan had trained her body and tongue to remain loose and smooth no matter how dire her predicament. This verbal sparring was far from her first.

"What do you expect, Lord Allastam? An expert team infiltrated our enclave to kill Master Avenazar—that is an undeniable fact. Should I discount my guards' testimonies and instead put my faith in you? You'd have me believe that the incredible timing of this attempt on Avenazar's life has nothing to do with your takeover of House Dathirii and the caravan we received as part of our brief alliance? That it's an unfathomable mystery if Diel vanished between Isandor proper and our walls, one in which you played no role?"

She snorted and placed her hands on her hips, allowing her words to sink in. Their bodies stood a mere foot apart, too close for comfort, but she refused to back down. A thin smile curved Allastam's lips.

"Why, that is no more preposterous than you and your master expecting me to believe an enclave of powerful mages isn't responsible for the scrying protections set on this city's most dangerous assassin. Or did you think I'd never put two and two together? That I wouldn't consider your people's disregard for our laws and love for violent scum?"

Jilssan stared at him hard, trying to remain impassive as her mind scrambled to figure out what Lord Allastam was rambling about. The assassin could only be Hasryan, but why would they waste time on shielding spells? Did Allastam think they'd hidden him? To what end? They had their own resources, as Drake Allastam had learned, and it wouldn't be worth the risk. She laughed. "This is preposterous."

"Is it? I'll have proof of your complicity soon enough." His smugness as he declared that was almost more than Jilssan could bear. She raised her eyebrows, and he took it as a challenge, adding with a sneer, "Isandor has its own scrying specialists, and I have the money to hire them."

She filed the information away, to examine once her position was less precarious. For now, the message was clear. The Myrians' brief alliance with Lord Allastam was already over. Mission accomplished, Jilssan thought, and she couldn't help her smile. If she could make the lord angry enough to forget Diel … "I wish you the best of luck, then. But you should have chosen your true allies more carefully, Lord Allastam. Next time, your son might not survive Avenazar's wrath."

Lord Allastam grabbed the front of her shirt with surprising vivacity, twisting it to secure his hold. Jilssan's heart jumped into her throat and she stepped back, only to find his cane behind her foot, disrupting her balance. She caught Allastam's forearm as she fell, and immediately cursed herself for the reflex.

"You're enjoying yourself too much," he said, and dropped her. Pain shot through her elbow as she cushioned her hard fall on the cobbled floor. "Drake's life is not a piece on your board game, to be lost to your lies."

Guards on each side advanced and drew spiked maces, the nasty-looking weapons killing Jilssan's witty retort before it crossed her lips. She scrambled back on her hands, snapping her words of power for speed and strength. The magic flooding into her muscles steadied her growing fears. She had come prepared for this eventuality and could get out of a fight. As long as she kept her head on her shoulders, and had all the guards accounted for. Jilssan's gazed flicked between them and their lord as Allastam strode after her. When he tried to smack her with his cane, she caught the gold-tipped tool, her movements a blur of speed, and tore it from his grasp. She sprang back to her feet, propping herself up with the cane and twirling it in front of her as the guards closed in on her. Lord Allastam stood within their circle, scowling.

"Don't forget yourself," Jilssan said. "We threw House Dathirii to the ground because they dared to interrupt Avenazar's business and threaten him. What do you think will happen if you attack us?"

"I think you arrogant people will learn not to lie to my face, betray me, then threaten Isandor's most powerful House."

Despite the serious of her predicament, a long, delighted laugh escaped Jilssan. How could she ignore the delicious irony of Lord Allastam, one of the most self-imbued nobles of Isandor, calling her arrogant? She tightened her grip on her newly acquired cane, knowing her chances of finishing this conversation without a fight were as slim as Avenazar's patience. Her fingers traced simple lines on the cane's heft, creating runic pathways through which she could channel her magic. It enveloped the golden tip first, stretching and sharpening it into a curved blade, then it sank into the wood, lengthening it into a longer, more flexible weapon.

Jilssan spun on herself slowly, keeping an eye on all five guards, praying the strength and speed coursing through her body would be enough. She'd hoped Lord Allastam would be too confused or flustered to attack outright, but it seemed it didn't matter whether or not he eventually understood someone had set their alliance up to fail: he would still take out his anger on her right here and now.

"I had been led to believe negotiations in Isandor were carried out peacefully," she said. "Is obedience to these customs only a pretence you maintain as a show of power?"

"Ah, well … I admit 'peaceful' has not been very present in my vocabulary as of late." He clucked his tongue, and Jilssan wondered how many of his teeth she could knock out with one solid blow. "Extortion and violence get me what I want a lot faster. Besides, I need you as insurance no harm will come to my family again."

"Charming." She wouldn't waste her time pleading, not even to point out Master Avenazar wouldn't bat an eye at eliminating her along with the House. With a last twirl of her bladed cane, Jilssan sealed the conversation. "Bring it on, then."

She said it but didn't wait for them to attack. Jilssan dashed towards a first guard, her enhanced speed placing her within range before he could raise his defences, and she smashed the side of the cane against his helmet, bending metal and crushing the skull under. He toppled to the ground like a doll and she spun on her heels, to glare at Lord Allastam. He blanched and backed away, perhaps realizing he'd be dead if she had picked him as the first target.

The other guards shook off their daze and advanced, spiked maces in hand, one of them circling back behind her. They approached from all directions at once, synchronizing so they could attack two at a time without ever getting in each other's way. Jilssan blocked a first strike then dodged a second, spinning on herself without pause to keep their assault at bay. Her cane-spear snapped around with great ease, and she thanked years of training with similar weapons for her ability to stay balanced despite the magically increased speed and strength of her blows.

The Allastam soldiers had clearly practised their dance for as long as she had hers, however, and while Jilssan managed to brush serious threats away, one blow clipped her shoulder and another tore through her left leg. Pain blanched her mind as blood poured out, leaving her panting. She gritted her teeth against it, pushing it back to focus on the fight. Jilssan still had one word of power—endurance—but it wouldn't save her against the multi-pronged assault. The guards had a pattern, though, a two-by-two back and forth they were forced to follow, that guided their movements in a way she could predict. If she used it against them, she might have a chance. Smiling, she bid her time, crouching, blocking, and dodging until they looped back to the familiar sequence.

Anticipating a low sweep from the woman behind her, Jilssan leaped up and spun around. The golden blade at the tip of her cane slashed through her throat, staining itself red, and Jilssan appreciated that she'd least ruined Allastam's fancy cane. She dashed forward, grabbing the dying guard and twisting the body between herself and the three other opponents. Someone's weapon buried into it with a dull thud. Jilssan thanked Keroth for her enhanced reflexes before throwing the corpse at the guards, forcing them to stumble backwards.

In the brief moment of respite, Jilssan cast another short spell and sliced the cane in a horizontal arc. The blood splatters at its tip hissed as they turned into acid and flew into the guards, eating armour and skin. All three of them screamed, though surprise must have played almost as much into the reaction as pain did. Jilssan didn't waste her opportunity: she sprinted towards the rightmost man and smashed his skull with a single blow.

The short burst left her covered in sweat. Speed and strength were powerful but demanding. Jilssan eyed the two remaining guards, her energy waning. Her head throbbed, her legs ached, and footsteps rang across the small forest gardens—more soldiers coming. She needed to get out of this fight and use what power she had left to shapeshift and fly away. The guards circled, wary, waiting. They must have noticed she'd slowed down, the wounds and spells taking their toll. With reinforcements on their way ...

Jilssan had to escape.

She sprang into action, dashing towards the guard closest to the exit. The blade of her staff caught the mace's swipe, then she smashed the guard's knee with the butt end. Jilssan didn't wait for him to hit the ground—his companion came too close behind. She set a foot on his shoulder, shoving him further down and using him as a springboard to leap away, aiming to change form mid-jump. Already, her muscles tightened as magic coursed through, preparing for the brutal shrinking into bird form.

A spike caught in her back as she pushed herself in the air, before her arms could shift into wings, her feet into talons. The metal dug into skin and muscles, striking her lower ribs with unsettling clarity. It ripped through her flesh as her movement continued, burning agony rippling through her back. Jilssan gasped and fell, landing hard, the last of her spells vanishing. Black smears blocked her vision and her mind rang with stunning pain, but she forced herself to scramble forward. Immobility meant death, and instincts drove her. The pebbles under her hands became blue grass. Her sight cleared as she reached the tree line.

Jilssan clawed at the tree and lumbered up, her back burning with every little movement. She turned around, the world spinning, her legs barely supporting her weight. She must have looked pitiful, leaning against a tree with blood running down her back, because Lord Allastam stepped from behind his remaining guards with a smirk.

"Not so smug now, are you?"

Jilssan groaned, her thoughts in a haze. As she fought for the consciousness to offer a witty reply, it occurred to her she might die here, today. She'd come ready for battle but hadn't expected it to happen, let alone for her to lose it. What was the point of Lord Allastam and Master Avenazar attacking each other if she perished and left Isra unprotected? Keeping her safe had been the goal of these machinations. She hoped the girl would have the sense to run before it was too late. At least she knew Diel and

Varden would make good on their promise.

"I might have … miscalculated," she whispered.

But so had he, coming this close, and Jilssan wasn't one to die without having the last word. With a smile, she shoved every sliver of energy into the tree behind her. Spindly branches sprouted all around her, growing at lightning speed. Some encased Jilssan in protective bark, but most flew straight towards the triumphant lord. His guards stepped in, using shields and maces to smash the branches. Yet as darkness closed in around Jilssan, she had the satisfaction of Lord Allastam's cry of rage and pain—his own blue tree cutting through his flesh.

Chapter Nineteen

ISRA stared at the heavy tome on Jilssan's desk, helpless and irritated. What did she hope to accomplish? Theories of magic had never been her strongest suit. Not that anything had been, really. She'd struggled with the logic underlying every rune and incantation then floundered to gather strands of power around her to cast even the simplest spells. It had taken her ages to master shapeshifting into a hawk. Why did she expect to understand Avenazar's incredibly complex spell?

But that's what Jilssan had asked, and Isra was determined to help. She'd first read through Jilssan's notes—scribblings about mental shields and other factors that could enhance one's defence against invasions of the mind—then she'd turned to the lengthy scroll with Avenazar's blocky, almost indecipherable scrawl. That had been a complete failure: apart from the commentary Jilssan had left in the margins to indicate which sections of the runes served what purpose, Isra had no clue what any of it meant. It stayed gibberish to her no matter how long she spent with it. So she'd turned to the massive tomes of research on the desk, and started reading.

Words blurred before her eyes, detailing the history of mind reading, the various types of protection devised through the ages, the process by which one could combine Mind and Body runes to access another person's memories—and here Jilssan had jotted down "Spirit rune?"—and more information than Isra could ever cram into her head. She spent the most time on the book about defences against attacks of the mind, hoping to glean something useful, scribbling her own notes on a separate parchment. Hunger snuck up on her as she studied, tightened her stomach until it became painful, then it vanished too, forgotten like the passage of time. Once, she remembered to drag herself back to her rooms to sleep, or made sure to have a meal. More often than not, she worked through the night, desperate to be helpful in some way, and her brown light hovered above her head, faithfully illuminating the area.

Belatedly, her mind sticky with fatigue, she eventually realized it was no longer necessary.

It must be morning, Isra thought, tearing herself from her current read, The Inner Workings of Divine Magic and Holy Relics. The tome had caught her attention: none of the others discussed divine magic. It'd seemed an odd choice, until she scanned the table of content and noticed a chapter about channelling divine energy into arcane spells. A great brazier had sprung into her mind, waves of heat rolling out of it and warming Keroth's temple. In front of it stood Master Avenazar and High Priest Varden, a throbbing link of magic uniting them. That was totally what Avenazar had been doing! Could they have quenched the fire, then? Would it have been enough to remove the main source of energy, or had it been already too late? But that was only one spell, and Avenazar hadn't needed an external source to assault Nevian. He'd done so with his own, considerable power. Still, if Jilssan had thought it was worth exploring …

Isra had been reading it late through the night, and now a good part of the morning. She stared at the pale sky with bleary eyes, wondering how that had happened again, and if every night had been like this for Nev Nev—a blur of words and theories glimpsed in dead hours, when at last he was alone.

Avenazar's angry voice boomed in the nearby corridor, giving her another terrifying taste of Nevian's life at the enclave.

"Jilssan! I've been waiting forever to know if the runt is dead! Where are you?"

Panic jolted Isra wide awake. She threw the tome on divine magic open, hiding its title and blanketing the parchments with Avenazar's spells on them, almost knocking down her inkwell in the hurry. She caught it just in time, righted it, then jumped to her feet and dismissed her magical light. She managed to spin around just as Master Avenazar flung the door open, slamming it against the wall.

He glared at her, his brow covered in sweat and his wounded wrist held close. Long seconds passed. He said nothing, his lips twitching, his breathing a dangerous whistle. Isra didn't dare move. Could he feel her fear? How terrified she was of his gaze examining every detail of her body, face, and hair—of every difference between her now and the thin blonde girl he'd known?

"Where is she?" he asked.

Isra's tongue remained stuck to the bottom of her mouth, thick and heavy. *Answer!* her mind screamed, but her body refused. No one was there to defend her. Avenazar snarled and closed the distance between them in three short strides, his left hand snatching her right arm. A primal yelp escaped Isra as she tried to scramble back, and her tongue loosened.

"In Isandor! She's in Isandor, m-meeting with Lord Allastam."

Doubts rose in her with every new word. Hadn't that meeting been yesterday? Isra had studied through the night, hadn't she? But then where was Jilssan? Fear once more paralyzed Isra. If Avenazar believed for even one second she had lied to him … Their eyes met for a brief moment—long enough to witness days of restrained anger brimming, waiting to be unleashed. Isra cast her gaze to the ground, shaking and sweating. "I'm sorry, Master Avenazar, she's not here. Whatever I can do to—"

Pain shot through her arm, shutting her down. She gasped as Avenazar released the agonizing magic he'd so often used on Nevian, and sank to her knees.

"Yes, grovel, as you always should have," he said. "You pathetic liar. How many have you deceived? What else have you been hiding, hm?"

Another blast rippled up her arm and tears started down Isra's cheeks. It hurt. It hurt *so much.* She wanted it to stop—needed it to stop. There had to be a way. Something to say, to placate him.

Words she was good with, no? But the pain took them all, searing them away until the only sound she managed was a scream. Avenazar intensified his magic for an agonizing eternity, then paused and yanked her back to her feet. He dug his fingers into her cheeks.

"Shall I find out? Scour your mind for your little secrets?"

Isra sobbed, dread mixing with the throbbing pain. Jilssan and Nevian had both entrusted her with precious information. If he searched her memories … She'd promised Nev Nev to keep his secret. She'd already left him to Avenazar's ire once; she wouldn't do it again. But how? Avenazar's massive presence pressed on all sides, demanding access, and her head ached as if her skull threatened to shatter under his assault. Tears rolled down her cheeks, and she grasped at what little she'd learned as protections—self-awareness, defence spells, blank minds. Perhaps if she thought of nothing but herself, she could do this.

Isra conjured an image of herself—flowing brown hair, thick eyebrows, and a strong nose, with skin a pale, red-tinged brown— on a white background. *Stay calm*, she admonished herself. *Stay calm and hold this.*

It lasted an instant, a flicker in time, present then gone. Avenazar completed his spell, invading her brain, and Isra's self-image shattered under the weight of her fears, of all the secrets she was desperately trying not to think about. She'd been so relieved to find Nev Nev alive. Now she wished it'd never happened. She wasn't good at this, couldn't bear the horrible pressure on her mind, scraping through it eagerly.

And she couldn't keep fragments of her chance encounter with Nevian from resurfacing.

Avenazar snatched them up, forcing Isra to relive it with frightening clarity. The pain receded for a moment as the wizard's energy focused on her memories, and she heard Nevian's words as acutely as she had on the first day. Avenazar's surprise, keenly present within her, turned into anger, then a terrifying, gleeful excitement—a predator presented with a new, particularly juicy prey.

The spell cut short and Avenazar dropped her. She fell to her knees like a ragged doll, nauseated with guilt, pain, and dread. Deflect, Jilssan had advised … and she had, however unwillingly. It'd stopped his attack. For now. Sooner or later, he'd wonder how long she'd hidden Nevian's location from them and return to punish her. But not before he'd taken care of his new target.

"Wonderful! Something to keep busy while I wait for Jilssan!" He cackled, and Isra didn't need to look up to know he was grinning. "I've been feeling better than usual, and there's nothing like a little magic to further push away one's bedridden days!"

Isra heaved wordlessly, trying to find her breath and fight her nausea. Tears rolled down her cheeks as Avenazar strode away, a new skip to his steps, and she flinched as the door slammed behind him. First she'd destroyed Nevian's cover at the enclave, and now she'd sent Avenazar after him. Nev Nev would be lucky to survive.

SCREAMS startled Larryn awake and he sprang to his feet, one hand reaching for his throat. Stone fingers and cold, windy bridges lingered in his mind, the haunting echoes of his fight pursuing him in dreams and wakefulness alike. He was in his kitchens, had been snatching precious minutes of rest against his door, where no one would know. Where maybe he would feel safe enough to forget the burning in his lungs or the blood over his face. No such luck; the screams had followed. Larryn sucked in a deep breath to calm himself and return to the routine of slicing vegetables and preparing dinner, when a second crash shook the Shelter's walls, then more yells and cries. Fear. Anger. A chilling, cackling laugh.

Larryn's heart jolted, his throat tightening. He hadn't imagined it! But who would fight in the Shelter? He'd made it clear early on that troublemakers would get barred, and with Hasryan around to enforce the rule these past years, no one had dared. Was that it? Did they think they could stop collaborating because his friend wasn't there to scare then shitless? Because he'd show them, scrawny as he was. Larryn raced out, his anger rising, a familiar, almost reassuring wave.

It petered out at the green glow emanating from his common room.

Magic, his mind registered, and his stride broke as the full scope of the sounds reached him. Footsteps hurrying out, the front door slamming, chairs crashing as they were overturned by … people running? And again that cackle, gleeful and confident. Someone was trashing the main area, scaring everyone out of his Shelter—an outsider with no fear of being mobbed. Larryn huffed and clenched his fists, burying his growing dread under an indignant scowl before he strode in, all bravado.

His patrons had scattered all over the Shelter's common room, leaving a wide circle open in the centre. Standing in the middle of it was a small man, no more than an inch above five feet, his bald head covered in sweat. He was grinning, cruel elation twisting his face as he wrapped bony fingers on a glowing green rope which had its other end looped around a table. Intricate patterns of golden filigree lined his sleeves—this asshole had more money there than all of the Shelter's patrons combined.

And Larryn knew these designs. Nevian's robes had featured a poorer version the night Cal had brought him to the Shelter, and he'd had them shoved in his face when hands had tightened on his throat, cutting off his air until his world had been reduced to his agonizing lungs. Myrian patterns. Avenazar. Had he come for Nevian, or to avenge the two comrades Larryn had killed? Did it matter? Larryn was dead. Deader than dead, even. So he did the only thing he could, when confronted with such odds: he slammed the door behind him and spat, "Put that down and get the fuck out of my Shelter."

A collective gasp followed his threat. Larryn glanced at his patrons, noticed how many held weapons both real or makeshift and waited, tense. They had been ready to fight, still were, and this knowledge helped the painful knots in his stomach. They would all die together, it seemed.

Avenazar's eyebrows shot up. "So this shithole is yours, hm?"

"Yeah, and I don't serve people who have money coming out of their asses." He stepped forward, wondering how pathetic his bravado looked from the outside. "Go away."

Larryn put every ounce of conviction he could into these last two words. As if he could do something against a wizard who'd wiped out entire chunks of Nevian's memory, whose raw power had razed half of his own enclave. Broken pieces of the first table lay near the fireplace, a testimony to what Avenazar could do, to what awaited Larryn. He didn't stand a chance.

"Wonderful!" Avenazar exclaimed. "I was hoping there'd be some resistance. I am, after all, terribly out of practice."

The table hurtled towards Larryn. With a yelp, he flung himself to the ground, but he couldn't avoid its foot completely. It clipped his arm and chest, slamming the breath out of his lungs and sending him tumbling. Sparks flew before his eyes and he hit the common room's wall, and sprawled on the floor. Larryn hacked and wheezed, desperate for some air. His lungs burned and his vision refused to clear. Avenazar would be upon him in an instant. He tried to get back up and managed to slide a knee under himself despite a solid dizziness.

Dimly, just above the ringing in his ears drowning out everything, he heard battle shouts. Larryn shook his head until his sight returned, blurred by tears. His people had rushed Avenazar, makeshift weapons in hand, hoping to overwhelm him with numbers. Larryn couldn't see the wizard behind his much taller patrons, only the green ropes hovering above. He forced himself to his feet, clenching his teeth against the throb in his chest. He had to help. Together they might stand a chance.

Avenazar's laugh doused Larryn's meagre hope. A force wave burst from the middle of the crowd, sending people flying and smashing against tables and walls, freeing the Myrian. Thick beads of sweat rolled down his forehead and he held his arm close, as if in pain. Good signs, except Avenazar was grinning, a wild light in his eyes. Enjoying himself. Revelling in how he'd scattered everyone, breaking bones and tables, destroying the Shelter—Larryn's Shelter. His only safe space.

Anger coursed Larryn, erasing pain and terror. He'd given this place everything, had carved a space for those who had nothing else, and he wouldn't let others' politics rip it away from him. He stalked forward, snatching the dagger always hidden in his boot, with no plans but the intent to stab. He'd killed before! He could do it again, he had to. Avenazar wouldn't take his home, or Nevian, not without taking his life, too.

A likely outcome.

Their gazes locked, and Avenazar's mouth quirked into a smile. "Adorable."

The green whips flew at Larryn, blurs of emerald power his eyes could barely track. They wrapped around his leg before he could dodge, and Avenazar yanked him off his feet with a laugh. Larryn dangled for one terrifying moment, his skull scraping the floor so many slept on at night, then other patrons rushed forward. Avenazar spun Larryn midair, using him to force everyone backward. Faces flew past his eyes, their expressions of fear and anger melting into one another. The wind cleared Larryn's head for a brief instant, then Avenazar slammed him into the ground.

Larryn's elbow smashed against the floor first and he screamed. Pain exploded up his arm as the bone splintered with an audible crack. Larryn felt the damage spread all the way to his shoulders, a climbing web of excruciating fractures. The world around him dimmed, buried under the agony. There was a rush of air—he was flying again—then he hit solid stones. The fireplace, shattering his back. Larryn moaned, barely aware of others calling his name as he flopped to the ground, his consciousness slipping away, escaping now while it still could. Distantly, he felt a rope tighten against his ankle, felt the floor move under him as he was dragged once more, and heard from far, far away a young, scared voice. Efua, he thought, but darkness took him.

DEMIROMANTIC.

Nevian let the word rest in his mind, prodding at its contour, its meaning, wondering at it and him. He had spent hours reading Cal's book, digging through accounts from people all over the land, trying to make sense of it all and, more importantly, of himself. All his life, he had assumed people exaggerated their stories of love, building flourishes around romance to elevate their relationships, to justify their need for companionship. It had all seemed alien, unfathomable, and irrational. How could anyone get so obsessed with others? Romantic attraction was how, apparently, and now that Vellien had left his side, Nevian understood. His heart fluttered at the thought of seeing them again and memories of their laugh—a charming little snort he'd grown exceedingly fond of—kept distracting him.

Demiromantic.

There were other options, other words he could have picked for himself. Grayromantic or quoiromantic or any of the myriad of experiences contained within this book—so many that Nevian's biggest reproach against its author was a failure to properly define these terms, or ol vague notion of 'romantic attraction'. Ol hadn't wanted to be restrictive, but Nevian liked boxes, liked to know what a word encompassed, what it really meant to him. It looked like he would have to decide that for himself.

Absorbed in his reading and thoughts, Nevian discarded the first distant crash. The Shelter was often noisy, and while it triggered terrible headaches in his early days here, he was mostly healed now and he'd learned to ignore the background chaos of rattling chairs and roaring laughter. He could filter out the usual racket in order to focus on the page before him.

All kinds, but not Avenazar's gleeful cackle.

It thundered through Nevian, freezing his world with its familiar cruelty, with the certainty of the fate it announced.

Avenazar had come for him.

He jumped to his feet, a thick sweat rolling down his forehead and spine. His legs gave out under him immediately, their strength stolen by despair. Why had he ever dared to hope his future would be otherwise? Why waste energy in rebuilding his life, one hour of painstaking study after another, one recovered memory at a time? One new bond at a time, in a community that had saved him, that accepted him. Nevian should have known better.

Avenazar had come for him.

The Shelter's residents were fighting him. Nevian could hear the tables crashing, the shouts and cries of pain from the common room. He gasped at Larryn's challenge, the pure suicidal act of provoking Avenazar. This wouldn't end well for anyone.

Nevian should help, but he couldn't move, couldn't stop his body from shaking or calm the wheezing of his breath. He scraped his nails against the wooden floor, fighting the panic and the rising guilt at his own immobility. Larryn deserved assistance—he'd fed Nevian, had let him stay despite the risks—but Nevian couldn't. He'd need to face Avenazar, to walk back into a nightmare he had barely escaped.

He squeezed his eyes against the nausea. What would even be the point of trying? What could he do, with his pitiful magic? You couldn't fight Avenazar. It was a waste of time, of energy, of life.

Larryn's pained scream echoed down the corridor, a stab into Nevian's stomach. He whimpered and pressed his forehead against the floor, his hands tightening into fists. Tears formed a solid lump in his throat. He should run, make good use of the time bought by this fight. But he couldn't move, couldn't even crawl an inch. All he could do was shake and shake and shake, and wait for his turn. It would come. Of that, at least, he was certain.

Efua's voice, high-pitched from anguish, pierced his panic as she called Larryn's name. Nevian froze and lifted his head. No no no no. She should have run. She had promised to run from the bad man. Did she not understand? She had to, was way too intelligent not to.

She shouldn't be here at all.

What if her turn came before his? What if Avenazar focused his attention on her? Lashed out against her? He'd hurt a child, would destroy her without second thoughts. He'd enjoy it, even, especially if he learned what she meant to Nevian.

Nevian grabbed the nearby chair and pulled himself up. The world spun under him, his head swam, but he held on tight until the worst passed. Efua hadn't run, and neither would he. Sooner or later, Avenazar would find him and take him back. There was no point in fighting it, had never been one. What could he do, except make it come faster and spare the others? It was the only rational thing to do, and he would force himself to do it.

Nauseous, his legs more wool than muscles, Nevian stumbled to his door. He leaned against the wall, sweat rolling down his back, his heart threatening to explode. Every step took forever, yet they all came a little more easily. Nevian focused on the destination. He could hear the front door's peculiar creak, over and over. Maybe the others were fleeing. Maybe they had taken Efua with them.

Her voice burst from the common room, full of tears and defiance. "Let him go! He's my friend!"

So much for that wish. His resolve hardened and he set his sweaty palm around the doorknob.

It was time. He could do this. He had survived it before, hadn't he? Best not to think of everything he was losing, of Cal's insistence to be a part of Nevian's days, of Efua's marvel at every new word learned, of Vellien's delicate presence and how they always checked in with Nevian, for even the smallest permission. He had allowed himself to hope Lord Dathirii would win this war, or that Avenazar wouldn't discover he was alive. How foolish. Life had never been that kind to him. But at least he'd had these brief moments, free and loved. Whether they'd make the future harder or easier, though, Nevian couldn't guess. With a long wheezing breath, he lifted his chin, and stepped inside.

Avenazar stood in the middle of wrecked tables and chairs, holding a limp Larryn midair with green ropes. Efua had run under him, as if to grab Larryn and pull him down, but Avenazar kept him just out of reach, mocking her frantic jumps. His cackles sent waves of panic through Nevian, and his arm hurt, throbbing as if Avenazar had already clutched it.

"I'm here." Nevian's voice crawled on the floor, a whisper desperate to go unheard. He gritted his teeth and repeated himself louder. "I'm here."

"Nevian!"

The fake delight in Avenazar's exclamation turned his legs into stone. Run! He had to run. But his feet were clamped to the ground. He couldn't. It was too late. Why had he walked right back into this nightmare? Countless hours of pain, of mockery, of debasing himself hoping to escape Avenazar's wrath for the day and study through the night awaited him. This horrible future tightened around him, a sea of despair ready to drown him.

Another voice buoyed him, filling his name with fear and respect and love as she spoke it. "Nevian."

Efua came running, and he stopped her with a glare. He was

nauseous, barely holding himself together, and any touch would worsen his state. Not to mention, Avenazar would never let her go if she hugged him. She stared, pain and confusion swirling in her big brown eyes. Nevian steeled his heart and strode past her. She would understand one day.

Nevian stopped next to Avenazar, his gaze firmly on the ground. He knew what to do. First he knelt, allowing Avenazar to look down on him, rather than up. It occurred to him he might die here and now, that Avenazar might simply finish what he'd started on winter's solstice. But he seemed in a good mood. Nevian had to try.

"I'm yours." He should have said more, but nothing else made it past his throat.

Avenazar dropped Larryn, and the body hit the ground with a thump. Nevian cringed but didn't turn, not even when Efua's tiny steps ran to it. If Avenazar thought he cared, they were dead.

"Finally, sensible words! Half the enclave seems to have forgotten what that means. You have no idea how I've missed you, Nevian."

Bony fingers clamped on Nevian's forearm. He whimpered and tried to pull away, the contents of his stomach hurtling up and to the floor long before Avenazar even assaulted him. Nevian had thought he could endure this without a word, that his discipline and willpower would see him through. He'd done it before, no? But his time at the Shelter had changed him, unravelling his defences, and he had no idea if he could rebuild them fast enough to survive. Avenazar's grip tightened and a wide grin spread on his face.

"I'm glad I didn't erase that out of your mind," he said. "Let's go.

I'll have ample time for your friends here once I've cleared this city of its elves."

Nevian managed to wipe his mouth, then the world around shimmered and blinked out, leaving him with nothing but the acrid taste of vomit on his tongue. He never looked back at Efua, yet he felt her eyes trail him all the way to the Myrian Enclave.

CHAPTER TWENTY

CAL had started doubting luck was enough.

Luck hadn't stopped Avenazar from learning Nevian was alive. It had not kept the monstrous wizard away from the Shelter, or spared Larryn from shattering his spine or breaking several ribs. Luck couldn't stall the internal bleeding now, and it didn't teach Cal the skills and finesse he needed to save Larryn. It wasn't enough. Tears had started flowing down Cal's cheeks, and he couldn't stop them. He stared at Larryn, his sobs mixing with Efua's. She'd stayed calm long enough to fetch him, had even managed coherent sentences as she explained what had happened, but the events had caught up to the poor girl.

Cal knelt at Larryn's side, exhausted from his last healing burst. He'd done everything he could, throwing his consciousness into Larryn's body, delineating the wounds before setting to work. But his technique was rough and unpractised, Ren's powers unsuited to curative tasks, and Larryn had multiple bones shattered, all over the place. He couldn't focus on one thing as he had with Hasryan's leg, back at the enclave, and before long he knew he was fighting a losing battle. Larryn needed a real healer.

He stumbled to his feet, wiping his tears then runny nose. His magic was depleted, a state not helped by his anger at Ren for allowing all of this to happen and letting Nevian be taken back to the enclave and the nightmarish life he'd endured far too long. What was the point of even guiding Cal to the kid in the first place? Around him laid the ruins of the Shelter, smashed tables and chairs everywhere, bowls of the morning's oatmeal splashed in strange patterns across the floor, with spoons and wooden cups close by. Most patrons had fled, but a few had sought brooms and set to work, slowly cleaning the disaster. If Xyr guidance was to bring him to the Shelter so shortly after the attack, then it was a cruel sort of luck.

"I'll be back," he told Efua. "Hold on tight. It'll be fine."

He couldn't muster any of his usual optimism. Larryn was dying a little more with every passing second, and Cal didn't know if he could run fast enough to save him. But he tried. He dashed out of the Shelter, his short legs pumping as he climbed stairs after stairs, leaving the dirty bridges of the Lower City behind, entering the too-clean upper layers of the city, where gold and networking could compensate for the shit luck that too often ruined Isandor's poorer inhabitants. His calves screamed from the ascent, his lungs burning despite the cold air, and his tears had returned, refusing to stop. Cal forced himself to keep going until he reached the foot of the tallest tower in Isandor, barely greeted the Brasten staff as he rushed inside, then hiked even higher, to the floor granted as guest rooms to the Dathirii.

The seemingly endless run up and up and up left him dazed, out of breath despite his good shape, his coat drenched in sweat, but he dragged his body to Vellien's door and hammered at it. Larryn needed a true healer, and Vellien … Vellien ought to know what had happened. They would want to be warned of Nevian's capture. No one answered, and Cal smashed his tiny fists harder against the door, the strength rising with his desperation.

Another door cracked open, farther down the round corridor. Cal spun about, wiping his tears in an attempt at dignity. Not that he really cared. One of his friends was dying, and the other in Avenazar's hands—not much better, all things considered. Dignity could wait.

Varden clung to his entrance, concern etched in his expression. Although it was well past noon, he wore his nightgown and seemed half-dazed. "Something happened," he said.

"Larryn's dying," Cal said—which meant nothing to Varden. He sniffled, pausing to gather his scattered thoughts. "Larryn's a friend. He's Arathiel's, too, and Hasryan's, and he owns the Shelter, where Nevian was hiding? And they were all keeping quiet but today Avenazar—" A sob choked Cal before he could explain more.

"Avenazar found them," Varden finished for him, his voice low with concern.

Cal nodded, wiping away the tears threatening to pour down again. "I need help. I wanted—Vellien could have … I'm not a healer, not a good one. I could only stall his bleeding but …"

The sleep clinging to Varden's posture melted away, and his shoulders straightened. "Vellien is supposed to return shortly, but we don't have to wait for them. I'm a healer. Give me a moment to dress."

He vanished into the room with a decisive pace. There had been a strange light in his eyes, an eagerness that cut off any of Cal's protests. Whether or not Varden ought to rest more didn't change how fast Larryn would die without help, and although the Isbari priest was still bone thin and had obviously been sleeping minutes ago, Cal doubted he could have convinced him to stay home.

Varden reappeared holding a winter coat, dressed in a clean doublet that had subtle flame patterns. Cal wondered if Branwen had found these for him—she had mentioned hunting down fashionable clothes for her friend while they'd stayed at Cal's, loudly recalling the amusing white shirt in his wardrobe that'd had fire sewn into it. Without another word, they hurried to the Brasten Tower's entrance where they asked the guards to get messages to Arathiel and Vellien.

Cal wanted to sprint all the way to the Shelter, but they'd only ran down a few flights of stairs before Varden's breath shortened. Exertion flushed his cheeks, and as they progressed, his pants turned into soft wheezes. Cal slowed to a brisk pace, hoping his shorter legs would help Varden stay behind. Another ten minutes later, however, Varden's condition hadn't improved. Cal stopped to check on him, and frowned as he noted his paleness and the sweat on his brow.

"Do you need rest?" Cal asked. "You shouldn't push yourself too hard."

"You said your friend was dying," Varden replied, catching his breath between words. He wiped his forehead then leaned forward, hands on his knees. "I'll rest once he's safe. Answer me this while I recover, though: is Nevian all right?"

Soft brown eyes met Cal's gaze and the tears returned in full force. He shook his head as they spilled down, his panicked mind rejecting words. Not that he'd be able to speak of them. His throat had tightened so much he could barely breathe, as if his body refused this new reality, too. Everything had gone wrong and he hadn't stopped it, couldn't even help with the aftermath. He hated it, hated feeling so powerless. Cal snorted, wiping his nose with cold hands before mumbling an apology. A simple question, and he'd lost his cool entirely. Varden crouched down and squeezed his shoulder.

"Let's take care of your friend first and set your mind at ease. It seems to me like you have enough running through it without worrying about whether or not I can handle the exertion."

He smiled, his expression warm and reassuring, and Cal remembered how Arathiel had done the same, on the winter solstice's night. A squeeze and a smile, the steady comfort washing away Cal's panic. They'd saved Nevian that night, and they could save both him and Larryn now, too. Cal wiped his tears and inhaled deeply. "You're right," he affirmed. "It'll be fine. I'm not powerless. I saved Nevian once, I convinced Arathiel to rescue Hasryan, and I helped to get you out of the enclave. It's not just luck."

"Luck might bring the opportunities your way, but you're the one who takes them. You're the one always ready to lend a hand." Varden straightened up. "I can never thank you enough for risking Avenazar's wrath for my sake. You had no incentive to, and every reason to refuse."

Cal looked up, his eyes wide. Something noble and solemn had slipped into Varden's tone. He didn't seem tired and emaciated anymore, but solid and reliable. A sense that no matter what, they could count on him to do the right thing, to be kind. It was a glimpse into the future, into whom Varden could be, given time away from Avenazar to bloom. Much like Nevian had slowly broken out of his shell during his stay at the Shelter. How much did they all stand to gain, with Avenazar gone? Cal's panic transformed, hardening into determination. It wasn't over yet.

"You're worth it," Cal said. "I'd save you a dozen times over if I had to."

Varden laughed and thanked him, his voice soft but pleased. "It's my turn to help now. Lead me to your friend."

A wide grin split Cal's face, and he stalked off once more with a strange headiness. Something in Varden's presence appeased his nerves and bolstered his confidence, and a strong urge to spend entire days around him washed over Cal. He recognized that feeling, that intense desire to make friends with someone and get to know them in and out. There would be time, Cal promised himself. Time for countless games of cards, late night talks about faith, and the opportunity to discover the exact shape of Varden's wonderfulness, and why he was worth not only of saving, but also of the highest honour: befriending.

VARDEN stared at the Shelter's unhinged door, fighting off ithe wooziness from their long run down to the bottom of Isandor and the stench of the area. His lungs burned, his breaths had turned into short gasps, and the surrounding filth clawed at his throat every time he tried to inhale deeper. Was this where Nevian had lived? The Shelter didn't look like much—flimsy walls squeezed between two towers, concealed in their shadows. Arathiel had spoken with such love of this place, however, and he knew gems could hide in the squalor of poor neighbourhoods. No one was more ingenuous than those with little means, and he'd found many great communities within the Isbari districts of Myrian cities.

Most of the stench vanished as he stepped inside, replaced by the scent of thick, warm oatmeal and … cinnamon? Varden's eyebrows arched; he hadn't expected something this expensive here. He set the thought aside as a girl came running for Cal, wrapping him into a tight hug. The common room had been otherwise deserted by most, with a handful of people carrying broken tables to the side. They all stopped working, their expressions revealing neither hope nor wariness. Varden focused on the young body in the middle of the floor and knelt next to it to examine the wounds.

His hopes that Cal's assessment of Larryn's state was an exaggeration born of panic vanished after a quick survey. True,

Cal had managed to slow the internal bleeding to a crawl, but it had caused major damage already, and it would kill him given enough time. Most of the interior tissues needed healing, including several broken bones. Even this surface assessment drained a lot of energy out of him. He could feel Larryn's entire body throbbing through his magic, a pulsing source of pain he struggled to keep at bay. Varden snatched his hand away and squeezed his eyes against the spinning of the room.

In the back of his mind, he sensed the embers of the night's fire beckoning to him. Varden hesitated. He'd called upon Keroth since his escape from the enclave, but always by relying on his personal strength and warmth. Never through a fire, not since Avenazar had forced him to use the temple's brazier and channel the divine flames into a wretched source of power. His throat tightened at the idea of reaching out once more, and he despised how tarnished this intimate touch with Keroth had become. What if Varden never found peace in it again? But a young man was dying, and Varden wouldn't have the strength to save him on his own. He shoved a burst of magic in the dying embers, igniting them, and even this brief burst felt right.

"Feed the fire," he demanded. "Keep it as big as you can. Burn the tables, if you must."

Varden let his link to the flames intensify as patrons found bits of woods to throw in it, and he studied his patient. Wasn't Larryn the owner of this place? He seemed too young for such responsibilities, barely out of his teenage years, if he was at all.

Compared to Nevian he was scrawny, as if his growth had been stunted, restricting his body to a pack of small wiry muscles instead of long stretched limbs. Pain and fear contorted Larryn's traits—an expression Avenazar too often left behind.

The thought stoked Varden's anger, and he didn't wait for it to abate before reaching for the flames behind him. Fire danced along his fingers, shedding a wavering light across the Shelter, rising in intensity as Varden drew more and more power from the brazier the others fuelled. How many lives would Avenazar destroy before someone stopped him? The wizard just took and took and took, leaving entire communities reeling, ruining even the deepest, most personal parts of those he targeted. Varden let his fury wash over him, refusing to calm the turmoil of emotion and seek serenity in the fire. Inner peace could wait; he had a young man's body to fix, a teenager to save, and a tyrant to destroy. Everyone wanted Varden to rest, but how could he? Every hour he spent recovering allowed Avenazar the same, and today proved they couldn't afford it.

Varden placed his palms on Larryn's chest, and the flames jumped to it with a flash. They surrounded the body, bright and tall, never scorching Larryn's skin or the ground under him. Power coursed through Varden and he spread it to Larryn, forcing bones to fuse together, straightening ribs where they belonged, knitting muscles back, and staunching the irregular bleeding. Larryn's breathing hitched for a moment, his entire body in shock from the brutal healing, then it evened out and deepened. Varden could have stopped there—should have, really, to let nature to calmly recover—but that allowed Avenazar more inflicted pain. He wanted to erase every trace of the attack.

Flames formed a spiralling link between the fire and him as he continued to draw strength from it, channelling Keroth through the intense heat. Sweat beaded on Varden's forehead as he smoothed out the rashes and contusions all over Larryn's body, healing them before they could even scar. Keroth's power rose within Varden, lighting up his mind, fanning his fury, heightening his perception of every wound. So much had been damaged inside Larryn through the years, so many broken bones, especially in his fingers. He could fix it all, and leave Larryn in a better physical shape than Avenazar had found him. Anything to spite the Myrian.

"Varden!" Cal's voice pierced through his heady rush, shattering the bubble he'd ensconced himself within. "I-I think you can stop. He's awake."

Varden was holding Larryn's hand, had even splayed his fingers apart. When had he … Varden dropped it, then the flames still curling around him. Larryn—wide awake, staring at him with obvious fear—snatched his hand back and pressed it against his chest.

"What the—"

A sudden rush of dizziness forced Varden to set his palms on the ground. He anchored himself to the fire behind, trying to make sense of what had just happened. Had he lost control? He'd been healing without pause, without regard for the person receiving his magic. And he had been *so angry*. That wasn't gone, though. Varden could feel it swirling inside of him, embers waiting to be rekindled. Waiting for him to set out after Nevian.

"I'm sorry," he said. "I'm done now."

Before Larryn could answer, the young girl sprinted across the room and threw herself upon him. Larryn hugged her tight, rubbing her back and whispering reassurances. She, however, was in no mind to be calmed. Her words flowed out, interrupted only by sobs. "I thought—you were bleeding and Cal looked—so scared—and I—and he was just f-flinging—and Nevian …"

"Nevian?" Larryn's voice caught as he repeated the name, and swept his gaze across the room, noticing for the first time who was obviously missing. He paled as understanding dawned, clung a little tighter to the girl, and scowled in Varden's direction. "Where's Nevian?"

It was once again the girl one answered. "He glared at me. L-looked at me all angry and-and walked to the bad man." She sniffed loudly then stepped away from Larryn, lifting her head to meet his gaze. Her shoulders squared and her voice, although still small and scared, steadied. "I shouldn't have been here. He'd made me promise to run and I broke my word."

Varden exchanged a glance with Cal, at a loss about what to say. He hadn't even had the chance to talk to Nevian since he'd escaped. Who was this girl? He tried to imagine the stiff teenager hell-bent on his studies spending time with a child, but Nevian would've just told her to leave. Yet it was obvious Nevian had a life here, one beyond books, and he'd hoped to keep it apart from Avenazar.

Larryn pulled Efua back to him, running his hand across her back. "He's not angry at you, Efua. I promise."

"He wanted you to be safe," Cal added, "and you are."

"He was so afraid when he made me promise."

Efua's voice had fallen into a whisper, and this time neither Cal nor Larryn answered. They stared at the floor, and the collective silence felt like mourning. Everyone knew how terrified of Avenazar Nevian had been. Yet he'd apparently walked directly to him to protect these people. His new home. Varden's hands balled into fists, and licks of flames formed around them.

"I'm going. Now. And soon he'll be safe, too."

His resolve was met by Cal's strangled exclamation. "What? How?"

"It's winter. They'll have lit fires to keep warm." He turned toward the Shelter's blazing flames. His head pounded from his burst of healing, yet the sight stirred the angry power still within him. Keroth wanted him to go, too. "I can fire-stride to the enclave from here."

"And then what?" Cal asked. "Face their guards alone? What about Avenazar?"

Varden gritted his teeth. He had no good answer, because

there were none. This was folly, but he couldn't stay here, couldn't abandon Nevian to his fate. "I'll figure it out."

"No!" Cal grabbed his wrist and stomped between the fire and him. Fear shone in his bright blue eyes. "I-I get it, Varden. I want him safe, too. But running here took too much out of you, and that healing … You can barely stand. We need to organize. We can send a team after him, like we did for you."

"You took ten days!"

Ten days of dank cells and torture. Ten days of pain and doubts and Avenazar playing with his mind, raking at Varden's sense of self until only the bare bones were left. His chest ached where Avenazar's link had dug into his skin and cold seeped into his mind, as it had then. Ten days. Ten days and this unholy, twisted spell at the end, threatening to break him at last. Varden clenched his hands, only to realize fire had jumped into his palms, nesting between his fingers, ready to be cast out. A hot wind was rising through the Shelter, and flames spun about him, almost lazily.

"Nevian is a teenager. He's suffered enough. I am not waiting on the pleasure of Lord Dathirii to pull him out of this nightmare. I already asked him, and his tower comes first."

"Of course." Larryn's tone dripped with bitterness, and he pushed himself to his feet. Dizziness caught up to him, forcing him to reach for Efua's lower shoulder and steady himself on her. She held him tight. "Towers and titles first, everybody's lives second. Typical."

A small cough interrupted the conversation from the doorway. Vellien stood against the wall, their face flushed, their breath short. How long had they been there?

"Will you … Will you wait on another Dathirii's pleasure?" they asked, and immediately grew even redder. "I-I came as fast as I could. I want to go, too. I know you can take me."

"I can," Varden confirmed, refraining himself from adding he wouldn't. He had no desire to drag patient, anxious Vellien into the Myrian Enclave, but this wasn't help he could refuse. Vellien's inner strength was undeniable, and Nevian might need a healer. Likely would, in fact. With Vellien's skill, however, Varden could conserve energy for their return trip.

"Then I'm coming too." Larryn wasn't asking, he was imposing himself, and he met Varden's gaze without hesitation. "Y'know, when Arathiel wanted a hand to rescue you, I turned him down. Everybody here counts on me for food and shelter, and I wasn't going to throw all of that away for a stranger. But that everybody, it includes Nevian. That kid saved my ass by walking into the common room, and I'm not gonna abandon him."

"You can barely stand," Varden pointed out.

"Neither can you."

"I draw my strength from Keroth and Their holy flames."

"Well, I draw mine from …" Larryn cast his gaze about, then let out a huff. He held Efua tighter, as if to comfort himself.

"You draw yours from spite," Cal said, "… and friendship. I

can lend you Ren's power, too. Xir luck."

Something passed between them—something Varden couldn't understand but which weighed the air and filled the Shelter even more strongly than the flames whipping about him. Larryn looked like he might refuse, out of guilt or shame or mix of the two, but he eventually nodded.

"Thank you, Cal."

He pulled away from Efua, gingerly walking closer to the halfling. Cal stepped forth with solemnity, then clasped a burned coin in Larryn's hands. "Listen to me, knucklehead. This coin has been with me since the day a prick flamed my parents' shrine and sent us running. It kept me safe through more than I can explain, and I'll want it back. You don't get to lose it, or fling it away in a fit of anger, or die holding it. Understood?"

"Cal …"

Their eyes locked, and after a long, rich silence, Larryn's face hardened. He nodded, wasting no more words in argument. Tiny hands wrapped around the coin, Cal began his blessing.

"Stride without fear and trust the future, for within every moment is threaded the fabric of luck, and Ren rewards the kind, the daring, and the ugly."

Varden's mouth quirked at the peculiar blessing, but any trace of doubts or mockery vanished when Ren's power spread out from the shining coin. It lay thick within the air, a sense of confidence and lightness, the almost careless assurance of those who know their fortunes will always remain good, no matter the odds. Keroth never felt this … light. They were the heavy warmth of a heated house in winter, comforting and steadying in adversity, or the all-encompassing raging flames of an inferno, inescapable and deadly. Ren's power was subtler, but that did not mean lesser.

Vellien perked up too, perhaps contrasting Alluma with the intense presence in the room. Their healing had always been threaded with kindness and wisdom, the knowledge of one who has experienced many lifetimes. The former might belong to Vellien, but not the latter. Varden wondered how that eternal understanding compared to Ren's easy confidence, born out of trust in the future rather than the teachings of the past.

Then it was gone, the intense presence receding completely, or almost. A trace remained, wrapping itself around Larryn, snug against him. Cal released the coin, his gaze lingering on it before he turned his entire body towards Varden, forcefully detaching himself from his holy symbol. Bruises had creased under his eyes.

"Here we go," he said, and his voice sounded strained. Next to him, Larryn was bouncing on his heels, brimming with energy. "Bring him back. I've yet to convince him to play cards with him."

Varden couldn't help his short laugh. "Now that would be the day. If we're not back within a few hours, something has gone wrong. Warn the others. And make sure this fire never dies. The brighter it burns, the easier our return."

Cal nodded, solemn. "You can count on us, sir! Efua and I

will be here waiting for you, stoking it with everything we can."

"Right. Then let's not waste another minute."

Varden threw his consciousness into the swirling flames. He pulled more from the brazier, wrapping them around Larryn and Vellien until they were connected, and he could feel their every breaths as surely as he did his. He let Keroth's power fill him, let Vellien's anxiousness and Larryn's jittery anger become a part of him and the flame, then he brought them into the Great Fire with a single stride. The ruined common room disappeared, leaving behind only bright, blazing heat.

Chapter Twenty-One

THE sharp tug on Nevian's belly vanished as the teleportation spell ended, and he landed in his quarters, toppling piles of books as high as he was. For a brief instant, the smell of old paper and the familiarity of his surroundings reassured Nevian, but Avenazar's fingers still dug in his wrists. The mage scoffed and shoved more of the thick tomes to the ground until they didn't dwarf him, and Nevian cringed at the heavy thump of books crashing to the floor. His concern for their well-being vanished as Avenazar turned to him. His stomach clenched, and he braced for Avenazar's overwhelming presence in his mind as the grip on his forearm tightened.

He knew this pain. He had endured it over and over before, and he could do it again—had to. Nevian might have given *himself* up, but he refused to *give* up. As long as he lived—a short time, perhaps, without Varden to heal him when Avenazar went overboard—he would cling to his goals and to the life he might one day build, away from his master. He just needed to endure. Nothing new there.

Yet when agony blazed through his arm, Nevian experienced Avenazar's assault differently that ever before. Instead of a bloated, unstoppable force, he faced a well-defined presence. Not only could he feel the limits of Avenazar's mind and power, but also his own. He knew the paths in his head now; he had explored them with Vellien, had repaired the damage to his memories with his partner. For a moment, the striking awareness stunned him. It reminded him of Varden's rekhemal, and how he'd become acutely perceptive of his mind and body when he'd first wrapped it around his arm. What would it feel like to wear the artifact now?

Avenazar left him no time for idle wondering, surging forward. Waves of pain washed over Nevian and he withdrew, scrambling out of the way. His mind screamed for him to find a corner and let it go—to hide until it passed, as he always had. But things were different. His weeks in the Shelter had done more than show him a new life, a community to return to. It had granted Nevian a self-awareness he'd never believed possible. He wasn't powerless; he could fight back, even if only a little. He wouldn't stop Avenazar, but perhaps he could redirect the destructive energy. Avenazar had always been easy to bait.

Baiting, however, meant sacrifices. He needed to occupy Avenazar, to let him obliterate at least part of what nestled in his mind. To choose what to lose, and what to keep.

With a sinking feeling, he pulled the strands of spellcasting knowledge forward, presenting first his hours of study at the Shelter, bent over his desk while desperately trying to retrieve what Avenazar had taken. The wizard's terrible glee coursed through Nevian, and as Avenazar focused on Nevian's just-recovered magic, Nevian hurried to shroud the threads of his life connecting to Vellien and Efua, burying them as deep as he could. Every instant drove him to work despite the growing burns of Avenazar's attacks, to bear the brunt of the erosive force as he concealed his affection for Cal, Larryn, and Varden. He left strands here and there, proof that he knew of them in case their absence alarmed Avenazar, then hid the essential parts. He could relearn magic, but he never wanted to forget the warmth everyone had brought to his life.

The task drained him, and soon the well-defined limits between Avenazar's mind and his own blurred. He forfeited, giving in to the agony and tiredness, and the clear paths sunk from his awareness as if in a mire. Nevian slunk away, sluggish, to weather the rest of the assault. Hoping, through the lancing pain, the shredding of his knowledge and self, that what he'd hidden would survive.

Avenazar's crushing presence vanished. It retreated as brutally as it had stormed in, and Nevian found himself on his knees, every muscle in his body clenched, his breath a wheeze. He flopped to the ground as soon as Avenazar released his forearm, utterly drained. His skull buzzed, and he was only dimly aware of Avenazar's heavy panting and his grunt of pain as he lumbered out of the room, leaving him half unconscious without even a word of mockery or warning to close his victorious and destructive return.

Nevian stayed on the floor, eyes squeezed shut, trying to fight the throbbing crowding his head and the darkness rising through him, a slow tidal wave of despair. He was alone again. At least he remembered Vellien and Efua and the others, and Avenazar hadn't found them in his mind. He hadn't looked for long, though, or it hadn't felt like it. He always lost track of time when under Avenazar's assault, but that last burst had seemed too short, especially considering the circumstances. Avenazar should have revelled in it, prolonged the agony until Nevian would die from it, or even beyond that.

Not that he'd complain. Nevian flipped on his back, staring at the ceiling of his room as he recovered. No towers of books hung in the periphery of his vision. He must have thrashed about, and most of the precious tomes had scattered around him, some pages folded or even torn. Nevian frowned, reached for one, and smoothed it out. The texture under his fingers calmed him, and he was still running his hands over the paper when the door cracked open.

A brown head peeked through, thick dishevelled hair framing a girl's unfamiliar face. Or … perhaps not. Something in the way she pressed her lips together, and in her gait as she dashed forward tickled his battered memory.

"Nev Nev!" she exclaimed, and all the guilt in her voice couldn't hide the happiness.

Recognition flashed through him. Hadn't Cal mentioned Isra had used transmutations to conceal her Isbari origins? He could see it, despite her flatter nose and thicker eyebrows, in her expression and body shape as she fell to her knees next to him. Somehow, she felt more approachable now, more relatable—another child forced to lie to survive. Nevian gathered his strength and sat up, one palm on the floor to fight the dizziness. No words left his parched throat, but Isra didn't need him to hold a conversation.

"I'm sorry! He stole from my mind, I promise. I tried to stop him, to keep everything hidden, but it hurt—"

Nevian interrupted her with a raised hand. Of course Avenazar had learned it through her. Who else even knew he was alive at the enclave? Bitterness lodged itself in his stomach and he stared at her, struggling to parse the truth of her words. Had she really tried, or had it been easier to deflect Avenazar's fury? Did it matter?

"I was …"

Happy, he thought, but he couldn't voice it. Not now, as the enormity of what he'd lost hit him in full force. Nevian pulled his legs close, wrapping arms around his bony knees as if hugging himself brought any comfort. Isra reached out, stopping herself before she touched him, perhaps remembering just in time how much he hated it. That was new. She had never cared before.

"I'm sorry," she said again. "Will they … will they come for you, like they did with Varden?"

Nevian didn't dare hope. Saving Varden had cost the Dathirii their home, no? He couldn't command Keroth's wrath, had nothing to offer to House Dathirii. Even if they wanted to, could they afford it now? How long would it take them?

"I will be dead before they get to it," he said. A toy to be played with, one ready to break, with no one around to mend it this time. "Avenazar will be back."

Isra paled. She didn't offer immediate reassurance or bland

statements of hope. Instead, her gaze unfocused and she stared ahead, her expressions shifting with the course of her thoughts. Nevian didn't know how to handle Isra now. Something had changed in her, and it went beyond her appearance.

"Perhaps I can find out what poison Jilssan's been using to keep Avenazar in bed, and away from us."

"What?" Jilssan had been poisoning Avenazar? Risked betraying him in such an obvious, direct fashion? The idea itself languished in his tired mind, too inconceivable to properly acknowledge. Was Isra mocking him? But her smile was weary, too, with none of the usual mischief that announced one of her games.

"She's been away from the enclave long enough for it to stop working," she said, "but with a new dose we can buy ourselves time until she returns."

"Slow down. Start at the beginning."

Jilssan wouldn't poison him without a plan. He doubted he could do anything to help. Avenazar would leave Nevian too exhausted to contribute—if he lived at all—but it gave Nevian something other than despair. He focused on Isra's words as she explained the aftermath of Varden's rescue, how Jilssan had been poisoning Avenazar and playing Lord Allastam against the Myrians. Except she'd been gone for so long now, and her plan was unravelling. Isra's voice had grown more panicked as she progressed, her hands twisting into the folds of her dress.

"And now I'm alone here and Avenazar is recovering, and I'm supposed create protection spells against him but I'm no good with theory, and even Jilssan's notes aren't doing much to guide me, and it's only a matter of time before Avenazar finds out and kills us all."

Nevian's heart stopped—not at the idea of Avenazar's discovery, it was too late for that. But defensive spells? Could he? He'd offered what magical understanding he'd regained as bait for Avenazar, to distract him while he shielded his cherished memories, yet it felt … intact? He tried to recall the basic runes and how Mind, Body and Spirit could interact and grinned as the knowledge flooded back in. Had Avenazar only sought to inflict pain? Or was he still too exhausted from days of poisoning? He *had* left awfully quickly.

"Show me," Nevian demanded.

Because unlike Isra, he'd almost never received assistance to master magic, had taught himself everything from too-complex books, learning to dismantle definitions and theories until he grasped their meaning. More importantly, he had a better understanding of how Avenazar worked than any other, and he'd recently devised a trick to avoid the brunt of an assault, even if only temporarily. His knowledge went beyond the abstract, and the idea that he could help counter Avenazar doused the burning despair that had lodged itself in him since first hearing his master's awful cackling laugh. He could fight back. Not just on a personal level, by preserving the pieces of himself that mattered most while waiting for doom to come, but by crafting this spell, too. He was not powerless.

"Here?" Isra asked.

Nevian shrugged and gestured at his tiny room. "What's more books in all of this mess?" He didn't dare leave and risk that punishment, but if Avenazar found Nevian studying, it would only amuse him. "Go get it, Isra. We don't have a minute to spare. He won't need to recover forever."

She jumped to her feet with a curt nod. "I wish you weren't here, but … I'm glad you're with me. One day I'll make everything up to you."

Nevian doubted that. Isra might try, but he didn't foresee his future lasting long enough for it to happen. And as annoying as Isra had always been—as hard as it was to forget she'd blown his cover and caused him so much pain—he could only hope she would get that chance.

THEY piled up the cluttered books across Nevian's floor in tall towers near the walls and rearranged the reference tomes, notes, and scrolls in the available space. His gaze stopped on each of his tools once more: Avenazar's actual spell, Jilssan's compiled annotations, first *From Emotional Empathy to Mind Control: A Survey of Mind Spells and Their Endless Possibilities*—a thick affair with little practical theory—second, *Into the Greatest Minds: Advanced Mind Spells*—a thin book with minimal fluff and many runes—third, *The Inner Workings of Divine Magic and Holy Relics*—a surprising choice from Jilssan—and finally a handful of others that spanned similar topic, but that Nevian discarded as of lower priority. Isra had re-explained what she'd already learned about the runes used by Avenazar and his exploitation of divine energy, then enumerated the basic defence types against mind spells with pride. She sounded like Efua when the girl sought praise, and it was all he could do not to snort.

"Where are those from?" he asked, voice flat.

"The *Survey* one. They included a chapter on protective measures."

Nevian dragged the heavy book closer to him and flipped through the pages until he found the right part. He couldn't help his smile; Avenazar would return, of course he would, but for now Nevian could dive into deep, pointed studies. A race against Avenazar's dismal health to unravel the most essential elements of mind spells and devise a way to block them. A chance to compare his startling experience earlier and theories of magic. Without another word to Isra, he dug into the work.

Time quickly lost any significance as Nevian absorbed everything he could about mind shields, traps, and various means of protection. He flipped back to previous chapters to better untangle their meaning on several occasions, and Isra often interrupted with questions of her own. She'd picked up the one discussing divine magic, and although the writing style wasn't particularly obtuse, she struggled with it. Her interrogations were so simple, and though it shocked him, he could only conclude she lacked certain basics that underlay most magical theory. A part of him wanted to grit his teeth and ignore it—he'd progress so much faster without her around—yet he thought of her subtle praise-seeking earlier, of the thrill he always felt when Efua finally grasped what he was trying to teach her, of how despite how brilliant the girl was, she needed someone to explain, and he pushed back his irritation at Isra's ignorance.

"Isra. Come here."

He sketched a few runes, starting with the simplest type and growing more complicated. She crawled up to where he lay on the floor and settled next to him, just far enough not to touch him.

"What are those?" he asked.

"Runes. I know runes, Nevian! I'm an apprentice too."

"Judging by your last question, you don't *know* know them. Do you want help, or not? Avenazar has erased this from my mind so often I'm convinced I developed muscle memory relearning it. It'll help you." And it would let him read uninterrupted.

She hesitated, staring at the runes and him in turn, then huffed in frustration. "All right. Try me."

Nevian had spent quite a few hours daydreaming about Efua moving from mundane reading to magic, devising methods to broach the basics without losing her into a sea of knowledge. Isra had a lot more practice under her belt already, so he skipped most of it and focused on the components of any given rune and the ways one could shape them to change a spell. Magic was everywhere, infinite and omnipresent, but one needed tools to grab it. Since she'd been reading through the book on divine magic as a source of power, he pointed the heart of the first rune to her, which determined how one nourished the spell. Most hearts linked to the self, pulling from the mage's energy to cast, but one could also store power in objects, or drain it from the living. He had Isra indicate where the heart was on the other runes he'd drawn, and her smile grew wide as she nailed each of them. Nevian couldn't help smile back.

"You should grasp what you're reading better now."

She sat up, staring at his parchment of drafted runes with renewed interest. After a moment, she turned to him, a mischievous grin in her eyes. "Thanks, Nev Nev. I'll stop bothering you now."

His lips parted for a retort, but denying it would be a lie. She laughed at his non-response, and he opted to focus on work. She was still annoying, joint studying or not.

They returned to their respective books, and Nevian relished the silence, the soft sound of pages being turned, and the occasional scratching of a quill. Isra no longer huffed in frustration every few minutes, and he could concentrate properly. He was blazing through the chapters when he ran into a peculiar note. In the margins of a paragraph, Jilssan had written in an elegant cursive the word 'rekhemal?'. Nevian's stomach twisted as he recalled how he'd use self-knowledge to protect himself from Avenazar, how he'd wondered specifically about the impact Varden's holy bandanna would have. He read the bracketed sentences beside the note with trepidation.

The more keenly aware one is of their mind's inner workings—the more acute and awake they are—the harder it becomes to invade it. As such, mind enhancements are one of the most subtle but best forms of protections against unwelcome intrusions. Unlike shields, they cannot be broken and must be circumvented.

"Isra ..." His voice came out as a croak, his throat dry. Had his hunch been spot on? "Did Jilssan have the rekhemal with her?"

She looked up. "What's that?"

"A holy bandanna used by Keroth's priests during the Long

Night's Watch. Varden must have had one on him when they—It's thick and black, with flames sewn where eyes would be if one ties it around their head."

Isra's eyes widened at his description. "Y-yeah, I saw that on her desk! Why? You think it matters?"

Nevian's pulse quickened. Isra had been reading a treaty on mixing arcane and divine magic, an odd choice Nevian had attributed to attempts to understand Avenazar's dominance spell. And while that might have been part of it … what if Jilssan had wanted to create a combined spell, too? What if she meant to place the rekhemal at the heart of her protection?

"Y-yes." His voice shook, and his hands, and all of his body, the rush of discovery piling upon his exhaustion, scattering his self-control. "It sharpens the mind and—here—" Nevian reread the passage aloud, struggling to stay calm as it echoed through him, a promise of a better future. "I doubt Avenazar's good at circumventing."

"That's brilliant! I'll get it for you." Isra jumped to her feet, brimming with delight. Before Nevian could place another word, she ran out of his quarters, thick hair flying behind her. As excitable as always.

Nevian tried to gather his thoughts as the door closed. The more keenly aware one is of his mind's inner workings … He'd spent so long knitting back memories with Vellien's help, rebuilding himself thread by thread, hour by hour. It'd been hard to ignore how intimate with Vellien the contact with had been, and in the process he'd never noticed how intimate with himself it was, too. Relief, pride, and anger whirled in him, and he steadied himself on the ground until the dizzy rush receded. He could defend himself. He'd done it already, in a fashion. He'd baited Avenazar, but what if he could learn to do even better, to create impossible pathways that couldn't be rammed through? How long could he keep Avenazar running in circles in his mind? What else could he do, once he could combine magic with self-knowledge? Nevian heaved a slow breath out, herding his thoughts back to the work at hand. After all, the opportunity to test out defences would come all too soon.

Chapter Twenty-Two

ISRA skidded to a stop in front of Jilssan's desk, bumping into the chair in her hurry. The sprint from Nevian's room left her breathless, her hair sticking to her forehead and the back of her neck and her legs on fire, yet it all paled compared to her excitement. Nevian was brilliant. He'd needed, what, a handful of hours to figure out where Jilssan had been headed? Perhaps even less. She'd spent days trying to unravel this and all she'd achieved was her brain turning into mush.

Of course, Nevian had known what the rekhemal was. And he'd had a lot of experience with Avenazar's spells, and had probably researched them before. And she'd given him the cliff notes. It made sense for him to be faster, but she couldn't help but be impressed, and a tad jealous. She shoved the feeling aside. Nevian had worked hard for his skills, and he'd been kind enough to stop and explain significant bits to her—Nev Nev, who never gave her anything unless she nagged, and even then, who'd always acted as though she didn't have the intelligence or drive to understand anything. She hadn't expected that and wasn't sure she deserved it. They were working together now, working to fix everything and start on a better footing, and she wouldn't waste her chance. She scanned the top of the desk until she spotted the black bandanna again, thrown into a delicate, open mahogany box with bright flame carvings. Isra snatched it up with a grin, lifting it at eye level to examine it.

The temperature in the room rose, a brutal heat wave that seemed to emerge from behind her. Isra's throat tightened and she spun around, fingers clenching on the rekhemal, half-convinced Keroth Themselves had come to avenge Their priest. The dying flames in Jilssan's fireplace roared to life, and Isra reached for the magic around her to harden and insulate her skin, readying for her inevitable struggle in capturing the currents of power. They stayed firm within her grasp—no twisting and bending out of shape as if growing more slippery as they neared her, no hardship to fuel spells she should know by heart. Instead, a thin sheen of blue effortlessly enveloped her, cutting off the worst of the heat. She didn't get long to marvel at her sudden skills: three figures emerged from the fire, wrapped in flames so bright she had to squint.

She gasped as Varden stepped out. Although his eyes had remained sunken and his skin tight over his bones, he'd regained some weight and seemed taller, healthier. Not hard, considering she'd last seen him falling under Avenazar's spell. His gaze flattened when it settled on her, and Isra knew he'd recognized her. Then he spotted the rekhemal, and the flames around him snapped, a reflection of his anger.

"What are you doing with that?"

"I—Jilssan had it!" She strode forward, directly into his fire, secretly pleased that her spell kept the heat at bay. Ignoring the scowls of Varden's elven companions, she handed him the bandanna. "I-I was fetching it for Nevian. He thinks it can protect him from Avenazar! You're here for him, aren't you?"

"Of course." Varden dropped the constant whirlwind of flames around him and the others.

"Then take it." Isra wriggled the rekhemal until Varden finally reached for it. He held it in his palms, running reverent fingers over the fabric before he pocketed it. She cleared her throat to get his attention back, even though the weight of his gaze unsettled her. "He's in his quarters, working out defensive spells. He … he'll be happy to see you. To get out of here."

"Great," one of Varden's friend said, a wiry man with angry cheekbones and skin almost as dark as hers. "Let's move before this place's massive asshole comes calling."

A shy smile appeared on the other companion's lips, and all three of them started off. Isra breathed more easily. Maybe they could do it. Avenazar had been tired, no? Maybe they could fix her wrongs and take Nevian away. He didn't deserve to be here, even if this afternoon had made her giddy, even if she didn't want to stay behind and face Avenazar alone.

Varden paused at the door, glancing back. "What about you?"

Isra hesitated. She wanted to go. Flee with them, if they'd have her, or run away on her own. But if she vanished, wouldn't Jilssan pay for it the moment she returned? Could she do that to her?

"I–I don't know. I don't even know where Jilssan is."

Varden's brow creased into a deep line. "I'm afraid I can't help you there. But you should leave, Isra. Run while you can."

Then he was off, stalking after his two companions and leaving her to her choices. Her heart hammered in her chest. Flee the enclave. Jilssan had told her to stay safe, no matter what. She should, she really should. She didn't want to just run, though. Not while everyone risked their lives to save Nevian, and not when Avenazar could pursue them and destroy this fleeting escape with a snap of fingers. They could take care of Nevian; she would deal with Avenazar.

THE enclave's fires burned in Varden's mind, countless individual torches only he perceived. Every time they stepped passed an open door, he reached out to the warmth in the fireplaces, dragging it into him, absorbing the power it contained and leaving cold, dry rooms behind. Flames licked his arms, climbing ever higher as they progressed, feeding his determination. He would not leave without Nevian, no matter what.

As his strength grew, he also became increasingly aware of Larryn's, of the subtle sheen covering him that flickered at the edge of his vision. Were all of Cal's blessings this powerful, or only this one? When it first flared, Varden tensed and stopped, waiting for what had provoked it. Something crashed around the corner, metal scraping on the stone floor, then a voice cursed about uneven tiles and hurting knees. With a quick glance between the three of them, they sprang into the closest room.

It was blessedly empty. Unsurprising, perhaps, considering how Cal's powers seemed to act. First they'd found Isra waiting for them, rekhemal in hand, and now this? They waited, their breaths shallow, as whoever had stumbled got back to their feet and strode past their door. Varden's gaze slid to the floor under his feet, its smoothness so remarkable it might have been wrought by magic, and smiled. Ren had tripped that guard as a warning, alerting them to the danger and slowing him down.

They counted a few seconds before slipping back out of the room, and Varden took the lead. Vellien had been muttering under their breath since they'd first left Isra behind. Praying, Varden concluded, and he wondered what precisely the elven teenager was asking of Alluma. Varden kept his flames at the ready in case Ren's luck didn't suffice. With every stride, his stomach clenched harder, fear tightening its grasp over it. It was difficult not to think of when he'd last traversed similar corridors, drawing upon meagre reserves to walk by himself, dragging his feet until they left the building and headed to Keroth's Temple. By the time they neared Nevian's door, the squeezing of his insides had turned into a painful stab, and Varden's only relief from it was in the flames around his body.

He completely missed the second flare of Larryn's aura, and the loud "Varden, wait! Shit!" came in too late. He stepped around the last corner as the echoes of laughter reached his ears, and faced a pair of guards three doors down—at Nevian's open door.

"Can't believe you understood those feverish mumblings right," one was saying. "This old coot crawls out of bed for an hour and this is what he does with it? Wouldn't want—"

"Shut up," his partner interrupted. She was staring straight at Varden, her gaze tracing the agitated flickers of Varden's flames. Her sword slid out of its scabbard as she shoved her companion towards the door. "Get inside. Hold the kid."

Varden never paused. The anger dormant in him flared back to life, stoking the fire surrounding him. As he strode forward, he blasted flames at the ceiling above the woman. "You have one chance to flee."

Her sword wavered, but her gaze did not. Varden met it and smiled. Very well, then. He had a lot to get out of his system.

Three arcs of searing flames burst from him. The first shot streaked down the corridor and hit her sword, turning it scalding hot. She dropped it with a yelp as the second snaked across the ground to wrap itself around her ankle, forcing her to dance back and pushing her off balance. The last was larger, blistering the air as it slammed in her chest. She screamed in pain and fell on her back, sword and armour clanking on the floor as Varden continued his advance. The guard scrambled away, panicked. He could kill her there and then, reducing her body to blackened bones and removing one Myrian minion from this blasted earth. Clean up. A tight ball of fire formed in the crook of his finger.

"Varden?"

Vellien's soft voice slashed through his anger and impulse to hurt, and Varden crushed what was left of it. Not on unknown goons, not when another solution was within easy reach. He threw the fireball to the ground at the woman's feet, shaping its explosion into a thick wall of flames that cut her off. Then he turned to the guard inside.

Tall and broad, he managed to tower over Nevian and was holding him by the scruff of his neck. Disgust at the touch was plastered over Nevian's expression, but the boy didn't wiggle or try to slip out. With an exemplar calm, he met Varden's gaze and said, "I need you to do this without burning the books."

Warmth bubbled through Varden at the request until it escaped in a frank laugh. Of course Nevian wouldn't want to lose the books. But beyond that, his complete trust that Varden could manage it—that Nevian didn't have to choose between his life and his knowledge—sent Varden's mind spinning with a mixture of joy and pressure. Could he do that? The guard clenched his sword harder. He looked like he wanted to pull farther back into the room, but the piles of tomes left him no space to manoeuvre.

"He's not going anywhere," he said. "Reinforcements will arrive."

Varden glanced at his wall of fire, and indeed the guard behind had fled. He should have brought up two of them, but he had no intention of staying long enough for it to matter. All of his stomach-churning fear had vanished, replaced by a heady confidence in his own power. With a dismissive shrug, he said, "Let them come. Do you truly think you'll fare better than your companion?"

"I have him." He gave Nevian a little shake, drawing a stifled moan out of him.

"Leave him alone!" Vellien exclaimed.

They stepped around Varden to see Nevian better, a trembling fury tensing their body. Nevian choked, his eyes widening in fear and yearning. When he managed to tear his gaze away and turn his attention back to Varden, his voice dropped to a whisper. "You're not alone?"

Varden smirked and squared his shoulder. "I am never alone."

He pushed power into the flames dancing around him, cancelling their heat so that nothing would catch fire but letting them rise up, occupying a terrifying space in Nevian's tiny room and crawling threateningly on the ceiling. Larryn moved to the other side of him, across from Vellien, drawing another gasp for Nevian. Neither of his two companions spoke, allowing him to lead, perhaps unsure of how Varden meant to get out of this pinch. Nevian had given him the solution: he wasn't alone, and Keroth's power was far from the only one at his disposal.

"I live and breathe by Keroth's blessing and strength," he intoned, his voice rising in a cadence not unlike a chant. "Today Alluma stands with me, protector of Their people, Their magic flowing in eternal cycles, preserving what matters through the trials of time. I come blessed with Ren's envoy, Xyr fortune invisible glitter showing me the path. And thus, with such guides by my hand, I need not worry about consequences."

He pulled without warning at both Larryn's and Vellien's power. The former gasped and stumbled forward as Varden burned through the aura of pure luck shimmering around him, reabsorbing its strength and shaping it into his flames. The golden glitter spread across the ceiling before falling into the room, covering the books for a few seconds before vanishing from all but a few.

Vellien had more practice wielding divine power and ceded to Varden, lending him their blessing and energy without hesitation. Varden weaved shields out of it, a plea to safekeep all that Ren's luck had touched within while he kept his fire away from allies. He worked quickly, giving himself no time for doubts. Between Ren's guidance and Alluma's protection, he had to trust this would succeed.

Varden set the entire room ablaze with holy flames.

The brazier lived through Varden, and in return, Varden lived through it. Every object, every movement, every crack and change of texture in the room sprang to life, myriads of sensation melding into his mind. A golden-green light settled over several books and parchments, spreading from them to Nevian, enveloping all in its protective magic.

The guard dropped Nevian as fire rushed him, raising his arm to shield himself. It wouldn't save him, but one couldn't fault him for trying. Nevian stumbled forward then dashed blindly through the room towards Vellien, never pausing at the bright flames. An agonized scream followed him as the brazier licked at the guard's skin, searing it. A few split seconds and he would die, burned to the core. Varden raised a hand, commanding the power of his temporary kingdom, and created a cooled vacuum around him.

"Move and perish," he specified.

From the terrified stillness of the man, he believed it. Good for him. Varden turned to Nevian, now by their side.

"I apologize. I did reduce many tomes to ashes. I suspect those mysteriously saved will be enough, however."

Nevian's gangly body was barely visible through the dancing flames around the room, yet the teenager managed to meet his eyes. With utmost serious, Nevian said "I have a diverging opinion of what constitutes 'enough' where knowledge and books are concerned. But I suppose I must accept this compromise now that everything else is ashes."

Varden snorted. "I suppose."

"They're just books, Nevian." Larryn moved into the room to pick up one and gingerly held it out. "You care too much about strings of small characters." Yet he continued gathering all those wrapped in the golden-green glow, obviously capable of seeing it.

"Home?" Varden asked. He could feel his strength slowly wane, with no fire but his own to feed it. The heady rush of power was dwindling, and he wanted to be safe before it left entirely.

"Home," Nevian confirmed, with a fondness Varden had

never heard before.

Smiling, he spun the flames around his companions and the blessed, protected material Larryn had been gathering, then stepped through the flame into the plane that connected all fires.

Chapter Twenty-three

TO THE non-initiated, the space between fires passed in a blur, an instantaneous warmth that wrapped itself around their body and released them on the other side. They could not see what Varden did, never experience the fiery landscape connecting all fires, Keroth's power flowing through the world into a unique tapestry. It blazed around them, flames twisting in a distorted reflection of the world. The enclave's walls rose, a darker, blocky shape, and right behind it danced Isandor's many spires. An arm's length from the wall, at most, the real world distance to it eaten up by flames.

Only the most powerful of Keroth's priests mastered this technique and were blessed with access to this serene, burning plane of existence. Or rather, only a few stepped in without losing their way forever. Acolytes who learned how to flamestride did so with an anchor, a High Priest who tied their spirits together and served as a safety line. By the time Varden had reached sufficient mastery, his only mentor was long gone, however. It hadn't stopped him. He'd read everything he could then stepped into the tiny fire of his chambers and willed himself to the kitchens', where most of the temple's Isbari were. He would chat late into the night with them, devouring whatever they offered to recover from the gruelling fire stride, then returned to his room. He'd burned himself at times, too exhausted to properly protect his spirit. For years, he'd practised on this short, easy distance.

Today's jump was longer, unfamiliar, and he had others to transport to safety.

Varden struggled against the pounding in his head and the fatigue pulling at his mind. He'd severely underestimated how much it'd take out of him to weave Alluma's and Ren's powers into Keroth's. Had anyone ever done this? He hadn't even considered it might be impossible, had just done it, the way he'd so often instinctively used Keroth's fire.

Focus, he berated himself.

Three souls counted on him and the slightest slip would leave them at the mercy of the ambient air, shimmering with scorching heat. Varden cast his gaze about, reorienting himself to trace their path forward.

The firescape was beautiful. Shapes twisted in an ever-shifting landscape, both familiar and alien, all shades of yellow and orange with occasional stripes of blue, green, and purple, the different colours marking a high concentration of various metal. The fire burned endlessly, soundlessly, a perfect, all-encompassing wall.

Nothing could touch him here. No soldiers, no wizards, no insults or weapons. He could rest, if he wanted. Stay here in a cocoon of fire, safe from the world and its never-ending battles, and rest at last. He was so very tired, after all, and he could not remember when he'd last been left completely alone, wrapped in warmth and silence, haunted by neither reality nor nightmares. Varden closed his eyes, hiding Isandor's twisted spires from his sight and mind, allowing the interfire space's enticing calm to envelop him. He was alone at last.

You're not, a small voice whispered, like the low crackle of a dying fire. Varden wanted to ignore it, to push it back into mutism, but the kernel of truth refused to be doused. He was not alone. He couldn't rest here, not now, not ever. The fire would consume his companions—righteous, angry Larryn; sweet, anxious Vellien; brilliant, prideful Nevian. Varden clung to their names, to them, and how they'd trusted him with their safety. He dragged himself out of his dangerous torpor, shaking off the urges to stay put. The firescape would kill them all if he didn't pull himself together.

With the worst of the sleepiness sloughing away, Varden felt his friends' presence again, the protective fire around them thinning fast. He gritted his teeth and rebuilt it in part, but he knew better than to reconstruct a full shield. The energy expended doing so would drain whatever he had left, and they'd never escape. What they needed was to get out—now. Except they seemed to have drifted, and the distorted shapes of Isandor's towers had vanished. Varden fought a thread of panic. It didn't matter. Moving through the firescape was a matter of willpower, and seeing his destination only eased the trip. It was not necessary. He could still do this.

Varden closed his eyes and focused on his memory of the Shelter—broken tables, a crying girl, the lingered scent of breakfast, and the rough, welcoming fireplace. He reached for Larryn's presence beside him, so integral to the place. As Varden tried to project himself into the Shelter, the sweet tranquility of this plane clung to him, like sticky webs refusing to release his mind.

It whispered to him. Avenazar had been to the Shelter, it wasn't safe, he knew of it. Best not to go.

Safer than here, where they would all burn.

The whispers insisted. Surely he could seek another refuge, somewhere far where they would all be safe, and he could return to the fire. Return here, to his cocoon of peace.

Varden tried to shake them off, but his grasp of the Shelter had already thinned, replaced by memories of serene meditation in the Keroth's temple's brazier. He fought against it and his growing exhaustion, forcefully bringing to mind the broken front door, Cal running to Larryn's side, the way patrons had wordlessly set to cleaning up. All the times Arathiel had spoken fondly of the place, of its music and how it'd welcomed him.

Memories of Arathiel crystallized into a strong presence, a clear beacon in the firescape. Varden clung to it, willing himself and the others forward. They sped through hills and farms of twisting fire until—between one heartbeat and the next—Isandor rose above them. Heat buffeted at Varden, a thousand tiny needles prickling at his skin, piercing his protection. He ought to rebuild them, but all strength had fled him, leaving him hollow and battered. Varden pulled even more of it away to wrap the others, snapping his eyes shut as sizzling pain ran across his back. The Shelter's fire burned bright, accessible at last, and Varden could almost see Arathiel stand in front of him. No, wait … he was there, right inside the Shelter, one arm stretched towards the flame.

About to get scorched.

With one last burst of energy, Varden ripped open the joint between the firescape and the Shelter, pushing everyone out. He stumbled forward as solid ground reappeared under his feet, dazed by pain and exhaustion alike, and strong arms caught him—only to let go immediately. Varden fell to his knee as Arathiel stepped back with a cry of pain. *Pain.*

Fire coursed down Arathiel's forearm, the flames searing his skin into a blackened crust with startling speed. Varden stared, stunned. How could it hurt Arathiel? How did the flame even affect him? Varden snapped back to his senses and reached to the fire, draining both the Shelter's blaze and the terrible flames running across Arathiel's arms into him, absorbing them as energy. Arathiel stood still, panting as he stared at his charred fingers, hand, and forearm.

"Snow," Varden said, and he sprang to his feet, grabbed Arathiel's elbow, and dragged him out, the world spinning around him with every step.

The other man caught on quickly and plunged his arm into the cleanest bank of snow. It hissed upon contact, then all sound stopped. They stayed there, crouching, their breath short, confused. Arathiel's gaze latched onto his burned arm now buried in the snow while Varden's travelled between him and the door.

"What—" they both started at the same time.

"You first," Arathiel added quickly, before offering Varden a pained smile.

"What happened? Did you reach into the flame?" He'd felt the familiar presence calling to him, pulling him back from the all-erasing fire.

Arathiel's smile turned sheepish. "I might have." He withdrew his arm from the snow, grimacing at every inch removed, then raised it. Everything from the tip of his fingers to his elbow was now a crusted, charred black. A line of the seared skin extended past that, as if a single flame had licked even farther up, burning him almost to the shoulder instantly. "It was foolish, but we could see your shadows flicker in and out of the fire, and they were growing paler. I wanted to catch you, I think."

"You did." Would Varden have made it out without that anchor? He should have been more wary of his low stamina, but the heady rush of combining Keroth's raw power with two other gods' had numbed his exhaustion until it was too late, and all four of them were already floating in the fire web. "I sensed you."

Arathiel's face lit and he picked up Varden's hand with his unburned one to squeeze it. "Don't do that again."

Varden laughed, his voice cracking from the weight of the last hours. "Save others? I don't think I can promise that."

Arathiel gave him a playful push. "I meant 'almost die' and you know that."

"Do I?"

Varden tilted his chin up with an impish smile. His gaze trailed Arathiel's jaw line, the ridge of his nose, his lips … A deep longing spread through Varden, warm and pounding, and his fingers twitched with the urge to draw, and touch, and hold tight against himself. At first he thought to push it back and keep the fire it lit in him for his sketches, but Branwen's encouragement ran in his mind. And why shouldn't he get this? Varden set his other hand flat on Arathiel's chest and leaned in closer. He could smell Arathiel now despite the smoke clinging to his nose; cedar leaves and cardamom.

"Perhaps you ought to watch over me more closely, then."

Arathiel's sharp and soft gasp was all the answer Varden needed. His blood pounded in his temples, his exhaustion washing away as he became heady with something better than power. Arathiel leaned in, gripping Varden hard. His breath was warm against Varden's ear as he whispered "I will."

Varden remained there for one blissful instant, exhaling slowly, basking in Arathiel's proximity. His hand slid down, then he stepped back, pulling himself out of Arathiel's space to stare at him. "I'll give you my word if you let me look at your wounds. You need a healer. Fire doesn't run up skin as if it's made of oil, and you don't usually feel pain. But it still hurts, doesn't it?"

Arathiel bit down on his lower lip and turned away with a shrug. His fingers slipped out of Varden's hand.

"I knew it," Varden pushed on, undeterred. "You don't fool me. First your back, and now your arm? I was there, Arathiel." He reached up, gently tilting Arathiel's chin so the other man looked at him again. "I remember your panic. Let me look into this with you. Tonight, just the two of us."

"Just us?" Arathiel repeated, and although doubts choked his voice, Varden detected a hint of willingness. A weakness to exploit, to get him to agree.

"Just us," he repeated. "You can't hide it forever, especially not the hand."

Arathiel wiggled his fingers with a grimace. Varden couldn't help but shudder at the grisly sight of blackened flesh, the skin ready to flake off. He reached out, gripping Arathiel's elbow. "It could infect, or fall off. How you're even standing is beyond me."

"I …" Arathiel trailed off with a frown, as if surprised he didn't have an explanation. "It's unpleasant, but I don't think it's the pain I should be feeling. It feels distant, like an aching memory of past agonies." He shrugged with a nonchalance that was obviously forced. "Let's return inside to wrap it. You must be cold."

Cold? While next to Arathiel? Varden couldn't feel the winter chill when his blood boiled like this, and every smile, shrug, or word spoken with that smooth, ember voice sent new waves of heat through his body. He kept that thought to himself, however. With a nod, Varden released Arathiel's arm and headed back inside.

NEVIAN stood in the middle of the Shelter, Efua's tiny arms wrapped tight around his waist, and tried to parse the last few hours. They had rescued him with such speed, despite his lack of inherent value to the fight. Nothing about him could help convince House Dathirii he deserved such a high-risk stunt.

But then, Diel Dathirii hadn't come for him: Varden had.

Varden, who had the most to lose, who knew better than anyone the extent of the risks. He'd strode in there, fire blazing at his arm and heels. Despite Larryn and Vellien by his side, it'd been hard to tear his gaze away from Varden and the raw power swirling around. The flames still danced in his mind, and Nevian closed his eyes to bask in the comfort they brought.

He was home. Safe, for now. Surrounded by people who liked him—loved him, even. This was his life, and he needed to learn to protect it before Avenazar returned.

Nevian squeezed Efua's shoulder, a signal for her to step back. As much as he loved her, the constant touch seeped into him, an alertness and discomfort he could no longer ignore. She hadn't believed he wasn't angry at her until he'd offered the hug, however—and then had asked him twice if he was sure he wanted it, refusing to move until he'd pulled her in himself. He smiled at her now, his heart tightening at the sight of her puffy eyes. He hoped she wouldn't get nightmares from this.

"I promise, when this is over, we'll read together again."

Nevian turned his attention to Vellien. It felt like ages since they'd seen each other, each day distorted and elongated into a small eternity. His expansive vocabulary vanished, entirely insufficient to encompass the soft warmth they brought him. So he smiled instead, keeping his eyes locked until Vellien's cheeks grew red.

"I'm so glad you're safe," Vellien whispered. "Are you all right? Do you need healing? A quiet space?"

"I'm … fine."

More so than he had any right to be. Exhaustion had started

taking root in him, yet everything else seemed as it should be. His mind wasn't scattered to the high winds, his hands didn't shake and his heart had returned to a slower, normal pace. He was fine, and that in himself troubled him. He shouldn't be, not after Avenazar had caught him.

"I shielded myself from him." Disbelief weighed each of his word. He'd found a theory to explain how he'd done it, had matched his experience of it with scholars' writings, and still he couldn't accept the truth of it. In all his years under Avenazar's yoke, he'd never once considered it possible to defend himself. His heart speeding him, Nevian turned to the pile of safeguarded papers Larryn had unceremoniously dumped on a table. "I think I could do it again. We could all do it, with time, and it's all thanks to you, Vellien!"

"M–Me?" They looked around the room as if they expected another Vellien to show up. "I wasn't even there! All I did was follow Varden and lend him what strength I could."

"You healed me. No, better: you helped me heal myself." Nevian's voice grew frantic and his hands flitted about as the theories coalesced in his mind. "When Avenazar crashed in, it wasn't this overwhelming rush of pain anymore. He was bloated and it hurt, but—"

He paused, struggling against the awful memories of that inescapable agony, crushing everything out of him. A thin sweat covered his forehead as he pushed on.

"I knew the landscape of my mind, because you helped me rebuild it, and I sheltered in it against the storm. Then Isra talked about research into protections and I asked to see it all, and I have the barebones of a spell in mind, one we might even imbue in an object, and it would make it harder for Avenazar to overpower any of us!"

The torrent of words only grew more energetic as he went on. This was why he was fine: he had work to do, a spell to keep him busy, something to obsess over. Something other than Avenazar's sickening touch and the emptiness of years stolen. Nevian's fingers tightened into his pants, dirty from sweat and dust, and continued, refusing to drop his focus from the challenges ahead.

"There is a way, but I can't figure it out here, waiting for Avenazar to return and finish what he started. I'll need resources. I'll need Varden to understand the rekhemal and divine magic, and I … I'll need you, to steady me through it."

Vellien met his gaze without hesitation, and the rest of the Shelter faded away as a pleasant heat spread through Nevian. He was glad for this excuse to see Vellien more, to slowly prod at his strange, swirling feelings and define them better, somewhere amidst all the work.

"Of course I'll be there. I missed you." They smiled at him, close to Nevian without ever touching him. "You should return with us to the Brasten Tower, Nevian. Nowhere is completely safe but we'll all be nearby, and they have a library. Besides …" Vellien's cheeks flushed deep *deep* shade of red, and they muttered "Most of the Dathirii family has been uprooted and lives there now. It'd be nice. You could meet them."

"Meet them," Nevian repeated, and he couldn't keep the fear out of his tone. What if they didn't like him? Found him too brusque and rude for Vellien? What if he was good enough for Vellien, but not for them, not for the noble elves of House Dathirii? If they were all so friendly to commoners, Larryn would not be here, in this Shelter. Not to mention, they might remember on behalf of which teen their entire war with the Myrian Enclave had started—for whom, ultimately, they had lost their home. Vellien had only good words for them, and yet …

"You'll be fine," Vellien said, sensing his doubts. "It doesn't have to be everyone at once. It's only sad Jaeger is still stuck in the Dathirii Tower, because you'd enjoy each other's company."

"The steward?" Nevian asked. Vellien had spoken a little about their family during the healing sessions, and that was the most sensible guess. Jaeger had always sounded organized and methodical.

"Yes. Will you come?"

Nevian glanced at Efua, then at the room around him. In all his time at the Shelter, he'd almost never been to the common area, yet its noise was as familiar as the creak of his bed. It had been silenced now, the harmony of conversations and music abruptly terminated by Avenazar. Perhaps he shouldn't have stayed here at all, but Nevian didn't regret it.

"I'll come," he said. "There is no more hiding, now."

It should terrify him, yet every time he thought of today's event, Nevian remembered the solid determination anchoring him through the pain, the sense of power and hope. They threaded through the fear, diminishing its hold over him until it no longer threatened to overwhelm him. Nevian would never be Avenazar's helpless toy again. When he next returned, he'd be ready for it.

Chapter Twenty-Four

H ER plan wasn't subtle, but Isra had no time to think of a better one. A blade. Poison. Shapeshifting. Those were her only tools, but she'd find a way. She had to. If she let Avenazar wake up, everyone would be doomed. *Do what needs to be done*, she told herself, clinging to Jilssan's words. Her stomach roiled in protest at the very thought, her palms sweaty on the letter opener's hilt. But this was the only way forward. For Nevian and Varden, back in the city. For Jilssan, whose betrayal wouldn't remain hidden for long. For herself, too, to atone for all of her mistakes.

Isra slipped into an empty study near Avenazar's rooms. These quarters had been meant for guests, but no one had resided at the enclave since its founding. Dust gathered on the furniture, and a thin cloud rose as she set down the tiny bottle she'd stolen from Jilssan's quarters—a small, unidentified vial she'd never seen until a few days ago. Isra sniffed it—the bitterness she expected was well hidden, almost imperceptible. The kind of clue a feverish, rash man would miss. She swallowed the large lump in her throat and forced a deep breath in, but no amount of steadying herself calmed the shaking of her hands as she poured the poison over her blade.

She had a weapon. She had poison. Now, for the shapeshifting.

Priestess Yavia had inherited the lead of Keroth's Temple after Varden's downfall, and with that responsibility had come the distasteful task of overseeing Avenazar's healing. She was a tall and spindly woman, with sharp features and a tendency towards silence. Isra had rarely dealt with her, avoiding the woman's judgmental pale eyes whenever possible, but she remembered enough of Yavia's face to mimic it. She hoped, anyway, because she had no better options.

Isra's right hand hung midair, letter opener at the ready to trace runes and call upon the threads of magic around her. She hesitated. Wearing another appearance wasn't new; she'd spent most of her life in a skin that wasn't hers, that she'd claimed as such through magic. But since the temple's collapse—since her father's amulet had shattered—she hadn't changed herself. She'd grown accustomed to the darker skin of her hands and the mass of hair tumbling down her shoulders. Despite the strangeness of it, it was liberating to be rid of that tiny voice whispering that she was a liar and that no one would love her if they knew.

They knew now, and if anything, they liked her even better.

With a deep breath, Isra sliced her shapeshifting rune through the air. Magic gathered around it, thick threads of light responding to her command with surprising ease. Why wasn't it slipping away? Twisting into unexplainable shapes? It hadn't done that either when she'd called a shield to defend herself earlier. Something had shifted when her amulet had shattered, an irrevocable change in her life she'd yet to fully understand. But Isra knew one thing: she meant to take full advantage of it.

She wrapped herself in magic, grinning at the surge of power running along her arms and diving deep within her, coursing through flesh and bones. Her body elongated, stretching and thinning at once, while her hair shortened into a dark, side-swept cut with bangs. Her lips dried, her skin wrinkled with age, and before long she could feel Yavia's long nails—her long nails— digging into her palms. Exhaustion seeped through her, replacing the surge of magical power. Not the mind-numbing blowback of using heavy spells, however. It was quieter, lodged within muscles and nerves, as if old age had caught up with her. Isra frowned. She hadn't meant for the spell to weaken her. Could shapeshifting magic have a mind of its own, drawing from subconscious ideas of others? She'd never transformed into someone else before, and her father's amulet had only created another Isra. Perhaps Jilssan knew more. Either way, the question had to wait for now.

It was time to kill Avenazar.

Isra wished she'd grabbed a few blank scrolls to make the letter opener more innocuous, but she'd hurried out at the first spark of an idea. Her heart thundered in her chest as she strolled down the corridor, forcing her steps to remain slow, calm. She wanted to run—to sprint in these old bones, burst into Avenazar's room, and be done with it.

To stab him, her mind provided, supplying Isra with specifics she would rather avoid. She quickened her pace, afraid to falter partway. You had to be ruthless to survive in Myria. Avenazar was a threat, and he was still weak. She set her hand on the doorknob and stared at it, all pale and wrinkled skin, the metal cold and smooth under her palm. Varden had come to save Nevian, but there was only one way to ensure they both stayed safe. Only this. Isra clung to this certainty and slipped into the room.

Avenazar had collapsed face first into his bed, still fully dressed in his Myrian robes. One of his legs hung over the side and he'd kept his wounded wrist clear of his stocky body, one elbow jutting out. The overall mess of limbs and half-upturned blankets reminded Isra of drunken teenagers who'd come home too stoned to properly prepare for bed. She stared, unsettled by the imagery, by how unimpressive the powerful wizard was, flopped down like this, robes clinging to his back. He moaned and shifted, startling Isra out of her contemplation. This was Avenazar, not some poor sod to be pitied. If he woke up now and guessed her ploy, he would kill her in an instant.

She padded across the room, her palms growing sweatier with every step. Nausea threatened to surge up and out, and she felt her heart beat all the way to her fingertips. Every moment now, she expected Avenazar to turn around, a sneer on his lips, and strangle her with those green whips of his. This had been a terrible idea. She wasn't an assassin, didn't have the skill or guts for this. Her flimsy disguise wouldn't save her, not from this big a mistake. Yet she made it all the way to the bed and held the letter opener two-handed above Avenazar's back, her entire arms shaking as waves of fear rose through her body, starting into her soles and mounting, up and up and up until she felt nothing but dizziness at the enormity of her actions.

The enclave's alarm went off.

It passed through Isra as a heavy pulse of unease weighing down her lungs and setting her nerves on edge, a signal that someone had pressed the trigger runes scattered across the grounds since the temple's collapse—one of Jilssan's only concessions to actual security. Isra buckled forward at the wave, but where it had hit her in an unmistakable yet ultimately discreet way, it crashed into Avenazar with full force.

The wizard jerked up with a pained and enraged cry, and Isra yelled at his sudden movement. Her heart skipped several beats and before she could think, she slammed the letter opener down, ramming it into the back of his shoulder with surprising strength. A scream escaped her lips as he fell back into the bed—she'd stabbed him! Stabbed Avenazar, hard and true, with a poisoned blade! The letter opener still jutted out of his shoulder and she stumbled back, her legs weak under her. Avenazar grunted and very slowly pushed himself back up, his eyes fluttering open. She needed to run. The magic holding her shapeshifted form started to slip, overwhelmed by her panic. Avenazar was staring at her now, his mouth twisting in a snarl as her body returned to normal.

"You're not Yavia," he spat.

Three crooked fingers sliced out from under him, power

pooling instantly between them and bursting forth as a green thread. It wrapped around Isra's arm, tightened painfully, and yanked her closer. She fell forward with a yelp, landing by the bed. Right beside him, within easy reach of his magic, of his mind crushing her again, tearing her into tiny pieces.

Isra squeezed her eyes shut and fought back the terrible futures her imagination conjured. Magic still coated her skin, and she grabbed for it before it all escaped. It twisted and turned under her grasp, shying away from the raw power of Avenazar's rope. The rope—it interfered! All her life she'd had a potent artifact at her neck, and all her life she'd struggled to control strands of magic in the world. That was why. Two powerful spells didn't naturally behave well together; they had to be forced! Thankfully, Isra had spent all her life doing just that.

She grappled the magic and coerced it back into her body. Power thrummed under her skin, waiting for her command— waiting for her to line up two coherent thoughts and escape. Avenazar's green rope sizzled against her forearm, hot and dangerous. She needed to escape, to become slippery, fluid. Willpower guided her magic, and her arm shrank, turning into clear water. Isra gasped as the change spread upward, to her shoulder and chest and legs. Her heart hammered and she let herself sink into the new form, splashing entirely onto the ground.

The world shut down around her, reduced to nothing but the cold wood under her, the lines and marks in its relief, and the vibration of Avenazar's frustrated scream. Thick energy slammed through her, causing her body to wobble. She needed to move.

Move. What a strange concept, to power herself through space, to displace her body through her own will. Isra struggled against the slippery consciousness, the heaviness of her human thoughts, as if they, too, had been liquefied. She pushed her form into pseudopods, water crawling across the floor, filling every crack on the way. Vibrations indicated nearby words in a specific rhythm. Chanting? She didn't know. She passed under the door, and released the magic.

Water surged upward as she reformed into a human body: bones and flesh and nerves. Isra's thoughts cleared, only to immediately turn into a pounding headache. She bit back a moan and sprinted off, eager to put as much distance between Avenazar and herself. She hoped the poison would keep him down, and the alarm would distract the guards.

The door behind her slammed open, pushed by green tendrils. Isra cursed and turned at the first corner, anxious to get out of Avenazar's sight. She was still looking over her shoulder when she ran headlong into a guard. Her head rang even worse, and for a moment her vision blackened. Too much magic, and yet … She wouldn't escape without more.

The woman was out of breath, and as surprised by the impact as Isra. She only stared, stunned, as Isra reached for the threads of power once more, and pushed herself into her familiar hawk shape. Arms turned into wings, hair into feathers, and she flew past the startled guard with a few quick flaps of her wings. This shape fit her, a comfortable form she'd long since adopted as part of her nature. Isra flew into the corridors, all senses tuned to the air currents around her until she found a room with an extinguished fireplace. She dove in, then up the chimney and into Isandor's cold winter day.

Hard wind buffeted her, pushing snowflakes into her wings, but the chill and exhaustion crawling into her bones couldn't douse Isra's elation. She was free, flying high into the sky after plunging a letter opener into Avenazar's back. She didn't know if he'd die from it, but at the very least she had bought everyone time.

Now she only needed to figure out where to go, and what in Keroth's holy flames had happened to Jilssan.

Chapter Twenty-Five

HASRYAN leaned on the warm bench, luxuriating in the magic keeping the wood under his ass hot and cozy even in the coldest winter chill. The Golden Plaza was the only public area in all Isandor where regular, I-don't-shit-gold-every-morning folks could enjoy these little marvels. It sat on top of the prestigious tower with the Golden Table, once the highest in the entire city, and while many spires had stretched far above it through the centuries since, it remained one of the most cherished locations in the city. Several businesses had crawled around it, including the *House of Delights*, a tiny establishment known for its many delicacies and, more importantly, great privacy.

Normally, Hasryan would avoid the plaza and its crowd, but Branwen had called him here, and he was desperate for something—anything—to fill his days. There hadn't been much for him to do since their return from the Enclave, and every outing he risked discovery, but the idleness ate at him more with every passing day. He needed to get away from Cal's place. No amount of divine statuettes or bright pillows could fill the emptiness Sora—and everyone else before her—had left with her departure. Hasryan hated staying behind. It gave too much space to the whispers in his head insisting they were *leaving him* behind.

"Ready?"

Branwen's voice startled him. She'd slid into the bench leaning against his while he'd been brooding, leaning casually onto it and stretching an arm out. He smirked but kept his gaze ahead. No meeting happening here.

"Whatever you need, love."

She choked at his 'love', and Hasryan enjoyed the rare noise of a Branwen caught off guard. He pulled his hood farther down and checked that his sleeves and gloves overlapped, properly hiding him, then closed his eyes and relaxed into the bench as if he was not Isandor's most infamous criminal, but a random, tired citizen enjoying the plaza.

"There's a merchant in the *House of Delights*, a certain Reinhaut Milar. He's here with a cargo of magical seeds, and Hellion is trying to buy them cheap and make them into the next big thing. Could well work, too; gardens are still in fashion."

"Can't have that happening," Hasryan said. This was familiar territory, and excitement built within him. He could use a routine job. "Scare tactics or physical impediments?"

"Scare." She rummaged into a bag with noisy gestures and muttered her next words, as if she was talking to herself. "Don't threaten him on our behalf, though. Just … convince him Hellion is not a safe investment in the current circumstances, and he'd do so much better if he spread his bets. Isandor *is* on his regular route, after all, and he should think of the future."

"Routine work, then." He'd done similar things a hundred times before under Brune's orders. Mild intimidation, he called it. Those Brune wanted to cow into full obedience often earned a trip to her egg-shaped cells, deep in her headquarters, so far from reach that not even the sun touched them. "What if I wanted to spice it up?"

Branwen froze for a split second, then offered a small, interested "oh?" and filched something out, as if the sound was meant for the content of her purse.

"Magical thingamabobs are what the Myrians first made their fortune on, isn't it? Aren't they territorial assholes who don't know shit about subtlety?"

"You could certainly say th—oh!" Branwen flung an arm over the bench, bumping his shoulder playfully as she did. "We are trying to undermine the trust between Lord Allastam and Avenazar, and if rumours spread that Hellion's treacherous deal doesn't even shield from the Myrians' wrath … That's—"

"Genius, I know," Hasryan completed for her.

Not that he'd thought through all these fancy ramifications. He'd just needed a pretend boss, and the Myrians offered one extra advantage: he wouldn't need to hide who he was. Let Allastam think the Myrians had protected him and stew in his anger.

"I can make that work. Any more info?"

Branwen snapped her bag shut and heaved a dramatic sigh, as if distressed. "Wide purple hat, big feather, not dressed to be comfortable in this cold. Oh, and Hasryan? Enjoy."

She stood up and stomped away, the perfect picture of an irritated lady. The clack of her knee-high boots on stone only added to the effect, and Hasryan allowed himself a moment to admire the strung-up, high-and-mighty gait she'd adopted, so unlike her easygoing nature. Simple and effective.

Now it was his turn to be the same, and Hasryan had no intention of letting her down.

REINHAUT Milar was a skeletal man whose bones rattled with every step, and whose thin coat couldn't keep Isandor's deadly gusts away. Full-body shudders wracked him as he hurried out of the *House of Delights*, past the plaza, and down a first flight of stairs. All his focus went to the bridges under his feet and the constant rubbing of his bare hands, and Hasryan had rarely found such an easy mark to follow. Poor man wouldn't notice a flying cow if it mooed at him.

Hasryan tracked him through most of the Middle City, biding his time. Isandor's irregular web of bridges and stairs meant many streets remained wide open, complicating any attempts to approach someone unseen and lead them into more secluded areas. He'd missed the squat buildings and compact roads of Nal-Gresh when he'd first arrived, but with time he'd learned to use the unique architecture to his advantage and enjoy the new challenge. An opportunity always emerged, especially once you reached the bottom half of the Middle City, and the space turned more cramped.

Milar turned onto a narrow bridge squeezed between the low half of the Serringer Tower and the last floor of another tower, and Hasryan took his chance. He dashed in after the man, catching up with a few confident strides, then threw an arm over his shoulder, spreading his cloak to cover their backs.

"Reinhaut Milar, what a pleasure to see you! You look awfully cold, my good sir. Allow me to keep you warm."

The merchant tensed and sputtered, but the cold tip of Hasryan's dagger pierced through his clothes before he could muster a protest and any screams died on his lips. With a steady pressure, Hasryan kept him walking, albeit more slowly.

"They warned me about this," Milar said. He had a husky voice, tense but not overly concerned. Not the simpering kind, then. "You don't scare me. Everyone in this city agrees your boss's got no bite."

Hasryan laughed. No need to even fake it! When it came to Diel Dathirii and underhanded tactics, 'no bite' was a perfectly good way to put it. But he wasn't here on their behalf, not as far as this little charade was concerned. Hasryan clapped the man's back as if they shared the funniest joke, then cut his laughter abruptly and dropped his voice to a low growl.

"Oh, my good sir, I'm afraid you've been ill-informed."

"Mister Diel Dathirii—"

"Did not send me," Hasryan interrupted, "and I daresay Master Avenazar is better known for his fangs than anything else."

Shock stopped Milar, and he stayed glued to this stone bridge, alone in the shadows of Isandor's towers. Hasryan slid away from him, keeping only the dagger near as he spun to the front and dipped into a low bow.

"You've heard, I see. Why the surprise, then? Has no one *warned* you that magical paraphernalia was our territory?"

Reinhaut Milar puffed his chest out, pressing it against the dagger's tip. He lifted his chin, and Hasryan had to appreciate the bravado. The twitch of his lips and dart of his eyes gave away some of his fear, but he remained far calmer than many targets before him.

"Say your piece."

Hasryan grinned and removed the dagger back with a casual flip. He let his wrist show with the movement, then tilted his head back so part of his face could be seen despite the hood. If Milar reported a dark elf to Lord Allastam, their little alliance would crumble.

"Allastam shouldn't have betrayed us. He's as good as dead—him, his family, and anyone who allies with him or his little underling houses. You want to sell these little seeds? You either come to us, or you change cities." Hasryan stretched, yawned, then stored the dagger and offered Milar a predatory grin. "That's the official bit, anyway. If you ask me? You should pack and run while you can. City's a mess, and the only profit in it is for cutthroats like me."

On most jobs, Hasryan would wait around and try to get some agreement, pressing the dagger in and growling scary things like 'Understood?'. He didn't think he needed to now. Reinhaut Milar didn't seem the type to fall for the usual intimidation routine, but scrambling all he thought he knew about the city's politics? Uncertainty could be the scariest trick of all. So Hasryan left him, turning his back and waving over his shoulder as he strode to the end of the tight passage, tugging on his hood and sleeves only as he re-emerged into the light.

A job well done, he thought, the restlessness of the past few days sloughing off his shoulders. Now if only Branwen could have more like these, dread might stop building with each day waiting for confirmation about Kellian's location and his next part in this shadow war.

CHAPTER TWENTY-SIX

ARATHIEL flexed his burned fingers over and over, engrossed by the jolt of pain every movement brought. His entire arm had throbbed all afternoon and evening, a sharp and distinctive sensation he hadn't felt in ages. The closest to it was the distant buzz across his back, which had started in the Myrian Enclave, when he'd fallen into the fire. It hurt, and the pain registered as familiar, as if he'd known it all his life despite its rarity. Arathiel felt so *alive*, and the exhilaration of it all scared him.

Soft fingers alighted on top of his own burned ones, stopping the incessant movement. Arathiel startled, heart somersaulting as his gaze found Varden's. He'd never heard him—of course not—and now he'd been caught in his morbid fascination. He tried to hide his embarrassment behind an awkward smile, but Varden's deep brown eyes pierced through it.

"I'm sorry," he said. "I should have knocked louder."

He didn't remove his hand, only slid on the bed right next to Arathiel, impossibly close. Even without detectable warmth or smell, Varden captured Arathiel's entire attention, sending a pleasant tingle through his body and mind. He forgot to breathe, forgot to answer at all. Varden's mouth quirked and he added with uncharacteristic shyness.

"I've been looking forward to this evening."

"Y-yes, to heal me."

Arathiel stumbled over the words. They both knew there was more, that their promise to meet alone held another one. Varden had shamelessly flirted with him earlier, and the thrill of it had left Arathiel grinning for the remainder of the day.

"Indeed, and I rested accordingly. Hours-long naps have become an inevitable part of my routine, it seems." Varden's exhaustion threaded his voice and weighed down his shoulders. "Sometimes I wonder if I'll ever recover."

"You might not." Recovery had grown into a foreign word for Arathiel. He would never regain all of his senses, but he'd learned to better read the world with what input he had left. "You'll adapt, however. We all find ways to deal with our new reality. Look at House Brasten, and all they changed in their home."

Not *theirs, his.* His family. His tower. It was still hard to think of himself as belonging here, in the home of his youth. Every morning, he woke to a ceiling both familiar and foreign, the recognizable cracks widened by the time, the etched relief smoothed away. Perhaps he should've asked for another room, but it was too late now, and in truth, he needed to grow accustomed to this new reality. Adaptation was more than physical.

"We'll see," Varden replied. "I have more pressing concerns than my recovery at the moment. Yours, for a start."

Arathiel laughed at the obvious change of topic. He wouldn't escape the promised healing session. "I must disagree with your priorities."

"How unfortunate that you don't set them." Varden met his gaze and squeezed the blackened hand very softly, sending an agreeable spike of pain through Arathiel. "Please. Let me see. Isandor has no better expert on burns."

Arathiel closed his eyes. He didn't want to say goodbye to the grounding hurt, but he had no argument to counter Varden. No one knew how the burns could affect his health, and with the way his body defied usual conventions, it'd be impossible to predict. Besides, he couldn't hide them forever. Best to take care of it now, with someone he trusted.

"All right," he said, reaching for the buttons of his shirt with his healthy hand. His fingers shook. "Don't panic when you see my back. It's … not like the hand."

The hand had charred black, but beyond a thin crust, it'd remain somewhat smooth. His back, however … he'd used mirrors to catch a glimpse, and the gruesome sight had left him nauseous. A single black line crossed the entirety of his brown skin, rising above the rest like a small mountain range. It had reminded Arathiel of meat forgotten on a fire, all dark, chunky, and twisted.

"I'll be fine," Varden reassured him. "I've seen many things over the years."

"You sound like you're an old man."

Arathiel finished unbuttoning his shirt, then turned around to offer Varden a clear view of his back before he slid the fabric down and exposed it. Varden's sharp gasp knifed through his heart, and Arathiel gritted his teeth. Here it was, the inevitable horror and pity. He clenched his fingers into the bed sheets to resist pulling his shirt back up.

A palm settled on the upper left of his back, pressing in hard so he could feel it. It didn't shake, and when Varden spoke, his voice remained steady. "Does it still hurt?"

"All the time." Arathiel frowned, unsatisfied with his own answer. "It's a slow burn, a prickle that is strangely familiar and distant, yet sometimes flares stronger … closer. That's not normal, is it?"

"We'll figure out what *your* normal is and work from there."

Arathiel wished he could make his normal the same as everyone else's, just this once. He kept the bitter thought to himself, instead offering a nod to Varden, who squeezed his shoulder in answer.

"I'm going to try to heal it. Brace yourself, and let me know if anything feels wrong."

"Wait." Arathiel tensed as a second hand placed itself on his lower back, on the other end of the scorched ridge. Others had tried to heal him before, to almost disastrous consequences. A memory scratched at the edges of his consciousness, of Cal fixing his open gash after he'd rescued Hasryan. Something is wrong, he'd said, struggling and sweating. "Be careful. Promise me you'll pull back if it becomes too much. Don't exhaust yourself over this."

"I would never," Varden replied, and the amused note in his voice pulled a grin out of Arathiel.

"Exhaust yourself, or pull back?"

Varden laughed, his voice melodious and reassuring. His thumbs pressed into Arathiel's back and rubbed tiny, almost imperceptible circles.

"I promise," he said, without specifying which.

Warmth spread from Varden's hands, sliding across Arathiel's skin and into the burns. Seconds trickled by, silent and still. Arathiel didn't dare breathe as he waited for a sign—a squeeze from Varden, a change in the throbbing, even a sharp stab of pain—anything, really, to let him know what was happening. The silence pressed on his lungs, and his mind conjured echoes of the Sapphire Guard healer who'd brought him from the brink of death, after he'd saved Hasryan. *Only magic holds his body together.*

The warmth across his back cooled, numbing the steady pain with it, and the shift drew Arathiel back to the present. He was with a healer he trusted now, competent and caring. He could relax into Varden's care and let him handle the situation. Whatever spell or phenomenon explained his problems, they could find out together. Varden released a slow sigh and inched his fingers along the burned line, flattening its ridge. Arathiel felt the skin resorb and smoothen with astounding acuity, then the pain was gone and nothing replaced it—nothing but the numbness that had followed him since the Well. Arathiel clenched his singed hand, trying to bury his bitterness under a renewed surge of pain.

Behind him, Varden moaned, a breathless and distant sound, and Arathiel's disappointment vanished.

"Varden?"

No reply came. Surely Varden was done now: Arathiel couldn't feel his wounds anymore—couldn't feel anything, really, from his lower back, not even Varden's own hands, so reassuring a few minutes ago. Arathiel's heart pounded with fear and guilt.

He whirled around, and Varden fell forward, into his arms. Arathiel caught him and held him by the shoulders as his eyes fluttered open.

"What ..." Varden squeezed his eyes back shut, then shook his head, as if chasing cobwebs out of it. "I'm sorry."

"Tell me." Arathiel's tone broke no disagreement. "Something was wrong, wasn't it?"

"Not at first."

Varden stopped there, biting his lower lip with open worry. A dangerous mix of frustration and desire welled up within Arathiel. He wanted to kiss Varden as much as he wanted answers.

"Tell me everything," he said. "Please, I deserve to know."

"I know. I'm trying to find words to explain. I'm much better with images, I'm afraid."

A shy smile curved his lips, sending Arathiel's heart into a flip. How did a single man get to be this beautiful? Did Varden even realize how irresistible he was when he did that? Probably not, or he'd wield it as the weapon it should be.

"It felt like being pulled in. A cold force held me still, leeching at my power. My arm's numb, from the tip of my fingers to my shoulder." He waved it for an instant, then smiled. "That's not all. Every living being is glued together by magic to some extent. It's everywhere around us, a weave holding the world. But within you it was ... stronger, I'd say? I could feel it pulsing. This Well must have changed your body on a fundamental level."

Arathiel let the information sink in. He'd known something was different—how could it not be?—yet hearing it explained added weight. Half-alive, the Sapphire Guard's healer had said. Perhaps that had been wrong. From the sound of it, he was half magic. Arathiel clenched his burned hand and pain washed over him, trying to fight back his rising tears. What was he supposed to do with this? Did he even belong to this world, or had he been deluding himself? The last few weeks had helped so much, grounded him into new friends and a new life, so why did he feel it all slipping away?

"You're hurting yourself." Varden wrapped his hands around Arathiel's fist, then unclenched the fingers one by one. "Let me heal it. I know what to look for now."

"I—"

Arathiel didn't want it gone. Would he sense anything again if he didn't hold this strange pain close? He didn't want to be half a magical being. He wanted to live a normal life, here, with this beautiful man in front of him, with his rediscovered family and all the new friends from the Shelter.

"I enjoy it," he admitted with undisguised anguish. "It hurts, but at least it's *something*. I want to feel …"

Arathiel trailed off, caught in the rawness of Varden's gaze. Tiny fires had lit in them, a swirl of determination, kindness, and desire that scorched Arathiel's throat dry. His lips parted, but his words had vanished, burned away in the intensity of the moment. Varden's shy smile flitted across his lips, as beautiful as ever, and Arathiel realized his earlier mistake. His companion knew exactly how to wield the weapon at his disposal.

Varden leaned forward and pressed his lips to Arathiel's. One hand gripped Arathiel's hip, pushing him against the bed's head, while the other grabbed his burned palm tighter. A jolt of pain coursed up his arm and spine, pursued by intoxicating shivers. Arathiel pulled Varden closer, hungry for more, desperate to feel the kiss as more than a distant press. Varden obliged, digging fingers into him, their touch clear and firm and deeply arousing.

Slowly, gently releasing Arathiel from his grasp, Varden withdrew. The shyness had given way to a knowing smirk. "Felt that?"

A sharp sound crossed Arathiel's lips, half sob and half laugh. He stole another pressing kiss from Varden, then ran a hand through his curls, focusing on the almost imperceptible tingle on his skin. His fingers trailed until his hand rested at the base of Varden's neck. He couldn't feel it under his palm, but Varden's cheeks had flushed from the touch.

"I certainly did," Arathiel said, his voice coarse. "I've been feeling a lot of different things about you recently."

"Great." Varden grinned even wider, and a tight chuckle escaped him. "Really great, even."

Arathiel couldn't tear his eyes away. Relief, nervousness, and confidence warred through Varden. One moment he was twisting his fingers and avoided looking at Arathiel's, the next he leaned into the hand at his nape with a smirk. Arathiel could've watched in silence for hours, but Varden quickly started babbling.

"I might have been a little impulsive there. I'm sorry, I was worried for you, and it's been a long time since I—a long and difficult one. I didn't—"

"Stop, Varden." Arathiel wrapped his arms around Varden,

pulling him close. "Please don't regret this kiss. When I imagine its taste, I imagine it must have a hint of sweetness, because that's what it was: the sweetest kiss I ever had. I'm glad I lived long enough to meet you, even if the Well was the price to pay for it."

"I'm glad I'm even there to meet." He snuggled into Arathiel's embrace, leaning his head on him. "But don't think I've forgotten your arm needs healing."

Arathiel snorted. Today he'd learned Varden could not easily be distracted. "You're too diligent a healer."

He didn't mind losing the grounding pain of his forearm as much if he received kisses and cuddles as a trade-off. Arathiel tightened his arms around Varden, wishing he perceived more of the comforting weight against him, or smelled the curly hair now inches below his nose.

"There is no such thing as too diligent a healer, Arathiel," Varden replied. "I'll see to it tomorrow morning, after I've slept. I'm afraid you're officially trapped under me."

Indeed, Varden had him against the bed's head. How tragic, to be forced to hold him for the coming night. "That's all right. You couldn't wish for a better human pillow than me. Whether you stay an hour or ten, I still won't feel the pins and needles."

Varden snuck his hand into Arathiel's, lacing their fingers together. "You're adorable."

"And you're tired. Hush and sleep, Varden. You need the rest."

He played with Varden's curls as the man's breath steadied, his mind floating in a strange bliss. How often had he daydreamed of this? They'd been idled thoughts, set aside while Varden recovered, but every conversation with the kind priest fuelled them. But it'd happened—a single, electrifying kiss, a breathless promise for more, a gentle night together. Arathiel grinned, tightening his grip on Varden.

It was easy, when overwhelmed by the strangeness of the Well and its inescapable impact on his life, to slip into despair and lose track of all he'd built since returning to Isandor. He had so many friends here already, and now Varden wanted him, too? Arathiel closed his eyes, returning to memories of Varden's tight grip on his hips, of his husky *"Felt that?"*.

Whatever horrible mysteries the future held for him, Arathiel refused to give in to sadness now. He meant to live a happy, fulfilling life, for whatever time he had left.

THAT night, Larryn prepared the worst meal the Shelter had ever seen. It was still solid nourishment, which was more than what most patrons would've had on their own, but he'd paid no mind to how he spiced the meat, overcooked the vegetables, and forgot the sauce entirely. Dry chunks of food piled at the bottom of bowls, sad little blocks that promised a chewy and bland experience.

No one had cared.

Patrons had trickled back to the Shelter throughout the day, banding together to right tables, set chairs around them, and pile debris in a corner, returning the common room to a hospitable state. Many had dared to knock on the kitchen's door, asking if he was all right or wanted help, telling him to forget cooking and rest, but he'd paid them no heed. Even though Larryn could barely keep on his feet, life at the Shelter needed to go on.

He ought to sleep and recover, but he feared his nightmares would return. Dead Myrians at night, and now live ones in the day. How had he gotten himself involved in this mess? This fight belonged to nobles high in their towers, not to him. Who would feed Isandor's homeless if he died? What would happen to everyone?

They would survive. Of course they would. His people were resilient, stubborn, and resourceful. They had weathered countless winters before he'd created this little haven, and if it vanished they would weather many more. He didn't want them to have to, however. Not without help—warm food, the occasional roof over their heads, the welcoming music, and the certainty of a safe place for them, in the company of others who struggled.

Larryn shouldn't have gotten involved, yet he knew he'd do it again in a heartbeat. It'd started with Nevian, and if avoiding Master Avenazar's ire meant he should have thrown a homeless teenager out, at the mercy of cold winters, unforgiving streets, and Avenazar's eventual attack, then he'd really had no choice. Besides, Avenazar was no better than any of the gold-coated nobles populating the highest levels of Isandor's towers, and Larryn had never been one to resist flipping off deserving assholes. Still, he liked it better when the Myrians wanted to poke holes into Drake instead of coming after his people.

He wished Nevian had stayed here, unwise as that was. Mostly for Efua's sake. She'd spent the rest of her day in his room, trying to read the small book he'd bought her, then fallen asleep on his bed. Larryn had tucked her in properly.

He ought to do the same with himself. Larryn rubbed his eyes and stared at the mess all over his kitchens' counters. The narrow work space had grown encumbered during the evening—he hadn't bothered to clean as he cooked. Even if he wanted sleep, he'd need to take care of that first. He had more meals to prepare, anyway. Besides, even the limited focus he put on his tasks stopped his mind from wandering to the half-burnt coin weighing heavily in his pocket.

Until Cal stomped right in, foregoing knocks or permission.

"I hear from our patrons that you refuse to rest from your near-death experience."

Larryn set his knife down and closed his eyes. Not now, he wanted to plead. He didn't trust himself to stay calm when all his strength was used to stay upright.

"They sent you to force me?"

Cal snorted. "No one's foolish enough to think that'll work."

Then what? Larryn turned around, but his answer came before he could even ask. Cal stretched up to slap a hand on his chest, and a burst of energy shot through Larryn, reinvigorating him. The flickering candles on his wall seemed to brighten, and each knife-inflicted scratch in his counter became a vivid etching under his fingers. What heaviness dragged his limbs vanished, and when Larryn inhaled a first, deep breath, he felt ready to take on the world.

"It won't last." Cal smirked, but his gaze avoided Larryn, scanning the kitchens instead. "Maybe the other patrons will get something edible out of your stubbornness, at least. Good night, Larryn."

Lost in all the new textures and sounds and the clarity of his brain, Larryn didn't react until Cal had his hands on the handle. The blessed coin had stayed in Larryn's pocket, heavy and warmer now, as if it'd absorbed part of the magical surge.

"W-wait!" Larryn called. "Don't you want it back?"

Cal stopped but did not turn around. "No, Larryn. Keep it. Its luck might protect the Shelter, or you. I think you'll know when to give it back."

Then he was gone, leaving Larryn to chew on his words. Cal had never explained how he'd acquired his holy symbol, but they'd all surmised from allusions to his past that he'd witnessed the fire twisting Ren's relief upon it. They didn't ask. If Cal—the cheerful friend who shared everything with everyone—wanted to keep this to himself, they'd respect that. This holy symbol meant the world to Cal, and Larryn didn't want that responsibility.

Didn't he have enough of those, already? He'd told Cal he'd earn the forgiveness, but he had no idea how to do that, or how to change for the better. This city had set anger deep within his broken bones, and Larryn *loved* the way it fuelled him. He didn't want to grow complacent or lose the drive of indignation. How else would he find the energy to feed everyone at the Shelter?

Friendship, he thought. That's what Cal had said, giving him the coin, that spite and friendship carried him forward. Larryn withdrew the holy symbol and stared at it, burnt silver against his brown palm. Cal hadn't fostered more responsibility on him. He'd blessed Larryn with a symbol of his trust in their friendship, and only once Larryn had earned it could he return that trust.

Chapter Twenty-Seven

I SRA blinked, unfocused eyes opening to a flurry of snowflakes blurring the dark sky above her. Cold had dug its claw deep into her, chilling her every bone, and her drenched robe had frozen under her. Had she collapsed there? Where was she? Isra fought her way through her sluggish mind, reaching for her last memories. She'd flown out of the enclave, strong winds and adrenaline carrying her into Isandor proper. That rush had vanished with brutal finality, however, and the intensity of the day's shapeshifting weighed her down.

Where had she gone? She couldn't remember the rest, only a daze of bridges, people avoiding her … flight again. She must have transformed one last time and … headed upward? Yes, she'd flown higher, she recalled that much.

Isra sat up, forcing weakened muscle to awaken and warm. Inches of snow slid off her body and hair, and she stared at them.

How long had she been lying there? She pressed numbed fingers against the stones under her. It felt so far away, and she was so cold.

Deep shudders shook her body from head to toes. Her teeth clattered, and fear wrapped itself tight around her lungs, pushing out a moaned sob. She could have died here. After stabbing Avenazar and escaping the enclave, she could have flown all the way here to die in the cold, and she still didn't know where *here* was. Hot tears slipped on her cheek, only to cool immediately in the ambient chill. She wanted somewhere warm and soft, with Jilssan laughing by her side and no thoughts of dying in the cold, or of Avenazar's anger, or-or anything, really! She wanted this nightmare to stop.

But it wouldn't, not on its own. Not if she stayed here crying over it. Isra wiped her tears away, ignoring her freezing skin, then struggled to wobbly legs. A powerful gust threw her back to the ground, to land painfully on chaffed palms, but she forced herself back up, slowly, spreading her feet to steady herself. She refused to die here.

Only snow-blurred skies expanded around her. None of Isandor's spires rose above, casting their oppressive dark shapes even in the night. She was at the top, the highest tower of the city. The Brasten Tower. Dimly, Isra recalled asking for directions now, then flying around to find a secondary entrance without guards. Landing on top, where a single door led down.

She stared at the terrace now, its garden buried under thick whiteness, the stone lamps throwing a pale blue light swallowed by the falling snow. The door traced a dark rectangle in the middle of it, challenging her. She hesitated. House Brasten was an enemy of the Myrian Enclave.

So am I, now, she reminded herself. She had stabbed Master Avenazar a few hours ago, hadn't she? If these people had taken in Varden, they'd accept her, too. They had to! And if they didn't, well, she might be warmer by the time they threw her out, right?

Her thin boots squished from cold water as she stumbled towards the door. Every single piece of clothing on her back had been drenched, and many had frozen over. Her feet hurt, a low, painful thrum that made them feel thrice their size. By the time Isra reached the door, the warmth seemed worth every risk. She pushed her way in, eager to take shelter from the unending winds.

Tiny stairs wound downward, lined with golden bulbs. Isra shoved her hands under her armpit, which only pressed her wet clothes against her skin. With a sound halfway between curse and moan, she started down, the echoes of her boots buried under the clattering teeth.

At least blessed warmth welcomed her inside, stronger as she got deeper into the tower. Isra could almost feel her bones thawing out, and with them, fresh tears pushed their way to the surface. She fought them back, admonishing herself. The stairs led to a simple wooden door, warm to her touch. Isra's heart jumped as she imagined how hot the room behind would be. Without thinking, she shoved it open and hurried through.

A curved spear point stopped her two steps within. Isra jerked back with a yelp. On the other end was a large black woman, her long twists held into a ponytail by a gold ribbon. The intricacies of her copper dress left little room as to her good standing—a noble, not a guard. Yet even to Isra's untrained eye, the lady's stance proved that she knew how to use her weapon. She was beautiful and commanding in a way Isra could only envy.

"State your name, purpose, and why I shouldn't call my guards on you."

Isra's legs turned into wool, and words lumped into her throat. Panic gripped her, and she couldn't get past the spear tip or the threat in this woman's voice. She would die here, now, cold and exhausted. All because she couldn't think, couldn't speak. Isra stumbled back with a sniffle, and when her heel hit the stairs, she fell into them.

The spear's tip lowered, and the other woman's gaze softened. "Please. You're in my quarters, dripping water on my floor, wearing robes from the Myrian Enclave. Tell me what you meant to accomplish."

"Warmth," Isra blurted, and that one word broke her dam, and everything else flowed after it in a stammered, disjointed plea. "I-I was so cold up there. I need warmth, and shelter, and is Varden here? I ran away. I stabbed Avenazar with a poisoned letter opener and ran away, but I don't think it was enough, and now he'll come after me. Please."

She forced herself to stop wringing her hands and looked up, past the spear tip and to her ... host? Full-body shudders still coursed through her, and water pooled around her ass, on the stone steps.

The lady set her spear against the door frame with a shake of her head, then helped Isra to her feet without a word. A firm hand on her shoulder guided her through the quarters, past a massive office offering an incredible view of Isandor. Snow obscured many of its lights, but Isra could make out the shape of lovely towers and bridges. The beautiful designs in the thick wooden desk, the rug under their feet, or the pottery that housed every plant indicated the work of master craftspeople, and the area reminded her of her father's office.

Which meant this regal woman …

"I–I'm sorry, I never asked for your name," Isra blurted.

"Can you not guess? You walked into my office and I am bringing you to my rooms. These are the highest quarters of the Brasten Tower."

Isra squeezed her eyes shut. She'd blundered directly into Lady Brasten's quarters—had been threatened at spear point by her! What a way to start a relationship. She felt like a fool, wet clothes dripping on the polished wooden floor.

"My apologies, Lady Brasten." She tried to sound gracious—not her best skill, truly. "I admit I'm a bit flustered."

"Understandable. I likewise apologize for your brutal welcome. These are dangerous times."

Lady Brasten pushed open one of the doors leading out of the office, and the warmth intensified. It enveloped Isra, prickling the tip of her fingers, sinking into her drenched robe. Bright flames danced in the fireplace before her, illuminating the lady's bedroom in a wavering light. Plush chairs flanked the fireplace, an intricate and graceful woodcarving in their armrests and back. Likewise, the curves of her bedhead combined strength and elegance, drawing the eyes without becoming overbearing. Isra's gaze moved from one gorgeous furniture to the next, drinking in the sights. The styles differed from her father's choices, yet the balance and wealth they spoke of reminded her of home. It was almost enough to forget the awful day.

"You have a beautiful room," she said.

"Thank you. Please, sit by the fire."

Isra staggered to a chair and collapsed in it. The heat caressed her skin, slowly pushing away the cold. She hoped her dripping skirt wouldn't drench the seats and ruin them, but Lady Brasten moved to the chest at the foot of her bed, her feet almost gliding over the ground. She searched through it and retrieved a large wool blanket, patterned into five wide stripes: green paling into white, then white turning to black. She threw it over Isra's shoulders, then strode to her wardrobe and withdrew a thick robe.

"Here you are. You should get out of your drenched clothes and into this marvel. It's enchanted to regulate temperature. Stay and warm yourself. You're as safe as possible here, given current circumstances."

Isra's weak fingers gripped the blanket as she tightened it around her shoulders, stunned by the kindness. Her tears threatened to return, but she fought them off. "Where are you going?"

"You wished to meet Varden Daramond, did you not?"

Isra swallowed hard, trying to erase the lump in her throat. "Y-yes." She had no idea what he'd say. He'd told her to run, hadn't he? Maybe he didn't hate her. Maybe he wouldn't be angry to see her here, in his refuge. She wondered if Nevian was here too, now, or if he'd returned to the Shelter. For a moment, she considered asking Lady Brasten, but Varden would know. She could wait. "Thank you. This is—I …"

"Don't worry about it," Lady Brasten said. "Master Avenazar's enemies will always be welcome into my tower. I accepted that risk when I accepted Lord Dathirii's request, and I will not renege on my duty."

Her voice had such a soothing cadence that despite witnessing Avenazar's power and ruthlessness over and over, Isra found herself believing in Lady Brasten. She needed this reassurance. Jilssan had vanished, and the disappearance weighed on Isra, a constant reminder that even the best could fail. Something had gone wrong, horribly wrong, the promises of safety let her cling to hope, feeble as it was. Her throat tight, she nodded, then repeated "Thank you."

Her relief was short-lived, interrupted by the distinctive click of a lock once Lady Brasten closed the door behind her. Isra's insides squeezed. Was the fire and promises of safety a lure? Did Lady Brasten plan to bring guards upstairs and throw her into a cell? But no. It wouldn't make any sense. Lady Brasten didn't need to trap her, not when she'd had a spear pointed at Isra, who'd been on the verge of hypothermia. Everything would be fine.

Isra stopped her hand-wringing, peeled off the cold and wet layers of clothes on her back, then wrapped herself in both the blanket and robe. Once changed, she dragged the seat closer to the fire, then huddled into it, feet drawn back to her. Her legs and arms prickled and hurt as they thawed and flared back to life, but she was no longer shivering uncontrollably. The thick blanket's warmth formed a shield, protecting the soft magical robe as it slowly warmed her naked skin. Isra exhaled and closed her eyes, relaxing into the chair, the comfort, and the welcomed safety.

VARDEN should have known he wouldn't get a full night of cuddling with Arathiel. His luck never held for long, and after what they'd done today, it was no surprise that consequences would catch up to them. At least the few hours of rest had energized him, and in truth the jolt of terror when Amake Brasten had found him entwined with Arathiel had destroyed any chance he'd sleep again tonight. Varden could still feel the tension in his body, the way he'd drawn fire close as self-defence, the certainty he'd pay for his love. He'd doused it as quickly as he could, reminding himself that he wasn't in Myria anymore, but his instincts didn't agree with the logic. Arathiel had placed a steady hand on his shoulder, squeezing harder than necessary, and Varden had clung to his voice as he fought against his panic.

"How did you know Varden would be here?" he'd asked.

Amake Brasten had laughed. "First, he wasn't in his room. Your friend Cal is a terrible gossip, and it seems he found himself mysteriously at a certain Shelter's window as the two of you flirted in the snow. I had to bribe him with a cheese-filled dinner for the details, but it was well worth it. I must say, he would be thrilled by my discovery tonight."

Even now, after he'd taken the time to wash his face, dress, and follow Amake Brasten upstairs, Varden still flushed at the memory. Arathiel had laughed, but Varden wasn't used to this openness. It rattled him, pushing against every reflex instilled in him by years of hiding. The still-erratic beat of his heart said he'd need to have a conversation with Arathiel about this. For now, however, he had another problem to focus on.

Isra had curled into a large chair, bundled under a heavy blanket. Thick wavy brown hair hid her features, but the steady rise of her chest made it clear she slept. Varden studied her for a moment, then turned towards Lady Brasten, still by his side. "She said she'd stabbed Avenazar?"

"Yes."

Varden stared at the teenage girl longer. She'd surprised him in the Myrian Enclave, offering him the rekhemal without hesitation and directing him to Nevian. The girl who'd denounced him as a traitor had changed by leaps and bounds since then.

"Can you leave us alone?"

Amake Brasten nodded. "I'll see what rooms we still have available. The halls have never been this full, but if this keeps up, I'll run out of space."

For a moment, Varden considered offering his quarters. The brutal awakening left him longing for a space of his own, however, and he discarded the idea. "We thank you, as always, for your hospitality. If she stabbed him and he survived …"

"Yes. He's liable to come here as soon as he recovers, isn't he?"

"I'm afraid so."

Amake left without another word. She no doubt had ample security measures to verify, in addition to her meeting with the steward to arrange rooms for Isra. Varden soaked in the silence for a while, allowing the beloved dance of the fire to further soothe his nerves. Then he cleared his throat to wake Isra up.

She jumped to her feet, whirling around and dropping the blanket to the ground. Her arms spread out, fingers crooking as she reflexively prepared to draw a rune. She stared at him, her heavy breathing easing as she recognized him and her surroundings. It seemed they shared the brutal awakenings tonight.

"Good evening, Isra," he greeted.

Isra avoided his gaze, instead bending down to pick up the blanket that had pooled at her naked feet. She threw it over her shoulders, cleared her throat, and muttered. "Good evening, High Priest."

The title jarred Varden, and he scowled at it. Hadn't he told her, in prison, that he was no longer a high priest? Keroth's church had reneged him. It chaffed that they'd abandoned him despite years of service, even though he'd expected no better.

"I'd prefer just Varden," he said. "Lady Brasten told me you wanted to talk to me."

Isra slid down into the chair, bringing her legs back up under the blanket. She'd rarely looked so young. "I … I wanted to talk to *someone*. I needed help—I still do. I don't know what to do anymore."

Varden pulled a second chair closer, sat at the edge of it, and stared at Isra. She sounded earnest, but he'd learned long ago not to trust her and the ways her mood could swing. He'd thought her spoiled, and while that had certainly played its part, he could tell now that much more had boiled under the surface.

"Help us or hide, whichever suits you best. You cannot go out while Avenazar lives, if he still does. You're one of us now— the targets, marked for death or worse by an abusive, powerful man. We're all here. Nevian, Diel Dathirii, myself … and now you."

"Aren't we making his task easier? He'll rip us all to pieces at once."

"Better that than to let him hunt us down one by one and die alone, don't you think?"

Varden's fingers clenched on the armchair, and he gritted his teeth. He hadn't been alone when Avenazar had descended upon him, but none of the gathered acolytes dared to stop him. It was worse, to be humiliated in front of everyone then thrown into a cell with nothing but hours of torture for company. Would Avenazar kill him this time around, or would he try his domination spell again? Varden forced himself to exhale slowly, calming the anger and fear swirling within him.

"We won't let him either way. We'll be ready when he comes."

Only faith underlay this belief, but he clung to it with absolute conviction. Keroth had set him on this path to face

Avenazar, and he'd see the task through to the end, through the rekhemal and the spell Nevian intended to devise around it. He hadn't had a chance to ask what it entailed yet, but they'd sit down together and build a way to counter Avenazar. It could be done. It had to be possible.

"Varden ..." Isra's voice trailed off, small and intimidated. She was half-hidden behind a blanket and struggled to meet his eyes. "What happened today—I'm sorry. Him going after Nevian ... th-that was me, too. N-not willingly!"

She added the last quickly, when Varden had risen from his feet, anger burning through him in an inexorable wave. For two years, he'd protected and healed Nevian, shielding the young apprentice to the best of his ability, finding secret kinship in his rebellion. He'd cared for the rude, standoffish teenager more than was wise, and they'd both paid the price for it. Even now, surrounded by allies and free to be himself, Varden felt more at home—closer to the humanity he'd worked so hard to preserve—alongside the young man. He gritted his teeth, gesturing for Isra to finish.

"He ripped it from my mind. But I'm sorry, because so many other times were my fault, too, and I didn't—I wasn't *thinking*." Her voice rose into a higher pitch, breaking at the end, and Isra paused to steady herself. "I know I've been bad, and I can't ever fix it, but I just—I'm sorry. I hurt *you*, too, provoked everything that happened to you, and here you are, comforting me."

Varden pressed his lips together, trying to juggle every

emotion tangled into him. He'd never forget Isra had been the one going to Avenazar, telling the wizard she thought he'd betrayed the enclave, causing him to attack him and both Nevian.

Yet he knew sooner or later, something would have made Avenazar turn on him, that Isra was a catalyst to inevitable pain, not the cause of it. And for once, her apologies seemed sincere. So much had changed, it was difficult to reconcile the crying girl in front of him now with the haughty Myrian he'd learned to avoid. A hardened part of him wanted to ignore her pain and sidestep shouldering her burdens, yet he found himself smiling instead, a hint of mockery in his voice.

"I was comforting you when you sought me out in a prison cell between two torture sessions too," he pointed out. "It's just ... it's who I am, I guess."

"You called me obnoxious." Isra pouted and crossed her arms, and the movement tugged at the blanket. "How is that comforting?"

Varden laughed, which only deepened her frown, but he couldn't quite bring himself to care.

"I can't be your emotional cushion, Isra," he said, "but I will accept your apology. You may have a lot to answer for and difficult work ahead of you, but you have time. You're a teenager. Learn from your mistakes and you'll be fine."

He pushed himself to his feet, startled at the exhaustion catching up to him, the blackness encroaching on his sight.

Webs of memories from his time at the enclave clung to his mind, weighing it down, sapping at his energy. Varden held the chair's armrest for a moment longer, allowing his vision to clear. Isra was staring at him, wide-eyed.

"Lady Brasten should have a room ready for you. Get rest. And …" Varden hesitated, wondering how much he could afford his next offer. Yet now that the idea had crossed his mind, he found he couldn't hold it back. "You're Isbari. If you have questions about our culture—food, beliefs, rituals, anything—I've been cut off for large parts of my life, but I'm sure I can answer some."

"I'm not—" She cut her protest short, and her face took on a solemn expression. Perhaps she understood the gravity of his offer, and how personal this knowledge was for him. Myrian church officials had done everything they could to keep him from reaching his community, and it wasn't until he'd entered adulthood and led his own services that he'd finally connected with them. Isra nodded. "I'll think about it. Thank you."

Varden extended a hand to help her out of the chair, and Isra grabbed it with force. Before he quite understood what had happened, she flung herself into him, tightening her thin arms around him and hugging him. He stiffened, unprepared for the show of affection and uncertain what to do about it. Without a word, Varden let the hug run its course, staring at the large fire while it passed, then squeezed Isra's shoulder as she stepped back.

"Let's go," he said. "You need rest."

So did he. Varden's fingers itched for a piece of charcoal and a moment of peace to draw several great fires, pouring the whirlwind of emotions the day had been, emptying his soul before he slept again. Without a word, he led Isra out of the room.

Chapter Twenty-eight

NEVIAN knocked at Varden's door early the next morning. Varden almost refused to budge, head ringing and limbs heavy from a too-short night. Wasn't he supposed to recover? But his daydreams of endless naps would need to stay in his imagination. Avenazar wouldn't wait for him to be fit to fight again. If Nevian believed he could help … Varden rolled out of bed, warning Nevian he'd need a minute.

Nevian held a small pile of books and scrolls, and he headed out as soon as Varden emerged, greeting him only with his name. Varden withheld any comment. Nevian's rough, busybody rudeness had a reassuring familiarity to it, and the silence gave him time to properly wake up.

They'd gone down two flights of stairs when a loud yawn startled Varden out of his tired reverie, and he caught the sound of footsteps coming up. Nevian hadn't slowed at all, even more lost in thoughts than he'd been, and Varden called his name right as they reached a landing.

"Someone's coming."

They leaned on the door as Diel Dathirii emerged from the stairs, a second yawn threatening to unhinge his jaw. He'd set a basket of various scrolls, candles, ink bottles and other miscellaneous items under the crook of his arms and had his eyes set on a jade statuette in his right hand. He startled when he noticed them, then dropped the carving with the rest and ran a hand through his hair.

"Didn't think I'd meet anyone this early!"

Exhaustion threaded his voice. Varden took in the dishevelled hair, the bags under his eyes and the stains at his fingertips, and added that to the fact Diel's bedroom was on the same floor as his, then reached the easy conclusion: he hadn't slept at all. From the hints Branwen had dropped, he had a difficult time doing so here, in a foreign bed without Jaeger. Varden thought of how comfortable Arathiel had been under him, how idyllic those few hours had been, and felt a pang of guilt. He didn't care to give that back to Diel, not when it meant putting Avenazar second. Maybe Diel needed a reminder of how this even started.

Varden let his hand hover near Nevian's shoulder. "I believe you've met young master Nevian?"

Varden's introduction was rewarded by a surprised flick of Nevian's gaze at the use of 'master', and the young man straightening up. He didn't have long to relish the reaction before relief washed away Diel's polite inquisitiveness.

"Oh, of course! You're the young apprentice I saved that day, when it all began." The elf surged forward, reaching for Nevian's shoulders. "I am so glad you're safe with us now."

Nevian jerked away from the extended hand, bumping into Varden in his attempt to dodge Diel's touch. A scroll on the top of his pile started rolling off, and Varden stopped it before it could fall.

"Saved?" Nevian repeated, his voice a fierce growl. "You provoked him. I would have died without Varden."

Was it petty, to enjoy how the smile froze on Diel's face? To relish the moment horrified realization danced through his face, fleeting as it was? Perhaps, but Varden figured it was better than getting angry at Diel for still not getting it. Even now, he bristled instead of admitting it.

"It seemed to me he was already well on his way to kill you, with or without my intervention." Diel pinched the bridge of his nose, squeezing his eyes shut. "I don't regret my actions, even now, with everything I've lost."

"Everything *you* lost? It's not about you," Nevian retorted. "We never asked for your help, but we're certainly paying for it. And now we'll fix it, too."

He strode down the stairs and past Diel with a great, indignant huff, and Varden pressed his lips hard to keep from smiling. Something had broken loose in Nevian since he'd left the enclave, and Varden enjoyed the little changes, like he'd both matured and stopped pretending to be an adult all at once.

"Well. That was …" Diel trailed off with a vague gesture.

"Expected?" Varden completed for him, knowing full well Diel had meant the exact opposite. "I hope your efforts to regain the Dathirii Tower are progressing at pace. Now if you'll excuse me …"

He offered a deferential nod then followed Nevian down the steps, leaving behind a speechless Diel. He had nothing to tell the man. An attack like what the Shelter had endured was exactly what he'd warned him about, when they'd first discussed their priorities. What could they have accomplished, if they'd moved against Avenazar immediately? He'd been bed-ridden, poisoned by his own lieutenant. That window would close soon—only Isra's attack kept it jammed open—but Varden himself had recovered since the explosion at the enclave. He wouldn't waste time or energy arguing with Diel Dathirii about the next move; he'd simply take it, alongside Nevian.

Besides, this would be an opportunity to check on the young wizard's state of mind, too. Yesterday was bound to have affected him.

Nevian, as it turned out, showed no sign of trauma or fatigue. Once they reached House Brasten's library, he scuttled through the rows, gathering every relevant tome and piling them next to those they'd salvaged from the Myrian Enclave. The eager bounce to his steps betrayed more joy than Varden had ever seen him acknowledge, and by the time he settled down to read, he was humming a soft and familiar music. It took a moment to place it, but when he realized Vellien had sung it by his bedside during his recovery, his face broke into a grin.

Varden settled into a chair, browsing the tomes Nevian had deemed useful as an excuse to subtly watch his companion's intense focus when Nevian seemed to remember him.

"Varden," he said, with honest surprise.

"You wished for my presence," Varden reminded him, mirth pushing through every word.

Perhaps the only reason Nevian didn't seem overly affected by yesterday's events was that he allowed nothing of the outside world into his bubble. It'd certainly match his behaviour at the enclave.

"I did." He blinked, as if chasing a deep, inconvenient daze, before turning back to the pile of tomes. "I'll have questions about the nature of your magic. Until then, you can do as you see fit." Varden's eyebrows shot up, but if his young friend noticed he was ordering him around, he showed no sign of it. He plunged back into his reading, muttering passages and scribbling notes on a nearby pad. The longer Varden watched, the more his desire to draw increased, and in time he slipped out of the airy library to retrieve Branwen's gifts and scratch that itch.

Most of their morning trickled by in relative silence. Nevian had him clarify a point here and there, but he otherwise seemed content to speak only to himself, repeating lines in the books or his notes as if they held great significance. The more time passed, however, and the more frustrated he grew, until his forehead thumped on the open pages.

"I'll never figure it out." The paper muffled his voice, so Nevian lifted his head again. "Jilssan believed it was possible, but I don't understand how. There is nothing practical in this essay!"

He sounded *so betrayed.* Varden stifled his laughter, before he drew Nevian's ire. He didn't want to insult the apprentice's absolute trust in dusty tomes.

"Perhaps I can help more than your text?"

Doubt creased a line in Nevian's forehead, and he crossed his arms in the most dramatic, prove-it-if-you-think-you're-better fashion. Varden wasn't sure how long he could keep himself from laughing—hadn't Nevian invited him for his knowledge?—so he nudged the conversation along.

"What do you need to know?"

"I need to understand how you do it," he said. "Your magic."

How …? Varden wouldn't know where to begin with this. He ran a hand through his curly hair, staining his forehead black with charcoal. "It simply happens, I suppose. I reach for Keroth and become a conduit for Their will, shaping it as I desire."

"You just … will it."

"Yes."

"But *how?*" Nevian insisted. "How do you 'reach'? What does that mean? You're no more practical than the essay."

"Not everything can be explained and controlled with charts or diagrams, Nevian. My faith guides me."

"If faith could defeat Avenazar, he'd be long gone," Nevian

muttered, turning back to his tome. "There has to be a way. A technique—something concrete I can use!"

"There certainly must be one. Avenazar succeeded. He exploited my ability to call upon Keroth—my communion with Them—and twisted it to fuel his spell."

Varden hadn't meant for bitterness to crawl into his voice, but bile and anger surged nevertheless. Nevian didn't notice. Nevian remained completely oblivious, his nose in the book again, mind no doubt on the theoretical aspects of spellcasting.

"The problem," he continued, "is that what Avenazar did is entirely different than our goal. He used you as a source of power—a conduit, like you said—but he dictated the end result. All he wanted was the raw magical energy you could provide. If I imitate that, it could destroy the rekhemal."

So Nevian's idea could destroy the rekhemal? No one had implied his holy artefact might be at risk until now, although Nevian had remained secretive about the exact nature of his plan.

"I might be more useful if you explained what you aimed to accomplish."

Nevian's mouth turned into a flat line and he paled. His secrecy worried Varden, but asking directly again was unlikely to get him to open up. He sighed.

"Very well, but don't forget what I told you when I first lent it to you. It could claim your soul."

Nevian snorted, but for the first time since they'd started

digging at books hours ago, he smiled and his shoulders relaxed. "I know you were pulling my strings. It only affects awareness. You … you wouldn't have given me something unsafe." His smile vanished, and he trailed the page with his fingers without reading. "I'm sorry I didn't warn you. When I returned the rekhemal to you, I knew about—I—"

"Nevian." Varden leaned over the table to reach out, stopping short only when he recalled how he jumped at unexpected contact. He set his hand down on the tome instead, near Nevian's own. "You were in an untenable position, but your only responsibility was to yourself. I would never ask you to willingly shoulder the risks Avenazar represents."

Nevian's fingers curled into shaking fists. They'd so rarely had the occasion to talk together, and never so freely. When Nevian looked up, Varden could watch track the rapid-fire emotions across his face, no longer contained and concealed. In the enclave, Nevian had bottled up all he could, desperate to remain as small and inconsequential as possible.

Slowly, Nevian straightened his back and met his gaze. "And if I meant to shoulder those anyway, would you stop me?"

Was this why he wouldn't share his plan? Had Nevian gotten it into his head that self-sacrifice was the only way to repay Varden for the pain endured? It seemed unlike him, but what did Varden know of Nevian, really? In the enclave, neither of them could be their full selves, and Nevian was still young, his personal growth stunted by Avenazar's abuse. Varden might have only witnessed the dedicated, pragmatic, and resilient student, but what else could Nevian bloom into, given the chance?

Varden prayed he would have it, and he wished he could ensure it happened. His first urge was to protect Nevian and keep him away from this plan and whatever danger it entailed, but would that be fair? Nevian had everything at stake here, and what he wanted to risk was his to decide. No one should take that from him.

"I would stop you from shouldering it alone," he answered at length.

Nevian's blue eyes widened in surprise; he must have expected a fight. He hesitated then, pondering his options now that Varden had changed the nature of his idea by insisting on sharing the risk, and eventually nodded. Though his agreement was silent and brief, Varden knew it would be unshakeable.

"Together, then. Tell me the plan."

Nevian snapped the book shut. A bright smile lit his face, fondness softening his otherwise harsh features.

"It starts with Vellien," he said, and it was all Varden could do not to go *ah*. "I'm not sure how to explain. When Avenazar attacked the night of the winter solstice, he destroyed so many memories. My mind was … messy. Ruined. We pieced it back together. Vellien didn't just heal me. They guided me through it, and let me rebuild as I wanted, at the pace I wanted."

Nevian's voice had started shaking now, and he found a

particularly interesting point at the table to stare at. "I didn't understand the significance until Avenazar returned and I—"

He paused, paler now, his eyes glazing over. Varden was about to tell him to take his time or stop entirely if he needed, but Nevian foresaw it and interrupted him with a lifted palm. He squeezed his eyes shut for another few seconds, then forged onward.

"Avenazar entered my mind and I discovered … I discovered I had control. He was there, and he was tearing at it, but he didn't know the paths. He perceived only what I allowed. I couldn't have thrown him out, but I led him in circles, flinging breadcrumbs of memories his way until he tired and left."

While Nevian had remained pale, he'd regained much of his countenance now, and Varden couldn't help but be impressed by his calm. Even faked, managing that veneer was an accomplishment in itself.

"I don't think it would have worked if he'd been healthy. The destruction at the Shelter must have taken a lot out of him, and he was feverish. Isra says Jilssan had been poisoning him. That must have helped."

"She's here now," Varden told him. "She tried to use that poison to kill him. We may have a few days of peace still."

Hope flitted through Nevian's gaze. "We might have time to work this out, then. This taught me how we can fight back. Because when he's in my mind—" He broke off, bringing one arm close to himself and clinging to it with his other hand.

"When he's in my mind, he's in unknown territory, and he doesn't even realize it. He's clueless. All he sees is a pathetic target, a toy to break over and over. But I'm not—I made myself more solid."

Nevian had always been solid. He might not see it yet, but he'd survived so much and always protected his core. Even now, remembered pain piercing through his voice like a thousand jagged edges, he radiated passion and pride. Varden had nourished flames all his life as part of his duties, and he vowed never to let that one die.

"The plan," Nevian said at last, oblivious to the quiet promise happening across from him, "is to trap him."

"Inside you?"

Alarm shot through Varden. This would be far worse than the terrible consequences of defeat. Could it even be called a win if Avenazar stayed within Nevian?

"N-no!" Nevian shuddered and squeezed his eyes, as if battling intense nausea. "I could never. I want to be, and live, and study. No. That's why I need the rekhemal and divine magic. Self-awareness gave me the tools to fight back, and it's how your artefact works: it grants one more awareness. With it on, I'd have an even stronger understanding of my own mind and a bigger advantage. But I ... I need it for its physicality, too, Varden. If I can figure out how to return a mind into a different body than the one it was attached to ..."

A cold horror trickled into Varden as he finally understood

the scope of Nevian's idea. "You want to trap Avenazar inside the rekhemal."

He had so little left from Keroth's Church now, and the rekhemal had been entrusted to him. He might no longer be a High Priest, but even if he never led another Long Night's Watch, to desecrate the rekhemal by shoving Avenazar's mind into it … It left him cold, as if the fire had been snuffed out of him.

"It's a holy relic, Nevian, not a mundane tool or container."

Nevian cringed at the flatness of his tone, but what else could Varden say?

"I understand." From the hint of stubbornness Varden detected, he guessed it wouldn't stop him. "We have no time to create another one, however, and from reading all these texts, I feel the particular nature of divine magic can help us circumvent Avenazar's defences and, well, and my own inexperience. I don't think I can pull out that complex a spell by myself."

"You believe I can?" Varden could understand why: he had performed incredible feats of magic with fire, and just recently combined the divine power of three different gods, but still.

"I don't know," Nevian answered. "I have no idea how to intersect arcane and divine. I can see similarities. I use runes as a tool to channel magic while you and your faith act as instruments for Keroth, but how can they merge? This is so beyond me, and the only time we have before Avenazar recovers is what Isra granted us. If only I knew …"

Nevian trailed off, frowning. He stared at a point ahead of him, lips moving as his mind worked. Varden waited and seconds stretched into minutes. Nevian tapped on the table, his irritation growing. At length, Varden prodded him.

"What is it?"

"A memory." Nevian inhaled deeply. "Something—someone—Avenazar erased."

"Someone who could help us now?" he asked. Memory had a way of pushing associations to the surface whether you wanted them or not. Perhaps if he jogged Nevian's, they'd find this erased person. But who could Nevian know that would help them? He'd almost never left the enclave. Almost. "Nevian. When you sneaked out into Isandor at night, what were you doing?"

Nevian's head snapped up and he jumped to his feet. "That's it!" He grabbed the table with both hands, a wide grin spreading across his face. "I was meeting with a mentor." Yet as memories rolled back in, Nevian's excitement dimmed. "She's ... she's Isandor's most dangerous mercenary leader, and warned me she wouldn't get involved. But I'm certain—the way she wields earth magic is unlike anything I've seen. It's not arcane, but she does perform that too. She was teaching me the runes. We need her help. She can create this spell, and I bet she can do it faster than any of us."

Varden had some reservations about the concept of hiring 'Isandor's most dangerous mercenary', but shady allies seemed a simple sacrifice to make. They'd worked with Jilssan already, so what was one more? Besides, mercenaries had one advantage: it was easy to know what they wanted from you. His smile stiff, his doubts clearly etched into his voice, Varden rose to his feet.

"Let's hope Lady Brasten grants us the required gold, then."

CHAPTER TWENTY-NINE

GREAT banners hung from the reception hall's high ceiling, depicting an intricate silver tree wrapped around a stylized D, the design sharp against the forest green background. Yultes stood alone in the midst of them, contemplating his handiwork. The reception hall had been arranged into two primary areas. One held an open floor for nobles to mingle, with waiters weaving through the crowd and a few tables lining the walls, for those seeking to acquire nourishment or refreshment in a more direct fashion. The second, farther from the main doors, contained the small stage and the commissioned lectern, along with two arcs of low, wide steps carved out of an old wood, rising like twisting branches, on which rising rows of staggered chairs fit with ease.

It had been a busy time, putting together Hellion's grand event. There had been so many details to think of—wine, food, seats, glasses, décor, invitations, what particulars to announce and what to keep secret ... Looking at the list Jaeger had first left him with overwhelmed him. Even with reluctant compliance from the staff, Yultes would have a hundred different things to manage, and he was quite frankly unused to this level of minutiae. But Jaeger had laughed at his dismay.

"When you build something, Yultes, you must set the foundations one brick at a time." The use of Diel's metaphor couldn't have been coincidence—not with Jaeger. "You already know what you want as a result. Quit worrying and get to work, and you'll be there before you know it."

At first, Yultes didn't understand the source of Jaeger's confidence in his abilities. He tried to bolster himself with it, pushing away his personal doubts, and did as told: he set to work. He held meetings with the household's staff heads, organizing the grand evening while sifting out how to cut corners in noticeable ways. And *that*, despite his inexperience, is what he excelled at. He drew upon countless attendances to similar parties, recalling the small details he and Hellion had sneered at. No wonder Jaeger trusted him to succeed. Yultes had been that judgmental noble unearthing every flaw in a soirée, sitting back with wine and friends to comment on them as if they were a slight to his person. He knew what an event hiding a slow decrepitude looked like, and he could create one.

Hellion had told him in no uncertain terms that today was a test of his competence, and Yultes agreed, albeit with different targets to reach. The Dathirii banners loomed over him, as if ready to pass judgment.

Most of them hadn't been unfurled in several decades, and although Yultes had ordered them cleaned, he'd asked for some to remain lacklustre. Dust dampened the rich green threads on many, and one even had tears near the bottom. Everything had gone through a similar treatment: the worn tablecloths on tables at the back, the notched and scratched wood of their rows of seats, the makeshift wooden scene which had last been used for Vellien's first concert—all of them stood as remnants of a more glorious past still clinging to relevance. He needed others to see it as clearly as he did now: Hellion's future meant going backward, and their fond memories of such times would not match reality.

Yultes breathed in deeply, relishing the stale scent of the hall. He'd scheduled the musicians late, so until Hellion's speech began, all the Dathirii nobles would have to occupy themselves would be each other, this unmistakable smell, and quickly depleting bites from the kitchens—his own purposefully erroneous estimation of their needs, since Nicole had wanted nothing to do with him. Only drinks would be served in abundance, and hopefully their emotions would run high rather rapidly, worsening any disappointment.

This was as good as it'd get. He ought to stop delaying, before the intended lateness turned into an issue for the second, riskier part of the evening. If Dathirii relatives still milled the stairs and corridors, Branwen might find sneaking in a far harder challenge, with or without help from Mia Allastam. With one last steadying breath, Yultes spun towards the main doors muffling the murmur of a crowd, and gestured at the staff members flanking them. They opened the hall, officially beginning the soirée.

Dathirii nobles streamed in, a sea of golden hair and pointed ears. Many already walked in pairs, cousins deep in discussion about the city's politics and business. He'd written the invitations to emphasize the importance of the occasion, and several Dathirii had dressed accordingly, opting for their best attire and transforming the crowd into a mass of green doublets, golden threads, and tree patterns. A conservative choice of fashion that'd spare them Hellion's unfavourable notice, no doubt. What would Branwen have worn, under such circumstances? The most extravagant, eye-drawing dress of her considerable wardrobe, or an outfit with House Allastam's colours as a statement about who truly owned the Dathirii Tower now. Or both, even. He smiled at the thought of his niece's imagined defiance—a happenstance that had grown more frequent over the course of their correspondence.

They'd exchanged a few letters through her intermediary, almost exclusively key business information, but he'd passed messages between Garith and her too, bearing witness to the incessant teasing between them. It'd left an indelible mark on him, to stand by Garith's desk and recite with dwindling calm the explicit details of her second encounter with one of Kellian's guards, followed by a quaint *"I hope your tower-contained chastity does not weigh too hard on you."*

Garith's chuckle had turned into a full laugh once he'd noticed the intense blush on Yultes' cheeks. "You made the mistake of mentioning you read these to me, didn't you? She's messing with *you* this time, not me."

He had indeed written that in his last letter. In his next, he took great care to state he and Garith considered selling her extensive and unique wardrobe to shore up House Dathirii's finances and asked which might fetch the best price. When her inflammatory reply came, he'd been more than happy to share with their coinmaster.

Yultes wished he could also discuss Branwen's potential fashion decisions for tonight's event with him, but he'd need a pretext to approach Garith without raising suspicions. Instead, he mingled with the other Dathirii as they drifted into the room, picking up glasses and quick bites before clustering together in small groups. Awkwardness tinged most conversations he joined, and many resorted to congratulating him about his new position before latching onto gossip from the city that had nothing to do with their own inner power struggle. Yultes kept his presence brief and straightforward, choosing to inflict the malaise of it on as many as he could. Through it, he purposefully avoided the back of the room, where Viranya Dathirii was talking with the rest of Hellion's most fervent champions.

She had adorned herself with brooches, rings, and earrings all bearing the Dathirii crest in an ostentatious display of pride only matched by her main interlocutor's braiding of hair and ribbons, which looped and twisted to create an artistic *D* with the forest-green ribbons. Iriel Dathirii had always taken great care of his shining golden hair—and often remarked on Yultes' own lacklustre white-sand tone. He had been the coinmaster when Yultes had joined the family, under Diel's father, and he'd never accepted being replaced by Garith. Along with the two of them, clad in an ornate breastplate that rivalled Kellian's decorative armour, stood Enmaris Dathirii, one of the few soldiers in the Dathirii guard that actually belonged to the noble house—the one who only ever agreed to work as a bodyguard to prestigious events.

Yultes had no particular urge to speak with them, but despite his best attempts to steer clear, Viranya spotted him flitting between two groups and called after him.

"Yultes, what a pleasant surprise! Please, come over and greet us properly." Yultes obeyed reluctantly, ignoring the implied 'as we deserve' at the end of her demand. She did not give him time to actually greet them. "We never truly chatted when you last interrupted me—you were in such a hurry!"

Coded message: she hadn't forgiven him this slight. No surprise there, if he was honest. "My apologies. I had much to accomplish in order to make tonight the event it deserved to be."

"I'm sure." She cast an unimpressed look at the room and granted him a most condescending smile. "So how does it feel to climb into such a prestigious position? We were just discussing how much we'd hoped to see it back within Dathirii hands."

Yultes forced a smile. "Then it is my utmost pleasure to fulfill your hopes."

Iriel huffed, lips pinched with discontent, and unlike his two companions, he dropped all pretence of niceties. "Life is, I'm afraid, full of disappointments."

"Indeed."

Yultes needed all his self-control to get this single word out. Iriel's disdain cut deeply, at wounds he'd done his utmost to heal or hide through the years. He'd worked hard and long to be accepted within House Dathirii, but it was never enough for these three. Hellion had promised it would be, one day, if he behaved properly and gave the family everything. So Yultes had—Trish was dead because he had—and it'd changed nothing. He'd failed, was still being set aside and demeaned by this small group he'd spent decades trying to impress.

Garith's laughter carried across the room, all charm and warmth, and it doused Yultes' bitterness. Someone in this family *had* accepted him. He had spoken directly to the loneliness lurking deep within Yultes and invited him to break it, if he dared. Would it be exchanging one set of behaviour for another, if he let that 'someone' Garith had perceived emerge and coalesce? And if it was, wasn't it worth the risk anyway? Yultes' gaze danced between Viranya, Iriel, and Enmaris, then he offered all three a slight bow.

"I like to think I'm exactly where I need to be, fulfilling Alluma's deepest wishes. Enjoy your evening."

Anger twisted their smiles, and Yultes drew great satisfaction from it. He did not give any the time to school their features or him, and simply walked away with his chin up.

BRANWEN resented having to sneak inside her own home, under the guise of an enemy soldier, during a soirée attended by most of her family but to which she had pointedly not been invited. The petty, dramatic part of her wished to stride into the room, flinging her nasal helmet to the side and shaking her hair out, claiming in front of all that Hellion was a fraud to mock, not a leader to follow. It would ruin his little evening and bring her great satisfaction.

Unfortunately, Yultes had kept this particular honour to himself—an egoist even when he helped, truly! At least he'd asked the next best thing from her, a favour they could all agree on: someone needed to extricate Jaeger from the Dathirii Tower tonight, before whatever humiliation Yultes had in mind for Hellion and the inevitable subsequent fury. Or, in Yultes' words, "There is only so much I can do to distract him from standards of leadership and respect he will never reach, especially with such a poignant reminder near at hand."

That had been a surprise—and a delight—to read. Sure, the rhythm of their exchanges had changed after she'd gotten Yultes to read some creative erotica aloud, but the tremendous skills with which her uncle cut Hellion to his core didn't match the tone of a reluctant helper, as she'd have expected. It was suspiciously too much, but if Yultes was playing a part, well, Branwen intended to enjoy the performance while it lasted. Besides, she'd have the opportunity to hear Jaeger's opinion on the matter soon. If he could trust Yultes after decades of enmity, they all could.

So she'd come prepared with this Alton-procured armour and with a small vial of the strongest soporific she could find on such short notice—which, thanks to Hasryan's tips for sellers, should knock out whoever watched Jaeger's door in a matter of seconds. Branwen wasn't used to such direct tactics, but after a brief planning session with Alton, it'd been clear that the Allastam guards knew each other too well for her to convincingly deceive them for more than a fleeting encounter. There'd be no luring this one away on false pretences.

She passed the reception hall, and her heart clenched at the murmur of a crowd drifting out of it. Despite herself, her steps faltered and she perked her ears, mentally untangling the voices until she identified their speakers. Here, the boisterous laughter of Aunt Ellie, there the sharp inflections of cousin Derral. She longed to join them and chat, longed for her old normal, with the Dathirii family around her. But for that, she had to keep going.

Branwen steeled herself against the nostalgia and started off again. Her fingers drifted against the uneven wood of their walls, so often walked past, but the echo of her steel boots on them was entirely unfamiliar, a jarring difference that set her ill at ease. As if the very tower rejected her as a stranger, unwelcome within its walls. She hated it, and that anger sped her steps, made her climb the stairs two by two until she reached the level with Yultes' old quarters. Jaeger's Allastam guard stood by the door, slouching and bored—a perfect target for her frustration.

She slipped the soporific vial into her palm and kept advancing. Hasryan had taught her a few techniques to get him to breathe in the vapours without causing a ruckus, but as he straightened from the wall and turned to her, Branwen forgot all of them. Her glare latched onto this single soldier, with dark indigo sleeves under his breastplate and the leafy A of Allastam's motif in white near the cuffs. She took in the beak nose, the clear blue eyes, the discontent twist of his lips, and she hated him outright. For a moment he became all his employer had inflicted upon her family, all the pain and fear of the recent weeks, all her love for Jaeger and Garith and Diel, who'd suffered more than anyone from this coup. Fury burned through her as she stomped down the corridor and—before he even realized the danger—smashed the vial in his teeth.

He cried out, the sound warping into a strangled choke as he breathed the volatile substance in. Branwen snapped out of her angry daze and reeled backward, covering her mouth and nose. "Don't get it all over you," had been Hasryan's main advice, and she sure had splashed a significant amount on her armour. Her mind slowed and the edges of her vision dulled as she watched the guard stumble forward, reaching for her. Branwen slapped his hand aside, striding farther away, and he collapsed within seconds. She stood there, panting and woozy, fighting her own soporific for Alluma-knew-how-long. Only once she was certain she wouldn't crumple did she move, knocking twice on Yultes' door before cracking it open.

When she stepped into the room, Jaeger was shoving a small purple flower into his mouth and chewing, his dark eyes on the door. Bruises painted his pale cheeks an ugly purple and yellow, but beyond them and a growing thinness, Jaeger remained strikingly unchanged. His long braid didn't have a hair out of place, and he'd selected a favourite combination of dark blue trousers and doublet over a simple white shirt. One might think nothing horrible had happened to him, and Branwen knew that was precisely the point. His quiet resilience shored up her own confidence.

"Don't tell me they feed you so little that you have to eat Yultes' plants to survive," she quipped, and she pulled her helmet off in one dramatic swoop.

His wariness melted away, transforming into joy more open than he ever displayed. "Branwen." He'd gasped her name, tasting it in wonder.

"The one and only!" She grinned at him and spread her arms. "We don't have much time, though. Pack up anything important."

Jaeger went rigid, and his brow creased. "You intend for me to leave."

He sounded … reluctant? Branwen scowled. "Obviously. If you trust Yultes, that is. He thinks the risk is too high for you after tonight."

A wry smile curved Jaeger's lips. "So he asked you to extract me, is that it? How touching."

Branwen didn't understand what amused him so. The guard outside wouldn't stay under forever, however, and she'd rather have left the Tower before he came to his senses or was found. "C'mon, Uncle. If not for yourself, do it for Diel. He's utterly hopeless without you, you should see him! Spends his day pacing aimlessly, loses himself in thoughts during important conversation … Lady Brasten's a fine ally, but by the time this is over, half our merchants will have signed with her instead. We need your unstoppable team back."

Jaeger's amusement vanished. "Perhaps it's time," he said, and longing seeped through his words. "I've taught Yultes what I could. I won't pretend I understand why he helps, but he seems genuine. The work we've done to undermine Hellion—ruining his mornings before important meetings, concealing funds, protecting the staff—wouldn't have been possible without him. I keep expecting the other shoe to drop, and for the old Yultes to return. Perhaps I ought to flee before it does."

By the bitterness in his tone at the end, he hated the idea of fleeing. Branwen set a hand on his forearm. "Don't think of it as a retreat. We simply need you on another frontline."

His eyebrows arched, and he cast her a knowing look, the 'don't think you can fool me about my own feelings that easily' one. It didn't stop him from dropping a quick kiss on her forehead before scouring the quarters for the rare belongings he meant to bring along. Once he'd packed a change of clothes, a single book, and an old quill, he turned and embraced the room with one last glance.

"Yultes will have to forgive me for the unwatered plants," he said, finality creeping into his voice.

Branwen set the Allastam helmet back onto her head, and they left.

CHAPTER THIRTY

THIS time, the silence in the corridors had an even more hostile quality to it, as if it existed for the sole purpose of echoing their every step louder. Branwen hurried along, all desire to banter with Jaeger quenched by the heaviness of the air around her. Her uniform might buy her a few seconds of hesitation in another Allastam guard, but with the vial of soporific shattered, she'd have only her wits to defend herself. Soldiers still surveyed most exits, but Yultes assured her he'd never seen any on the doors leading in and out of Camilla's private quarters. They'd locked those and called it a day—not that a lock would've stopped her, even if she didn't have her aunt's keys in her pocket right now.

First, though, Branwen needed to stop in her own quarters. Working her network without access to her usual disguises had severely hampered her ability to reach some informants, and she couldn't ignore this opportunity to grab a few outfits. Besides, she and Jaeger would stand a much better chance of escaping if they could pass for house staff. After some makeup and the right clothes, all they'd need would be to look preoccupied and fake a conversation about chairs or papers Hellion had urgently demanded they'd fetch, and they'd be left alone. Hopefully, she could fit it all in half an hour—she didn't dare take more, even if Hasryan had guaranteed at least two hours of sleep from that soporific.

They reached her rooms unimpeded, and Branwen's throat tightened as she closed the door behind them. Sneaking through her home had weighed on her; corridors once beloved could now betray her with every corner, and enemies could hear the stairs creak under her steps instead of family. The Dathirii Tower had been taken from them. Not her quarters, though. Everything inside was as it should be, and the familiarity of it all wrapped around her heart and eased the tension in her shoulders. She was home. Not for long, not under pleasant circumstances, but she was. How she wished she had time to revel in it.

"Undo your braid," she told Jaeger.

His head whipped towards her. "What?"

"You heard."

She grinned at how flustered the thought made him, and he must have caught the mischief in her eyes, as he tilted his head to the side and quirked an eyebrow in silent disapproval. Branwen's chest expanded tenfold, and her love for Jaeger spread from there to her entire body, a quiet and peaceful warmth that both energized and choked her. She'd never stopped moving since they'd lost the Dathirii Tower, never slowed to examine the gaping wounds inflicted upon her, lest they paralyze her. Here, in the sanctity of her quarters, it hit her fast and hard, leaving her speechless.

Jaeger's expression softened, his voice falling into a whisper. "I suppose if I must."

"Y–yes!" She cleared her throat and wrangled her emotions back under control. "It's too recognizable. I could spend hours on your disguise and everyone would still know you from a mile away because you never change hairstyles."

"My apologies. I did not think consistency was such a crime." The eyebrows returned, arched and amused.

He reached for his braid, and Branwen watched, mesmerized, as agile fingers untied it and made quick work of the tangled strands. How often had he undone Diel's hair during cozy nights together? How often had he done hers, for that matter? She longed for her younger days, when Diel or Jaeger would sit behind her and listen to her endless rambles while they braided and pinned her hair. She'd loved the sharp pulls on her hair, the touch of their fingers against her scalp, the intimacy of the moment. Gods, returning to her quarters was turning her into a melancholic sop. She ought to get a hold of herself.

Her throat tight, Branwen headed into the depths of her walk-in. Her fingers trailed every attire as she passed it, and the ever-changing textures soothed her. Her hands ached with the urge to pull the dresses out, to admire once again the beauty of her collection, but she forced her mind away from it. Priorities. First, she needed her House Lorn courier outfit and a proper binder to go with it, then the puffy-sleeved top and loose pants for her foreign tailor persona, and finally the low-cut, sleek dress and makeup essential to lounging at The Silken Rose, where nobles sought high-class escorts—many of whom Branwen had grown fast friends with throughout the years. She kept her eyes peeled as she unearthed those specific needs for anything she could use for Jaeger. His long slender body would float in most of her clothes, and she'd have to get creative to fit them to him. When her gaze locked on a deep purple masculine robe meant to be wrapped over the body and often worn with pants, she squealed with glee and yanked it off its support.

"Now that's a worrisome sound," Jaeger commented from her main rooms.

She strode out of the walk-in, every outfit draped over her forearm. "Aren't you excited? I might take offence."

Her voice trailed off, breath stolen by the sight of Jaeger. He'd perched on a stool, his back and shoulders straight, perfectly situated in the window's light as if posing for a painting. His dark hair cascaded all around him in bouncing waves, and he'd thrown it all to one side, concealing most of his bruises behind a black curtain. The moonlight slid across his cheekbones and pointed chin, sharpening them, and she'd swear his eyes had turned a darker shade of blue. Branwen had always known why her uncle loved Jaeger—quick-witted, dependable, and attentive as he was—but now she understood the other half of the equation.

"Oh, Jaeger. You absolutely must do this more often." Especially in front of Diel. If Ren smiled on her tonight, she'd be there to see his reaction when Jaeger walked into the Brasten Tower looking like *that*.

"It makes it hard to work."

"It makes you look like the brooding hero every girl swoons over, deep and dark secrets reflected in perfect eyes, mysterious as the moon."

The thought amused Jaeger, and the reserved tilt of his smile only amplified the effect. "You can see why I won't, then."

"What a shame. Imagine how crestfallen Garith would be if you were to tear all eyes away from him and to yourself? The worst day of his life!"

The laughter breaking out of Jaeger was as loose as his hair—frank and bouncing off the walls, released with abandon so raw it left Branwen unsettled. She'd never heard Jaeger so frayed and honest before, it gripped her into the same sort of unhealthy fascination as Diel's scatterbrained pacing had. All her life, these two men had provided solutions to all of her problems—the miracle worker and his steady anchor, always present, always reliable. She wished she'd never seen the cracks in them, never been forced to hold on while they crumbled. But it was almost over. Once they were reunited, they could heal.

Three sharp knocks at the door killed Jaeger's mirth, and they turned to it, horror sinking deep in their stomach. In the silence that ensued, the clink of steel was unmistakable. Guards.

"Open up!" a woman called.

Branwen's gaze slipped to the window. How far was the closest bridge? Curses, she should have set some furniture in the way, to buy themselves some time in case this happened. Her quarters had felt too safe, a haven in which no harm would come to them. Jaeger caught her gaze, tucked his hair behind his ears, and walked to the entrance, sliding the calm steward mask into place. She slunk out of view, on the other side the door, retrieving the long dagger at her hip. Her eyes snagged on the bruises across Jaeger's cheek as he opened the door, and she gripped her weapon tighter. She wouldn't let them give him another set without a fight.

"Ah, Jaeger," Hellion said, his tone all pleasant charm, "I believe Miss Branwen is with you?"

Five guards flanked Hellion as he pushed his way into the room—too many for her to assault. He had dressed in his finest clothes, an elegant doublet with long sleeves buttoned loosely over a white shirt. Delicate branches had been twined into his hair, braiding part of it and allowing the rest to flow behind in a river of gold. Ready to impress the crowd of Dathirii he should have been idly chatting with.

Branwen stifled a cry of rage, anger, and fear roiling inside of her. How had he known? She could only think of one way—one person who'd known she'd come and could tell him—and she hated it. She had wanted to trust Yultes, to believe he meant his scathing words about Hellion and held sincere doubts about his past mistakes. But he'd always been a slimy bastard, and it seemed that hadn't changed.

She stomped forward, shoving herself between Jaeger and Hellion. The Allastam soldiers encircled them, dousing any thoughts of escape. She jutted her chin up.

"Hellion! I don't remember inviting you inside my quarters."

"And I'll forgive you the offence," he replied, inclining his head with exaggerated magnanimity. She almost punched him there and then. "If you'll come with me to our beautiful reception. After all, the rest of the family is there. It'd be a shame for you to miss it."

Soldiers grabbed her arms, making it clear that the invitation, candid though it was, could not be refused. Good. Whatever games Hellion was playing, she'd relish a chance to ruin it.

YULTES hadn't anticipated how much work it'd be, the day of the reception, to turn it into the perfect disaster. By the time he'd finished gliding through the crowd to greet all the Dathirii present, he'd already witnessed several incidents. A waiter had bumped into Jayna Dathirii, her entire tray of spicy shrimp and cheese starters spilling all over the elf's gorgeous white-and-green dress, and the sommelier had dropped a bottle of wine while advising guests on their choice, shattering it on their smooth wooden parquet. Across the room, a chair's leg had cracked and given it, sending Iriel sprawling with glorious, humiliating cacophony, and an unexplained, musty odour had been gaining in strength throughout the evening. Every time, he was called upon to find a solution or run interference on behalf of the staff, sparing them from the worst of punishment or promising the irate noble they'd see to the details in the morning, but they couldn't afford to fire people here and now, during the event.

The incidents targeted random nobles, so no one would suspect foul play directed at Hellion, and held little connection to each other. They created small grievances that in a well-planned reception would be easily forgotten, but which made the lack of decent music and plentiful food all the more striking. It'd seemed a great strategy, but after two hours placating members of his family or scrambling to identify the source of the stink, Yultes regretted every single decision that had led him to it. When Hellion slid through the crowd and touched his shoulder, he barely remembered to smile through his frazzled exhaustion.

"Hellion!" he exclaimed. "How has your evening been?"

A lot hinged on this. Yultes had hoped that enough Dathirii would cozy up to him and flatter his ego to keep Hellion from noticing the awful degree of disorganization of the night, but he'd been so swept up in rectifying accidents and smoothing away indignation he hadn't kept track of his old friend. Hopefully, the number of times he'd indicated to other Dathirii that their new leader would love to hear from them had sufficed to occupy him.

He did seem in exceptionally good spirits—more so than Yultes had seen him since Diel had returned, certainly. At his question, he released a sing-song hmm and wiggled his fingers midair.

"How to say it? My pleasant but disappointing evening has recently taken a turn for the better. Apologies for the delay on the schedule regarding my speech, but I do believe I'm ready to begin."

"Delay?"

The word escaped Yultes before he could think better of it, and Hellion's eyebrows rose, his mouth twisting briefly in a grimace before sliding back to a convivial smile.

"You hadn't noticed," Hellion said.

A stranger might have mistaken his mild tone for unconcerned surprise, but not Yultes—never Yultes. After decades at Hellion's side, striving to gain and keep his approval, he'd learned to catch the slightest hint of disappointment. Every conversation had been a chance to prove himself or, more accurately, an opportunity to fail Hellion's standards and be rejected. That hadn't changed, and the touch of scorn in Hellion's statement sent reflexive fear and guilt coursing through Yultes.

"N-No, I've been …" He trailed off, halting his wave towards the new chair they'd provided to replace Iriel's. Excuses didn't matter with Hellion.

"All forgiven, my friend." Hellion squeezed his shoulder. Neither the declaration nor the gesture brought Yultes any relief. It was never that easy. "You've clearly had a lot to handle. I'll make sure you can rest properly after this. But for now, let's tie up the evening with some exquisite surprises, shall we?"

He slid away from Yultes without waiting for an answer—not that Yultes had any to give. No, he only had questions right now, each of them as terrifying as the other. Had Hellion meant he'd replace Yultes with another, more competent steward, thus granting him a vacation? And what surprises? They hadn't discussed his speech beyond the great thematic lines. As Yultes watched his devious old friend climb onto the stage, he felt like he had somehow missed the one detail that would ruin their plans.

Staff ushered the gathered Dathirii crowds towards the seating area, away from the long tables of starters and drinks as Hellion strode to the lectern, and in the absence of music—which would normally pause to encourage guests to follow indications—it took an awkward time to get everyone situated. Yultes drifted through the crowd, helping wherever he could, and almost ran face first into

Garith. The young coinmaster snorted at him.

"Yultes," he greeted, stiffly. "You're dreadful at this."

It stung, even though they'd agreed on snippy hostility beforehand. Yultes struggled to keep his face amused and aloof. "Yes, I'm sure a party without several litres of beer sloshed around and constant base innuendos isn't up to your standards. Thank you for the compliment."

He hurried along before he could hear Garith's snarky comment, but the laughter of those around him clung to Yultes regardless. He yearned for a friend in the crowd, to be honest and vulnerable with, to let go of the tight control he'd kept on who he allowed others to perceive. Yultes didn't even know what he'd say then, but the nugget of desire for it within him had grown into an all-consuming need and the brief, scathing encounter with Garith left him standing in a sea of elves he ought to call family, suffocating in his own isolation. If nothing changed, he would be the one to break.

"My beloved Dathirii, I am so pleased to see you all gathered here."

Hellion's sweeping declaration grounded him back to the present, and all the work he still needed to accomplish. He couldn't break now. What sort of architect would that make him if he collapsed before the towers he'd built? This nightmare evening was almost over, and he only had to hold on.

"The last weeks marked an important turn in our family's destiny. We have lived through difficult times, watched our reputation plummet into insignificance and our great, beautiful name be spoken with derision and pity. But *we* deserve better. We are an old and glorious line, more resilient and experienced than any of the human Houses in Isandor. We should be respected and hailed as leaders, not mocked and discarded!"

Hellion threw his arms out with calculated dramatic flair, and a few of the elves whispered in indignation and assent. Enmaris' gravely voice rose above the tumult with a firm "Absolutely!" and a resounding clap of hands. Yultes suspected that unlike him, they'd read the speech beforehand and knew when and how to react to best support it.

With every word, Hellion outlined the great future he envisioned: a flourishing partnership with House Allastam, new profitable deals with merchants that held large and steady businesses, reinstating House Dathirii as a respectable noble line and being known once more as sensible lawmakers rather than dangerous troublemakers. That last earned him a few grumbles from the elves around Garith, but by now most of the gathered Dathirii listened with careful interest.

Diel might have led the house for about a century, but many present today remembered his father before, and some had seen Isandor's founding alongside the old elf. Yultes had listened to Hellion and his close circle speak of those days with unabashed fondness, but those discussions had always held layers of bitterness for him. He and his brother had arrived in Isandor with no titles and no coins to their names, low-lives who'd have been disregarded without a second thought if not for their elven blood and the headstrong campaign Diel's sister had mounted. She'd been smitten with Lehran the moment they'd met—and he, with her, really. Many of Hellion's friends considered their inclusion in House Dathirii an affront, and Iriel had once called it the beginning of the end, even if it predated the death of their beloved Lord Dathirii. In the golden days Hellion now evoked, Yultes had no place in House Dathirii. Sometimes he wondered if that had changed at all.

"Change, however," Hellion went on, "must come from the inside. We will look to the future with fresh eyes and fresh ideas. After all, how can we expect others to believe in our transformation if we, ourselves, stagnate? As such, I have reached a few key decisions."

Curious whispers coursed through the crowd, and Yultes stiffened, his lungs tightening. He'd brought the impetus for this, pushing for Hellion to forget Jaeger and look forward, but none of these decisions had been discussed with him. In retrospect, Hellion's excellent mood earlier seemed ominous.

"In time, we will need to stop relying on House Allastam's gracious help to protect us from harm. As chagrined as I am by my brother's continuous absence, he must be replaced. As such, Lord Enmaris Dathirii will tackle the difficult challenge of rebuilding our Dathirii guards, many of which have deserted with their captain."

Not a single soul in this room actually believed Hellion cared about Kellian. The two had been at odds since forever, and neither made much secret of it. The animosity for Hellion had extended throughout the Dathirii Guards, even if most knew better than to express it outright, and with two of their own killed during his takeover, it didn't surprise Yultes they'd chosen not to return to their post at all.

"It will be an honour, milord," Enmaris replied, his booming voice covering the crowd's murmurs.

Yultes fought to keep disdain from twisting his lips at the use of titles. They'd lost those, or had Hellion forgotten? That was the only reason the rest of Isandor hadn't come knocking in outrage that Lord Allastam had so blatantly participated in another family's inner struggle. But Hellion couldn't sell a grandiose future of riches and good reputation if he reminded his closest allies that they now belonged to the rabble they despised.

After Enmaris, Hellion transferred the liaison to House Allastam to Jayna, who'd had the misfortune of the encounter with shrimp starters earlier. A few stains still marred her dress, but she lifted her head with pride. Jayna was a younger Dathirii with a sharp tongue and an intimate understanding of when to bow and flatter, and when to negotiate and placate. Yultes gritted his teeth; he'd always known his previous job would need to be reassigned, but he'd expected Hellion to consult him about the best person for it. He swallowed his bitterness, reminding himself that none of it mattered if he was, truly, working to unseat his old friend. He forced himself to meet the young elf's searching gaze, smile at her, and mouthed congratulations.

"And finally, it is my utmost pleasure to return the position of Dathirii Coinmaster into the capable and experienced hands of Lord Iriel Dathirii. He has long held it, and I—"

"Apologies, oh great Lord Dathirii, but I must beg to differ." Garith had hopped to his feet, dragging all eyes away from Hellion. "This may come as a surprise to you, used as you are to bootlicking and eager assent, but the Dathirii books are mine and I do not intend to pass them to one of your cronies."

Iriel sprang to his feet with an angry "How dare—", only to stop as Hellion raised a calming palm. He cut a striking figure, up on the wooden stage, his golden hair braided into a crown-like branch, his demeanour as collected as ever. The lectern and height conferred on him gravity and authority. As Hellion's smirk widened, Yultes couldn't help but think of him as the leader, and of Garith as a rebellious child.

"I believe you'll surprise even yourself, if you but hear me out fully."

By Garith's derisive snort, he had a healthy dose of doubts about that. Yultes could only hope so. Without Garith's assistance, none of the last weeks would have been possible. The creative bookkeeping had allowed them to hide staff wages, pretend Hellion had limited gold to negotiate with during trade deals, and even slowly build a reserve for Diel's return. The excuses were often flimsy, but Hellion relied on Yultes' assurance the numbers were true. Iriel Dathirii would not be fooled so easily.

"This takes us to my next key decision," Hellion said, "but before, I think we ought to welcome the guests we've found snooping around the tower. They'll want to hear it, too."

Yultes' blood ran cold. Only one person should have been snooping around tonight, at his request. He'd trusted Branwen to get in and out of the Tower without issue, Jaeger in tow. One less problem to worry about, he'd thought—he hadn't realized Hellion would pile new ones at his feet.

A side door by the stage opened, and two Allastam soldiers dragged Branwen in. She resisted every step of the way, clad in her own set of their armour, cursing at them that she could walk, thank you, and did they really have to be so upset about their sleeping comrade? Not that she was sorry, of course. Why be sorry when they didn't belong here at all?

Yultes schooled his face into polite shock, fighting off an urge to smile. Not that he needed to worry about others staring at him. All eyes were to the front, with various levels of surprise and indignation on the Dathirii's visages. Did they resent one of their own being mishandled, or were they angry Branwen had used the reception to sneak around?

"Branwen!"

Her head snapped up when Garith called her name, and she stopped squirming to grin and chirp a bright "Cousin!" at him as he bounced down the slow stairs, golden hair flying behind him.

He halted after three strides when a third Allastam guard entered with Jaeger in tow. The whole room of Dathirii elves froze.

Jaeger walked with calm, glacial dignity, his chin raised and his paces even. Flickering light from a chandelier above caressed his bruises in brief moments, bringing them to life in sharp and ephemeral reminders of the violence Hellion had visited upon him. His long dark hair cascaded around his shoulders and back, out of any braids for the first time in centuries, and it morphed his entire presence. When he turned dark eyes to the crowd, the collected professionalism they'd all grown used to had vanished, replaced by a smouldering intensity few could withstand. Yultes' throat dried, but unlike many who averted their gazes or pointedly turned it to Hellion, he stared back. Branwen played at defiance, but in Jaeger, it burned low and strong, ready to be unleashed.

"I don't believe they need any introduction." Hellion's affable tone hadn't changed at all. If anything, he'd grown warmer, more satisfied and self-confident.

"I can introduce my fist to your face," Branwen offered.

"My, have your manners vanished with your title, beloved niece? I assure you, that'll be quite unnecessary."

Hellion dismissed the idea with a simple wave, then turned back to the seated nobles. He was fully in control now, poised and calm in a way Yultes hadn't seen since he'd grabbed the family's leadership. Both Branwen's and Garith's outburst had only contributed to his self-possessed aura.

"I offer you a new future for House Dathirii, one of greatness borne from sound, pragmatic decisions and cunning deals. We are elves, and time is on our side. But many have lost track of that. They are bound by impulses, and look only to the present and immediate past. I won't force them into our future."

Branwen caught his gaze while Hellion went on, and the fury burning in there startled him. She mouthed a slow 'asshole', but there was no playful smirk with it, none of the conspiring humour they'd shared over secret messages. She didn't mean Hellion; she meant him. Oh, Alluma guide him, she thought he'd betrayed them. Of course she did! He'd known of her coming, had been Hellion's ally for decades, and now his old friend was commanding an entire room with great presence, following his plan. He had advised Hellion to frame Diel as a past to cast aside. He'd been right, too! Most Dathirii listened with rapt attention, the air tense with febrile hope. They had watched Diel's war drain their resources, lost their titles from it, and many would gladly follow Hellion down another path, especially one that echoed a misremembered, glorious past.

Yultes allowed himself a moment to relish the thrill of success. Perhaps Diel was right. Perhaps he could be a great architect, if he set his mind to it. Hellion's speech had only been half the plan, however, and it was high time to bring Hellion's image of control and presence crashing down around him.

Yultes' gaze swept the room for the young butler charged with the most crucial part of the evening, and signalled for him to move to the next step.

JAEGER forced his shoulders to remain squared and proud, his chin tilted up, and his eyes straight ahead, glaring at the space above the gathered Dathirii elves. Many stared at him still, and for the first time in decades, their condescension needled at him. He'd long made his peace with the idea Hellion's close circle would always deem him inferior, but other Dathirii had warmed up to him over the course of his stewardship—or so he'd thought. Up on the stage, held by a guard from another House, he felt exposed, as if offered up for evaluation to those gathered. A guest, Hellion had called him, as if he didn't belong to the family.

They'd like that, wouldn't they? Hellion had hearkened back to the glorious days of Diel's father, when the great noble elves of House Dathirii did not mingle with commoners. Every word of his speech painted a future without Jaeger in their midst—not as Lord Dathirii's steward, and certainly not as Diel's lover. His very existence within the Dathirii Tower prohibited the dream Hellion tried to conjure.

Jaeger held no illusion Hellion intended to fix that tonight. He braced himself, unwilling to give an inch to fear. He had little control over his future, at the moment, but he would greet what came with dignity. When Hellion turned back to them again, a paternalistic smile to match his description of the Dathirii defying him as remnants of the past, Jaeger met his gaze, unflinching.

"You're free to go," Hellion said, dripping with fake magnanimity.

Free to go? Shock spread through Jaeger, and Branwen gave voice to it.

"What?"

Garith's voice echoed her, farther into the room, and Hellion laughed at them, their surprise obviously pleasing him. He wiggled his fingers at the guards, and they released Jaeger's forearm.

"You heard me quite perfectly the first time, I'm certain. House Dathirii deserves solid foundation. We are those." He encompassed the gathered elves with a sweep of his arm. "I will not cling to a dysfunctional past. We're moving forward, with those who believe in the future I propose. Everyone else is free to leave. Go."

Silence draped the room, heavy and stifling. The constant murmurs of whispered conversation had disintegrated with the announcement, swallowed by the weight of the choice offered. Jaeger already knew his answer. He would not be erased from his home and its history, a footnote deemed unworthy of them. He hadn't accepted to escape with Branwen for his own sake, but to ground Diel in their fight. It ate at him, to delay his reunion even further when a clear path to his love lay at his feet, but Jaeger couldn't take it. If he left, he ceded this battlefield to Hellion.

Defiance swelled in his chest, borne by the anger and frustration of endless days trapped in rooms that weren't his, in a tower that should have been his home. Jaeger would not play by Hellion's games, no matter how tempting the prize.

"No."

His voice cracked the air like a whip, shattering the silence. Hellion whirled towards him, outrage contorting his face. Before a single word could slip through his lips, something snapped above their heads, then another. Hellion's retort morphed into an undignified scream as the Dathirii banner above him crashed down. Its top wooden pole smashed into his back, sending him sprawling, then it rolled away, unfurling its forest-green fabric and the elegant D of their family's crest.

Symbolic and humiliating, Yultes had promised. You could hardly beat the dusty banners of your illusory great past striking you down in your crowning moment.

Two more banners snapped, almost an echo to his thoughts. One fell right behind the last row of chairs, but the second crashed into a section of the seated Dathirii. They scrambled away with indignant and fearful cries, and all around the room, elves hurried away from the shadow of banners and the threat of a collapsing decor.

Branwen grabbed his hand, jolting him back to their present. Around them, the three Allastam guards exchanged uncertain glances and made no move to seize them again. Garith was cutting through the press of the crowd, towards them.

"Come on," Branwen said. "He said we were free to go, didn't he?"

"No." Jaeger slipped his hand out of hers. "I can't go."

"But—"

"I will not leave my home."

Jaeger cast his voice out, and it sliced through the chaos of panicked elves, slowing their jostling and stopping Garith in his tracks. They stared at him, mouth agape with a surprise he shared. Jaeger preferred to avoid attention, not command it. Not today. Today, he needed them to listen and let his every word sink in.

"I've lived here for a century. It is as much mine to love and inhabit as it is any of yours, and I will not abandon it to Hellion's despicable, soulless future." He pushed the fallen banner's pole with the tip of his toe, sending it rolling off stage and crashing to the ground. "House Dathirii has a heart, and its home knows it is missing. I've served it for decades, and I refuse to be erased from it. I'm staying, and I'm fighting until there are no more Allastam soldiers within our walls, and the House is back in hands that care for it more than their personal glory."

He swept his gaze across the room one more time, then pushed back the loose hair that'd once again fallen over his eyes and turned to Branwen. She was staring at him, lips parted as if she'd seen a ghost and for a moment Jaeger lost track of what he'd been about to say. Had he really been that shocking? A quick blush climbed to his cheeks, and he cleared his throat.

"Tell Diel I love him, but he needs to get a hold of himself. House Dathirii is waiting for him."

"Jaeger ..."

She trailed off, abandoned words, and engulfed him into a hug. Branwen squeezed him so tight and so long his lungs started to burn, but he closed his eyes and let himself melt into her warmth. When she stepped back, her eyes gleamed with tears.

"Right. I'll pass your message. Good luck."

And she strode off, leaping down the stage and walking through the gathered Dathirii. They parted at her approach, some with scorn but many more with eagerness and good words. She slowed, exchanging well wishes with them without ever truly stopping—not until she reached Garith. They didn't touch, didn't even say a word to each other. They had never needed to, these two, despite all the banter they loved to share. They stared at each other with gravitas they rarely held, and a small circle of Dathirii bloomed around them, keeping a respectful distance. Jaeger thought of Diel's plan, how he'd meant for the pair to one day lead House Dathirii, and he could see it now. Then they nodded to one another, in perfect synchronism, and Branwen continued on her way.

Jaeger watched her leave through the great main doors, dignified even in her soldier's disguise, barely aware of the hands once more clenching his forearm and the servants rushing to help Hellion from under his banner.

"Come on," Yultes whispered in his ears. "If you insist on staying, it's best you're out of sight by the time he regains control of himself."

Most of the room had stopped paying attention to him. Jaeger closed his eyes, drained from his brief time in the limelight, and let Yultes pull him away.

Chapter Thirty-One

"Explain."

Hellion's command greeted Yultes the moment he stepped into the office, chilling him to the bone. By the time he'd returned to the reception hall, the banner had been removed from Hellion, and Jayna Dathirii—newly nominated and gifted with a small connection with Alluma—had tended to the worst of his concussion. He'd stormed out of the room without another word, taking refuge in Lord Dathirii's quarters. Yultes had apologized to all and set the house's staff to cleaning while the rest of the elves either hung around discussing the day's events or escaping the cursed evening.

None of Hellion's close circles followed him. They knew better than to risk his ire at times like these, and vanished to their own quarters. Yultes steeled his nerves and climbed the many staircases as if walking to his own execution. The humiliation had worked perfectly, and Jaeger had doubled down on its symbolism to deadly results. The low intensity he'd carried with him onto the stage had exploded in a heart-stopping speech, and Yultes prayed Hellion's head had rung too hard for him to hear it. Whoever paid the price for today might well depend on what Hellion had perceived, in those few stunned minutes under the banner.

"Are you hurt?" Yultes asked, avoiding the demand.

Hellion's beautiful hair was dishevelled, the crown of branches askew on his head, and an ugly red still flushed his cheeks. He seemed otherwise unharmed, however, and was already tending to the lost dignity with a sizable glass of wine. The lit fireplace danced before his eyes, and he'd yet to turn towards Yultes or even spare him a glance.

"This banner ruined everything, Yultes. I have never been this humiliated, and I will know who's to blame."

"Accidents—"

"That was no accident!" Hellion whirled on him with a shriek, leaping out of his seat with unbridled rage. His earlier calm had vanished, crushed under the Dathirii banner along with his dignity. "Banners don't simply fall from the ceiling en masse. Nor does our hired staff show such blatant incompetence and clumsiness. Did these people mysteriously grow three thumbs when leadership passed from Diel to me? And, for that matter, did the musician just happen to cancel last minute?"

Yultes' throat dried. This was it, then. Hellion had put all the pieces together, and one could only notice so many issues before he attributed them to the organizer, rather than the individual involved. The vacations he'd threatened Yultes with earlier seemed even more ominous now. Hellion stalked towards him, trembling with indignation.

"When I told you this was a test of your competence, did you think I merely meant coordinating?" Hellion asked. "Someone was bound to tamper with our plans, and your job was to catch them in the act and stop them. Clearly, you've failed in a spectacular manner."

Air escaped Yultes' lungs as surely as if he'd been punched. Hellion's suspicions had slid right off his back, refuse coursing down the shitslides to go splash someone else. He trusted Yultes so thoroughly and implicitly that the simplest answer to the night's sabotage had been discarded completely.

It would be so easy, to name the servants who had installed the banners, to let the fault fall on their shoulders and dodge all blame. They had letters from Jaeger urging them to follow Yultes' orders, but would Hellion even look at them? To share those would betray his promise to shield them to the best of his ability, however. He had already lost Hellion's trust; he didn't want to lose Jaeger's and the staff's.

"If I've failed you, then I should bear responsibility for—"

The slap came hard and fast, and Yultes staggered backward under the force of his surprise. His cheek burned where Hellion had hit him, the sting of his friend's many rings forming nodes of pain.

"I don't care for your grovelling right now. I'm ordering you to investigate. Find me the culprits."

"What for? Making examples of the rebellious ones will not scare the others into submissions." He didn't think this argument would work on Hellion, but his mind was spinning on itself, desperate for something better. Until he found it, he'd need to buy time. "Fear isn't what you excel at—not as much as smooth promises, negotiations, and charm."

How hollow the affirmation felt when his heart raced with terror, his cheek still stinging from the slap. How often had he picked apart every word and emotion he shared with Hellion with intense care, afraid of disappointing his friend? Hellion wielded words as his favourite weapon, and he'd instilled into Yultes a healthy fear of what he could do with them.

"Do you hear yourself, Yultes?" Hellion reached for his chin, and his nails bit into Yultes' skin as he dragged him closer. "I asked you to be my right hand, not to become Jaeger. I will not debase myself to charming servants. They should fear me—and they should fear you, too."

His cologne snaked around Yultes, filling the air with overpowering flowery odours, muddling his thoughts. The smell had a familiar and reassuring quality to it, from countless hours close to Hellion, listening to his advice. His old friend released the iron grip on his chin and patted his cheek with gentle affection. His voice softened.

"Your job is to dominate them, not befriend them. Don't demean yourself, Yultes. Our House can trace its elven lineage back to the very start of Isandor, and centuries still beyond. You're a Dathirii noble and it's time you act as one. Forget the rabble and find me those responsible, or create them."

"I'm not a noble, not anymore. Neither are you."

This time, Yultes anticipated the slap and braced for it. It stung nonetheless, but he ground himself in the pain. Hellion's call to their title and lineage had jarred him out of his daze. Those values had held no place for him when he'd first arrived, and he'd spent decades struggling for acceptance against them.

But there was an extra layer of absurdity in Hellion's desire to define his worth as elven in nature. Yultes remembered the ancient traditions of his village, nestled deep in the forest, and the ceremonies of his childhood celebrating the unique cycles of their lifestyle. He had lived them, unlike Hellion, who for the most part inhabited a world dominated by human conception of time, gender, and nobility. In attempting to fit in, Yultes had buried any talk of his village, ashamed of their exile from it, of the strange traditions tied to Meltara, the Water Dancer, rather than Alluma. Of the blessing They had granted to his brother, which had led to his departure. Yultes had wanted to fit in, to become worldly and respected.

Perhaps Hellion had a point, and he should take more pride in who he'd been before arriving in Isandor. One had to wonder how much that young Yultes and the person Garith perceived in him had in common. He might well have changed beyond recognition, but there was, truly, only one way to find out.

"I have made many grievous mistakes in my life, my friend—more than you know, even—but this isn't one of them."

"What are you saying, Yultes?"

Hellion's voice rumbled out, smooth and dangerous—a warning.

Familiar fear jolted through Yultes as he recognized the threat. Do not overstep. Do not question. Would Hellion slap him a third time, if he dared to do so? In the past, the punishment had been verbal, insults and implied threats about his future within Hellion's group or House Dathirii as a whole.

How often *had* Hellion lashed out with words? Yultes couldn't begin to count, and even without adding Lady Viranya and the others to the tally. But Hellion had been trying to help, hadn't he? He'd taught Yultes how to behave within noble circles, to honour the Dathirii name that had been bestowed upon him. As a friend … right?

Doubts wrapped around his heart, which beat in time with the sting of his twice-slapped cheek. Had Hellion ever been his friend? Or had he spent decades nourishing his shame under the guise of coaxing him to become a proud Dathirii, more worthy of that honour? Had he seen in Yultes someone in need of help and guidance, or had he detected an easy prey, someone to groom and keep close at hand? How much of his life had been a tapestry of lies? Yultes burned with the desire to confront Hellion, to spill the swirl of questions within him and let the world answer them. But he couldn't. If Hellion confirmed his doubts, he'd break.

Instead, Yultes drew in a shaky breath, steadying his voice. He may not have it in him to ascertain the truth about his relationship to Hellion, but he could no longer pretend to eat the lies whole. That, too, had grown beyond him.

"You taught me my title was meaningless if I did not earn it. So is yours."

Terrible anger flashed through Hellion's expression, and every inch of Yultes quivered at its sight. Decades of experience screamed for him to stop before it was too late. He hurried on, words stumbling one after the other in a rush.

"A noble is graceful, diligent, and cunning," he recited. "Those are your words, yet you would ask me to scapegoat a Dathirii servants and terrorize them with an outsider's soldiers? To smash a toy to pieces because it doesn't work quite how we'd have wanted? You make me think of Lord Allastam—impatient, choleric, and clumsy. His House is graceless and blunt, brute force instead of delicate artifice. It has nothing in common with the House Dathirii you promised tonight, the one you made me dream of, and I'll take no part in building it. Come seek me when you've found your poise again."

He turned heels, his head ringing with his own daring, his hands shaking as he reached for the handle, opened the door, and strode out of Hellion's room, leaving him to chew on his words. Never in his life had Yultes refused his friend, let alone demand better from him. From the sound of glass shattering on the door behind him, there would be hell to pay for his defiance.

DIEL'S face fell when she walked through the door alone. By the way he stood in the middle of his room, his body half-turned towards her, he'd been pacing again. Unsurprising, truly. Despite what she'd told Jaeger, Diel had been more active over the course of the last few days. He'd met in person with many of the trade partners that had followed them, written to the nobles who used to liaison with House Dathirii, hoping to force them to acknowledge him, and meddled with Hellion's prospective trade deals. His energy came in waves, however, and learning what she'd planned for the night had obliterated any focus he'd had. He must have spent all night thinking of Jaeger and now, instead of pure adoration blazing through his face, she got to watch his dreams shatter, and the pointless struggle to hide the extent of his disappointment.

"I'm sorry," she said, each word as heavy as her heart.

He offered a wobbly smile, then gestured for her to sit at the edge of the bed. He dragged his desk's chair closer and settled with such slow, controlled movement she knew he was making an effort not to crumple into it.

"Tell me," he whispered.

So she did, sparing no details of her evening or her suspicions about Yultes. Diel grimaced at those, and argued with her that it might be more complicated—his optimism had survived, it seemed—but she had no intention to trust his advice again. When at last she repeated Jaeger's message for Diel, her uncle laughed, his smile soft and affectionate.

"I wish I could have seen him."

Deep longing threaded his voice, and his fingers traced the seam of his pants as if it was dear to him. He sighed, a young boy full of yearning for his first love, and Branwen couldn't hold her smirk.

"If I'm honest, Uncle, I'm not sure you'd have survived it. With the braid down, the thunderous passion of his voice, the confidence with which he claimed the room? It takes a man stronger than you are to withstand that."

Diel's lips parted, but no sounds crossed them and his cheeks turned a deep red. Branwen grinned at his embarrassment, clinging to the simple joy of teasing him to soothe the ache in her heart. She desperately wished she could have brought him Jaeger instead of his words, and that failure weighed on her. What had she accomplished by sneaking into the Dathirii Tower? Even her disguises had stayed in her quarters, forgotten in the chaos. Tonight had been a disaster.

"Branwen," Diel said softly, "You couldn't have stopped tonight from happening."

"I just—I wanted him with us so badly, you know?"

She choked on her words partway through, frustration and sadness rising within her in unexpected waves. Branwen flattened her hand on the bed sheets under her, feeling for the texture, grounding herself as tears fought their way up. She'd kept her calm since they'd lost their home, but every reunion with a new family member chipped at her defences. Hearing her name in Garith's voice had torn through her, red-hot longing and love, and now everyone's absence hurt more keenly than ever.

Diel slid besides her, wrapping his arm around her and pulling her close. She leaned hard into him, settling her head onto his bony shoulders. When he squeezed, her tears flowed out, down her cheeks and on his velvet shirt. Branwen felt childish—no one had died, and Hellion had been thoroughly humiliated—but she had worked so long and hard over the last weeks, and tonight her prize had slipped through her fingers. No matter what they did, they hit a wall, and all those she loved were trapped on the other side. Something, somewhere, would have to give—or she'd be the one to break first.

Chapter Thirty-Two

LARRYN perched on his Shelter's roof, legs tucked close to himself to fight off the cold piercing through his coat. At least the biting wind slicing between Isandor's towers kept him awake. His every muscles ached, nightmares still plagued him, and most of the time he could barely keep moving. Only one thing reliably pushed away the fog of exhaustion: Cal's coin.

His fingers tightened around its cold metal, and he retrieved the holy symbol from his pocket. Cal's blessing washed away years of anxiety, replacing fears for his future and the Shelter with a certainty that somehow, no matter the luck needed, all would solve itself. Larryn had never realized how much he carried in his mind until it was gone. No more questioning where everyone's next meal would come from, if Yultes' stream of gold had disappeared for good. No more worrying about what people would do or say if they learned he had a Dathirii father. No more berating himself for his inability to read or count, and his unsuitability as a role model for Efua. The endless string of battles that had been his life would finally halt—Ren would see to it.

Larryn rubbed his thumb over the deity's carved figure on the coin. Was that how Cal always felt? Perhaps the secret to his hopeful outlook on life hid in Ren's continuous blessing of certainty. But Cal still worried quite a lot, usually about others. Luck didn't explain his kindness or his patience. He deserved the best, and right now, Larryn was far from meeting that requirement. He barely felt alive without Ren's symbol to clear his mind. Mindlessly, he flipped the perfectly balanced coin into the air.

A soft thump behind startled him. Larryn sprung to his feet, snatching the coin midair and almost dropping it from his cold fingers. He whirled to face whoever had joined him on the roof, clenching Cal's precious symbol, his heart hammering against his chest. Hasryan finished heaving himself up before dusting snowflakes off his dark cloak and the pulled hood hiding most of his white hair. In the dim light of the Lower City, it made him almost impossible to see—probably the point, Larryn realized.

"What a superbly warm weather! Perfect to spend the night in reflective silence on the roof," Hasryan declared. "Excellent choice."

"I'm freezing my ass off."

Hasryan laughed and pulled the hood down. "Then what are you doing here? I thought I'd need to sneak into—is that Cal's coin?" He lunged for it, plucking it out of Larryn's fingers before his friend could protest. "It is! Why do you have that?"

"Luck."

Hasryan's usual good sense of humour must have stayed home, because he glared at Larryn. "Use more words."

"He gave it to me to keep me safe when I rescued Nevian." Larryn extended his palm, motioning for Hasryan to return it. Cal had entrusted *him* with his coin, and it felt wrong to leave it in anyone else's hands, even Hasryan's.

After a moment of hesitation, Hasryan offered it back. "I heard Avenazar came here."

"Swooped in and ruined everything, cackling with glee. That bastard's got sadism in his blood." Larryn's grip on the coin tightened, but even the certainty of Ren's luck could not keep the rising tide of fear. "What was Lord Dathirii's plan, exactly? Make Avenazar angry and watch while he destroyed everything? Is that what he's waiting for: deaths from the poor and the defenceless, so he can prove what a dangerous, uncontrollable murderer this asshole is?"

Larryn's voice rose to a higher pitch, and he let the fury propel what the coin couldn't, replacing his exhausted terror with the will to spite that had driven him through so much of his life.

"It's always the same. Nobles start shit high above in their towers, and when the spires crumble, who gets crushed under them? We do. Stuck down here trying to protect ourselves, but nothing's gonna protect us from the likes of Avenazar. I almost *died*. Nevian got dragged back to the enclave, at his mercy—not much better than dead for him. We rescued him, but Varden lost his way through his flamy planescape or whatever, and we almost all died there, too. That includes Vellien, ya know? Don't they care about them? I just—what … what are they waiting for, Hasryan?"

"I don't know, but I'm not waiting anymore."

Cold determination studded Hasryan's voice, and Larryn paused and *really* looked at him. His cloak enveloped him, blurring his body shape into an amorphous darkness. Under it, Hasryan wore long sleeves of black cotton, black gloves, and soft-padded boots—all designed to make him silent and difficult to spot in the night.

"You're up to no good."

Hasryan spread his hands, palms out, and grinned. "Me? I would never."

"Spit it out. You know I ain't stopping you."

"I'm glad," Hasryan said, as if there had been any doubts. "I'm taking Lord Allastam off the board, and then Master Avenazar if I can. They want me to believe the moral thing to do is to politic our way out of this, but I'm not buying it anymore. Good people could die with every day we waste, and I've killed folks far less deserving than these two assholes."

His hands fell to the pommels of the two daggers by his side, and Larryn recognized the electrified blade he'd stolen from the guards' headquarters—Brune's cursed gift. Hasryan thumbed it with a loving caress, and when he spoke again, his voice betrayed his worries.

"I'm ill prepared for this. I wish I'd spent the last days studying the Allastam Tower, learning its patterns, mapping a route, that sort of stuff. But all I'll have is our old sneak-ins together, to drink on one of their balconies. I figured I'd drop by, to see my best friend before I went."

Larryn hated the sound of that—like a goodbye. "Stay safe, Hasryan. The Dathirii aren't worth dying for."

"But it's not just the Dathirii anymore, is it?" Hasryan met his gaze, red eyes glinting in the diminished light. "It's you and the Shelter, too, and Arathiel and Cal. You're all worth the risk. Life wouldn't be the same without your constant rants."

He shoved Larryn playfully, and Larryn countered with a swift shoulder check. The brief tussle that ensued warmed him like a newly kindled fireplace, its familiarity grounding. Life kept kicking the two of them down, destroying their attempts to build something better for themselves, but somehow they stayed together through all that shit, finding small ways to hang onto the tiniest improvements. They'd always have each other's company, no matter what else came their way.

"Don't die on me," Larryn said. "I'll have breakfast waiting for you."

"Deal." Hasryan squeezed his arm, then twirled on himself and stepped towards the edge of the low roof. "To a bright dawn, with none of these bastards alive to ruin our delicious breakfast."

He saluted and let himself fall off. Larryn ran after him, but by the time he got to the edge, Hasryan was one shadow among hundreds, and he never spotted him.

WINTER nights were an awful time to spider along tower walls. Snow turned the stones slippery, his fingers grew numb from freezing, and the wind threatened to unhinge him and send him plummeting to his death. Every entrance had a guard posted near it, however, even the servants', limiting his options. So he'd padded his way to the side most shielded from the winds, chose an area where few candles brightened the rooms, and started the climb up.

The Allastam Tower was shaped like a three-stranded helix, two whites and one black, and the unique structure forced Hasryan to climb in a diagonal and occasionally perform a switch from one strand to another. The smooth stones' scarce handholds turned the jumping manoeuvre into a dangerous, reckless act, and Hasryan almost slipped more than once. Under his thick hood and heavy cotton clothes, he was sweating profusely and his heart ached from exertion and stress.

Relief flooded through him when he reached the darkened window he'd been aiming for and its much larger windowsill. This one didn't open at all, however, forcing him to keep his slow trek upward, to another window. Hasryan tested it—locked. Holding on as he was, he'd have a hard time picking that. His gaze trailed up, to his next options, and snapped to the balcony. There. It'd be locked, too, but Hasryan would have two feet under him at least. Muscles and lungs straining, he pushed himself up again, one handhold at a time until he clambered over the railing. No light escaped through the room's curtains, and once he pressed his ear to the glass, he heard nothing. Satisfied, he set to work on the lock.

The cold made his fingers clumsy, he shivered from his sweat cooling off in the biting winds, but with time and focus he managed to hook the mechanism inside, push it up, and undo the lock proper. It settled with a soft click, and Hasryan slipped into the room with childish excitement.

He stepped into a room almost devoid of furniture. Three bookshelves lined the left wall, all empty except for a single pile of tomes and an old, rusted lamp, and a bedside table with a broken leg waited besides them. Nothing but silence and dust filled the rest of the space.

This was familiar territory, easier than unexpected breakfasts and other social engagements. Sneaking and killing had been part of his life for more than a decade, and they fit him like well-worn gloves. It felt good, to put his peculiar skill set to use and finally move the needle in their favour with it. Hasryan pressed his ear to the door, listened for the tower's inhabitants, and once confident he'd be alone, he unlocked it and stepped into the corridor. His earlier worries had given way to professional focus.

Runes along the top of the walls thrummed to life, emanating a soft blue light. They gleamed only in a tight area around him, shedding enough illumination to see his path without casting a glare that'd bother sleeping residents. Very clever for them, and awful for him. *This* was why he needed preparation.

Hasryan stretched up and tapped the runes, to no avail. He didn't know shit about magic, either, and doubted it'd be wise to waste time here. At least the glow didn't have a long range. If he kept his ears peeled, he might hear servants before they noticed it. He hoped. He set off, steps slow and measured, annoyed at the enchantment for depriving him of shadows to skulk in.

As predicted, the glow tracking him turned a simple infiltration into an endless game of cat and mouse. Hasryan's acute hearing helped him detect others, and the helix shape of the tower bent everything, creating twisting corridors with limited vision ahead. It helped to keep out of sight, but he was still forced to backtrack and hide into unlocked quarters over and over, wasting precious time. Curse it, he'd wanted to search for their cells—not the official ones, for which they were bound by law to inform the Sapphire Guard about their prisoners, but the secret ones. Everyone in the Lower City's underground knew the biggest houses hid a plethora of locked rooms in which they could do whatever pleased them. If Kellian Dathirii was in here instead of in Brune's headquarters, that's where Hasryan would have found him.

He'd never have time for that, however, not with how long he needed to weave his way farther up the tower, where Lord Allastam's quarters would be. Hasryan already suspected the Myrian Enclave would have to wait for the next night. Cal had told him some girl had poisoned Avenazar, so at least he might have a bigger window of opportunity there.

A scream bounced down the corridor, muffled by distance or a door. Hasryan froze at it, but curiosity soon had him threading closer.

"What are you doing?"

Fury and pain weaved through the choked voice, and Hasryan followed it until he found the door with soft candlelight under. Slowly, he moved to the one across the hall and tested the handle. Unlocked—Ren must be smiling on him.

"Please hold still, milord," a second voice said, calmer.

"Hold still? I bet this cut hurts more than giving goddamn birth! Quit complaining and do your job. Or do I need to hire a better physician to attend me?"

Hasryan hung to their every word. Who but Drake had been wounded recently? This wasn't him, though. Hasryan would recognize his nasal voice anywhere. There was something familiar to the casual arrogance and the rhythm of speech. Attitudes were taught, weren't they? They'd always known Drake took after his father.

"I assure you, there is no need," the physician replied in a soothing tone. "I can stop the pain."

"You've said that before! Make sure it doesn't come back this time." A thump of wood on the floor echoed out of the room. "I want to be hale and healthy when I make her pay. No one's answered my demands for ransom and reparation, so they don't care either way. She's all mine."

The sadistic pleasure sent a shiver down his spine. This was definitely Lord Allastam, Hasryan decided. How terrible, that he could recognize a man he'd never met before only on the strength of his assholery and his obvious love for retribution. What little he knew of Allastam kindled only rage in Hasryan, and no compassion.

He edged closer to the door, a familiar thrill coursing through his veins. Yet even as Hasryan's hands drifted to his daggers, a pang of guilt needled at him. He'd promised Sora he wouldn't do this. How could he hold that word, though, when he could hasten this conflict's end with a single kill? She didn't need to know. No one needed to know.

A flash of light spilled out of Allastam's room, followed by a heavy sigh of relief. Hasryan pushed his guilt aside. If this bastard was getting healed, then it might be over soon. He had to be ready.

"Here," the physician said, and there was a clink of vials. "If it reopens again or turns too painful, use this. It'll close it up and sustain you for a few hours, saving you another trip down here."

"This works on anyone? For any wounds?" Allastam asked.

Hasryan shuddered at what purpose that question might have. Somehow, he doubted Allastam would use emergency healing kindly. The physician must have agreed, as their tone hardened.

"It's for *you*."

His only thanks was a small grunt. Allastam got up—first his cane thumped the floor, then slippered feet. Hasryan leaned back into his hiding place—a sick room with a single empty bed and dusty shelves—and waited for his mark to come out, ready to pursue.

Lord Allastam's greying hair stood on one side of his head, displaced by sleep, and in the dim blue lights from the wall, the bags under his eyes seemed deeper and darker. He clung to an old wooden cane, the paint chipped away by years, with no fancy design to its pommel that Hasryan could notice. The night robe and slippers had an obvious high quality to them, softer and comfier than anything Hasryan had ever tried on, but if it weren't for them, the Head of House Allastam would've looked a tired, ordinary man. How at odds with the arrogant, backstabbing lord that had overtaken House Dathirii. Hasryan had seen more than one target look frail and vulnerable, however; looks were deceiving when it came to brutal ruthlessness. He waited to ensure the physician stayed in their room, then padded out of his hiding place and followed.

To his surprise, Lord Allastam didn't head upwards, towards his personal quarters, but continued down the spiralling passage, whistling to himself with blood-chilling joy. Hasryan shivered. *She's all mine*, he'd said of his prisoner. Whoever this unfortunate soul was didn't have a great night ahead of her, if that was the direction Allastam was heading. And if so, she might share a cell with Kellian.

Every step Allastam took likely brought him closer to these secret cells, but how long could Hasryan track him while the very corridors announced his presence? He had a careful balance at play here—if he killed him early, he also risked the body discovered before he reached the cells. He'd have to let professional instincts guide him. Hasryan slid Brune's electrified dagger out of its sheath and, confident Allastam was far enough not to notice the blue glow, and followed him through the tower.

The twisting corridors seemed to go on forever, the stop-and-go nature of this trailing exercise made worse by the curves of the walls and the passage of a pair of soldiers, once. Allastam had stopped by them, whispering a few instructions before moving on, still humming, but Hasryan was forced to hide until the two soldiers had walked well past him before he resumed.

He caught up to Lord Allastam in time to spot him bifurcate into a side corridor, the blue runes marking his position fading out instead of following him. If that enchantment existed only in main passages, this might be his chance. Hasryan's strides lengthened, his fingers tightened over his dagger. He heard the slide of Allastam's slippers around the bend—casual steps, unwary. Good.

When he rounded the bend, Allastam was less than five feet away, still clueless. His heart pounding, Hasryan dashed forward. His left arm reached for Allastam's mouth even as the right one rose, flipping his grip on the dagger. He grabbed the man and brought him hard against his body, muffling the surprised shriek as he slid the weapon under Allastam's ribs, slicing upward until his blade hit the sternum. Blood spurted out, warm against his fingers, as lightning sizzled across the old man's torso. He screamed into Hasryan's palm and his cane dropped to the ground, its echo deafening.

"Y'know," he whispered, "I never even killed your wife."

Allastam jerked against him—the last throes of a dying man. The routine was almost comforting, in a way. Hasryan hadn't lost the needed decisiveness and—

Bright white light blinded him, and Allastam bit into his hand before elbowing him hard. Hasryan stumbled backward, choking down his yelp and blinking. He reflexively fell into a low crouch—just in time for the air above his head to swoosh. The cane?

It smacked his temple, sending him sprawling to the side. How was Allastam moving so fast? How was he even alive? That stab should have gone to his heart, and no one had ever survived that before. Hasryan blinked again, and his vision cleared right as the cane came down hard on him. He blocked with his forearm and gasped as pain spread through it.

Electricity crackled in the dark corridor—his own weapon, now in Allastam's clutches. The older man panted hard, his nightshirt stained red, a bright look in his eyes and a wide smile on his lips. Brune's dagger in one hand, his cane in the other. The stab mark shone with the same light that had blinded Hasryan—the same as the physician's, he realized.

"Stabbing me isn't the most convincing argument, wouldn't you say?" He raised the jagged blade to his eyes with a smirk. "And with the same weapon, no less."

Hasryan didn't wait for more mockery. He flung his second dagger at Lord Allastam, catching him between two ribs. The older man staggered as Hasryan scrambled up, eager to finish an already too-messy kill, but Allastam forced him back with another swipe of his cane. He stared at his electrified dagger, willing it to return, but the moment he'd released it in Allastam's wounds, he'd given his enemy an opportunity to claim it. Which left him without weapons. Time to get creative.

"Didn't want to sully anything else on you," he said. "That one's cursed."

In the split-second Allastam glanced at the dagger, Hasryan barrelled forward. A predictable cane swept for his head, but this time Hasryan threw himself down under it, sliding feet first into Allastam's legs. His fingers clamped onto the physician's needle as he passed it, and with the other hand he yanked hard on Allastam's nightshirt, destroying his already precarious balance.

Allastam collapsed on Hasryan, but the yank had sent atrocious pain through his forearm, stunning him, and bony fingers clasped his chin before he could recover from it. Cold metal slipped at the base of his neck, the tip of his own dagger slicing the muscles tying it to his shoulders. Red–hot agony spread through the juncture, then the electricity dancing on his jagged blade jumped to the rest of his body. The last thing Hasryan knew was Lord Allastam's soft voice whispering into his ears.

"Don't worry. We know how to treat the scum of the earth here."

Character Guide

THE following is a list of characters featured in *City of Deceit* with short descriptions to help readers navigate the story. The "titles" assigned to each character are meant to poke fun at them—don't take them too seriously.

House Dathirii

<u>Diel Dathirii (Lord Dathirii), Eternal Idealist, he/him</u>
Head of the Dathirii House, loves political fights and people, but none more than Jaeger.

<u>Jaeger, Stalwart Steward, he/him</u>
Diel's personal steward, the logistics behind the passion, a stickler for titles even for his long-time love.

<u>Branwen Dathirii, Master of Disguises, she/her</u>
Dathirii spymaster, her heart is as big as her multi-gender wardrobe.

<u>Garith Dathirii, Number One Flirt, he/him</u>
Dathirii coinmaster. Has ladies over at irregular hours, beware.

Vellien Dathirii, Anxious Healer, they/them
Dathirii priest of Alluma, youngest cousin. Would sing more if it didn't focus everyone's attention on them.

Camilla Dathirii, Tea of Kindness, she/her
Diel's aunt, has retired from wilder years to grant tea, cookies, and wisdom to those in need.

Kellian Dathirii, Stiff Guard, he/him
Captain of the Dathirii Guards, spends many hours wishing people would stop taking huge risks. Vanished.

Yultes Dathirii, Professional Impostor, he/him
Once main Dathirii liaison to House Allastam, now Hellion's steward. Diel's step-brother and Larryn's father. Is great at lying to himself and others.

Hellion Dathirii, 'Cunning' Shitlord, he/him
Yultes's "best friend", Lord Allastam's underling. Took over the Dathirii Tower to prove elves and nobles are superior.

House Allastam

Lord Allastam, Bitter Crusader, he/him
Head of House Allastam. Would watch the world burn to get his way and avenge his murdered wife.

<u>Drake Allastam, High on Privilege, he/him</u>
Lord Allastam's son, heir to the house leadership, typically responds to 'no' and 'fuck you' with violence. Long history of harassing Larryn.

<u>Mia Allastam, the Discreet Daughter. she/her</u>
Lord Allastam's daughter. Won't let chronic pain and the family's overbearing protectiveness keep her away. The only person Drake listens to.

House Brasten

<u>Amake Brasten (Lady Brasten), Slicing Politician, she/her</u>
Head of House Brasten, ready to own the Golden Table on her own if needed.

<u>Arathiel Brasten, Drifter from the Past, he/him</u>
Stayed trapped for a hundred and thirty years in a mysterious Well that drained his senses. Stayed at the Shelter in secret until people needed saving. Member of the Halfies ~~Trio~~ Quartet.

<u>Oloan Brasten, Twin Coinmaster, he/him</u>
One of House Brasten's twin coinmaster.

<u>Lindi Brasten, Afflicted Dancer, she/her</u>
Arathiel's sister, sick when he left for the Well. Dead.

The Shelter

<u>Larryn, Anger Stew, he/him</u>

Owner of and cook at the Shelter. Rages against the machine (and everyone else, really). Member of the Halfies ~~Trio~~ Quartet.

<u>Hasryan, Assassin Seeks Friends, he/him</u>

Once Brune's favourite assassin, now helps House Dathirii. His sass is as deadly as his blades. Member of the Halfies ~~Trio~~ Quartet.

<u>Cal, Luck's Generous Hand, he/him</u>

Priest of Ren, the luck deity. Lover of cheese, quick to develop friend crushes and act on them. Member of the Halfies ~~Trio~~ Quartet.

<u>Nevian, Stubborn Pupil, he/him</u>

Avenazar's old apprentice, now hiding at the Shelter. Still determined to learn magic—and now, to teach it to Efua.

<u>Efua, Genius Letter Girl, she/her</u>

Orphan living at the Shelter. Larryn's unofficial little sister. Works as a letter delivery girl.

<u>Jim, Hard-Working Father, he/him</u>

First owner of the shelter. Adoptive father for Larryn and Efua. Dead.

The Myrian Enclave

<u>Master Avenazar, Destructive Ego, he/him</u>
Head of the Myrian enclave. Ruthless and powerful mage who avenges every slight. Grievously wounded (for now).

<u>Master Jilssan, Ambitious Pragmatic, she/her</u>
Transmutation specialist and Isra's master. Always ready to do what it takes to survive.

<u>Isra, Conflicted Princess, she/her</u>
Jilssan's apprentice. Is learning to untangle herself and be a better person, one clumsy step at a time.

Other Figures of Note

<u>Varden Daramond, Gentle Flames, he/him</u>
High Priest of Keroth, imprisoned for treason. Talented artist, loving soul, powerful fire-wielder.
<u>Sora Sharpe, Unapologetic Law Enforcer, she/her</u>
Investigator for Isandor's Sapphire Guards in charge of finding Hasryan. Hates political games.

<u>Lai, Confident Informant, ne/ner</u>
An informant for Sora Sharpe. In a queerplatonic relationship with one of House Dathirii's kitchen boys.

Brune, Ruthless Mercenary Leader, she/her

Leader of the Crescent Moon mercenary, powerful mage, Hasryan's old boss. Has hands in every pockets. Loves the colour brown.

Nicole, Iron-Grip Cook, she/her

In charge of the Dathirii's kitchens. Knew Larryn's mother. Don't mention Yultes to her.

Alton, Considerate Spy, he/him

Serves House Allastam. Part of Branwen's network of spies and friends. They disagree on fashion, though.

Lord William, Single Noble, he/him

Presides the Golden Table but has no House. Loves drama in many shapes.

Noble Families of Isandor

House Lorn

Founding family, and currently the biggest family in Isandor. Holds more seats on the Golden Table than any other House.

House Allastam

Second biggest family in Isandor. Its rise to power can be attributed almost entirely to the current Lord Allastam.

House Balthazar

A rising star in Isandor politics. Its wealth increase is recent but, speculation says, unlikely to last. Third biggest house.

House Dathirii

Founding family and the only elven noble house.

House Brasten

House of medium importance. Has managed to retain a seat on the Golden Table despite the family's often deadly hereditary illness.

House Carrington

Founding family that fell from power after a botanical spell gone wrong infected and killed half their family. Still sits at the Golden Table.

House Serringer

Small house that has a fur monopoly. One seat at the Golden Table.

House Almanza

Minor Isandor house. One seat at the Golden Table.

About the Author

Claudie Arseneault is an asexual and aromantic-spectrum writer hailing from the very-French Quebec City. Her long studies in biochemistry and immunology often sneak back into her science-fiction, and her love for sprawling casts invariably turns her novels into multi-storylined wonders. Claudie is a founding member of The Kraken Collective and is well-known for her involvement in solarpunk, her database of aro and ace characters in speculative fiction, and her unending love of squids.

You can also always find all of her books at
claudiearseneault.com

WANT MORE?

At The Kraken Collective, we know how frustrating it can be to reach the end of a book and want more. Within the following pages, you'll find books with a similar feel to help you scratch that reading itch and why we're recommending them.

We hope our suggestions will help you find your next favourite read!

Shades and Silver
by Dax Murray

Looking for more speculative queer stories that deal with identity, acceptance, and figuring out where (or with whom) you belong? In *Shades and Silver*, by Dax Murray, every Ástfríður may command and bend a metal of the earth. But Britt does not know which metal to choose, and Astrid has never felt the pull of metal at all. *Shades of Silver* is a gorgeous fantasy with two non-binary characters and intriguing metal-centered worldbuilding.

The Ice Princess's Fair Illusion
by Dove Cooper

City of Deceit gives a lot of room to exploring aromantic identities, but if you're looking for more, check out *The Ice Princess's Fair Illusion*, by Dove Cooper. A sapphic, queerplatonic retelling of King Thrushbeard told in free verse, *Ice Princess's* touches on many facets of asexuality and aromanticism, from compulsory heterosexuality to the choosing (or eschewing) of labels. Truly a gem of a story.

Learn more about these and other titles at
www.krakencollectivebooks.com

Acknowledgements

Remerciements

WOW, it has been a while. Five years, in fact, since I first published *City of Strife*, and a lot certainly happened since, pandemic included. So before I move on to thanks, here is the small story of *City of Deceit*.

Early in 2019, I sent my draft for the third and "final" book to my editor for a developmental edit. It was a monster of a draft, almost 200,000 words, and I couldn't tell if I should make drastic cuts or split the book in two. They were adamant: split, and give everything time to breathe. Which I could have done there and then, except in the meantime I had grown a superb obsession with *Devil May Cry*, and my brain lived and breathed fanfiction. There was no way it could wire itself to the daunting process of properly untangling the plot lines and reworking the entire book to make it two. I poked at it every now and then, jutting ideas for when I'd be ready to come back.

That happened in January 2020. I sat down, full of New Year Motivations ™, and slowly reread the two first books, my current draft, and my edit notes. I was a little rusted, but by the end of February, I had a solid plan.

I think you can see where this is going. Like many others, I was well and truly derailed by the pandemic.

Yet here I am. And I owe it first to S. L. Dove Cooper, my editor and friend, who believed in this book more steadfastly than even I could. Your encouragements and firm comments are half the reason it got where it is. So many other writer-friends greeted me back with joy and encouragements when I set back down to work—Cedar, RoAnna, Sandstone, Painter, Candace, Lyssa—and so many readers cheered on me as I poked my head back on social media. You've all reminded me of why I loved writing and loved this series.

But it's been five years, and as I said, five years is a long time. *City of Deceit* wouldn't *be* without friends outside of my writing communities : Marianne, Audrey, Elianne, Jonathan, who bring me such joy every week; Ash, Ren, Liz, Sofia, Henna, Vane, Toni, and Sumi, who've filled a year of my life with excitement, laughter, and self-confidence I'd lost (and continue to do so today).

And finally, I cannot overstate how blessed I am with the best family and partner. You've been there since Day 1, and it has meant the world.

Thank you all <3